KING OF THE NORTH

HARRY TURTLEDOVE

BAEN

KING OF THE NORTH

Copyright © 1996 by Harry Turtledove

All rights reserved, including the right to reproduce this book or portions thereof in any form.

A Baen Books Original

Baen Publishing Enterprises
P.O. Box 1403
Riverdale, NY 10471

ISBN: 0-671-87715-1

Cover art by Ken Tunell

Map by Eleanor Kostyk

First printing, April 1996

Distributed by Simon & Schuster
1230 Avenue of the Americas
New York, NY 10020

Printed in the United States of America

She was beautiful.
         She was divine.
                  But *he* was the Fox.

In the middle of the clearing stood a comely naked woman with long dark hair, twice as tall as the Fox, who held in her right hand an axe of Gradi style.

"Voldar," Gerin whispered. In the silence of his mind, he thanked his own gods that the Gradi goddess had chosen to meet him in a dream rather than manifesting herself in the material world.

She looked at him—through him—with eyes pale as ice, eyes in which cold fire flickered. And he, abruptly, was cold, chilled in the heart, chilled from the inside out. Her lips moved. "You meddle in what does not concern you," she said. He did not think the words were Elabonian, but he understood them anyhow. That left him awed but unsurprised. Gods—and, he supposed, goddesses—had their own ways in such matters.

"The northlands are my land, the land of my people, the land of my gods," he answered, bold as he dared. "Of course what happens here concerns me."

That divinely chilling gaze pierced him again. Voldar tossed her head in fine contempt. Her hair whipped out behind her, flying back as if in a breeze—but there was no breeze. In face and form, the Gradi goddess was stunningly beautiful, more perfect than any being the Fox had imagined, but even had she been his size, he would have known no stir of desire for her. Whatever her purpose, love had nothing to do with it.

She said, "Obey me now and you may yet survive. Give over your vain resistance and you will be able to live out your full span most honored among all those not lucky enough to be born of the blood of my folk."

He said, "I'll take my chances. I may end up dead, but that strikes me as better than living under your people—and under you. Or I may end up alive and free. Till the time comes, you never know—and we Elabonians have gods, too."

Baen Books by Harry Turtledove

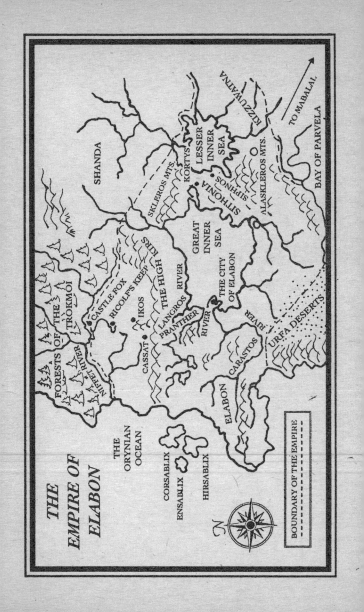

THE
EMPIRE OF
ELABON

THE
ORYNIAN
OCEAN

CORSABLIX
ENSABLIX
HIRSABLIX

BOUNDARY OF THE EMPIRE

FORESTS OF THE
TRÖKMOI

NIFFET RIVER

SHANDA

CASTLE FOX

RICOLF'S KEEP

IKOS

CASSAT

SKLEROS MTS.

THE HIGH KIRS

LANGROS RIVER

PRANTHER RIVER

GREAT
INNER
SEA

KORTYS

LESSER
INNER
SEA

SIPHNOS

VINHONIA

SITHONIA

ALASKLEROS MTS.

KIZZUWATNA

TO MABALAL.

BAY OF PARVELA

THE CITY
OF ELABON

VINHONIA RIVER

ELABON

CARASTOS

URFA DESERTS

N

I

Gerin the Fox looked down his long nose at the two peasants who'd brought their dispute before him. "Now, Trasamir, you say this hound is yours, am I right?"

"Aye, that's right, lord prince." Trasamir Longshanks' shaggy head bobbed up and down. He pointed to several of the people who helped crowd the great hall of Fox Keep. "All these folks from my village, they'll say it's so."

"Of course they will," Gerin said. One corner of his mouth curled up in a sardonic smile. "They'd better, hadn't they? As best I can tell, you've got two uncles, a cousin, a nephew, and a couple of nieces there, haven't you?" He turned to the other peasant. "And you, Walamund, you claim the hound belongs to you?"

"That I do, lord prince, on account of it's so." Walamund Astulf's son had a typical Elabonian name, but dirty blond hair and light eyes said there were a couple of Trokmoi in the family woodpile. Like Gerin, Trasamir was swarthy, with brown eyes and black hair and beard—though the Fox's beard had gone quite gray the past few years. Walamund went on, "These here people will tell you that there dog is mine."

Gerin gave them the same dubious look with which he'd favored Trasamir's supporters. "That's your father and your brother and two of your brothers-in-law I see, one of them with your sister alongside—for luck, maybe."

Walamund looked as unhappy as Trasamir Longshanks had a moment before. Neither man seemed to have

1

expected their overlord to be so well versed about who was who in their village. That marked them both for fools: any man who did not know Gerin kept close track of as many tiny details as he could wasn't keeping track of details himself.

Hesitantly, Trasamir pointed to the hound in question—a rough-coated, reddish brown beast with impressive fangs, now tied to a table leg and given a wide berth by everybody in the hall. "Uh, lord prince, you're a wizard, too, they say. Couldn't you use your magic to show whose dog Swifty there really is?"

"I could," Gerin said. "I won't. More trouble than it's worth." As far as he was concerned, most magic was more trouble than it was worth. His sorcerous training was more than half a lifetime old now, and had always been incomplete. A partially trained mage risked his own skin every time he tried a conjuration. The Fox had got away with it a few times over the years, but picked with great care the spots where he'd take the chance.

He turned to his eldest son, who stood beside him listening to the two peasants' arguments. "How would you decide this one, Duren?"

"Me?" Duren's voice broke on the word. He scowled in embarrassment. When you had fourteen summers, the world could be a mortifying place. But Gerin had put questions like that to him before: the Fox was all too aware he wouldn't last forever, and wanted to leave behind a well-trained successor. As Trasamir had, Duren pointed to the hound. "There's the animal. Here are the two men who say it's theirs. Why not let them both call it and see which one it goes to?"

Gerin plucked at his beard. "Mm, I like that well enough. Better than well enough, in fact—they should have thought of it for themselves back at their village instead of coming here and wasting my time with it."

He looked to Trasamir and Walamund. "Whichever one of you can call the dog will keep it. Do you agree?"

Both peasants nodded. Walamund asked, "Uh, lord prince, what about the one the dog doesn't go to?"

The Fox's smile grew wider, but less pleasant. "He'll have to yield up a forfeit, to make sure I'm not swamped with this sort of foolishness. Do you still agree?"

Walamund and Trasamir nodded again, this time perhaps less enthusiastically. Gerin waved them out to the courtyard. Out they went, along with their supporters, his son, a couple of his vassals, and all the cooks and serving girls. He started out himself, then realized the bone of contention—or rather, the bone-gnawer of contention—was still tied to the table.

The hound growled and bared its teeth as he undid the rope holding it. Had it attacked him, he would have drawn his sword and solved the problem by ensuring that neither peasant took possession of it thereafter. But it let him lead it out into the afternoon sunlight.

"Get back, there!" he said, and the backers of Trasamir and Walamund retreated from their principals. He glared at them. "Any of you who speaks or moves during the contest will be sorry for it, I promise." The peasants might suddenly have turned to stone. Gerin nodded to the two men who claimed the hound. "All right—go ahead."

"Here, Swifty!" "Come, boy!" "Come on—good dog!" "That's my Swifty!" Walamund and Trasamir both called and chirped and whistled and slapped the callused palms of their hands against their woolen trousers.

At first, Gerin thought the dog would ignore both of them. It sat on its haunches and yawned, displaying canines that might almost have done credit to a longtooth. The Fox hadn't figured out what he'd do if Swifty wanted no part of either peasant.

But then the hound got up and began to strain against

the rope. Gerin let go, hoping the beast wouldn't savage one of the men calling it. It ran straight to Trasamir Longshanks and let him pat and hug it. Its fluffy tail wagged back and forth. Trasamir's relatives clapped their hands and shouted in delight. Walamund's stood dejected.

So did Walamund himself. "Uh—what are you going to do to me, lord prince?" he asked, eyeing Gerin with apprehension.

"Do you admit to trying to take the hound when it was not yours?" the Fox asked, and Walamund reluctantly nodded. "You knew your claim wasn't good, but you made it anyhow?" Gerin persisted. Walamund nodded again, even more reluctantly. Gerin passed sentence: "Then you can kiss the dog's backside, to remind you to keep your hands off what belongs to your neighbors."

"Grab Swifty's tail, somebody!" Trasamir shouted with a whoop of glee. Walamund Astulf's son stared from Gerin to the dog and back again. He looked as if somebody had hit him in the side of the head with a board. But almost everyone around him—including some of his own kinsfolk—nodded approval at the Fox's rough justice. Walamund started to stoop, then stopped and sent a last glance of appeal toward his overlord.

Gerin folded his arms across his chest. "You'd better do it," he said implacably. "If I come up with something else, you'll like that even less, I promise you."

His own gaze went to the narrow window that gave light to his bedchamber. As he'd hoped, Selatre stood there, watching what was going on in the courtyard below. When he caught his wife's eye, she nodded vigorously. That made him confident he was on the right course. He sometimes doubted his own good sense, but hardly ever hers.

One of Trasamir's relatives lifted the hound's tail.

Walamir got down on all fours, did as the Fox had required of him, and then spat in the dirt and grass again and again, wiping his lips on his sleeve all the while.

"Fetch him a jack of ale, to wash his mouth," Gerin told one of the serving girls. She hurried away. The Fox looked a warning to Trasamir and his relatives. "Don't hang an ekename on him on account of this," he told them. "It's over and done with. If he comes back here and tells me you're all calling him Walamund Hound-Kisser or anything like that, you'll wish you'd never done it. Do you understand me?"

"Aye, lord prince," Trasamir said, and his kinsfolk nodded solemnly. He didn't know whether they meant it. He knew he did, though, so if they didn't they'd be sorry.

The girl brought out two tarred-leather jacks of ale. She gave one to Walamund and handed the Fox the other. "Here, lord prince," she said with a smile.

"Thank you, Nania," he answered. "That was kindly done." Her smile got wider and more inviting. She was new to Fox Keep; maybe she had in mind slipping into Gerin's bed, or at least a quick tumble in a storeroom or some such. In a lot of castles, that would have been the quickest way to an easy job. Gerin chuckled to himself as he poured out a small libation to Baivers, the god of barley and brewing. No reason for Nania to know yet that she'd found herself an uxorious overlord, but she had. He hadn't done any casual wenching since he'd met Selatre. *Eleven years, more or less*, he thought in some surprise. It didn't feel that long.

Walamund had also let a little ale slop over the rim of his drinking jack and drip onto the ground: only a fool slighted the gods. Then he raised the jack to his mouth. He spat out the first mouthful, then gulped down the rest in one long draught.

"Fill him up again," Gerin told Nania. He turned back to Walamund and Trasamir and their companions. "You can sup here tonight, and sleep in the great hall. The morning is time enough to get back to your village." The peasants bowed and thanked him, even Walamund.

By the time the man who'd wrongly claimed the hound had got outside of his second jack of ale, his view of the world seemed much improved. Duren stepped aside with Gerin and said, "I thought he'd hate you forever after that, but he doesn't seem to."

"That's because I let him down easy once the punishment was done," the Fox said. "I made sure he wouldn't be mocked, I gave him ale to wash his mouth, and I'll feed him supper same as I will Trasamir. Once you've done what you need to do, step back and get on with things. If you stand over him gloating, he's liable to up and kick you in the bollocks."

Duren thought about it. "That's not what Lekapenos' epic tells a man to do," he said. " 'Be the best friend your friends have, and the worst foe to your foes,' or so the poet says."

Gerin frowned. Whenever he thought of Lekapenos, he thought of Duren's mother; Elise had been fond of quoting the Sithonian poet. Elise had also run off with a traveling horse doctor, about the time Duren was learning to stand on his feet. Even with so many years gone by, remembering hurt.

The Fox stuck close to the point his son had raised: "Walamund's not a foe. He's just a serf who did something wrong. Father Dyaus willing, he won't take the chance of falling foul of me again, and that's what I was aiming at. There's more gray in life, son, than you'll find in an epic."

"But the epic is grander," Duren said with a grin, and burst into Sithonian hexameters. Gerin grinned, too. He was glad to see knowledge of Sithonian preserved here in the northlands, cut off these past fifteen years and more from the Empire of Elabon. Few hereabouts could read even Elabonian, the tongue in their mouths every day.

Gerin also smiled because Selatre, having first learned Sithonian herself, was the one who'd taught Duren the language. The boy—no, not a boy any more: the youth—didn't remember his birth mother. Selatre was the one who'd raised him, and he got on so well with her and with his younger half brothers and half sister that they might have been full-blooded kin.

Duren pointed eastward. "There's Elleb, coming up over the stockade," he said. "Won't be too long till sunset." Gerin nodded. Ruddy Elleb—actually, a washed-out pink with the sun still in the sky—was a couple of days before full. Pale Nothos floated high in the southeast, looking like half a coin at first quarter. Golden Math wasn't up yet: she'd be full tonight, Gerin thought. And swift-moving Tiwaz was lost in the skirts of the sun.

Walamund had his drinking jack filled yet again. The Fox brewed strong ale; he wondered if the peasant would fall asleep before supper. Well, if Walamund did, it was his business, no one else's. He'd hike back to his village in the morning with a thick head, nothing worse.

From the watchtower atop the keep, a sentry shouted, "A chariot approaches, lord prince." On the palisade surrounding Castle Fox, soldiers looked to their bows and bronze-headed spears. In these troubled times, you never could tell who might be coming. After a short pause, the sentry said, "It's Van of the Strong Arm, with Geroge and Tharma."

The soldiers relaxed. Van had been Gerin's closest friend since before the great werenight, and that had been . . . Gerin glanced up toward Elleb and Nothos once more. Those two moons, and Tiwaz and Math, had all been full together nearly sixteen years before. Sometimes, that night of terror seemed impossibly distant. Sometimes, as now, it might have been day before yesterday.

Chains creaked as the gate crew lowered the drawbridge to let Van and his companions into Fox Keep. The bridge thumped down onto the dirt on the far side of the ditch surrounding the palisade. Not for the first time, Gerin told himself he ought to dig a trench from the River Niffet and turn that ditch to a moat. *When I have time*, he thought, knowing that likely meant *never*.

Horses' hooves drummed on the oak planks as the chariot rattled over the drawbridge and into the courtyard. "Ho, Fox!" Van boomed. The outlander was driving the two-horse team, and in his fine bronze corselet and helm with tall crest could easily have been mistaken for a god visiting the world of men. He was half a foot taller than Gerin—who was not short himself—and broad through the shoulders in proportion. His hair and beard were still almost all gold, not silver, though he was within a couple of years of the Fox's age, one way or the other. But the scars seaming his face and arms and hands gave proof he was human, not divine.

Yet however impressive the figure he cut, Walamund and Trasamir and all the peasants who'd accompanied them to Castle Fox stared not at him but at Geroge and Tharma, who rose behind him in the car. Trasamir's eyes got very big. "Father Dyaus," he muttered, and made an apotropaic sign with his right hand. "I thought we were rid of those horrible things for good."

Van glared at him. "You watch your mouth," he said, a warning not to be taken lightly. He turned back to Geroge and Tharma and spoke soothingly: "Don't get angry. He doesn't mean anything by it. He just hasn't seen any like you for a long time."

"It's all right," Geroge said, and Tharma nodded to show she agreed. He went on, "We know we surprise people. It's just the way things are."

"How'd the hunting go?" Gerin asked, hoping to distract Geroge and Tharma from the wide eyes of the serfs. They couldn't help their looks. As far as monsters went, in fact, they were very good people.

Tharma bent down and slung the gutted carcass of a stag out of the chariot. Geroge grinned proudly. "I caught it," he said. His grin made the peasants draw back in fresh alarm, for his fangs were at least as impressive as those of Swifty the hound. His face and Tharma's sloped forward, down to the massive jaws needed to contain such an imposing collection of ivory.

Neither monster was excessively burdened with forehead, but both, under their hairy hides, had thews as large and strong as Van's, which was saying a great deal. They wore baggy woolen trousers in a checked pattern of ocher and woad blue: a Trokmê style.

Pretty soon, Gerin realized, he was going to have to put them in tunics, too, for Tharma would start growing breasts before too much time went by. The Fox didn't know how long monsters took to reach puberty. He did know Geroge and Tharma were about eleven years old.

Monsters like them had overrun the northlands then, after a fearsome earthquake released them from the caverns under the temple of the god Biton, where they'd been confined for hundreds, maybe thousands, of years. The efforts of mere mortals hadn't sufficed to drive the monsters back, either; Gerin had had to evoke both Biton, who saw past and future, and Mavrix, the Sithonian god of wine, fertility, and beauty, to rout them from the land.

Before he'd done that, he'd found a pair of monster cubs and had not killed them, though he and his

comrades had slain their mother. When Mavrix banished
the monsters from the surface of the world, Biton had
mocked his sloppy work, implying some of the creatures
still remained in the northlands. Gerin had wondered
then if they were the pair he'd spared, and wondered
again a year later when a shepherd who'd apparently
raised Geroge and Tharma as pets till then brought
them to him. He thought it likely, but had no way to
prove it. The shepherd had been maddeningly vague.
He did know no other monsters had ever turned up,
not in all these years.

Having two monsters around was interesting,
especially since they seemed bright for their kind, which
made them about as smart as stupid people. They'd
grown up side by side with his own children, younger
than Duren but older than Dagref, the Fox's older son
by Selatre. They were careful with their formidable
strength, and never used their fearsome teeth for
anything but eating.

But soon Tharma would be a woman—well, an adult
female monster—and Geroge mature as well. The Fox
was anything but certain he wanted more than two
monsters in the northlands, and just as uncertain what,
if anything, to do about it. He'd kept putting off a
decision by telling himself he didn't yet need to worry.
That was still true, but wouldn't be much longer.

"Take that in to the cooks," he told Geroge. "Venison
steaks tonight, roast venison, venison ribs—" Geroge
slung the gutted deer over his shoulder and carried it
into the castle. Tharma followed him, as she usually
did, although sometimes he followed her. She ran her
tongue across her wide, thin lips at the prospect of plenty
of meat.

"I need more ale," Walamund muttered. "We're
supposed to eat alongside those horrible things?"

"They don't mind," Gerin said. "You shouldn't, either."

Walamund sent him a resentful glare, but the memory of recent punishment remained fresh enough to keep the serf from saying anything. Geroge and Tharma came out into the courtyard again, this time accompanied by Dagref and his younger sister Clotild, and by Van's daughter Maeva and his son Kor.

Behind the children strode Fand. "You might have told me you were back," she said to Van, a Trokmê lilt to her Elabonian though she'd lived south of the Niffet since shortly after the werenight. A breeze blew a couple of strands of coppery hair in front of her face. She brushed them aside with her hand. She was perhaps five years younger than Van, but beginning to go gray.

He stared over toward her. "I might have done lots of things," he rumbled.

Fand set hands on hips. "Aye, you might have. But did you, now? No, not a bit of a bit. Hopped in the car you did instead, and went off a-hunting with not a thought in your head for aught else."

"Who would have room for thoughts, with your eternal din echoing round in his head?" Van retorted. They shouted at each other.

Gerin turned to Nania. "Fetch them each the biggest jack of ale we have," he said quietly. The serving girl hurried away and returned with two jacks, each filled so full ale slopped over the side to make its own libation. Gerin knew he was gambling. If Van and Fand were still angry at each other by the time they got to the bottom of the jacks, they'd quarrel harder than ever because of the ale they'd drunk. A lot of the time, though, their fights were like rain squalls: blowing up suddenly fierce while they lasted, and soon gone.

Maeva gave Dagref a shove. He staggered, but stayed on his feet. The two of them were very much of a size, though he had a year on her. Maeva showed every promise of having much of her father's enormous physical prowess. Gerin wondered if the world was ready for a woman warrior able to best almost any man. Ready or not, the world was liable to face the prospect in a few years.

Clotild said, "No, Kor, don't put that rock in your mouth."

Instead of putting it in his mouth, he threw it at her. Fortunately, he missed. He had a temper he'd surely acquired from Fand. Four-year-olds were not the most self-controlled people under any circumstances. A four-year-old whose mother was Fand was a conflagration waiting to happen.

Van and Fand upended their drinking jacks at about the same time. Gerin waited to see what would happen next. When what happened next was nothing, he allowed himself a tiny pat on the back. He glanced over at Fand. Hard to imagine these days that he and Van had once shared her favors. Getting to know Selatre afterwards was like coming into a calm harbor after a storm at sea.

The Fox shook his head. That that image occurred to him proved only that he'd done more reading than just about anyone else in the northlands (which, though undoubtedly true, wasn't saying much). He'd never been on the Orynian Ocean—which lapped against the shore of the northlands far to the west—or any other sea.

Shadows lengthened and began to gray toward twilight. A bronze horn sounded a long, hoarse, sour note in the peasant village a few hundred yards from Fox Keep: a signal for the serfs to come to their huts from out of the fields, both for supper and to keep themselves safe from the ghosts that roamed and ravened through the night.

Van looked around to gauge the hour. He nodded approval. "The new headman keeps 'em at it longer than Besant Big-Belly did," he said. "There were times when he'd blow the horn halfway through the afternoon, seemed like."

"That's so," Gerin agreed. "The peasants mourned for days after that tree fell on him last winter. Not surprising, is it? They knew they'd have to work harder with anybody else over them."

"Lazy buggers," Van said.

The Fox shrugged. "Nobody much likes to work. Sometimes you have to, though, or you pay for it later. Some people never do figure that out, so they need a headman who can get the most from 'em without making 'em hate him." He was happy to talk about work with his friend: anything to distract Van from yet another squabble with Fand.

Fand, however, didn't feel like being distracted. "And some people, now," she said, "are after calling others lazy while they their ownselves do whatever it is pleases them and not a lick of aught else."

"I'll give you a lick across the side of your head," Van said, and took a step toward her.

"Aye, belike you will, and one fine day you'll wake up beside me all nice and dead, with a fine slim dagger slid between your ribs," Fand said, now in grim earnest. Van did hit her every once in a while; brawling, for him, was a sport. She hit him, too, and clawed, and bit. The outlander was generally mindful of his great strength, and did not use all of it save in war and hunting. When Fand was in a temper, she was mindful of nothing and no one save her own fury.

Van said, "By all the gods in all the lands I've ever seen, I'll wake up beside somebody else, then."

"And I pity the poor dear, whoever she is," Fand shot back. "Sure and it's nobbut fool's luck—the only kind a fool like you's after having—you've not brought me back a sickness, what with your rutting like a stoat."

"As if I'm the only one, you faithless—!" Van clapped

a hand to his forehead, speechless despite the many languages he knew.

Gerin turned to Trasamir, who happened to be standing closest to him. "Isn't love a wonderful thing?" he murmured.

"What?" Trasamir scratched his head.

Another one who wouldn't recognize irony if it came up and bit him on the leg, the Fox thought sadly. He wished he had the wisdom of a god, to say the perfect thing to make Van and Fand stop quarreling. With that, he'd probably need other divine powers, to make sure they didn't start up again the moment his back was turned.

Selatre came out to the entrance to the great hall. "Supper's ready," she called to the people gathered in the courtyard. Everyone, Van and Fand included, trooped toward the castle. Gerin chuckled under his breath. He hadn't known what to say to get Van and Fand to break off their fight, but Selatre had. Maybe she was divinely wise.

The notion wasn't altogether frivolous. Selatre had been Biton's Sibyl at Ikos, delivering the prophecies of the farseeing god to those who sought his wisdom, until the earthquake that released the monsters tumbled the god's shrine in ruins. Had Gerin and Van not rescued her while she lay in entranced sleep, the creatures from the caverns below would have made short work of her.

Biton's Sybil had to be a maiden. Not only that, she was forbidden so much as to touch an entire man; eunuchs and women attended her. Selatre had reckoned herself profaned by Gerin's touch. Plainly, she would have preferred him to leave her in her bed for the monsters to devour.

So matters had stood then. Now, eleven years, three living children, and one small grave later, Selatre tilted up her face as Gerin came back into Castle Fox. He brushed his lips against hers. She smiled and took his hand. They walked back toward the Fox's place of honor near the hearth and near the altar to Dyaus close by it. The fat-wrapped thighbones of the stag Van, Geroge, and Tharma had killed smoked on the altar.

Selatre pointed to them. "So the king of the gods gets venison tonight."

"He'd better not be the only one," Gerin said in a voice intended to carry back to the kitchens, "or there'll be some cooks fleeing through the night with ghosts baying at their heels to drive them mad."

A serving girl set rounds of thick, chewy bread on the table in front of each feaster. When another servitor plopped a couple of still-sizzling ribs on Gerin's flatbread, it sopped up the grease and juices. The Fox reached out to a wooden saltcellar in front of him and sprinkled some salt onto the meat.

"I wish we had pepper," he said, fondly remembering the spices that had come up from the south till the Empire of Elabon sealed off the last mountain pass just before the werenight.

"Be thankful we still have salt," Selatre said. "We're beginning to run low on that. It hasn't been coming up the Niffet from the coast as it used to since the Gradi started raiding a couple of years ago."

"The Gradi," Gerin muttered under his breath. "As if the northlands didn't have troubles enough without them." North of the Niffet lay the forests in which the Trokmoi dwelt: or rather, had dwelt, for the fair-haired barbarians had swarmed south over the Niffet near the time of the werenight, and many still remained: some, like Fand, among Elabonians; others, such as Gerin's vassal Adiatunnus, in place of the locals, whom they had subjected, driven away, or slain.

The homeland of the Gradi lay north of the Trokmê

country. Before coming down into Elabon, Van had been through the lands of both the Gradi and the Trokmoi. Gerin had seen a couple of Gradi at Ikos once, too: big, pale-skinned men with black hair, sweltering in furs. But, for the most part, the Trokmoi had kept the Elabonians from learning much about the Gradi and having much to do with them.

So it had been for generations. As Selatre had said, though, the Gradi had lately begun harrying the northlands' coastal regions by sea. Maybe they'd got word of disorder in the northlands and decided to take advantage of it. Maybe, too, their raids had nothing to do with whatever was going on locally, but had been spawned by some convulsion in their own country. Gerin did not know.

"Too much we don't know about the Gradi," he said, more to himself than to anyone else. Though he styled himself prince of the north, his power did not extend to the coast: none of the barons and dukes and petty lordlets by the sea acknowledged his suzerainty. If they were learning about the seaborne raiders, they kept that knowledge to themselves.

Selatre said, "I've been through the scrolls and codices in the library. Trouble is, they don't say anything about the Gradi except that there is such a people and they live north of the Trokmoi."

Gerin set his hand on hers. "Thanks for looking." When he'd brought her back to Fox Keep from Ikos, he'd taught her letters and set her in charge of the motley collection of volumes he called a library, more to give her a place of her own here than in the expectation she would make much of it.

But make something of it she had. She was as zealous now as he in finding manuscripts and adding them to the collection, and even more zealous in going through the ones they had and squeezing knowledge from them.

If she said the books told little about the Gradi, she knew whereof she spoke.

She glanced down at the table. Compliments of any sort made her nervous, a trait she shared with Gerin and one that set them apart from most Elabonians, for whom bragging came natural as breathing.

"What are we going to do about the Gradi, Father?" Duren asked from across the table. "What can we do about them?"

"Watch and wait and worry," Gerin answered.

"Are they just raiding, do you suppose, or will they come to settle when they see how fragmented that part of the northlands is?" Selatre asked.

The Fox picked up his drinking jack and raised it in salute. "Congratulations," he told his wife. "You've given me something brand new to worry about. Here I spend half my time trying to figure out how to bundle the Trokmoi back across the Niffet from what ought to be a purely Elabonian land, and now I have to think about adding Gradi to the mix." He gulped ale and spat into the bosom of his tunic to avert the evil omen.

Selatre sent him a look he could not fathom until she murmured, "A purely Elabonian land?"

"Well, in a manner of speaking," he said, feeling his cheeks heat. Selatre's ancestors had dwelt in the northlands for years uncounted before Ros the Fierce added the province to the Empire of Elabon. They'd taken on Elabonian ways readily enough, and most of them spoke Elabonian these days, which was what had led him to make his remark. Still, differences lingered. Selatre's features were finer and more delicate than they would have been had she sprung of Elabonian stock: her narrow, pointed chin was a marker for those of her blood.

"I know what you meant," she said, her voice mischievous, "but since you pride yourself on being so often right, I thought surely you would take the correction in good part."

Gerin enjoyed being told he was wrong, even by his wife, no more than most other men. But before he could come back with a reply sardonic enough to suit him, one of Walamund's relatives shouted at Trasamir, "I know how you got that cursed dog to come when you called it. You—" The suggestion was remarkable for both its originality and its obscenity.

The Fox sprang to his feet. He could feel a vein pulse in his forehead, and was sure the old scar above one eye had gone pale, a sure sign he was furious. And furious he was. "You!" he snapped, his voice slicing through the racket in the great hall. Walamund's kinsman looked over to him in surprise. The Fox jerked a thumb toward the doorway. "Out! You can sleep in the courtyard on the grass and wash your mouth with water, not my good ale, for I'll waste no more of that on you. On your way home tomorrow, think about keeping your mind out of the midden."

"But, lord prince, I only meant—" the fellow began.

"I don't care what you meant. I care what you said," Gerin told him. "And I told you, out, and out I meant. One more word and it won't be out of the castle, it'll be out of the keep, and you can take your chances with wolves and night ghosts where no torches and sacrifices hold them at bay."

The foul-mouthed peasant gulped, nodded, and did not speak. He hurried out into the night, leaving thick, clotted silence behind him.

"Now," Gerin said into it, "where were we?"

No one seemed to remember, or to feel like hazarding a guess. Van said, "I don't know where we were, but I know where I'm going." He picked up Kor, who'd fallen asleep on the bench beside him, and headed for the stairs. Fand and Maeva followed, off to the big bed they all shared. The quarrel between Van and Fand hadn't flared again, so maybe it would be forgotten . . . till the next time, tomorrow or ten days down the road.

Once upon a time, Duren had been in the habit of falling asleep at feasts. Gerin sighed; remembering things like that and comparing them to how matters stood these days was a sign he wasn't getting any younger.

He looked around for Duren and didn't see him. He wouldn't be out in the courtyard, not with only a drunken, swill-mouthed peasant for company. More likely, he was back in the kitchens or in a corridor leading off from them, trying to slip his hands under a serving girl's tunic. He'd probably succeed, too: he was handsome, reasonably affable, and the son of the local lord to boot. Gerin remembered his own fumblings along those lines.

"Dyaus, what a puppy I was," he muttered.

Selatre raised one eyebrow. He didn't think she'd done that when he first brought her to Fox Keep; she must have got it from him. "What's that in aid of?" she asked.

"Not much, believe me," he answered with a wry chuckle. "Shall we follow Van and bring our children up to bed, too?"

Their younger son, named Blestar after Selatre's father (Gerin having named Duren and Dagref for his own brother and father, whom the Trokmoi had slain), lay snoring in her lap: he had only a couple of years to him. Dagref and Clotild were both trying to pretend they hadn't just yawned. The Fox gathered them up by eye. "Upstairs we go," he declared.

"Oh, Papa, do we have to?" Dagref said through another yawn. Along with belief in the gods, all children seemed to share an abiding faith that they had to deny the need for sleep under any and all circumstances.

Gerin did his best to look severe. Where his children

were concerned, his best was none too good, and he knew it. He said, "Do you know what would happen to anyone else who presumed to argue with the prince of the north?"

"You'd cut off his head, or maybe stew him with prunes," Dagref said cheerfully. Gerin, who'd been taking a last swig from his drinking jack, sprayed ale onto the tabletop. Dagref said, "If Duren argued with you, would you stew *him* with prunes? Or isn't he part of 'everybody else'?"

Down in the City of Elabon, they'd had special schools to train the officials who interpreted the ancient and complex code of laws by which the Empire of Elabon functioned. The hairsplitting in which those schools indulged had once struck Gerin, who reveled in minutiae himself, as slightly mad: who could not only make such minute distinctions but enjoy doing it? Watching Dagref grow, he regretted being unable to send the boy south for legal training.

When he got upstairs, he opened the door to the chamber he shared with his wife and children and went inside to bring out a lamp. He lighted it at one of the torches flickering in a bronze wall sconce in the hallway, then used its weak glow to let Selatre go into the chamber and set Blestar at the edge of the big bed. Dagref and Clotild took turns using the chamber pot that stood by the side of the bed before getting in themselves, muttering sleepy good-nights. The straw in the mattress rustled as they lay down.

"Don't blow out the lamp," Selatre said quietly. "I need the pot myself."

"So do I, as a matter of fact," the Fox answered. "Ale."

He wondered if Duren would disturb them, coming back later in the night. He didn't think so; he doubted his elder son would be sleeping in this bed tonight. Just in case, though, he shut the door without barring it. After he shoved the chamber pot against the wall so Duren wouldn't knock it over if he did come in, he blew out the lamp. Darkness and the heavy smell of hot fat filled the bedchamber.

The night was mild, not so much so that he felt like getting out of tunic and trousers and sleeping in his drawers, as he would when summer came, but enough that he didn't drag a thick wool blanket up over his chin and put a hot stone wrapped in flannel by his feet. He sighed and wriggled and twisted away from a stem of straw that was poking him in the ribs. Beside him, Selatre was making the same small adjustments.

Blestar snored on a surprisingly musical note. Dagref and Clotild wiggled around like their parents, also trying to get comfortable. "Stop poking me," Clotild complained.

"I wasn't poking you, I was just stretching out," Dagref answered, maddeningly precise as usual. "If I poke you, that's something I do on purpose." Usually, he would add, *like this*, and demonstrate. Tonight he didn't. That proved he was tired. Clotild didn't snap back at him, either.

Before long, their breathing smoothed out. Gerin yawned and stretched himself—carefully, so as not to bother anyone else. He yawned again, trying to lure sleep by sympathetic magic. Sleep declined to be lured.

Selatre was breathing very quietly, which meant she too was likely to be awake. When she slept, she sometimes snored. Gerin had never said anything about it. He wondered if he did the same. If he did, Selatre hadn't mentioned it. *Wonderful woman*, he thought.

Her voice reached him, a tiny thread of whisper: "Have you fallen asleep?"

"Yes, quite a while ago," he answered, just as softly. Dagref hadn't poked Clotild. Selatre did poke him now, right in the ribs, and found a sensitive spot. He had all he could do not to writhe and kick one of his children.

She started to poke him again. He grabbed her arm and pulled her close to him, that being the fastest way he could think of to keep her questing finger from making him jerk again. "You cheat," she said. "That's the only ticklish spot you have, and you won't let me get to it."

"I cheat," he agreed, and covered her right breast with his left hand. Through the thin linen of her long tunic, her nipple stiffened at his touch. The feel of her body pressed against his made him stiffen, too. He felt one eyebrow quirk upward into a question, but she couldn't see that in the dark. He put it into words: "Do you think they're sleeping soundly enough yet?"

"All we can do is find out," she answered. "If they do wake up, it would fluster you more than me. I grew up in a peasant's hut, remember: the whole of it about the size of this room. I never imagined having so much space as I found first at Ikos and then here at Fox Keep."

Thinking of the raised eyebrow he'd wasted, he said, "Well, if my ears turn red, it'll be too dark for the children to notice." He kissed her then, which struck him as a better idea under the circumstances—and, indeed, generally—than talking about his ears. His hand slid down from her breast to tug up the hem of her tunic.

They didn't hurry, both because they didn't want to wake the children and because, after a good many years together, friendly familiarity had taken the edge off passion. Presently, Selatre rolled over onto her side, facing away from Gerin. She lifted her top leg a little to let him slide in from behind, a quiet way of joining in more ways than one. Her breath sighed out as he entered her to the hilt. He reached over her to tease at her nipple again. The edge might have gone from their passion, but a solid core remained.

After they'd finished, Selatre said, "Did you put the

pot by the wall? I think I'd better use it again." She slid out of bed and groped her way toward it. Gerin, meanwhile, separated his clothes from hers and got back into them. He suspected he had his drawers on backward, but resolved not to worry about it till morning.

When Selatre came back to bed, she put her drawers and tunic back on, too, then leaned over and unerringly planted a kiss on the end of his nose. He squeezed her. "If I wasn't sleepy before," he said, "I am now—or pleasantly tired, anyhow."

Selatre laughed at him. "You saved yourself in the nick of time there, didn't you?"

"Considering the history of this place since I took the rule after my father was killed, how could I do it any other way?" Gerin replied, and settled down to sleep. Laughing still, almost without voice, Selatre snuggled against him.

His eyelids were growing heavy when the bed frame in the next chamber started to creak. Selatre giggled, a sound different from her earlier laughter. "Maeva must have stayed awake longer than our brood did."

"Or maybe Kor woke up, just to be difficult," Gerin answered. "He has his mother's temper, all the way through. He'd better be a good swordsman when he grows up, because I have the feeling he'll need to be."

Selatre listened to the noises from the far side of the wall for a moment, then said, "His father's quite the mighty swordsman, by all I've seen."

"That's true any way you care to have it mean," Gerin agreed. "It's because of that, I suppose, that he and Fand are able to make up their quarrels. I almost wonder if they have them for the sake of making up."

"You're joking," Selatre said. After she'd thought it over, though, she shook her head against his chest. "No, you're not joking. But what an appalling notion. I couldn't live like that."

"Neither could I," he said, remembering fights he'd had with Fand back in the days when she was his lover as well as Van's. "My hair and beard would be white, not going gray, if I tried. But one of the things I've slowly come to figure out through the years is that not everybody works the same way I do."

"Some people never do figure that out." Selatre yawned. "One of the things I've slowly come to figure out over the years is that I can't do without sleep. Good night."

"Good night," Gerin said. He wasn't sure his wife even heard him: now her breathing was as deep and regular and—he smiled a little—raspy as that of their children. Sleep swallowed him moments later.

The peasants set out for their village early the next morning, Trasamir Longshanks leading Swifty the hound on a rope leash. Walamund's relative, rather to the Fox's disappointment, seemed not much worse for wear after his night in the courtyard. Uncharitably, Gerin wondered how often he'd passed out drunk between houses in his hamlet.

Bread and ale and cheese and an apple did for Gerin's breakfast. He was going down to see how the apples were holding out in the cellar when the lookout yelled, "A horseman approaching from out of the south, lord prince."

Gerin went out to the doorway of the great hall. "A horseman?" he called up. "Not a chariot?"

"A horseman," the sentry repeated. "One of our men, without a doubt."

He was right about that. The idea of getting up on a horse's back rather than traveling in wagon or chariot or cart was new in the northlands. As far as Gerin could discover, as far as widely traveled Van could say, it was new in all the world. One of the Fox's vassals, Duin the Bold, had come up with a trick that made staying mounted much easier: wooden rings that hung down from either side of a pad strapped around the horse's girth, so a man could use his hands for bow or spear without the risk of going over the animal's back.

Duin, though, had died fighting the Trokmoi just after the werenight. Without his driving energy, the device he invented advanced more slowly than it would have otherwise. If your father had ridden to war in a chariot, and your grandfather, and *his* grandfather . . .

"It's Rihwin the Fox, lord prince," the sentry reported when the rider came close enough to recognize him.

"I might have known," Gerin muttered. That was true for a couple of reasons. For one, Rihwin had been some time away from Fox Keep. A couple of times a year, he went out to see how his numerous bastards were doing, and, no doubt, to try to sire some more of them. He had a fair-sized troop of by-blows scattered widely over the lands where Gerin's suzerainty ran, so his expeditions ate up a good deal of time.

And, for another, his love for the new extended to more than women. He'd come north with Gerin from the civilized heart of the Empire of Elabon bare days before the werenight for no better reason than that he craved adventure. Had riding horses been old and chariotry new, he would no doubt have become an enthusiastic advocate for the chariot. As things were, he probably spent more time on horseback than any other man in the northlands.

The gate crew let down the drawbridge. Rihwin rode into the courtyard of Fox Keep. He waved a salute to Gerin, saying, "I greet you, lord prince, my fellow Fox, valiant for your vassals, protector of your peasants, mild to merchants, and fierce against your foes."

"You've been in the northlands fifteen years and more now," Gerin said as Rihwin dismounted, "and you still talk like a toff from the city." Not only did Rihwin have a soft southern accent, he also remained fond of the elaborate phrasing and archaic vocabulary nobles from the City of Elabon used to show they had too much time on their hands.

A stable boy came up to lead Rihwin's horse to its stall. "Thank you, lad," he murmured before turning back to Gerin. "And why should I not proclaim my essence to the world at large?" A hand went up to the large gold hoop he wore in his left ear. So far as Gerin knew—and he likely knew more of the northlands than anyone else alive—no other man north of the High Kirs followed that style.

"Rihwin, save for keeping you out of the alepot as best I can, I've long since given up trying to make you over," he said.

Rihwin bowed, his handsome, mobile features twisting into a sly smile. "No small concession that, lord prince, and in good sooth I know it well, for where else has the victorious and puissant prince of the north retreated from any venture to which he set his hand?"

"I hadn't looked at it so," Gerin said thoughtfully. "You tempt me to go back to trying to reform you." Rihwin made a face at him. They both laughed. Gerin went on, "And how is your brood faring these days?"

"I have a new daughter—the mother says she's mine, anyhow, and since I lay with her at around the proper time, I'm willing to believe her—but I lost a son." Rihwin's face clouded. "Casscar had only three years: scarlet fever, his mother said. The gods be kind to his ghost. His mother was crying still, though it happened not long after I saw her last."

"She'll be grieving till they bury her," Gerin said, remembering the loss he and Selatre had had. He shook his head. "You know you shouldn't risk loving a child when it's very small, for so many of them never do live to grow big. But you can't help it: it's how the gods made us, I suppose."

About half the time, maybe more, a remark like that would have led Rihwin to make a philosophical rejoinder, and he and Gerin could have killed a pleasant stretch of time arguing about the nature of the gods and the reasons they'd made men and women as they had. The two of them were the only men in the northlands of whom Gerin knew who'd had a proper education down in the City of Elabon. That perforce kept them friendly even when they wore on each other: in an important way, they spoke the same language.

But now Rihwin said, "The other thing I wanted to tell you, lord prince, is something interesting I heard when I was out in the west, out well past Schild Stoutstaff's holding. When I went that way a few years ago, I met this yellow-haired Trokmê wench named Grainne and, one thing leading to another, these days I have myself a daughter in that village. The gods grant she does live to grow up, for she'll delight many a man's eye. She—"

Gerin stared down his nose at him. "Has this tale a point? Beyond the charm and grace of your daughter, I mean? If not, you'll have to listen to me going on about my children in return."

"Oh, I do that all the time anyhow," Rihwin said blithely, "whereas you need only put up with me a couple of times a year." Gerin staggered back as if he'd taken a thrust mortal. Chuckling, Rihwin said, "As a matter of fact, though, lord prince, the tale indeed has a point, though I own to being unsure precisely what it is. This village, you see, lies hard by the Niffet, and—"

"Did you get word of more Trokmoi planning to raid or, worse, settle?" Gerin demanded. "I'll hit them if you did, and hit them hard. Too cursed many woodsrunners this side of the Niffet already."

"If you will let me finish the tale, lord prince, rather than consistently interrupting, some of these queries may perhaps be answered," Rihwin replied. Gerin kicked at the grass, annoyed at himself. Rihwin had caught him out twice running now. The southerner went on, "Grainne told me that, not so long before I came to visit, she'd seen a new kind of boat on the river, like nothing on which she'd ever set eyes before."

"Well, what does she know of boats?" Gerin said. "She wouldn't have been down to the City of Elabon, now would she, to watch galleys on the Greater Inner Sea? All she'll have ever seen are little rowboats and rafts and those round little coracle things the Trokmoi make out of hides stretched over a wicker frame. You'd have to be a Trokmê to build a boat that doesn't know its front from its backside." He held up his hands. "No. Wait. I'm *not* interrupting. Tell me how this one was different."

"The Niffet bends a trifle, a few furlongs west of Grainne's village," Rihwin said. "There's a grove of beeches at the bend, with mushrooms growing under them. She was out gathering them with a wicker basket— which she showed me as corroborating evidence, for whatever it may be worth—when, through a screening of ferns, she spied this boat."

"Eventually, my fellow Fox, you're going to tell me about it," Gerin said. "Why not now?"

Rihwin gave him a hurt look before going on, "As you say, lord prince. By her description, it was far larger than anything that moved on the water she'd ever seen before, with a mast and sail and with some large but, I fear, indeterminate number of rowers laboring to either side."

"A war galley of some sort," Gerin said, and Rihwin nodded. Gerin continued, "You say she saw it through ferns? Lucky the rowers didn't spot her, or they'd likely have grabbed her and held her down and had their

fun before they cut her throat. That'd be so no matter
who they were—and, so far as I know, nobody's ever
put a war galley on the Niffet. Do you suppose the
Empire of Elabon has decided it wants the northlands
back after all?"

"Under His indolent Majesty Hildor III?" Rihwin's
mobile features assumed a dubious expression. "It is,
lord prince, improbable." But then he looked thoughtful.
"On the other hand, we've had no word, or next to it,
out of Elabon proper since the werenight, which is,
by now, most of a generation past. Who can say with
certainty whether the indolent posterior of Hildor III
still warms the Elabonian throne?"

"A distinct point," Gerin said. "If it is the imperials—"

Rihwin raised a forefinger. "As you have several times
in the course of this conversation, lord prince, you
break in before I was able to impart salient information.
While the ship and men Grainne saw may have been
Elabonians, two significant features make me doubt
it. First, while her Elabonian is fluent—much on the
order of Fand's, including the spice thereof—she could
not follow the sailors' speech. Admittedly, the ship
was out on the river, so this is not decisive. But have
you ever heard of an Elabonian ship mounting the
shields of oarsmen and warriors between rowing
benches?"

Gerin thought back to his days in the City of Elabon,
and to the galleys he'd seen on the sea and tied up at
the quays. He shook his head. "No. They always stow
them down flat. Which leaves—"

He and Rihwin spoke together: "The Gradi."

"That's bad," Gerin said. He kicked again at the dirt
and paced back and forth. "That's very bad, as a matter
of fact. Having them raid the seacoast is one thing. But
if they start bringing ships up the Niffet . . . Father
Dyaus, a flotilla of them could beach right there, a few

furlongs from Fox Keep, and land more men than we could hope to hold away from the walls. And we'd have scant warning of it, too. I need to send out messengers right away, to start setting up a river watch."

"It will not happen tomorrow, lord prince," Rihwin said soothingly. "Grainne watched this vessel turn around at the river bend and make its way back toward the west. The Gradi have not found Castle Fox."

"Not yet," Gerin answered; he borrowed trouble as automatically as he breathed, having seen from long experience that it came to him whether he borrowed or not, and that it was better met ahead of time when that proved possible. The Gradi, however, were not the only trouble he had, nor the most urgent. He asked Rihwin, "When you rode out to visit all your lady loves, did you go through Adiatunnus' holding?"

"Lord prince, I had intended to," Rihwin answered, "but when I came up to the margins of the lands he rules as your vassal, his guardsmen turned me away, calling me nothing but a stinking southron spy."

"He's not yet paid his feudal dues this year, either." Gerin's dark eyebrows lowered like stormclouds. "My guess is, he doesn't intend to pay them. He's spent the last ten years being sorry he ever swore me fealty, and he'll try breaking loose if he sees the chance."

"I would praise your wisdom more were what you foresee less obviously true," Rihwin answered.

"Oh, indeed," Gerin said. "All I had to do to gain his allegiance last time was work a miracle." Adiatunnus had made alliance with the monsters from under the temple at Ikos; when, at Gerin's urging, Mavrix and Biton routed them from the northlands, the proud Trokmê chieftain was overawed into recognizing the Fox as his overlord. Now Gerin sighed. "And if I want to keep that allegiance, all I have to do is work another one."

"Again, you have delivered an accurate summary of

the situation," Rihwin agreed, "provided you mean keeping that allegiance through peaceable means. He may well prove amenable to persuasion by force, however."

"Always assuming we win the war, yes." Gerin's scowl grew blacker still. "We'll need to gather together a goodly force before we try it, though. Adiatunnus has made himself the biggest man among the Trokmoi who came over the Niffet in the time of the werenight; a whole great host of them will fight for him."

"I fear you have the right of it once more," Rihwin said. "He has even retained his stature among the woodsrunners while remaining your vassal, no mean application of the political art. As you say, suppressing him, can it be done, will involve summoning up all your other retainers."

"Which might give Grand Duke Aragis the excuse he needs to hit my southern frontier," Gerin said. "The Archer will recognize weakness when he sees it. The only reason he and I don't fight is that he's never seen it from me—till now."

"Will you then let Adiatunnus persist in his insolence?" Rihwin asked. "That would be unlike you."

"So it would," Gerin said, "and if I do, he'll be attacking me by this time next year. What choice have I, my fellow Fox? If I don't enforce my suzerainty, how long will I keep it?"

"Not long," Rihwin answered.

"Too right." Gerin kicked at the dirt once more. "I've always known I'd sooner have been a scholar than a baron, let alone a prince." With old friends, Gerin refused to take his title seriously. "There are times, though, when I think I'd sooner have run an inn like Turgis son of Turpin down in the City of Elabon than be a prince—or practiced any other honest trade, and some of the dishonest ones, too."

"Well, why not run off and start yourself an inn, then?" Rihwin poked his tongue into his cheek to show he didn't intend to be taken seriously. His hands deftly sketched the outlines of a big, square building. "By the gods, I can see it now: the hostelry of Gerin the Fox, all complaints cheerfully ignored! How the dour Elabonians and woad-dyed Trokmoi would throng to it as a haven from their journeys across the northlands to plunder one another!"

"You, sirrah, are a desperately deranged man," Gerin said. Rihwin bowed as if he'd just received a great compliment, which was not the effect Gerin had wanted to create. He plunged ahead: "And if I did start an inn, who'd keep the Trokmoi and the Elabonians—to say nothing of the Gradi—from plundering *me*?"

"By all means, let us say nothing of the Gradi," Rihwin said. "I wish my lady love there had never set eyes on that ship of theirs. Father Dyaus willing, none of us will see such ships with our own eyes."

But Gerin refused to turn aside from the inn he did not and never would have. "The only way to keep such a place is to have an overlord strong enough to hold bandits at bay and wise enough not to rob you himself. And where is such a fellow to be found?"

"Aragis the Archer is strong enough," Rihwin said teasingly. "Were I a bandit in his duchy, I'd sooner leap off a cliff than let him get his hands on me."

Gerin nodded. "If he were less able, I'd worry about him less. But one fine day he'll die, and all his sons and all his barons will squabble over his lands in a war that'll make the unending mess in Bevon's holding look like a children's game by comparison. We'll not have that here, I think, when I'm gone."

"There I think you have reason, lord prince," Rihwin said, "and so, being the best of rulers, needs must continue in that present post without regard for your obvious and sadly wasted talents as taverner."

"Go howl!" Gerin said, throwing his hands in the air. "I know too well I'm stuck with the bloody job. It *is* a hardship, you know: on account of it, I have to listen to loons like you."

"Oh! I am cut to the quick!" Rihwin staggered about as if pierced by an arrow, then miraculously recovered. "Actually, I believe I shall go in and drink some ale. That accomplished, I shall take more pleasure in howling." With a bow to Gerin, he hied himself off toward the great hall.

"Try not to drink so much you forget your name," Gerin called after him. The only answer Rihwin gave was a finger-twiddling wave. Gerin sighed. Short of locking up the ale jars, he couldn't cut Rihwin off. His fellow Fox didn't turn sullen or vicious when he drank; he remained cheerful, amiable, and quite bright—but he could be bright in the most alarmingly foolish ways. Gerin worried about how often he got drunk, but Gerin, by nature, worried about everything that went on around him.

Right now, though, worrying about Rihwin went into the queue along with worrying about the Gradi. Both were a long way behind worrying about Adiatunnus. The Trokmê chieftain was liable to have the strength to set up on his own if he chose to repudiate Gerin's overlordship, and if he did set up on his own, the first thing he'd do would be to start raiding the lands of Gerin's vassals . . . even more than he was already.

The Fox muttered something unpleasant into his beard. Realizing he never was going to be able to drive all the Trokmoi out of the northlands and back across the Niffet into their gloomy forests came hard. One of the bitter things life taught you was that not all your dreams came true, no matter how you worked to make them real.

Up in the watchtower atop Castle Fox, the lookout shouted, "A chariot approaches, lord prince!"

"Just one?" Gerin asked. Like any sensible ruler, he made sure trees and undergrowth were trimmed well away from the keep and from the roads in his holding, the better to make life difficult for bandits and robbers.

"Aye, lord prince, just the one," the sentry answered. Gerin had chosen his lookouts from among the longer-sighted men in his holding. As it had a few times before, that proved valuable now. After a few heartbeats, the lookout said, "It's Widin Simrin's son, lord prince."

The drawbridge had not gone up after Rihwin arrived. Widin's driver guided his two-horse team into the keep. Widin jumped out of the car before it stopped rolling. He was a strong, good-looking young man in his late twenties, and had held a barony southwest of Fox Keep for more than half his life: his father had died in the chaos after the werenight. Whenever Gerin saw him, he was reminded of Simrin.

"Good to see you," Gerin said, and then, because Widin's keep was a couple of days' travel away and men seldom traveled without urgent need, he added, "What's toward?"

"Lord prince, it's that thieving, skulking demon of an Adiatunnus, that's what," Widin burst out. Worrying about the Trokmoi was already at the head of Gerin's list, which was the only thing that kept it from vaulting higher. Widin went on, "He's run off cattle and sheep both, and burned a peasant village for the sport of it, best I can tell."

"Has he?" Gerin asked. Widin, who had never studied philosophy, did not know a rhetorical question when he heard one, and so nodded vigorously. Gerin was used to such from his vassals; it no longer depressed him as it once had. He said, "If Adiatunnus is at war with one of my vassals, he's also at war with me. He will pay for what he's done to you, and pay more than he ever expected."

His voice held such cold fury that even Widin, who'd brought him this word in hope of raising a response, drew back a pace. "Lord prince, you sound like you aim to tumble his keep down around his ears. That would be—"

"—A big war?" Gerin broke in. Widin nodded again, this time responsively. Gerin went on, "Sooner or later, Adiatunnus and I are going to fight a big war. I'd rather do it now, on my terms, than later, on his. The gods have decreed that we can't send all the woodsrunners back over the Niffet. Be it so, then. But we can—I hope—keep them under control. If we can't do even that much, what's left of civilization in the northlands?"

"Not much," Widin said. Now Gerin nodded, but as he did so he reflected that, even with the Trokmoi beaten, not much civilization was left in the northlands.

II

Chariots and a few horsemen rolled out of Fox Keep over the next couple of days, heading east and west and south to summon Gerin's vassals and their retainers to his castle for the war against Adiatunnus. He sent out the men heading west with more than a little apprehension: they would have to pass through Schild Stoutstaff's holding on the way to the rest of the barons who recognized the Fox as their overlord, and Schild, sometimes, was almost as balky a vassal as Adiatunnus himself.

Duren went wild with excitement when Gerin decided on war. "Now I can fight beside you, Father!" he said, squeezing the Fox in a tight embrace. "Now, maybe, I can earn myself an ekename."

"Duren the Fool, perhaps?" Gerin suggested mildly. Duren stared at him. He sighed, feeling like a piece of antiquity unaccountably left adrift in the present-day world. "I don't suppose there's any use telling you this isn't sport we're talking about. You really maim, you really kill. You can really get maimed, you can really get killed."

"You can prove your manhood!" No, Duren wasn't listening. "Tumbling a serving girl is all very well—better than all very well—but to fight! 'To battle your enemy with bright-edged bronze'—isn't that what the poet says?"

"That's what Lekapenos says, all right. You quoted him very well." Gerin looked up to the sky. What was

36

he supposed to do with a boy wild for war? Did justifying being wild for war by quoting from the great Sithonian epic poem mean Duren was properly civilized himself, or did it mean he, as the Trokmoi sometimes did, had acquired a civilized veneer with which to justify his barbaric impulses? Father Dyaus gave no answers.

Van came out of Castle Fox. Duren ran over to him, saying, "It'll be war! Isn't that wonderful!"

"Oh, aye, it's wonderful, if you come through in one piece," Van answered. Duren took the half of the answer he was hoping to hear and went into the hall, singing a bloodthirsty song that had nothing to do with Lekapenos: Gerin knew the minstrel who, fool that he was, had translated it from the tongue of the Trokmoi. Van turned round to look after Duren. He chuckled. "The fire burns hot in him, Fox."

"I know." Gerin didn't try hiding that the fire didn't burn hot in him. He said, "This is needful, but—" and shrugged.

"Ahh, what's the matter? You don't want to be a hero?" Van teased.

"I've *been* a hero, over and over again," Gerin answered. "And what has it brought me, besides always another war? Not bloody much."

"You hadn't decided to be a hero when you went to rescue Selatre from the monsters, you wouldn't have the wife you've got now," his friend pointed out. "You'd not have three of your children, either. You might still be sharing Fand with me instead, you know." Van rolled his eyes.

"Now you've given me a defense of heroism indeed!" Gerin said. Both men laughed. Gerin went on, "But I don't see you rushing toward the fight the way you once did, either."

Van looked down at his toes. "I'm not so young as I used to be, either," he said, as if the admission embarrassed him. "Some days, I'm forced to remember it. My bones creak, my sight is getting long, my wind is shorter than it used to be, I can't futter three times a night every night any more—" He shook his head. "If you knew how long you were going to be old, you'd enjoy the time when you're younger more."

Gerin snorted. "If you'd done any more enjoying while you were younger, either you or the world wouldn't have lived through it. Maybe you and the world both."

"Ah, well, you have something there," Van answered. "But it's like you said, Captain: I've been a hero, too, and now what am I? I'm the fellow who, if some Trokmê brings me down and takes my head to nail over his doorposts, I turn him into a hero. So they come after me, whatever fight I happen to be in, and after a while it starts to wear thin."

"There you have it," Gerin agreed. "After a while, it starts to wear thin. And the ones who do come after you, they're always the young, hot, eager ones. And when you're not so young any more, and not so eager any more, and it has to be done anyhow, then it turns into work, as if we were serfs going out to weed the fields, except we pull up lives instead of nettles."

"But nettles don't uproot themselves and try pulling you up if you leave 'em in the fields," Van observed. He looked thoughtful. "Can't you magic Adiatunnus to death, if you don't fancy fighting him?"

"Not you too!" The Fox gave his friend a massively dubious look. Hearing vassals and peasants plead cases before him for years had given him a first-rate look of that description. Hardened warrior though Van was, he gave back a pace before it. Gerin said, "I could try spelling Adiatunnus, I suppose. I would try it, if I didn't think I was likelier to send myself to the five hells than the cursed Trokmê. Putting a half-trained wizard to work is like turning a half-trained cook loose in the kitchen:

you don't know what he'll do, but you have a pretty good idea it'll turn out bad."

"Honh!" Van shook his head again. "All this time as a prince, and you still don't think you're as good as you really are. All the magics you've tried that I know of, they've worked fine."

"That's only because you don't know everything there is to know," Gerin retorted. "Ask Rihwin about his ear one day. It's not a story he's proud of, but he may tell it to you. And if you try working a spell with death in it, you'll get a death, all right, one way or another."

"What's the good of having all those what-do-you-call-'ems—grimoires—in your book-hoard if you won't use 'em?"

"I didn't say I wouldn't use them," Gerin snapped. "I do use them—for small things, safe things, where even if I go wrong the disaster will be small, too . . . and for things so great that having the magic fail won't be a bigger catastrophe than not trying it. Putting paid to Adiatunnus is neither the one nor the other."

"Honh!" Van repeated. "I may be turning into an old man, but you're turning into an old woman."

"You'll pay for that, by Dyaus!" Gerin sprang at the bigger man, got a foot behind his ankle, shoved, and knocked Van to the ground. With an angry roar, the outlander hooked an arm around the Fox's leg and dragged him down, too, but Gerin managed to land on top.

Men came running from all parts of the keep to watch them wrestle. As Gerin tried to keep Van from tearing his shoulder out of its socket, he reflected that they'd been grappling with each other for too many years. When they'd first begun, his tricks had let him beat Van as often as he lost. Now Van knew all the tricks, and he was still bigger and stronger than the Fox.

"I'm the prince, curse it," Gerin panted. "Doesn't

that entitle me to win?" Van laughed at him. Any ruler in the northlands who tried to make more of his rank than was due him got laughed at, even Aragis.

Strength wouldn't serve, the usual tricks wouldn't serve, which left—what? Van tried to throw Gerin away. To the outlander's surprise, Gerin let him. The Fox flew through the air and landed with a thud and a groan, as if he'd had the wind knocked out of him. Blood up, Van leaped onto him to finish the job of pinning him to the dirt.

Gerin stuck an elbow right into the pit of the outlander's stomach. Van folded up. It wasn't anything he wanted to do, but he couldn't help himself; he had to fight to breathe, and, for the first moments of that fight, you always seemed to yourself to be losing. Gerin had no trouble pinning him instead of the other way round.

Van finally managed to suck in a couple of hissing gasps. "Fox, you—cheat," he wheezed, his face a dusky red because he was so short of air.

"I know," Gerin said cheerfully. When his friend could breathe again, he helped pull him to his feet. "Most of the time, they pay off on what you do, not how you do it."

"And I thought I had all your tricks down." Van sounded chagrined, not angry. "It got to the point where you hadn't come up with anything new in so long, I didn't think you could. Shows what I know."

"Shows I got tired of having that great tun you call a body squashing me flat every time we wrestled," Gerin answered. "Actually, I used that ploy of seeming helpless against Aengus the Trokmê—remember him? The chief of the clan Balamung the wizard came from? I let the air out of him with my sword, not my elbow."

"Felt like your sword," Van grumbled, lifting up his tunic as if to see whether he was punctured. He had a red mark where Gerin's elbow had got home; it would probably turn into a bruise. But, considering the scars that furrowed his skin, reminders of a lifetime of wandering and strife, the mark was hardly worth noting. He rubbed at himself and let the tunic fall. "I should have been wearing my corselet. Then you'd have banged your elbow and not my poor middle."

"And you talk about me cheating!" Gerin said, full of mock dudgeon.

"So I do," Van said. "D'you care to wrestle again, to see if you can befool me twice?"

"Are you daft?" Gerin answered. "These days, it's a gift from the gods when I can fool you once. I'm going in for a jack of ale to celebrate." Van trailed after him, undoubtedly having in mind a jack of ale with which to drown his own discomfiture.

Before Gerin got to the entrance of the great hall, someone small came dashing out and kicked him in the shin. "Don't you hurt my papa!" Kor shouted. When Gerin bent down and tried to move him aside, he snapped at the Fox's hand.

"Easy there, boy." Van picked up his son. "He didn't do me any great harm, and it was a fair fight." No talk of illicit elbows now. Van carefully gentled Kor down: his son took after Fand in temperament, and Gerin supposed the patience Van needed to live with her—when he did live with her—came in handy for trying to keep the boy somewhere near calm, too.

After his ale, Gerin went out to the peasant village close by the keep. He had a pretty good notion of how the village stood for supplies and how much it could spare when his vassals and their retainers started arriving for the fight against Adiatunnus. The short answer was, not much. He wanted to see by how much the long answer differed from the short one.

The old village headman, Besant Big-Belly, would

have whined and wheezed and pleaded poverty. His replacement, Carlun Vepin's son, was working in the fields as Gerin approached. The Fox nodded approvingly. Besant hadn't been fond of work of any description. Since his passing, yields from the village had gone up. That probably meant Gerin should have replaced him years before, but far too late to worry about that now. One of the five hells was said to have enormous water wheels in which lazy men had to tread forever, emptying buckets of boiling water onto themselves. For Besant's sake, Gerin hoped that wasn't so.

When Carlun spotted Gerin, he came trotting over to him. "Lord prince!" he called, giving the Fox something between a nod and a bow. "How may I serve you this afternoon?"

"How's your store of grain and beans and smoked meat and such holding up?" Gerin asked, hoping he sounded casual but doubting he sounded casual enough to make Carlun give him a quick, rash answer.

He didn't. The headman's face was thin and clever. "Not so well as I'd like, lord prince," he answered. "We had a long, hard winter, as you must recall, and so didn't get to plant till late this spring. The apples haven't been all they should on account of that, either, and the plums are coming in slow, too, so we've been drawing on the stores more than I would if I had other choices. Cabbages have done well, I will say," he added, as if to throw the Fox a bone of consolation.

"Let's have a look at the tallies for what you've used up," Gerin said.

"I'll fetch them, lord prince." Carlun trotted off toward the wattle-and-daub hut he shared with his wife and their four—or was it five?—children. He came out a moment later with a couple of sheets of parchment.

Even before the werenight, Gerin had begun teaching a few of the brighter peasants in his holding to read.

His time in the City of Elabon had convinced him ignorance was an enemy as dangerous as the Trokmoi. When he'd begun his scheme, he hadn't thought of its also having thoroughly practical uses: a man who could read could keep records much more accurate than those proffered by a man relying solely on his memory.

Carlun probably inked his pen with blackberry juice, but that didn't bother the Fox. Neither did the headman's shaky scrawl. Here was the barley, here was the wheat— Gerin took a look at the records, took a look around the village, and started to laugh.

"Lord prince?" Did Carlun sound a trifle apprehensive? If he didn't, he should have. But he did: he was clever enough to know he hadn't been clever enough with the records.

"You'll have to do better than that if you're going to cheat me," Gerin said. "Not mentioning the storage pits off to the east there and hoping I wouldn't notice doesn't do the job. I remember you have them even if you didn't write anything about them here."

"Ah, a pestilence!" Carlun said. Like the Fox, he kicked at the dirt in anger and frustration. Carlun World-Bestrider, for whom he was named, had been the greatest emperor in Elabonian history. Now he saw even his little headmanship in danger. If Gerin raised someone else to take his place, he'd never live it down, not if he stayed in the village till he was ninety. "What—what will you do with me, lord prince?"

"Hush. I'm not finished here yet," Gerin said, and then fell silent again while he methodically went through the rest of the parchment. Carlun waited and squirmed. The Fox looked up. "You're right. The cabbages have done well."

Carlun jerked as if a wasp had stung him. Then he realized Gerin hadn't ordered him cast down from his small height. Gerin, in fact, hadn't said anything about his fate at all. "Lord prince?" he asked in a tiny voice, as if not willing to admit hope still lived in him.

"Oh, aye—about you." The matter might have slipped Gerin's mind. He turned brisk: "Well, it's simple enough. You can't be headman here any more. That's pikestaff plain."

Carlun took the blow like a warrior. "As you wish, lord prince," he said tonelessly. "Dare I ask you to give me leave to travel to some village far away in the lands you hold? That way, maybe, my family and I will be able to hold up our heads."

"No, that's impossible," Gerin said, and, for the first time, Carlun's shoulders slumped in dismay. Gerin went on, "Can't do it, I'm afraid. No, I'm going to move you into Fox Keep instead."

"Lord prince, I—" Carlun suddenly seemed to hear what the Fox had said. He gaped. "Into Fox Keep?" His gaze swung toward the timbers of the palisade. "Why?"

With a lot of lords, the question wouldn't have needed asking. You brought a peasant inside a keep so you could take all the time you wanted tormenting him with all the tools you had. But Gerin did not operate that way, and never had. He took a certain somber pride that his serfs understood as much.

It was, evidently, the only thing Carlun understood. In an exasperation partly feigned and partly quite genuine, Gerin said, "Father Dyaus above, man, don't you see you're the first of all the peasants I've taught who's ever tried to cheat me with words and numbers?"

"I'm sorry, lord prince," Carlun said miserably. "If only I could have another chance, I'd serve you well."

"I'll give you another chance," Gerin told him, "and a proper one this time. How would you like to keep accounts for all the lands I hold, not for this one little village? I've been doing it myself, but each day is only so long. Oh, I'll look over your shoulder, and so will Selatre, but I've dreamt for years of finding a man at home with numbers to whom I could give the job. If you're at home enough with numbers to try cheating with them, you may be the man to try. If you make good, you'll be better off there than you ever could be here, headman or no. Are you game for it?"

"Lord prince!" Carlun fell to his knees. "I'll be your man forever. I'll never cheat again, not by so much as a bean. I'll do whatever you ask of me, learn whatever you set before me—"

Gerin believed the last part. He was less sure of the rest. He'd been down to the City of Elabon and seen how arrogant imperial treasury officials—indeed, all imperial officials—could get. He didn't want men acting in his name behaving like that. Going through histories and chronicles, though, warned him they were liable to behave like that no matter what he wanted them to do. Despite Carlun's fervent protestations, they were also likely to see to it that silver and grain and other good things ended up in their hands rather than in the treasury.

"Get up," he told Carlun, his voice rough. "You're already my man forever. I'll thank you to remember it in better ways than this." He shook the offending parchments in Carlun's face. The headman quailed again. Gerin went on, "The other thing to keep in mind is, you're like a dog that's bitten once. If you cheat again and I find out about it, you'll wish you'd never been born, I promise you that. I've never crucified a man in all the years I've ruled this holding, but that would tempt me to change my mind."

"I already swore, lord prince, I'd not take even a bean that wasn't mine, and I meant every word of what I said." Carlun gabbled out the words. Was he trying to convince himself as well as the Fox? No, probably not,

Gerin decided. He meant what he said—now. But it was a rare treasurer who died poor. Gerin shrugged. Time would tell the tale.

"I didn't mean to frighten you—too much," Gerin said, with a grin lacking only Geroge's fangs to make it truly fearsome. Carlun had picked a stupid way to cheat the first time. As he got more familiar with the numbers he juggled, he was liable to get more adept at concealing his thefts, too. Again, though, time would tell. "Go on, go let your wife know what we're going to do, then head up to the keep. Tell Selatre what I've sent you for—and why."

"Y-yes, lord prince," the newly promoted larcenous headman said.

But when he turned to go, Gerin held up a hand. "Wait. If you're leaving the village, with whom should I replace you?"

An evil gleam kindled in Carlun's eyes. "The one who complains most is Tostrov Waterdrinker. I'd like to see how he'd shape in the job if he had it."

"Tostrov?" Gerin rubbed his chin. "Aye, he does complain a lot, doesn't he? But no, he has no other virtues I can think of. No one would pay him any mind. Try again, and seriously this time."

"Aye, lord prince." Carlun hesitated, then said, "The man my sister married, Herris Bigfoot, is no fool, and he works hard. People respect him, too. You could do worse."

"Mm, so I could. I'll think on that," Gerin said. He slapped the parchments against his knee. They made a dry, rustling sound, as if they were dead leaves rubbing one another. "Now, back to the business I came here for. With that stored grain you didn't bother writing down"—he watched in some satisfaction as Carlun went pink—"how are you fixed for stores?"

He thought about adding something like, *If you still*

tell me you're starving, I'm going to open up those storage pits and see for myself. In the end, he didn't; he wanted to see how Carlun would react without the goad. The headman hesitated, visibly thinking through the answers he might give. Gerin hid a smile: no, Carlun wasn't used to dealing with someone who was liable to be trickier than he. After a pause that stretched a couple of heartbeats too long, he replied, "Lord prince, we're— not too badly off, though I hate to say that so early in the year."

"And you have plenty of cabbages," the Fox added. Carlun squirmed. "Well, never mind that. We'll need some of what you have, to feed the warriors who'll be gathering here for war against Adiatunnus."

Carlun licked his lips. "You'll be drawing more than the customary dues from us, then?"

Was that a hint of reproach in his voice? It was, the Fox decided. He eyed Carlun with a mixture of annoyance and admiration. The headman would not have dared protest to any other ruler in the northlands: of that Gerin was sure. Most overlords thought, *What does ruling mean but taking what I want and what I'm strong enough to grab?* But the Fox, so far as he could, tried to substitute custom and even the beginning of law for naked theft.

He fixed Carlun with an unpleasant stare. "I could say the overage is forfeit as punishment for trying to cheat me." After watching the serf writhe, though, he said, "I won't. It's not the village's fault you cheated. It had better not be, anyhow." He stared again.

"Oh, no, lord prince," Carlun said quickly. "My idea. All mine."

No one from the village had come to complain he was cheating the Fox. Maybe the other peasants hadn't known. Maybe they'd hoped he'd get away with it. No proof, and Gerin didn't feel like digging. "I'll believe you," he said, "No, I won't simply take it. For whatever we exact over the set dues, I'll ease your labor in the forests and on the Elabon Way and such."

"Thank you, lord prince," Carlun said. Before Gerin could find any other awkward questions with which to tax him, he hurried back toward the village. The Fox had told him to do so, after all, and didn't take offense.

Still holding the parchments, Gerin stood a while in thought. From what he knew of Herris Bigfoot, Carlun's brother-in-law wouldn't make a bad headman. The only trouble he foresaw was that he hadn't taught Herris to read. Record-keeping here would go downhill for a while.

Or would it? Herris wasn't stupid. Maybe he could learn. You didn't need to know much in the way of reading and writing to keep track of livestock and produce. The Fox shaded his eyes with one hand and peered out over the fields. He was starting to have trouble reading these days, having to hold manuscripts farther from his eyes because his sight was lengthening. Out past arm's length, though, nothing was wrong with the way he saw.

There stood Herris, talking and laughing with a woman who, Gerin saw, was not Carlun's sister. He shrugged. He hadn't heard anything to make him think Herris was doing anything scandalous, so he wouldn't worry about this. He went over to Herris, noting as he did so that the barley was coming in well.

Carlun's brother-in-law watched him approach. Herris' friend quickly got back to work weeding. "You want something with me, lord prince?" Herris asked. "I saw you talking with Carlun, and—"

"How would you like his job?" the Fox asked bluntly.

The woman busy pulling weeds let out a startled gasp. Herris scratched his head. He didn't look or act as sharp as Carlun, but Gerin knew that didn't necessarily mean anything. After the pause for thought, Herris said, "It depends, lord prince. How come you don't want him there no more?"

Gerin nodded in approval—loyalty to your kin seldom went to waste. He explained the new post for which he wanted Carlun (though not the cheating that made him think Carlun might be right for it), finishing, "And he said you'd do for headman here. Thinking about it, I'd say he's likely right, if you want the job."

"I do, lord prince, and thank you," Herris said. "I'd've felt different, I expect, if you were giving him the sack for no good reason."

"No," Gerin said, again not mentioning he had a good reason if he wanted to use it. He smacked the rolled-up parchments against his leg once more. "There is one other thing—I know you don't have your letters, so I'm going to want you to learn them if you can. That way, you'll have an easier time keeping track of things here."

Herris pointed to the accounts Carlun had kept. "May I see those, lord prince?" Gerin handed them to him. He unrolled them and, to the Fox's surprise, began to read them out. He stumbled a couple of times, but did well enough on the whole.

"I *know* I didn't teach you your letters," Gerin said. "Where did you learn them?"

Herris looked worried. "Am I in trouble, lord prince?" Only after the Fox shook his head did the peasant say, "Carlun taught 'em to me. He didn't know he was doing anything wrong, swear by Dyaus he didn't. He learned 'em to me and a couple-three others, he did. It was a way to pass the time, nothin' more, that's for true."

"It's all right," Gerin said absently. "Don't worry about it." He shook his head, altogether bemused. So they'd been learning letters in the peasant huts, had they, instead of rolling dice and drinking ale? No, more likely alongside of rolling dice and drinking ale. A lot of nobles in the northlands reckoned serfs nothing more than domestic animals that chanced to walk on two legs. The Fox had never been of that school, but this caught him off guard. If you let learning put down one root, it would put out half a dozen on its own—unless, of course, the Trokmoi yanked them all out of the ground. "Can you write as well as read?" he asked Herris.

"Not as good as Carlun can," the peasant answered, "but maybe good enough so you can make out the words. The numbers, they're not hard."

"No, eh?" Was he boasting? Gerin decided to find out. "Take a look at the numbers on these sheets here. Tell me what you think is interesting about them."

Herris scratched his head thoughtfully, then went over the records his brother-in-law had kept. Gerin didn't say anything, but rocked from heels to toes and back again, giving Herris all the time he wanted. He couldn't think of a better test for the prospective headman's wits and honesty both.

He was beginning to think Herris either less honest or less bright than he'd hoped when the peasant coughed and said, "Uh, lord prince, is there another sheet somewheres?"

"No." The Fox kept his voice neutral. "Should there be?"

"You said you were giving Carlun this fancy spot at Fox Keep?" Herris asked. Gerin nodded. Herris looked worried. "Him and me, we've always got on well. I'd hate to have him think I was telling tales, but . . . we've got more grain than these here parchments show."

"Herris!" The woman who was weeding spoke his name reproachfully. Then, too late, she remembered with whom he was talking. She bent down and started pulling plants out of the ground as fast as she could.

"Good," Gerin said. "You'll do. You'll definitely do."

"Lord prince?" Herris was floundering.

"I never told Carlun not to cheat me," the Fox explained. "Of course, that was only because it hadn't occurred to me he'd try, but still, the fact remains, so how am I to blame him? In a way, I'm glad to see learning take hold, with him and with you. But only in a way— bear that in mind. I've warned him what will happen if he tries any more cheating, and I would advise you to think very hard about that, too. Do we understand each other?"

"Oh, yes, lord prince," Herris said, so sincerely that he either meant it or was a better liar than Gerin thought. One way or the other, the Fox would find out.

Chariots began rattling into Fox Keep, by ones and twos and sometimes by fours and fives. As they arrived, Gerin's vassals hung their armor on the walls of the great hall. The firelight from the hearth and torches made the shining bronze molten, almost bloody. That seemed fitting, for bloody work lay ahead.

Bevander Bevon's son said, "Lord prince, is all quiet with Aragis the Archer? If the grand duke gets wind of what we're about here, he's liable to jump us while we're busy."

"I've worried about the same thing myself," the Fox agreed, eyeing Bevander with considerable respect. The man was not the greatest warrior the gods ever made, but he knew intrigue. He and his father and brothers had fought a multicornered civil war for years; any man who couldn't keep track of who'd last betrayed whom soon paid the price.

Bevander went on, in meditative tones, "Or, on the other hand, Aragis might want to let us fight Adiatunnus and *then* attack. If we and the Trokmoi were both weakened, he might sweep us all into the Niffet and style himself king."

"If he wants the title, he's a fool, and whatever else Aragis is, he's no fool," Gerin answered. "I have a better claim to call myself king than he does, by the gods, but you don't see me doing it. If any man styles himself king, that'll be a signal for all the other nobles in the northlands to join together and pull him down."

"If any man styles himself king who hasn't earned it, you mean," Bevander said. "If Aragis beats you and the woodsrunners both, who could say he has no right to the title? You should use some of your magic powers, lord prince, and see what Aragis intends when you move against the Trokmoi."

Like so many other people in the northlands, Bevander was convinced Gerin had strong magical powers because he'd cleared the land of the monsters from under Biton's shrine at Ikos. The Fox knew only too well that had been two parts desperation to one part sorcery. He hadn't advertised the fact, wanting his foes to think him more fearsome than he was. That created another problem, as solutions have a way of doing: his friends also thought him more fearsome than he was.

Now, though, he paused thoughtfully. "I may do that," he said at last. Scrying was not likely to be a form of magic particularly dangerous to his health. He didn't know how accurate the spells would prove; in peering into the future, you tried to navigate through a web of possibilities expanding so rapidly that even a god had trouble following the links.

Bevander beamed. "May you have good fortune with it," he said. He swelled with the self-importance of a man who's had a suggestion taken.

Gerin eyed him as he walked away, strutting just a little. He had wit enough to be dangerous had his ambition matched it. Having obtained the lion's share of Bevon's barony for backing the Fox in the last fight against Adiatunnus, though, he'd been satisfied with that—and with finally getting the upper hand on his brothers—ever since.

For his part, Gerin was satisfied to remain prince rather than king. The only trouble was, no one believed him when he said as much.

Selatre came into the library. "Hello," she said to the Fox. "I didn't expect to find you here." Ever since he'd taught her to read, she'd taken the chamber where he stored his scrolls and codices as her private preserve.

"I'm getting away from the racket of my barons," he said, and then, because he didn't like telling her half-truths, "and I'm looking in the grimoires to see what sort of scrying spell I can cast that's least likely to turn me into a salamander."

"I wouldn't want that," Selatre said seriously. "Salamanders aren't good at raising children, let alone running a principality." She walked over and ran a hand down his arm. "I suspect they're also, mm, less than desirable in certain other areas."

"I daresay you're right," Gerin answered. "The gods only know how we'd manage to put a pond in the bedchamber." As Selatre snorted, he went on, warming to the theme, "Or we could go up to the Niffet and make sport there, always hoping no big pike came along at the worst possible moment."

"I'm leaving," Selatre said with more dignity than the words really needed. "It's plain enough you won't keep your mind on what you're doing if I'm here to distract you."

The Fox grinned over his shoulder, then returned to the grimoires. If half what they said was true, seeing into the future was so easy, no one should ever have needed to consult Biton's Sibyl down at Ikos. Of course, if half what the grimoires said was true, anyone who read them would have more gold than he knew what to do with and live to be three hundred years old. Knowing which grimoire to trust was as important as anything else when it came to sorcery.

"Here, this ought to do it," the Fox said at last, picking a spell from a codex he'd brought back from the City of Elabon. He closed the book, tucked it under his arm, and carried it out of Castle Fox and over to the small hut near the stables where he worked his magic.

Every time he went in there, even if it was for nothing more elaborate than trying to divine where a sheep had strayed, he wondered if he would come out again. He knew how much he knew—just enough to be dangerous—and also how much he didn't know, which gave him pause about using the knowledge he had.

He opened the grimoire. The divining spell he'd chosen, unlike a lot of them, required no wine. Wine grapes would not grow in the northlands. Even if they had, he would have been leery of using what they yielded. His previous encounters with Mavrix, the Sithonian god of wine, made him anxious never to have another.

"Oh, a pestilence," he muttered. "I should have brought fire with me." After filling a lamp with perfumed linseed oil, he went back to the castle, got the lamp going at a torch, and carried it over to the hut. He felt stares at his back; if his vassals hadn't noticed before what he was doing, they did now. Whatever enthusiasm they had, they hid very well.

He set the lamp on a wooden stand above his worktable. That done, he rummaged in a drawer under the table till he found and pulled out a large quartz crystal. The grimoire said the crystal was supposed to be flawlessly pure. He looked at it, shrugged, and started to chant. It was what he had. If he didn't use it, he couldn't work the spell.

As with a lot of spells, this one had the more difficult

passes for the left hand. The Fox suspected that was intentional, to make the spells more likely to fail. It bothered him not at all, since he was left-handed. His magic did not go wrong on account of clumsiness. Lack of training and lack of talent, however, were something else again.

"Reveal, reveal, reveal!" Gerin shouted in tones of command, holding the crystal between the elevated lamp and the table.

A rainbow sprang into being on the grimy tabletop— getting it spotlessly white, as the grimoire suggested, had struck the Fox as more trouble than it was worth. As the magic began to unfold, he reckoned himself vindicated. He had seen, over the years, that the men who wrote tomes on magic had a way of worrying more about form than about function.

The rainbow vanished. A white light filled the crystal. Gerin almost dropped it in alarm, but held on when he realized it wasn't hot. Surely the little smudges and chips that white light revealed would not matter to the spell.

He concentrated his own formidable wits on Aragis the Archer, visualizing the grand duke's craggy, arrogant features: by his face, Aragis might have been half hawk on his father's side. The brain behind that harsh mask was alarmingly keen—nearly as good as Gerin's, if focused more on the short term and the immediate vicinity.

So what was Aragis plotting now? If the Fox locked himself in battle with Adiatunnus, what would the grand duke do?

As soon as Gerin fully formed the question, a beam of light stabbed out from the glowing crystal down onto the tabletop. The Fox sucked in a quick, startled breath. There sat Aragis, with what looked like a mixture of distaste and intense concentration on his face. Gerin looked closely, trying to be sure he was reading the expression correctly. His rival seemed shrouded in shadow.

Aragis suddenly rose. The perspective shifted. The strings of oaths Gerin let out had nothing to do with the spell. Maybe purity of materials and cleanliness of scrying surface mattered more than he'd thought. A view of Aragis grunting in the smelly castle latrine was less edifying than the Fox had hoped. No wonder the grand duke's expression had been as it was. Had he obtained relief for the problem troubling him? Gerin would never know.

The light from the crystal faded. Evidently that was the only glimpse of Aragis Gerin would get. He swore again, half in anger, half in resignation. Sometimes his magics worked, sometimes he made an idiot of himself and wondered why he ever bothered trying. At least he hadn't come close to burning down the hut, as had happened before.

Unlike most of Gerin's vassals, Bevander could guess why Gerin had gone into the hut in the first place. Looking very full of himself, he walked up to the Fox and asked, "What news of Aragis, lord prince? Will he bedevil us if we war with Adiatunnus?"

"I don't really know, worse luck," the Fox answered. "The spell I tried turned out to be full of shit." He wasn't often able to tell literal and symbolic truth at the same time, and savored this chance the way a litterateur savored a well-turned verse. All the same, he would have traded the witticism for a real look into the future.

Every time his vassals rode away from Fox Keep at the end of a campaign, Gerin forgot how much chaos they brought while they were there. Part of that came from packing a lot of fighting men into a compact space and then having to wait for the latecomers before everyone could go out and fight. If they couldn't battle their foes, a lot of the Fox's troopers were willing, even eager, to battle one another.

Some of those fights were good-natured affrays that sprang from nothing more than high spirits and a couple of mugs of ale too many. Some had the potential for being more serious. Not all of Gerin's vassals loved one another. Not all of them loved him, either. Schild Stoutstaff was not the only man who would have liked nothing better than to renounce his allegiance to the Fox—had he not had Adiatunnus hanging over his southern border.

Gerin did his best to keep known enemies among his vassals as far from each other as he could. For years, he'd been doing his best to keep those vassals from going on with their own private wars. "And you've done well at it, too," Van said when he complained aloud one day: "better nor I ever thought you could. A lot of the feuds that were hot as a smith's fire when first I came here have cooled down in the years since."

"And a lot of them haven't, too," Gerin said. "Drungo Drago's son remembers that Schild's great-great-grandfather killed his own great-great-great-grandfather in a brawl a hundred years ago, and he wants to pay Schild back. And Schild remembers, too, and he's proud of what his flea-bitten brigand of an ancestor managed to do."

"Isn't that—what do you call it?—history, that's the word I want?" Van said. "You always say we have to know history if we're going to be civilized, whatever that means. Do you want Drungo and Schild to forget their blood feud?"

"I want them to forget their blood vengeance," Gerin answered. "The old quarrels get in the way, because the new one we have is more important—or it ought to be more important. The way some of my vassals eye some of the others, you'd think they came here for their own private wars. As far as they're concerned, fighting mine is a nuisance."

"Only one way to deal with that," Van said. "So long as they're more afraid of you than they are of each other, they'll do as you like."

"Oh, they know I can thump them like a drum if I have to, and they're too fractious to join together and cast me down, for which the gods be praised," the Fox replied. "But that isn't what brings them together here. The one they're really afraid of is the cursed Trokmê."

Van scratched a scar that wandered down into his beard. Himself afraid of nothing this side of angry gods, he found fear of a foe hard to fathom. At last, he said, "There's that, too, I suppose. Anyone who thinks the woodsrunners make good neighbors has been chewing the wrong leaves and berries: I give you so much."

Vassals hastily moved aside from the doorway to the great hall. Gerin understood that a moment later, when Geroge walked outside. Even without armor, the monster was a match for men who wore bronze-scaled corselets and helms and carried spears and shields. A couple of minor barons had already urged the Fox to get rid of Geroge and Tharma both. He'd invited them to try it, with no more additions to nature than the monsters enjoyed. They hadn't urged twice.

Geroge came up to Gerin at a sort of lumbering trot. "Something wrong?" the Fox asked. As best he could tell, Geroge looked troubled. The monster's features were hard to read. The forward stretch of the lower half of his face made his nose low and flat, and heavy brow ridges shadowed his eyes. Had a creature half-wolf, half-bear walked like a man, it would have looked a lot like him.

He was also right on the edge of the transition from

child to adult, and no more easy with that than anyone else. "They laugh at me," he said in his rough, growly voice, pointing with a clawed forefinger back toward the great hall. "They should be used to me by now, but they call me names."

"Why don't you grab one of them and eat him?" Van said. "He won't call you names after that, by the gods."

"Oh, no!" Geroge sounded horrified. As best the Fox could tell, he looked horrified, too. "Gerin taught Tharma and me never to eat people. And we couldn't eat enough of them to keep the rest from hurting us."

"That's right," Gerin said firmly, giving Van a dirty look. He'd worked hard trying to humanize the monsters, and didn't appreciate having his work undermined. "That's just right, Geroge," he repeated, "and you reasoned it out very well, too." For their kind, Geroge and Tharma were both clever. He never failed to let them know it.

Geroge said, "What do we do, then? I don't like it when they call us names. It makes me mad." He opened his mouth very wide. Examining the sharp ivory within, Gerin knew he would not have wanted the monster annoyed at him.

He said, "If they bother you again, *I* will eat them."

"Really?" Geroge's narrow eyes widened.

"Er—no," the Fox admitted. He had to keep reminding himself that, even though Geroge was bigger and much more formidably equipped than he, the monster was also as literal-minded as a child half his age. "But I will make them very sorry they insulted you. They have no business doing it, and I won't stand for it."

"All right," Geroge said. Like a child with its father, he was convinced Gerin always could and would do exactly as he promised. Gerin had to bear that in mind when he spoke with the monster. If he didn't deliver on a promise . . . he didn't know what would happen then, or want to find out.

"Anyone who bothers you will answer to me, too," Van rumbled. That made the monster happy; unlike most mere mortals, Van was still stronger than Geroge, and also unintimidated by his fearsome looks. That made him a hero in the monster's eyes.

"Let's go hunting," Geroge said. "We need more meat with all these people crowding the keep. We always need more meat." His tongue, long and red and rough like a cat's, flicked out to moisten his lips. He didn't just need meat—he needed to hunt more meat.

"You won't hear me say no," Van answered. He went back into the great hall, emerging a moment later with a stout bow and a quiver slung over his back. He affected to despise archery when fighting men—he preferred a long, heavy spear that he handled as if it were a twig used for picking teeth—but proved his skill as a bowman whenever he went after game.

Geroge hurried away, too, returning momentarily with Tharma. Both monsters were chattering excitedly; they were about to go off and do something they loved. With so many warriors in the keep, the drawbridge was down. Flanked on either side by a monster, Van tromped out of the keep and headed for the woods.

No one would call Geroge and Tharma names while they were out hunting. Even if a warrior came upon them in the woods, he would think several times before drawing their notice, much less their anger. Gerin had hunted with them, many times. Out among the trees, they sloughed off a lot of the cloak of humanity they wore inside Fox Keep. They were more purely predators in the woods, and less inclined to put up with nonsense from people.

Gerin, much to his own regret, had to put up with a lot of nonsense. He sometimes thought that the hardest part of the ruler's art. He'd never been one to suffer fools gladly. In his younger days, he'd never been one to suffer fools at all. He would either ignore them or insult them till they went away. First as baron, though, and then as self-styled prince, he'd gradually become convinced the number of fools was so high, he made too many enemies by treating them all as they deserved. Little by little, he'd learned patience, though he'd never learned to like it.

Rihwin the Fox and Carlun Vepin's son came out of the great hall together. Seeing them so sent alarm through Gerin. Carlun had already figured out on his own how to get into trouble, and if by some chance he hadn't, Rihwin would have taken care of that small detail for him. Rihwin could get anyone, from himself up to and including gods, into trouble.

To Gerin's relief, his fellow Fox said something to Carlun that seemed to rub the ex-headman the wrong way. Rihwin laughed out loud at that. Carlun looked angry, but didn't do anything about it. In his place, Gerin wouldn't have done anything, either. Carlun had spent a lifetime with hoe and shovel and plow, Rihwin just as long with sword and bow and spear. If you weren't trained from childhood as a warrior, you were a fool to take on a man who was.

Laughing still, Rihwin gave Carlun a mocking bow and went on his way. Carlun saw Gerin and hurried over to him. "Lord prince!" he cried, his face red with frustrated, impotent fury. "They scorn me, lord prince!"

He might have been Geroge, though he expressed himself better. On the other hand, the warriors could twit him with impunity; he wasn't liable to tear them limb from limb if they pushed him too far. "What are they calling you?" Gerin asked.

"They've given me an ekename," Carlun said indignantly. "One of them called me Carlun Inkfingers, and now they're all doing it." He held out his hands to the Fox. Sure enough, the right one was stained with ink.

Gerin held out his hands in return. "I have those stains, too, you'll note," he said, "and rather worse than you: being left-handed, I drag the side of my hand through what I've written while that's still wet."

"But they don't call you Gerin Inkfingers," Carlun said.

"That's true. I've given them reason to hang a different sobriquet on me," Gerin said. "You could do that. Or you could take pride in the one they've given you, instead of letting them make you angry with it. Most of them, you know, couldn't find their own name on a piece of parchment if it stood up and waved to them."

"I don't like trying to deal with so many of your warriors," Carlun said, sticking out his lower lip like a sulky child.

"Then it's back to a village for you—a village far away," Gerin told him. "You won't be headman there, either— you know that. You'd just be a serf among serfs for the rest of your life. If that's truly what you want, I'll put you and your family on the road tomorrow."

Carlun shook his head. "I don't want that, lord prince. What I want is revenge, and I can't take it. They'd kill me if I tried." His eyes swung in the direction Rihwin had gone.

"If you tried sticking a knife into one of them, he would kill you," the Fox agreed. "There are other ways, though, if you think for a bit. A man with armor can stand off several without. And a man who knows reading and numbers, if you put him in with folk who don't—"

He watched Carlun's eyes catch fire. That amused him; clever as the ex-headman was, he hadn't yet learned to conceal his thoughts. And, a moment later, the fire faded. Carlun said, "You warned me, lord prince, what would happen if you caught me cheating. I don't like the warriors' mocking me, but you would do worse than mock."

Though he did not smile, the Fox was pleased he'd put a healthy dose of fear in Carlun's soul. He answered, "I didn't say anything about cheating—certainly not about cheating me out of my due. But if a man insults you, he should hardly be surprised if you reckon up what he owes his overlord with very close attention to every detail. Do you understand what I'm saying?" He waited for Carlun to nod, then went on, "It's not as satisfying as smashing a man in the face with an axe, maybe, but you're not there so he can smash you in the face, either."

Carlun went down on one knee and seized Gerin's right hand in both of his. "Lord prince," he said, "now I understand why you have gone from victory to victory. You see farther ahead than any man now living. Teach me!"

That evening, in some bemusement, Gerin said to Selatre, "There I was, explaining how to avenge yourself on someone who'd offended you without getting killed in the process, and he ate it up like a bear in a honey tree. Have I made him someone who will aid me better, or am I turning him into a monster more dangerous than any of Geroge and Tharma's unlamented cousins?"

"You can't be sure, one way or the other," she answered, sensible as usual. "For all you know, you may be doing both at once. He may end up being a useful monster, if you know what I mean."

"Which is fine for me, but not so good for him," Gerin answered. "Maybe I should have just sent him off to another village and had done with it. That would have been simplest, and it wouldn't have shown poor Carlun temptations the likes of which he's never seen before."

"Nonsense," Selatre said crisply. "If he hadn't known about temptations like that, he wouldn't have tried cheating you in the first place. Now you have him working for you, not against you."

"People like Carlun, the only ones they work for are themselves," Gerin replied with a shake of the head. "The way you get them to do what you want is to make them see that going your way sends them along their own path better than anything else they could do."

Selatre nodded. "Aye, I can see that. You've done it for Carlun, plain enough. By the time he's through with your vassals, they'll be lucky if they have a tunic and a pot of beans apiece to call their own."

She laughed, but the Fox began to worry. "Can't have that. If he squeezes them too hard, they'll blame me. Just what I'd need—rebellions from men who've always been solid backers."

"You'll curb him before it comes to that," Selatre said confidently. She had more confidence in Gerin, sometimes, than he had in himself.

"The gods grant you're right," he said.

From Fox Keep, the land sloped down to the Niffet a few furlongs away. Gerin drilled his vassals on the expanse of grass and bushes where sheep and cattle usually grazed. Some of the warriors grumbled at that. Drungo Drago's son complained, "This practicing is a silly notion, lord prince. We go off, we find the cursed Trokmoi, and we smash 'em into the ground. Nothing to worry about in any of that." He folded massive arms across a wide chest.

"You're your father come again," Gerin said. Drungo beamed, but Gerin had not meant it altogether as a compliment. Drago the Bear had been strong and brave, but up to the day he clutched his chest and keeled over dead he'd not been long on thought.

"Aye," several men said together. "Turn us loose on the Trokmoi. We'll take care of what happens next."

"You practice with the bow, don't you?" the Fox asked them. They nodded. He tried again: "You practice with the spear and the sword, too?" More nods. He did his best to drive the lesson home: "You practice in your chariots, I expect, so you can do the best job of fighting from them?" When he got still more nods, he bellowed, "Then why in the five hells don't you want to practice with a whole swarm of chariots together?"

He should have known better than to expect logic to have anything to do with their answer. Drungo said, "On account of we already know how to do that, on account of we've all been in a bunch of fights already."

"Brawls," Gerin said scornfully. "Every car for itself, every man for himself. The woodsrunners fight the same way. If we have an idea of what we're going to do before we do it, we'll have a better chance of winning than if we make it up as we go along. And besides" —he pointed off to the right wing— "we'll be trying something new on this campaign."

"Yes, and those fools on horses' backs aren't worth anything, either," Drungo said, eloquently dubious, as his gaze followed the Fox's finger.

"You *are* your father's son," Gerin told him, feeling old. Sixteen years ago now, back before the werenight, Drago had mocked Duin the Bold, claiming the art of equitation was more trouble than it would ever be worth. They'd almost brawled then. Now Gerin was going to find out whether Duin had known what he was talking about.

When his overlord pointed to him, Rihwin the Fox waved from the stallion on whose back he perched. He led a couple of dozen mounted men, most of them only half his age. His years were the main reason Gerin, halfway against his better judgment, had placed him in command of the riders. With luck, he would have more sense than the hotheads he led, but he was also living proof that experience did not necessarily bring maturity.

"We'll try another practice charge," Gerin said to Drungo. "Maybe you'll see what I'm driving at." He had thought about giving up the chariot himself and going over to riding a horse, but his long partnership with Van and their driver Raffo had kept him in the car.

He brought down his arm. The chariots jounced across the meadow in a line less ragged than it had been a few days before. And over on the right flank, the horses moved faster than any team hauling car and warriors both. They also made their way without effort over ground that would surely have made a chariot flip over. Rihwin even leaped his horse across a gully: you would have had to be mad to urge a team to try such a stunt (which might not have deterred Rihwin, but would have given anyone else pause).

"There," Gerin said when the exercise was over. "Do the lot of you think this business of riding horses may have something to it after all?"

Again, Drungo spoke for the conservative majority, just as Drago had in his day: "Maybe a small something, lord prince, but no more than that. Horses for scouts and for flank attacks: aye, I'll give you so much. But it's the chariots that'll finish the foe."

As he was still fighting from a chariot himself, Gerin could not very well argue with that. In fact, he more or less agreed. Having stood up against a chariot charge, he knew how it turned opponents' blood to water and their bones to gelatin. The drum of the hooves, the rattle and bang of the cars as they thundered down on you, the fierce cries of the warriors standing upright in them, weapons ready to hand . . . If you could stand up against such without quailing, you were a man indeed. Cavalry alone would not be nearly so fearsome.

What he said, then, was, "We will be using the cavalry on the flanks, to disrupt the charge our foes try to make against us. We've not done that before, not in war. That's why I've been bringing us out here the past few days: so we could see how it would go, see how the flank chariots need to stick close to the riders and how the riders can't get too far out in front of the chariotry—"

"Well, why didn't you say so, lord prince?" Drungo demanded.

The Fox couldn't decided whether to throttle his literal-minded vassal or merely to pound his own head against the side rail of his car. By Drungo's self-righteous tones, the notion that they had been out there for any reason save Gerin's perverse obstinacy had till that moment not penetrated his thick skull and actually reached his brain.

After a long sigh, the Fox said, "We'll try it again, this time charging down toward the Niffet. If the woodsrunners on the north side are peering across, as they likely are, we'll give them something new to think on, too."

They pounded down toward the Niffet, as he'd ordered, and then, after a pause to let the horses rest, back up toward Fox Keep. The men on the palisade there gave them a cheer. Gerin took that as a good omen. Very often, looking bloodthirsty was a sign you would fight well.

"You know something, Fox?" Van said as Raffo drove the chariot at a slow walk toward the drawbridge. "By the time Duren's son is the big man here, most of his warriors will be on horseback, and they'll listen to the minstrels' old songs about chariot battles and wonder why the singers couldn't get it right."

"D'you think so?" Gerin said. Van's big head bobbed

up and down. That surprised Gerin; in matters military, the outlander was for the most part as conservative as Drungo. "Well, you may be right, but I'd bet on the bards to change their tunes by then."

He thought about what he'd just said, then shook his head. "No, I take that back. You're likelier to be right than I am. The minstrels have a whole great store of stock phrases and lines about chariots, same as they do about keeps and love and everything else you can think of. If they have to start singing about horses instead of chariots, their verses won't scan."

"And most of 'em, being lazy as everybody else, won't have the wit to come up with anything new on their own, so we'll hear the same songs a bit longer yet, aye." Van cocked his head to one side, studying the Fox. "Not everybody would up and own he was wrong like that."

"What's the point to defending a position you can't hold?" Gerin asked. Put that way, it made sense to the outlander. He nodded again, jumped down from the chariot, and headed into Castle Fox afoot.

Gerin let Raffo drive him into the stables. There, his lungs full of the green, grassy smell of horse manure, he said to Rihwin, "You did well in the practice. I want to see how well your lads fare at charging home with the spear and at archery from horseback, too."

"I'd not care to be a man afoot trying to stand against me when I have a leaf-pointed spear of shining bronze aimed at his belly," Rihwin replied, sounding a bit like a bard himself. "Riding him down or putting the point through his vitals should be no harder than gigging trout from a stream."

Gerin shook his head in bemusement; he'd been on the other end of this same conversation with Van a few days before. "Except the trout aren't trying to gig you, too," he pointed out, his voice dry. "And except that you mostly won't be going up against men afoot. How will you do against chariotry?"

"We'll ride over them like—" Rihwin paused to catch an elusive simile and caught sight of Gerin drumming the fingers of one hand into the palm of the other. His flight of fancy came back to earth with a thud. "When we fight the battle, we'll know, lord prince. With luck, we'll come at them from directions they'll not expect."

Gerin thumped him on the shoulder. "Good. That's what I'm hoping you do. I don't ask miracles, you know: just that you do what you can."

"Ah, but, my fellow Fox, miracles are so much more dramatic—the stuff of which the minstrels sing for generations yet unborn."

"Aye, with formulas that should have died of old age but haven't," Gerin said, now picking up the discussion he'd just been having with Van as if it hadn't stopped. "Besides, the trouble with miracles is that, even if you do get 'em, you'd almost rather not: getting 'em is a sign of how bad you need 'em, as much as anything else."

He did not mention the couple he'd pulled off, though they went a long way toward proving his point. By the gleam in Rihwin's eye, he was about to bring them up, but he suddenly thought better of it; if it hadn't been for him, at least one and maybe both of them would have been unnecessary.

What he did say, after a few heartbeats' hesitation, was, "For a man who has accomplished as much as you have, lord prince, you've left the bards surprisingly little about which to sing."

The converse of that was, *For a man who's accomplished as little as you, Rihwin, you've given the bards all too much fodder*. Gerin did not say that. Rihwin was as he was, charm and flaws engagingly blended. You enjoyed him, admired his courage, and hoped he was seldom in a position to do you much harm. That hope, however, did not always work out.

"Let's go into the great hall," Gerin said, also a little more slowly than he should have. "We'll drink some ale and hash over how best we can make horses and chariots work together."

"I'm for that," Rihwin said. "I have several ideas we've yet to try, which, if they work as I hope, bid fair to make that cooperation easier to effect." Rihwin always had several ideas. Out of any given batch, some would work. The trouble was figuring out which ones before you tried them all, because those that failed had a way of failing spectacularly.

In the courtyard, Duren was patiently standing alongside Dagref, helping his half brother improve his form at archery. Under Duren's tutelage, Dagref let fly. He whooped in delight when he hit the target.

Watching them, Rihwin sighed. "There are times, my fellow Fox, when I envy you—oh, not so much your children, but having them all here so you can see them every moment as they grow. It's not like that with my brood of bastards."

Gerin exhaled through his nose. "If you'd wanted a wife, plenty of barons had daughters or sisters they'd have pledged to you. We both know that's so." He didn't come any closer to mentioning that Rihwin would have been betrothed to Elise, back before the werenight, if he hadn't gone and disgraced himself as the betrothal was about to be announced. Instead, he went on, "Plenty of barons would pledge you a daughter or sister even now. You have but to seek a bit."

Rihwin sighed again, on a different note. "You, my fellow Fox, are fortunate enough to enjoy waking in the same bed each morning, and to enjoy the company of the same lady—and an excellent lady she is; mistake me not—when not in that bed. In my opinion, the chances of finding a woman who both makes a pleasing bedmate and is interesting when vertical as well as horizontal are lamentably low. Were I wed, I fear I should be bored."

"You don't know till you look," Gerin said stubbornly. "If you're unhappy with your life as it is, wringing your hands and moaning won't make it better."

" 'Unhappy' perhaps takes the point too far," Rihwin answered. "Say rather I recognize its imperfections, but also realize it would have other imperfections, likely worse ones, did I change it."

"And you the one who usually plunges ahead without the least thought of consequences," Gerin exclaimed. "You'd best have a care, or you'll get a name for prudence."

"Father Dyaus avert such a twisted fate!" Rihwin cried. Both men laughed.

In the great hall, the kitchen servants had set a big jar of ale in the middle of the floor, the pointed tip stabbed through the rushes strewn there and into the dirt below. Gerin and Rihwin got drinking jacks, filled them with the dipper, and joined a crowd of warriors at a table arguing over what they'd done and what still needed doing.

"A good strong spear thrust into a man from horseback, now—that'd do some damage," Schild Stoutstaff declared. He pointed to his own weapon hanging on the wall, which had given him his sobriquet. His thinking lived up to the ekename. He nodded to Gerin. "This time, lord prince, maybe we'll be rid of that cursed Trokmê for good."

"Aye, maybe," Gerin said. He suspected that, if Adiatunnus was beaten, Schild would promptly forget as many of his own feudal obligations as he could. He'd done that before. The only time he remembered he owed service was when he needed protection.

Well, he was here now. That would do. Gerin poured out a small libation to Baivers, then stuck his forefinger into the drinking jack and used ale to draw cryptic lines on the tabletop in front of him. "Here—these are the chariots," he told Rihwin, pointing. "And *these* are your horses. What you need to—"

He didn't get to finish explaining what Rihwin needed to do. The lookout's horn blew, a higher, clearer note than the one the village horn used to call the serfs back from the fields at close of day. Normally, the sentry up in the watchtower just called out when he spied someone. He saved the horn for times he really needed it.

After he sounded the warning note, he shouted something. Through the racket and chatter in the great hall, Gerin couldn't hear what he said. He got to his feet and started for the doorway. He hadn't gone more than a few steps when a man came running in, yelling, "Lord prince! Lord prince! There's boats in the Niffet— big boats—and they're heading this way!"

III

"Oh, a pestilence," Gerin said as men exclaimed and cried out all around him. Unlike his vassals, he was angry at himself. After Rihwin had told him of the galley his leman had seen on the Niffet, he'd intended to station riders along the river to bring word if more such came up it. As sometimes happens, what he'd intended to do didn't match what he'd actually done.

Too late for self-reproach now. He ran outside and hurried up onto the palisade. One of the warriors already up there pointed out to the Niffet. Gerin had to choke down sardonic thanks. The ships out there, all five of them, were quite easy enough to find without help.

He saw at first glance that they weren't Elabonian war galleys. Instead of the bronze-clad rams those carried, these ships had high prows carved into the shapes of snarling animals and painted to look more ferocious. *Grainne might have mentioned that*, he thought, absurdly aggrieved the woman had left out an important detail.

The galleys strode briskly up the Niffet, propelled against the current by a couple of dozen oars on either side. They turned sharply toward the riverbank as they drew nearest to Fox Keep, and grounded themselves on that muddy bank harder than Gerin would have liked to endure were he aboard one of them. As soon as they were aground, men started spilling out of them.

"Arm yourselves!" Gerin shouted to his vassals, some of whom had followed him out into the courtyard to

73

see what the fuss was about. "The Gradi are attacking us!"

That sent the nobles running back into the great hall—or trying to, for at the doorway they collided with others trying to get outside. After much screaming and gesticulating, pushing and shoving, that straightened itself out.

Meanwhile, the warriors from the ships pounded toward Fox Keep at a steady, ground-eating trot. As they drew nearer, Gerin got his first good look at them: big, bulky fellows with fair skins and dark hair. They wore bronze helms and leather jerkins and tall boots, and carried a shield on one arm and a long-hafted axe in the other hand.

"Gradi, sure enough," Van said from beside the Fox. Gerin jumped; his attention on the invaders, he hadn't noticed the outlander ascending to the palisade.

Rihwin the Fox had been right behind Van. "My leman surely saw one of those ships, lord prince," he said, pointing out toward the Niffet.

"If I thought you were wrong, I would argue with you," Gerin said. For a moment, gloom threatened to overwhelm him. "This is what I feared worst when I heard your woman's news: these cursed raiders sweeping down on us by surprise, hitting us with no warning—"

To his amazement, both Van and Rihwin burst into raucous laughter. Van said, "Mm, Captain, don't you think it's the Gradi who're liable to get the surprise?" He half turned and waved down into the courtyard, which was aboil with a great host of the most ferocious—or at least the most effective—warriors the northlands knew.

"Just so, lord prince," Rihwin agreed. "Had they chosen another time to come, they might have done you grievous harm: truth. But now, with so many bold and valiant men assembled here, they are more apt to find themselves in the position of a man who bites down hard on a stone, thinking it a piece of fruit."

"Put that way—it could be so," Gerin said, that choking depression lifting almost as fast as it had settled on him. He looked out over the wall again. The Gradi had got close enough for him to hear them singing. He had no idea what the words meant, but the song sounded fierce. Some of the raiders carried long ladders. A corner of the Fox's mouth quirked upwards. "Aye, let 'em try to storm the keep, and see how much joy they have of it." He thumped Rihwin on the shoulder. "And you, my fellow Fox, gather up your horse-riders and prepare your mounts. Readying the chariots would take a long time, but we can loose you against the foe at a moment's notice."

Rihwin's eyes shone. "Just as you say, lord prince." He hurried down off the walkway, shouting for his horsemen.

Gerin's eyes went to the peasant village not far from Fox Keep and the fields surrounding it. Not since the year of the werenight, most of a generation before, had the serfs come under attack. The older men and women, though, knew what to do, and the younger ones didn't take long to figure it out: as soon as they spied the war galleys landing, they all ran for the woods not far away. The Fox hoped they wouldn't peep out from the edge of the forest, either, but would keep running to get away from the invaders.

Some of the Gradi peeled off toward the villages. "They'll steal the animals and burn the huts," Gerin said mournfully.

"Let's make 'em thoughtful about the keep," Van answered. "They haven't got the strength to coop us up in here, though they don't know that yet, either. We'll give 'em one set of lumps, then another."

The Gradi started shooting fire arrows at Fox Keep.

A good many of the logs of the palisade, though, were still painted with the gunk Siglorel Shelofas' son had used to keep Balamung the Trokmê from burning the keep with magic fire during the chaos after the werenight. Even all these years later, flames would not catch on them.

Elabonians on the walkway shot back at the Gradi. A couple of the big, burly men out on the grass crumpled. One of them thrashed about, clutching at his shoulder. The other lay very still; the arrow must have found a vital spot.

"Ladders! Ladders!" The cry came from two sides of the palisade at once. One of the ladders peeked over the top of the log fence only a few yards from where Gerin stood. He rushed toward it, and reached it at the same moment as a Gradi swarmed up and tried to scramble onto the walkway.

The raider bawled something at him in an unintelligible language—and swung his axe through a deadly arc. But the Fox ducked under the stroke and thrust the point of his sword through the Gradi's throat before the fellow could fully protect himself with his shield.

The Gradi had eyes bright and blue as a lightning bolt. They went wide in horror and shock. The heavy axe dropped from his hand. He clutched at the spurting wound as he slipped and slid down the ladder. Cries of dismay from below said he was fouling the men behind him.

Gerin leaned forward and shoved at the top of the ladder with all his strength. Two arrows whipped past his head; the fletching on one of them brushed his cheek as it flew past. He ducked away, fast as he could. The Gradi on the bottom part of the ladder shouted as it leaned away from the wall and toppled over with a crash. He looked again. Three or four of them were writhing at the bottom of the ditch. If he had any luck, they'd broken bones.

The cry of "Ladders!" rose again and again, now from all four sides of the square palisade. Three of the ladders went over faster and more easily than the one Gerin toppled—his men had remembered the forked poles kept on the walkway against just such an emergency. At the fourth one, though, around the far side of Castle Fox from Gerin, cries of alarm and the clash of metal against shields and metal against metal said the Gradi had gained a lodgement. Elabonian warriors rushed toward the fighting to hold them in check.

Down in the courtyard, trying to reach the drawbridge through chaos, came Rihwin the Fox and most of his horse-riders. "Let down the bridge!" Gerin yelled to the gate crew. He had to shout several times to gain the crew's attention, and several more to make them believe him. With a squeal of chains, the bridge fell.

The Gradi outside Fox Keep roared in triumph when the drawbridge came down. Maybe they thought their own folk were opening it, to let them into the keep. If they did, they discovered their mistake in short order. A few of them started over the bridge. Rihwin, leading his riders out, skewered the leading Gradi on his spear. His followers rode down the others, trampling them or knocking them into the ditch around the palisade. The shouts of triumph turned to shouts of alarm.

Rihwin and his horsemen smashed through the Gradi who swarmed near the drawbridge and then galloped off toward the stragglers who'd decided to plunder the peasant village. Some they rode down, some they shot with arrows, some they speared. Had the Gradi stuck together in a tight formation, they might have been able to fight back. Instead, they scattered. A running man was no match for a man aboard a speeding horse.

With the riders gone, the Gradi tried once more to

rush in over the drawbridge. Gerin's men met them at the gate, slashing with swords, thrusting with spears, and putting their bodies between the invaders and the courtyard.

Gerin hurried down to the yard to help drive away the Gradi. And, step by step, he and his men did exactly that, forcing their bigger foes back across the drawbridge and then gaining the grass on the far side.

That seemed to discomfit the Gradi. Instead of sweeping all before them, here they were swept instead. Gerin pointed toward the Niffet. "Get torches!" he cried. "We'll burn the bastards' boats and see if they can swim home!" His vassals roared in fierce approval. As he'd hoped, some of the Gradi understood Elabonian. They yelled in alarm. Some of them, at first a trickle and then a great flow, began streaming away from Fox Keep and toward the great river.

Gerin looked southward. He wished Rihwin would come galloping back and hit the invaders while they were in disorder. It was probably too much to ask for, but—

No sooner had he wished for it than Rihwin, at the head of most of his riders, charged down on the Gradi. Every once in a while, Rihwin did something right, and, when he did, it was as magnificent as any of his failures. As he'd predicted and as he'd proved by the village, foot soldiers had enormous trouble standing against onrushing horses with armored men on top of them. Neither he nor Gerin had imagined how much alarm the horses would create in a foe. The Gradi were seeing mounted men for the first time, and did not like what they saw.

Neat as you please, Rihwin snatched a torch out of the hand of a running Elabonian and urged his horse ahead until the animal seemed to be all but flying over the ground. He darted past the Gradi as if their rawhide boots had been nailed to the grass and flung the torch into one of the war galleys.

They still had men aboard their ships, to protect them if something went wrong with the attack on Fox Keep. Gerin expected one of those men to douse the torch before the ship caught. But Rihwin's spirit was rewarded with a gift of luck. The torch must have landed in a bucket of pitch or something equally inflammable, for a great pillar of black smoke rose from the galley.

The Gradi howled as if they were being burned. Gerin's men, for their part, howled too, but with fierce joy in their voices. Not all the Gradi gave way to despair, though. A big fellow turned and slashed at the Fox with his axe. Gerin turned the blow with his shield, and felt it all the way up his arm to his shoulder. He knew he had to be careful; the axehead, if it squarely met the facing of the shield, was liable to bite straight through and into his arm.

He thrust at the invader with his sword. The Gradi also got his shield up in time to block the stroke, although he seemed cautious and tentative in meeting a left-handed swordsman.

Clank! A rock the size of a man's fist bounced off the side of the Gradi's helmet. He staggered. His blue, blue eyes suddenly looked distant, his face blank, as if he were drunk. Taking advantage of a stunned man was anything but sporting. The Fox cut him down without a qualm.

"Well done, Father!"

Gerin whirled around. There stood Duren, a helm on his head, a shield on his arm, a sword in his hand—his right hand, for he hadn't taken after his father there. The blade had blood on it.

"Get back to the keep," Gerin snapped. "You've no business here."

"Who says I haven't?" his son retorted. "Who do you

think threw that rock at the Gradi? You'd still be fighting him if I hadn't."

Gerin started to shout at Duren, but closed his mouth with a snap before angry words came out. If his son was big enough to do a man's job on the battlefield— and evidently he was—how could the Fox order him back like a boy? The plain truth was, he couldn't.

"Be careful," he said gruffly, and then, "come on."

A pig darted across the field, squealing and threatening with its tushes anyone who came near. Gerin wondered whether some Gradi had hoped to take it away as loot, or whether they'd simply broken the pen confining it to let it run wild. It headed off toward the woods. If one of the villagers didn't track it down there pretty soon, it would be a wild animal again; the difference between domestic swine and wild boars wasn't great.

As the Gradi neared their galleys, they found a shield wall, behind which the men not fighting pushed the surviving ships back into the Niffet and began boarding them. The warriors of the shield wall refused to give ground, but fought in place till they were killed. Their stubborn resistance let most of their comrades escape.

The torches the Elabonians flung at the galleys fell short and died, hissing, in the Niffet. A couple of archers had fire arrows ready to shoot. Most of those missed, too, but one stuck in the timbers at the stern of a ship. Gerin's men cheered at that. The Fox hoped the Gradi wouldn't note the little fire till it had grown into a big one. A bend of the Niffet carried the raiders out of sight before he could find out.

Wearily, he turned and looked back toward Fox Keep. The meadows his chariotry had been churning into a rutted mess now had bodies scattered over them. Some of his men were methodically going from one Gradi on the ground to the next, making sure those bodies were dead ones.

"Take prisoners!" he shouted.

"Why?" Drungo Drago's son shouted back. He was about to smash in the head of a fair-skinned Gradi down with an arrow through the thigh.

"So we can squeeze answers out of them," Gerin told him. "You need to be a patient man to go around questioning corpses." Drungo stared at him, then decided it was a joke and laughed. Had Gerin been the Gradi writhing on the ground in front of him, he didn't think he would have found that laugh pleasing to the ear.

His own men had taken hurts, too. Parol Chickpea, who was a good enough warrior to have lived through a lot of fights but not good enough to come through them unscathed, was binding up a cut on his shield arm. One of the northerners' axes must have hacked right through the shield, as had almost happened to Gerin.

Schild Stoutstaff was hobbling around, using his spear as a stick. When Gerin asked how he was, he gritted his teeth and answered, "I expect I'll heal. The cut runs up and down" —he pointed to his calf— "not straight across. If I'd got it that way, the bastard would have hamstrung me."

"Go back to the keep and have them wash it out with ale," Gerin told him. "It'll burn like fire, but it makes the wound less likely to rot."

"I'll do that, lord prince," Schild said. "You're clever about those things, I can't deny." He limped back toward the castle, blood soaking the bandage he'd ripped from his tunic and trickling down his heel onto the grass.

Gerin headed back to Fox Keep at a pace no better than Schild's. Not only was he weary past belief, almost past comprehension, but he also wanted a closer look at the damage his holding and his army had suffered. Hagop son of Hovan, his neighbor to the east, whose holding had acknowledged his suzerainty since not long after the werenight, crouched by a corpse that looked like him—maybe a younger brother, maybe a son. He did not look up as the Fox walked by.

The thump of hooves on turf made Gerin turn his head. Rihwin the Fox was having a little trouble controlling his horse, which might not have cared for the stink of blood so thick in the air even human nostrils could smell it. The animal kept rolling its eyes and trying to sidestep, almost as if it were skipping. It snorted, and looked for a moment as if it would rear, but Rihwin, leaning forward and speaking to it in a coaxing voice, persuaded it to keep all four feet on the ground.

"By Dyaus All-Father, my fellow Fox, you couldn't have done that better if we'd done nothing but practice it for the past year," Gerin told him. He turned and pointed back toward the war galley Rihwin had fired, which still crackled and burned and sent a great cloud of smoke into the sky. "And that—that was better than I'd dared hope."

"It did work rather well, didn't it?" Rihwin said. "We were here, we were there, with almost no time between being one place and the other. And wherever we were, the Gradi gave way before us, though they have a name for ferocity." He looked back at the carnage on the field and shook his head. "So much happened so fast. Astonishing, lord prince."

It wasn't done happening yet, either. Not quite all the Gradi had been flushed out of the village south of Fox Keep. There was fighting on the winding lanes that ran through the huts of the village. Gerin watched a couple of raiders flee into the forest with Elabonians pounding after them. "If the troopers don't get them, the serfs likely will," he said. "If they don't have ambushes set already, I miss my guess. And they know those woods the way they know the feel of their wives' backsides in their hands."

"Or maybe the backsides of their neighbors' wives," Rihwin said.

"If they're at all like you, that's probably the way of it," Gerin agreed.

Rihwin glared, then started to laugh. "That barb has too much truth in it for me to deny."

"Hasn't stopped you before," Gerin said, which got him another glare.

Back at Fox Keep, the men on the palisade raised a cheer when they recognized their overlord. "We beat the bastards back," one of them shouted, and in a moment they all took up the cry. The ditch around the palisade was full of dead Gradi. A few live men were trapped down there, too. They'd leaped in to try to swarm up the scaling ladders, only to find that those went down almost as fast as they went up.

Gerin looked with some curiosity from them to his troopers who peered over the top of the palisade to watch them. "I'd have expected you to have finished them by now," he called to his men.

"If you want us to, we will, lord prince," Bevander Bevon's son called back. "Your wife said you'd be likely to want them alive for questioning, and when the lady Selatre says something, we know it's best to listen to her."

That might have been because the warriors respected Selatre's own good sense, or because they still felt awe for the god who had spoken through her and wondered whether Biton might still inform her thoughts. Gerin sometimes wondered that himself. He said, "She's right, of course." However she did it, she knew him almost better than he knew himself. Walking up to the edge of the ditch, he called down to the Gradi, "Surrender and you'll live."

For a moment, the big men down in there did not respond. He wondered if they knew Elabonian. Then one of them said, "We live, you make us slaves?"

"Well, of course," Gerin answered. "What else am I going to do with you? Give you a barony? Turn out my peasants so you can have a farm?"

"You make us slaves, what we do?" the Gradi asked.

"Whatever I tell you to do," the Fox snapped. "If you're a slave, that's the end of the stick you're holding. If I put you in the mines to grub out copper or tin, you do that. And if I have you walking a water wheel, you walk it and thank the gods you're alive to do the walking."

"My gods, Voldar and comrades, they ashamed if I do these things," the raider replied. Drawing a dagger from a sheath on his belt, he muttered something in his own guttural language and plunged the knife into his chest. He tried to cry out, but blood pouring from his mouth and nose drowned his words. Slowly, he crumpled.

As if watching him inspired them, the rest of the Gradi also slew themselves—except for two who slew each other, each ramming his knife into the other's throat at the same instant. "Voldar!" each cried the moment before his end came.

"Father!" Duren said, gulping. He'd come through his first battle fine—better than Gerin had, at about the same age—but this . . .

"I've never seen anything like it in all my life," the Fox said. He was sickened, too. Facing death on the field was one thing. If you were a warrior, that was what you did, not least so you could reap the rewards of triumph. But to embrace death as if it were a lover . . . you had to be mad to do that, he thought.

"Is Voldar their chief god?" Duren asked, seeking, as men will, an explanation for the inexplicable.

"I don't know," Gerin said. "Too much about the Gradi I don't know. Van went through their country; maybe he can tell us something of what gods they have." Something else occurred to him. He raised his voice to a great shout: "Bind the prisoners well. Don't let them harm themselves."

From the palisade, Bevander said, "None of the warriors who made it up to the walkway by that one ladder yielded. They all fell fighting."

"That, at least, doesn't surprise me," Gerin answered. "Their blood was up, and so was ours. Even if they had tried to surrender, we might have slain them out of hand. This, though—" He pointed down into the ditch, then shook his head. The most articulate man in the northlands save perhaps Rihwin, he was speechless in the face of the self-murdered Gradi.

He looked over the battlefield till he spotted Van of the Strong Arm. He waved to him, but the outlander did not see. The Fox turned to Duren. "Go fetch Van here. Because he went through the country of the Gradi, he's two ahead of anyone else around."

"Aye, Father." Duren loped off. Gerin looked at him with a small stir of jealousy for his son's limber youth. He could feel himself stiffening up already; for the next couple of days he'd be hobbling around like an old man.

Van came trotting back with the Fox's son. If he felt any twinges, he didn't let on. "They killed themselves?" he called to Gerin. "That's the tale the lad here tells."

"See for yourself." Gerin pointed down into the ditch. "Some of them called on Voldar as they did it. Is he their chief god?"

"She—goddess," Van answered. "She's cold as ice, any way you care to take that. They love her madly, the Gradi do, though they know she doesn't love them." He shrugged. "If they didn't love her, they say, the land they live in would be bleaker yet, though how that could be, I tell you, is past anything my poor wits can fathom. But she's that kind of goddess. If I were one of hers, I'd not want to make her angry at me, and that's for true."

"Surrendering after you've lost a fight would anger her?" the Fox asked.

"So it would, to hear the Gradi tell it." Van frowned. "Or so I thought I heard it, not knowing their tongue any too well, and so I remember it, not having been in the Gradi country for going on twenty years now."

"As I told Duren, you may not know much, but whatever you do know puts you ahead of everyone else here," Gerin told him. "Do you still remember any of what you learned of their speech?"

Van's frowned deepened. "A few words come back, no more—no surprise, when for so long I've used Elabonian and a bit of the Trokmê tongue and none of the rest of the languages I once knew."

"Let's go talk to a prisoner." Gerin headed toward a Gradi down on the ground with one of his own men squatting beside the fellow. Not far away lay a bronze axe. The Gradi tried to hitch himself toward it, but the Elabonian wouldn't let him. The blood-soaked bandage on the raider's thigh showed why he couldn't do more.

He glared up at Gerin, gray-blue eyes blazing. But the blaze slowly faded, to be replaced by a puzzled look. The Fox had seen that before, on the faces of men who would bleed to death soon. He said, "Why did you strike Fox Keep?"

The Gradi didn't answer. Maybe he didn't understand Elabonian. Maybe he didn't understand anything, not any more. He nudged Van. The outlander spoke, haltingly, in a language that seemed to be pronounced farther back in the throat than Elabonian.

Something like intelligence came back into the Gradi's face. He answered in the same tongue. "He says it doesn't matter what he tells us now. He's died in battle. Voldar's handmaidens will carry him off to the golden couches of the afterworld and lie with him whenever he likes, and give him roast meat and beer when he doesn't feel like futtering."

"If it doesn't matter what he tells us, ask him again why he and his comrades hit Fox Keep," Gerin said.

Van repeated what he'd said before, whatever that was. Again, the Gradi answered without hesitation. Van translated: "He says, to kill you and take your land and—something." The outlander scowled. "Bring it under Voldar and his other goddesses and gods, I think he means."

"Just what we need," Gerin said unhappily. "The Trokmoi are already here in the northlands in numbers enough to let their bloodthirsty gods contend with Dyaus and the other Elabonian deities. Will we have a three-cornered war among gods as well as men?"

No sooner were the words out of his mouth than he realized the war might have more than three corners. Selatre's Biton was ancient in the northlands, far more ancient than the Elabonian presence here. And Mavrix, originally from far Sithonia, manifested himself in this land as a fertility god even if wine grapes would not grow here.

The Gradi spoke again, dreamily, as if from far away. Gerin caught the name Voldar, but had no idea what else the raider was saying. Van asked a question that sounded as if he were choking on a piece of meat. The Gradi answered. Van said, "He says Voldar and the rest like this land. They will make it their home, and change it to suit them even better." He ground up some turf with the sole of his hobnailed boot as he twisted a foot back and forth. "I think that's what he says. It's been a demon of a long time, Fox."

Whatever the Gradi had said, they weren't going to

get anything more out of him. He slumped forward, took a last few rattling breaths, and lay still. The blood from the thigh wound had not only soaked the rough bandage Gerin's man had given him, it also puddled beneath his body.

"Let's go on to another one, Captain," Van said to the Fox. "We need to nail that down. If their gods are fighting for them right out in the open, like I thought from what he said, we've got troubles. Your Dyaus and the rest, they let people do more unless you really shout to draw their notice."

"I wish I could say you were wrong," Gerin answered. "The other half of the loaf is, when you have drawn their notice, you almost wish you hadn't. I don't like dealing with gods."

"You don't like dealing with anything stronger than you," Van said shrewdly.

"You're right about that, too." The Fox paused thoughtfully. "You know, I've never truly evoked an Elabonian god. Mavrix is Sithonian, and Biton got adopted into our pantheon. I'm not eager to start, mind, but I haven't."

"Don't blame you," Van said. "But if the Gradi do and you don't, what does that leave? Leaves you in a bad place, you ask me."

"I'm already in a bad place," Gerin told him. Van looked a question his way. He explained: "Somewhere in there between being born and dying, I mean."

"Oh, that bad place," Van said. "The others are worse yet, I hear, but I'm in no hurry to find out."

Over the next few days, several of the wounded Gradi found ways to kill themselves. One threw himself down a stairway and broke his neck, one hanged himself with his belt, one bit through his tongue and choked to death on his own blood. The determination required for that chilled Gerin. Was he supposed to stuff rags into the mouths of all the prisoners?

A few of the raiders, though, lacked the fortitude of their fellows and seemed to resign themselves to captivity. They did not ask the Fox what he would do with them after they healed, as if, not hearing it from his lips, they could pretend they did not know.

He didn't push the issue. Instead, he asked them as many questions as he could, using Van's halting command of their speech and the smattering of Elabonian some of them had acquired. The picture he got from them was more detailed than the one the first dying Gradi had given him, but not substantially different: they'd come to stay, they like the northlands fine, and their goddesses and gods had every intention of establishing themselves here.

"You yield to them, they let you be their slave in this world, in next world, too," said one of the prisoners, a warrior named Kapich. Like his countrymen, he took their victory and the victory of their deities for granted.

"Look around," the Fox suggested. "Look where you are. Look who is the lord here." He phrased that carefully, not wanting to remind the Gradi of his status so strongly that he would be inspired to kill himself.

The raider looked at the underground storeroom where he was confined. He shrugged. "All will change when this is the Gradihome." He used Elabonian, but ran that together, as his people seemed to do in their own language. His eyes were clear and innocent and confident. He believed what he was saying, believed it so strongly he'd never thought to question it.

Gerin, by his nature, questioned everything. That made him perhaps a broader and deeper man than any other in the northlands. But the Gradi's pure and simple faith in what he said was like an armor the arrows of reason could not pierce. That frightened the Fox.

He waited unhappily for Adiatunnus to take advantage of the disruption of the planned Elabonian attack to launch one of his own. Had he been in Adiatunnus' boots, that was what he would have done, and the Trokmê's mental processes were less alien to him than those of the Gradi.

And, when from the watchtower the lookout spied Widin Simrin's son approaching in his chariot, Gerin was sure the blow had fallen. The only reason Widin and his men weren't already at Fox Keep was so they could absorb Adiatunnus' first onslaught and keep him and his woodsrunners from penetrating too deeply into territory the Fox held.

The drawbridge came down with a thud: now, although Castle Fox bulged with men, the bridge stayed up till newcomers were identified. Gerin waited impatiently at the gatehouse. "What word?" he called before Widin had even entered Fox Keep.

His vassal, almost as urgent, jumped out of the chariot and hurried over to him. "Lord prince, the Trokmoi have suffered a great defeat!" he said.

"That's wonderful!" Gerin said, as all the men who heard burst into cheers and swarmed round to pound Widin on the back. Then the Fox, with a keener ear for detail than his comrade, noticed what Widin had said—and what he hadn't. "You didn't beat the woodsrunners yourself, did you?"

"No, lord prince," Widin answered. "Some of them have entered my fief, but as refugees and bandits, not an army."

"Well, who did beat them, then?" Drungo Drago's son demanded, bushy eyebrows pulling together in puzzlement. He was brave and strong and honest and had not a dram of imagination in his head or concealed anywhere else about his person.

"The Gradi, they said," Widin replied. "Four boatloads

came down a tributary of the Niffet, grounded themselves, and out poured warriors grim enough, by all accounts, to have turned even Adiatunnus' stomach."

"I wonder if those were the four boatloads who got away from us," Gerin said, and then, in thoughtful tones, "I wonder whether I want the answer to that to be yes or no. Yes, I suppose: if they have enough warriors to assail Adiatunnus and us at the same time, they've put a lot of men into the northlands these past few years."

"Don't know the answer either way, lord prince," Widin said. "From what the Trokmoi who fled 'em told me, they landed, stole everything that wasn't roped down, killed all the men they could, kidnapped some women, and sailed off with the wenches still screaming on their ships. Adiatunnus' men couldn't very well go after them."

"No more than we could." Gerin pointed toward the Niffet. "I wish that Gradi ship hadn't burned altogether. We need to start learning more about how to make such ships for ourselves."

"As may be, lord prince," Widin said with a shrug. "What matters is, the woodsrunners got badly hurt. But then, I hear the same thing happened here."

"If I hadn't been mustering men to move against Adiatunnus, you'd be telling your story to the Gradi here," Gerin said.

"That wouldn't be so good," Widin said; the Fox thought the understatement commendable. His vassal went on, "If the Gradi hadn't hit the Trokmoi, though, I might not be around to tell you my tale, so I suppose it evens out, in a way."

"I suppose it does," Gerin agreed. His scowl was directed at the world at large, and especially at the western part of it where the Gradi congregated. "What's really happened is that the raiders have knocked me and Adiatunnus both back on our heels. That's bad. If they're doing the moving and we're being moved, that

makes them the strongest power in the northlands right
now."

"You'll check 'em, lord prince," Widin said with the
unbounded faith of a man who had watched the Fox
overcome every obstacle since he himself was a boy.

Gerin sighed. "I wish I knew how."

The underground storerooms of Castle Fox made
good places to stash prisoners, as Gerin had long since
found. He had several Gradi down there now, and had
not lost any of them in a good many days. He'd counted
on that. One of the things he'd seen over the years was
that not everyone could live up to a strict code of
conduct. The Gradi came closer to managing than most,
but they were human, too.

It was dark underground, dark and dank. Gerin carried
a lamp as he headed down to a makeshift cell for another
round of questioning with one of the captured raiders.
As the Gradi was nearly Van's size and not of the sort
of temper given to inspiring trust, Gerin also brought
along Geroge and Tharma. If anything or anybody could
intimidate the prisoner, the monsters were the likeliest
candidates.

He unbarred the door to the chamber where the Gradi
was confined and went in. The raider had a lamp inside,
a small, flickering one that filled the room with swooping
shadows but didn't really illuminate it. Gerin half
expected the Gradi's eyes to reflect the light he carried,
as a wolf's would have, but his prisoner was merely
human after all.

"I greet you, Kapich," Gerin said in Elabonian.

"I greet you, Gerin the Fox," Kapich returned in the
same language. He was more fluent in it than any other
Gradi at Fox Keep, which was one reason Gerin kept
interrogating him.

He walked farther into the chamber. That let Geroge

and Tharma come in behind him. Their eyes did give back the lamplight, redly. Their kind had lived in caverns subterranean for uncounted generations; they needed to be able to seize on any tiny speck of light they could.

Even Gerin's lamp, though, was not very bright. Kapich needed a moment to realize the Fox hadn't just brought a couple of bravos with him, as he'd done on earlier visits. The Gradi sat up on his straw pallet. "Voldar," he muttered, and then something unintelligible in his own language.

"These are my friends, Geroge and Tharma," the Fox said cheerfully. "They're here to make sure you stay friendly and talkative."

Kapich didn't look friendly and he'd never been what anyone would have reckoned talkative. Staring toward the two monsters, he said, "You have bad friends."

"I have bad taste in all sorts of things," Gerin agreed, cheerful still. "I'm keeping you alive, for instance." That brought Kapich's pale glare back to him. He went on, "Now tell me more of what you Gradi aim to do with the land here once you have it."

"There is to tell not so much," Kapich answered. "We make this land into a new Gradihome, we live here, our goddess and gods live here, we all happy, all you other people serve us in life, Voldar and others torment you forever when you die. It is good."

"I'm glad someone thinks so, but it doesn't sound any too good to me," the Fox said. If that bothered Kapich, he did an astonishingly good job of concealing it. Gerin said, "Why do you think you and your jolly crew of gods and goddesses can settle down here without regard for anybody else?"

"Because we are stronger," the Gradi said, with the irksome self-assurance of his kind. "We beat you people at every fight—"

"What are you doing here, then?" Gerin broke in.

"Almost every fight," Kapich corrected himself. "Here, you were lucky. We beat the Trokmoi at every fight, too. Voldar and the gods beat down their gods, too, drive them away. Your gods—" For a moment, his self-assurance cracked. "If your gods let you rule over things like that" —he pointed to the two monsters— "they must have some strength."

"I'm not a thing," Geroge said indignantly. "Do you hear me calling you a thing? You should know better than to call names." Had Gerin been admonished to mind his manners by anyone with such an impressive set of dental work, he would have seriously considered it.

"It talks!" Kapich said to him. "It is not a hound only. It talks. Your gods will indeed be more trouble than the . . . holy foretellers said."

"And what did the holy foretellers foretell wholly wrong?" Gerin asked.

The wordplay made Kapich frown and mutter; Gerin resolved not to waste his wit on those who couldn't follow it. After puzzling out what he meant, the Gradi said, "They said your gods were foolish and they were weak because this was not their proper home and they had no traffic with that home."

Gerin plucked at his beard. The holy foretellers had a point. In a way, the Elabonian gods were immigrants here, as were those of the Gradi pantheon. And, indeed, the northlands had been cut off from the Elabonian heartland for most of a generation now. But if Dyaus and Baivers and Astis the goddess of love and the rest of the deities who had made their way north with Ros the Fierce were not at home here by now, then they were nowhere at home. They'd had centuries to grow acclimated to the northlands and have the landscape accept them. The Fox was sure the Gradi foretellers had blundered there. How to make them pay for the error?

Had he been one of the heroes of whom the minstrels sang, he would have come up with an answer on the instant and been able to use it within days, if not right away. As he was, however, an ordinary man in the real world, nothing occurred to him. He asked the Gradi, "What do you mean, you'll make the northlands into another Gradihome? What does that entail?" He'd heard the phrase before; he wanted to be sure he understood its meaning.

Kapich stared at him, plainly thinking the question either foolish or having an answer so obvious, it needed no explaining. But explain he did, in condescending tones: "We make this country over, to suit us better. It is too hot now, too sunny. Our gods do not like this; it makes them squint and sweat. When they are at home here, they will shield us from the nasty heat."

Were the Gradi gods strong enough to do that? Gerin didn't know. He didn't want to find out, either. Kapich thought they were. That probably meant they thought they were, too, which meant they'd try.

What little he knew of the land from which the Gradi came derived from Van's accounts of his travels through it. By the outlander's tales, it was a country of snow and rock and stunted trees, where the farmers grew oats and rye because wheat and barley wouldn't ripen in the short, cool summers, a place where berries took the place of tree fruit and wolves and great white bears prowled through the winters.

"I thought you were coming here because you liked our land and our weather better than your own," he said to Kapich. He had a hard time imagining anyone not wanting to escape from the grim conditions Van had described.

But the Gradi shook his head. "No. Voldar hates this hot country. When it is ours, she will make it comfortable. Some of our rowers, in working the oars, fall into a faint from the heat. How do we do a man's deeds while we bake in an oven?"

"If you wanted a cold country, you should have stayed in the one you had." That was not Gerin, or even Geroge: that was Tharma, who usually held her tongue.

"If we are strong enough to take this one, our gods are strong enough to make it fit what we want—and what they want," Kapich answered.

"Do your gods ever want something different from what you want?" the Fox asked, probing for weaknesses.

Kapich shook his head again. "How could that be? They are strong. We are weak. We are their thralls, to do as they will with us. Is it not the same among you here, you and the Trokmoi?"

Gerin thought of his own efforts, some even successful, to trick the gods into doing what he wanted rather than the other way round. "You might say that," he answered, "and then again you might not." Kapich stared at him in incomprehension.

He left the Gradi and went up to the great hall, Geroge and Tharma following. Geroge asked, "Can his gods really do that, what he said they could?" The monster sounded like a boy asking his father for reassurance the sky couldn't really freeze and shatter and fall on his head during a cold winter.

Gerin was as close to a father as Geroge had among the world of men. As far as he was concerned, that meant he had a father's obligation to be honest with the young monster. He said, "I don't know. I've never had to deal with the gods the Gradi follow till now."

"You'll find a way around them." Tharma spoke confidently. As children are convinced their fathers can do anything, she was certain the Fox would be able to fend off Voldar and the rest of the dark deities from the dark, gloomy land the Gradi called their own.

As Widin Simrin's son had shown, most of Gerin's

subjects felt that same confidence in him. He wished he had more of it himself. As far as he could see, he'd been lucky in his dealings with gods up to now. When you were dealing with beings far more powerful than you were, how long could your luck last? Could you make it stretch for a whole lifetime? *Of course you can,* Gerin thought wryly. *If you make a mistake while you're treating with a god, you don't have any more lifetime after that.*

Van got up from the table where he'd been sitting. "You look like a man who could use a jack of ale, or maybe three," he said.

"One, maybe," Gerin said while the outlander plied the dipper. "If I drink three, I'll drink myself gloomy."

"Honh!" Van said. "How would anyone else tell the difference?"

"To the crows with you, too," the Fox said, and poured down the ale Van had given him. "These Gradi, you know, they're going to be nothing but trouble."

"No doubt," Van said, but more as if relishing than abhorring the prospect. "You ask me, life gets dull without trouble."

"No one asked you," Gerin said pointedly.

His friend went on as if he hadn't spoken: "Aye, betimes life gets dull. I've put down so many roots here at Fox Keep, oftentimes I think I'm all covered with moss and dust. Life here can be a bore, for true."

"If things get too boring, you can always fight with Fand," the Fox said.

Van tried to ignore that, too, but found he couldn't. "So I do," he said, shaking his head as if to shake off a wasp buzzing around it. "So I do. But she fights with me as much as I fight with her."

That, Gerin knew from experience, was also true. "Maybe it's love," he murmured, which drew an irate glare from Van. The outlander's eyes didn't quite focus and were tracked with red, which made Gerin wonder how many jacks of ale Van had had. His friend didn't test his enormous capacity as often as he once had, but today looked to be an exception.

"If it is love, why do we go on sticking knives into each other year after year?" Van demanded. Given Fand's habits—she'd stabbed a Trokmê who'd mistreated her—Gerin wasn't so sure his friend was using a metaphor till the outlander went on, "You and Selatre, a year'll go by between harsh words. Me and Fand, every peaceful day is a battle won. And you call that love?"

"If it weren't, you'd leave it," Gerin answered. "Every time you have left, though, you've come back." He raised a sardonic eyebrow. "And wouldn't you be bored if you didn't quarrel? You just said you thought peace and staying in one place for years were boring."

"Ahh, Fox, you don't fight fair, hitting a man on the head with his own words like that." Van hiccuped. "Most people—Fand, f'r instance—you say something to 'em and they pay it no mind. But you, now, you listen and you save it and you give it back just so as it'll hurt worst when you do."

"Thank you," Gerin said.

That got him another dirty look from the outlander. "I didn't mean it for praise."

"I know," the Fox answered, "but I'll take it for such all the same. If you don't listen and remember, you can't do much." He turned the subject: "Do you think the Gradi can do as they say they will—them and their gods, I mean?"

"That's the question, sure as sure," Van said, "the one we've been scratching our heads about since they tried to tear the keep down around our ears." He peered down into his jack of ale, as if trying to use it as a scrying tool. "If I had to guess, Captain, I'd say they likely can . . . unless somebody stops them, that is."

"Unless *I* stop them, you mean," the Fox said, and Van nodded, his hard features unwontedly somber.

Gerin muttered something coarse under his breath. Even Van of the Strong Arm, who'd traveled far more widely than he himself ever would, who'd done things and dared things that would have left him quivering in horror, looked to him for answers. He was sick of having the weight of the whole world pressed down on his shoulder. Even a god would break under a burden like that, let alone a man likely more than half through his appointed skein of days. Whenever he wished he could rest, something new and dreadful came along to keep him hopping.

"Lord prince?"

He looked up. There stood Herris Bigfoot, his expression nervous. The new village headman often looked nervous. Gerin wondered whether that was because he worried about his small job as the Fox did about his larger one or because he had something going on the side. "Well?" he said, his voice neutral.

"Lord prince, the village suffered when the Gradi came here," Herris said. "We had men killed, as you know, and fields trampled, and animals run off or wantonly slain, and some of our houses burned down, too—lucky for us it wasn't all of 'em."

"Not just luck, headman." Gerin waved to the warriors sitting here and there in the great hall, some repairing the leather jerkins they covered with scales of bronze to make corselets of them, others fitting points to arrows, still others sharpening sword blades against whetstones. "Luck had a bit of help here. If we hadn't driven the Gradi away, you'd have had a thin time of it."

"That's so." Herris bobbed his head in his eagerness to agree—or at least to be seen agreeing. "Dyaus praise all your brave vassals who kept those robbers from hauling everything back to their big boats. Still and all, though, some bad things happened to us in spite of how brave they fought."

"Ah, now I see which way the wind blows," Gerin said. "You'll want me to take that into account come fall, when I'm reckoning up your dues. You'll be missing people and animals, you'll have spent time you could have been weeding on making repairs, and so forth."

"That's it. That's right," Herris exclaimed. Then he noticed Gerin hadn't promised anything. "Uh, lord prince—will you?"

"How in the five hells do I know?" the Fox shouted. Herris sprang back a couple of paces in alarm. Several of the warriors looked up to see why Gerin was yelling. A little more quietly, he went on, "Have you noticed, sirrah, I have rather more to worry about than you or your village? I was going to fight a war against the Trokmoi. Now I'll have to fight the Gradi first, and maybe Aragis the Archer off to the side. If anything is left of this principality come fall, I'll worry over what to do about your dues. Ask me then, if we're both alive. Till then, don't joggle my elbow over such things, not when I'm trying to figure out how to fight gods. Do you understand?"

Herris gulped and nodded and fled. His sandals thumped on the drawbridge as he hurried back to the village. No doubt he was disappointed; no doubt the rest of the serfs would be. Gerin resolved to bear up under that. As he'd told the headman, he had more important things to worry about.

To his own surprise, he burst out laughing. "What's funny, Fox?" Van demanded.

"Now I understand what the gods must feel like when I ask them for something," Gerin said. "They're really doing things that matter more to them, and they don't like being nagged by some piddling little mortal who's going to up and disappear in a few years no matter what they do or don't do for him. As far as they're concerned, I'm an annoyance, nothing more."

"Ah, well, you're good at the job," Van said. Gerin wondered whether his friend intended that as a compliment or a sly dig. After a moment, he shrugged. However Van intended it, it was true.

Gerin drew his bow back to his ear and let fly. The sinew bowstring lashed his wrist. The arrow flew straight and true, into the flank of a young deer that had wandered too close to the bushes behind which he sheltered. The deer bounded away through the underbrush.

"After him!" Gerin shouted, bursting from concealment. He and Van and Geroge and Tharma pounded down the trail of blood the deer left.

"You got him good, Fox," Van panted. "He won't run far, and we'll feast tonight. Venison and onions, and ale to wash 'em down." He smacked his lips.

"There!" Gerin pointed. The deer had hardly been able to run even a bowshot. It lay on the ground, looking reproachfully back at the men who had brought it down. As always when he saw a deer's liquid black eyes fixed on his, the Fox knew a moment's guilt.

Not so Geroge. With a hoarse cry, the monster threw himself on the fallen deer and tore out its throat with his fangs. The deer's hooves thrashed briefly. Then it lay still.

Geroge got to his feet. His mouth was bloody; he ran his tongue around his lips to clean them. More blood dripped from his massive jaws down onto the brownish hair that grew thick on his chest.

"You didn't need to do that," Gerin said, working hard to keep his voice mild. "It would have been dead soon anyhow."

"But I *liked* killing it," Geroge answered. By the

way his deep-set eyes glittered, by the way the breath whistled in and out of his lungs, he'd more than liked it. It had excited him. The suddenly rampant and quite formidable bulge in his trousers suggested the same thing. He didn't yet realize the excitement of the hunt could be transmuted to other excitements, but he would soon.

And what then? Gerin asked himself. It was another question that refused to wait for an answer, especially when he saw how Tharma looked at Geroge. Everything seemed to be descending on his head at the same time: the Trokmoi, the Gradi, the gods, and now the awakening of the monsters. It wasn't fair. You could deal with troubles when they came singly. But how were you supposed to deal with them when you couldn't handle one before the next upped and bit you?

Maybe you couldn't. He'd learned a long time before that life wasn't fair. You had to go on any way you could. But having all his problems so compressed seemed . . . inartistic, somehow. Whatever gods were responsible for his fate should have had more consideration.

Van drew his bronze dagger. "After I gut the beast, what say we make a fire and roast the liver and kidneys right here? Meat doesn't get any fresher than that."

Geroge and Tharma agreed so readily and so enthusiastically that, even had Gerin been inclined to argue, he would have thought twice. But he wasn't inclined to argue. Turning to the monsters, he said, "Gather me some tinder, would you?"

While they scooped up dry leaves and tiny twigs, Gerin found a stout branch on the ground and a good, straight stick. He used the point of his own dagger to bore a hole in the branch, then wound a spare bowstring around the stick and twirled it rapidly with the string. Van was even better with a fire bow than he was, but the outlander was also busy butchering the deer, and Gerin had made plenty of fires on his own. If you were patient . . .

He worked the string back and forth, back and forth. The stick went round and round, round and round in the hole. After a while, smoke began to rise from it. "Tinder," he said softly, not breaking his rhythm.

"Here." Geroge fed some crumpled leaves into the hole—not too many, or he would have snuffed out the sparks Gerin had brought to life. He'd done that before, and Gerin had shouted at him for it just as if he weren't physically far more formidable than the Fox. Gerin breathed gently on the sparks: blowing them out was another risk you took. Presently, they grew to flames.

"There ought to be a way to do that by magic," Van said, impaling a chunk of liver on a stick and handing it to Geroge.

"I know several, as a matter of fact," Gerin answered. "The easiest will leave you exhausted for half a day. . . . No, that's not so; the one for the flaming sword won't, but that one takes ingredients that aren't always easy to come by and, if you do it wrong, you're liable to burn yourself up. Sometimes the simplest way is the best one."

"Aye, well, summat to that, I suppose," the outlander admitted. "But still, a clever fellow like you ought to be able to figure out an easy way to make the kind of magic you need."

"I have trouble enough working magic," Gerin exclaimed. "Expecting me to come up with new kinds is asking too much." Wizards who could do things like that wrote grimoires; they didn't go from one book of spells to another picking out the simplest things to try and hoping they worked.

Geroge toasted his chunk of liver over the fire. After a moment, Tharma joined him. The savory smell of roast meat drove the thought of magic from the Fox's mind. The meat wasn't well roasted; both foundling monsters had accepted the notion that meat needed cooking before being eaten, but they'd accepted it reluctantly, and ate even roast meat bloodier than was to Gerin's taste.

They were also halfhearted about any notions of manners. With their teeth, they hardly needed to cut bites from a slab of meat so they could chew them. They just bit down, and a juicy gobbet disappeared forever every time they did.

Van handed Gerin a kidney on a stick. He cooked it a good deal longer than the monsters had their pieces of liver. "I wish we had some herbs, or even a bit of salt," he said, but that was almost ritualistic complaint. The strong, fresh flavor of the kidneys—which went stale so quickly after you killed an animal—didn't need enhancement.

Van roasted the deer's other kidney for himself. When he lifted it away from the flames, he took a bite and then swore: "Might as well be right out of your five hells, Fox: I just burned my mouth."

"I've done that," Gerin said. "We've all done that. We ought to bring the rest of the carcass back to the keep."

The outlander checked the sun through the forest's leafy canopy. "We still have some daylight left. I don't feel like going back yet. Suppose I do the heart in four parts and we cook that, too?"

"Do that!" Geroge said, and Tharma nodded. Any excuse to eat more meat was a good one for them.

"Go ahead," Gerin said after he too gauged the sun. "The cooks will jeer at us for stealing the best bits ourselves, but that's all right. They didn't catch the beast, and we did."

Before slicing up the heart, Van kicked the pile of guts away from the fire. He frowned a little. "Not so many flies on 'em as I'd've thought."

"It's been a cool spring. That has something to do with it," Gerin said. Then he too frowned. Sometimes the most innocent remark, when you took it the wrong way—or maybe the right one—led to fresh ideas . . . and fresh worries. "Is it a cool spring because that's how it happens to be, or is it a cool spring because the gods of the Gradi are getting a toehold here and want it to be cool?"

"You have a cheerful way of looking at things, don't you, Fox?" Van handed him a piece of the meat he'd just cut. "Here, get some fresh heart in you."

Gerin snorted. "You have been at Fox Keep a goodish while, haven't you? When you first got here, you never would have made a joke like that."

"See how you've corrupted me?" the outlander said. "Bad jokes, staying in one place for years at a time, having brats and knowing it—I probably sired some out on the road, but I never stayed in one place long enough to find out. It's a strange life settled folk live."

"All what you're used to," Gerin said, "and by now you've been here long enough to be used to this."

He glanced over to Geroge and Tharma. Sometimes the two of them—especially Geroge—would closely follow human conversation. Humans were all they knew, and they wanted to fit in as best they could. Today, though, both of them seemed more intent on the roasting quarters of heart than on what Gerin was saying. He didn't let that bother him as much as he would have a few years before. He'd done a better job of making them into more or less human beings than he'd ever expected.

No. He'd made them into **more** or less human children. He still had no proof their true essence would stay hidden as they matured. He still had no idea what to do with them as they did mature, either. The just thing would be to let them grow up as if they were people, and to treat them as such unless and until they gave him some reason to do otherwise. The safe thing would be to put them out of the way before he had to do it.

He took his piece of roasted heart off the fire, blew on it, and took a bite. The meat was tough and chewy, and he lacked the teeth to slice effortlessly through it as Geroge and Tharma had. He sighed. The safest thing would have been to put them out of the way as soon as they came into his hands. He hadn't done that then, fearing the hands of the gods, not his own, had true control over their fate. He still feared that now. He'd do nothing—except worry.

Van's teeth were merely human, but he made short work of his chunk of deer heart. He licked his fingers and wiped them clean on the grass, then dug around with a fingernail to rout out a piece of meat stuck somewhere in the back of his mouth. "That hit the spot," he said. "Enough to make my belly happy, not so much that I won't be able to enjoy myself come supper."

"The way you eat, the only thing that amazes me is that you're not as wide as you are tall," Gerin said.

Van looked down at himself. "I am thicker through the middle than I used to be, I think. If I get too much thicker, I won't be able to fit into my corselet, and then what will I do?"

"Save it for Kor," Gerin answered, "unless Maeva takes it before he has the chance."

"You had that thought run through your head too, eh?" Van started to laugh, but quickly swallowed his mirth. "It could happen, I suppose. There's not a boy her age can match her, and she's wild for weapons, too. Whether that'll still be so once she sprouts breasts and hips—the gods may know, but I don't. She'll not be one of the common herd of women any which way; so much I'll say already."

"No," the Fox agreed. In musing tones, he went on, "I wonder, now: is there any such thing as 'the common herd of women,' once you come to know 'em? Selatre wouldn't fit there, nor Fand, the gods know" —he and Van both chuckled, each a little nervously— "nor Elise, either, thinking back."

"You seldom speak of her," Van said. He scratched at his beard. "To a shepherd, I suppose, each of his sheep is special, even if they're nothing but bleating balls of wool to the likes of you or me."

"I know that's so," Gerin said, warming to the discussion. "I've seen it with my own eyes. It makes you wonder, doesn't it? The better you know the members of a class, the less typical of the class they seem. Does that mean there really isn't any such thing as 'the common herd of women'?"

"Don't know if I'd go so far," Van answered. "Next thing, you'll be saying there's no such thing as a common grain of sand or a common stalk of wheat, when any fool can see there is."

"A lot of times, the things any fool can see are the things only a fool would believe," Gerin said. "If you looked hard enough, I daresay you could find differences between grains of sand or stalks of wheat."

"Oh, you could, maybe," Van allowed, "but why would you bother?"

A question like that, intended to dismiss a subject, often started Gerin thinking harder. So here; he said, "I can't tell you why you might want to know one grain of sand from another, but if you could tell which stalk of wheat would yield twice as much as the others, wouldn't you want to do that?"

"You have me, Fox," his friend said. "If I could do that, I would. I can't, not by looking. Can you?"

"No, though I wish I could." Gerin paused. "I wonder if I could make a magic to see that. Maybe with barley, not wheat: Baivers god of barley knows I've never scanted him, and he might lend me aid. That would be a sorcery worth taking risks for, if I could bring it off."

He wondered if he knew enough, or could learn enough here in the northlands, even to plan such a spell. Or rather, he started to wonder; Geroge's formidable yawn distracted him. The monster said, "I'm bored, sitting around here. Can we go back to the keep now?"

"Aye, we can." Gerin climbed to his feet. "In fact, we'd better, so we're there before sunset. With the deer, we have enough for a decent offering for the ghosts, but you don't want to use such things if you don't have to."

They tied the carcass to a sapling, which they took turns shouldering by pairs as they carried it to the chariot waiting at the edge of the woods. The car had been crowded for four, and was all the more crowded for four plus a gutted deer, but Fox Keep wasn't far.

When they got back, a stranger waited in the courtyard. No, not quite a stranger; after a moment, Gerin identified him: "You're Authari Broken-Tooth, aren't you? One of Ricolf the Red's vassals?"

"Your memory is good, lord prince," the newcomer said, bowing. "I am Authari." When he opened his mouth to speak, you could see the front tooth that gave him his sobriquet. "But I am not Ricolf the Red's vassal. I came here to tell you, Ricolf has died."

IV

"But he can't have done that," Gerin exclaimed: looking back on it, surely one of the more foolish things he'd ever said. Authari was polite enough not to point that out; Authari, whatever else he was, was usually polite. Gerin recovered his wits and went on, "I am in your debt for bringing me the news. You will, of course, stay the night and sup with me."

"I will, lord prince, and thank you," Authari said, bowing again. "It happened four days ago now. He was drinking a cup of ale when he said he had a headache. The cup fell out of his hand and he slid off the bench. He never woke up again, and half a day later he was dead."

"Worse ways to go," the Fox remarked, and Authari nodded. Like most men, both of them had seen a great many worse ways. But that was not the point of this visit, and Gerin knew it. "The succession to his barony—"

Authari coughed. "Just so, lord prince: the succession to his barony. Several of Ricolf's vassals banded together and bade me tell you—"

"Tell me what?" Gerin said, his voice deceptively mild. "What have you and your fellow vassals of Ricolf's to tell me? In law, his heir is surely my son Duren, as he has no sons of his own living."

"Were you still wed to his daughter Elise, lord prince, no one would contest Duren's right of succession," Authari replied. The Fox did not believe that for an instant, but waited for the minor noble to go on. After

109

a moment, Authari did: "By her own actions, though, if tales be true, Elise severed her connection with you. And Duren has been raised here, not in the holding of Ricolf the Red. But for the thin tie of blood, we keepholders have no reason to feel any special loyalty toward your son, and would sooner see one of our own number installed in Ricolf's place."

"Of course you would," Gerin said, mildly still. "That way, when, a year and a half down the line, the rest of you decide you don't care for whichever of your number you've chosen, you can go to war against him with a clear conscience and make his holding as much a mess as Bevon's ever was."

"You misunderstand," Authari said in hurt tones. "That is not our concern at all. Our fear is having foisted upon us a youth who does not know the holding."

Gerin felt his patience leaking away like grains of sand—whether individually identifiable or not—between his fingers. "Your concern is, if Duren takes over Ricolf's holding, you'll all have to become my vassals as well as his. There—now it's out in the open."

"So it is." Authari sounded relieved—he hadn't had to come right out and say it himself. "No one denies you're a good man, lord prince, but we who served Ricolf value our freedom, as true men must."

"You value freedom even more than law, seems to me," Gerin replied, "and when you use the one to flout the other, soon you have neither."

"As may be." Authari drew himself up to his full height. "If you seek to install Duren by force of arms, I must tell you we shall fight."

At most times, that threat, if it could be so dignified, would have made Gerin laugh. Lands where the barons did acknowledge his suzerainty surrounded the holding of Ricolf the Red. The main reason Ricolf had never sworn fealty to him was that he'd been too embarrassed to ask it of the older man after Elise ran away with the horseleech. He could easily have summoned up the force to quash Ricolf's restive vassals . . . were he not facing war with Adiatunnus and a bigger war against the Gradi. He did not need distractions, not now.

And then Authari said, "If you seek to interfere with our freedom, I must tell you we have friends to the south."

"You'd call on Aragis the Archer, would you?" Gerin said. Authari nodded defiantly. "I ought to let you do it," the Fox told him. "It would serve you right. If you think you wouldn't fancy being my vassals, you deserve to be his. First time anyone stepped out of line, he'd crucify the fool. That would make the rest of you think— if anything could, which I doubt."

Authari's angry scowl showed the stump of his front tooth. He shook a finger in Gerin's face. "Now that's just the kind of thing we don't want in an overlord— showing off how much better than us he thinks he is. Aragis would respect us and respect our rights."

"Only goes to show how much you don't know about Aragis," Gerin answered with a derisive snort. But then he checked himself. The more he antagonized Authari, the more the loon and his fellow fools were liable to summon Aragis to their aid. Since the Archer's forces would have to pass through areas under Gerin's control, that would touch off the long-threatened war between them . . . at the worst possible time for the northlands as a whole.

"We may not know about Aragis, by Dyaus, but we know about you," Authari said. "And what we know, we don't trust."

"If you know me, you know my word is good," the Fox said. "Has anyone ever denied that, Authari? Answer yes or no." Reluctantly, Authari shook his head. When he did, Gerin went on, "Then maybe you'll hear out the proposal I put to you."

"I'll hear it," Authari said, "but I fear it may be another of your tricksy schemes."

Gerin thought seriously about taking Authari up onto the palisade and dropping him headfirst into the ditch around Fox Keep. But his head was so hard, the treatment probably would neither harm him nor knock in any sense. And so the Fox said, "Suppose we ask the Sibyl at Ikos who the rightful heir to Ricolf the Red is? If the oracle says it should be one of you people, I won't fight that. But if Duren should succeed his grandfather, you accept him without any quarrels. Is that just?"

"Maybe it is and maybe it's not," Authari answered. "The god speaks in mysterious ways. We're liable to get an answer that will just keep us squabbling."

"Some truth to that," Gerin said, not wanting to yield any points to Ricolf's vassal but unable to avoid it. "And, of course, people of bad will can deny the meaning of even the plainest verses. Will you and your fellows swear a binding oath by the gods that you'll do no such thing? I will—and I trust Biton's judgment, however he sees the future."

Authari gnawed at his underlip. "You're so cursed glib, lord prince. You always have a plan ready, and you don't give a man time to think about it."

As far as the Fox was concerned, planning came as naturally as breathing. If Authari hadn't thought he might suggest the Sibyl as a means of resolving their dispute, Authari hadn't looked very far ahead. Silently, Gerin sighed. People seldom did.

At last, much more slowly than he should have, Authari said, "I'll take that back to my fellows. It's worth thinking on, if nothing else."

"Don't spend too much time thinking about it," Gerin said in peremptory tones. "If I have to, I can ravage your countryside and maybe take several of your keeps before Aragis could hope to get far enough north to do you any good." With luck, Authari had no idea how reluctant he was to launch such a campaign. Still sharply, he went on, "You'll ride out tomorrow. Ten days after that, I'll follow, and meet you at Ricolf's keep to hear your answer. Don't think to waylay me, for I'll have plenty of men along to start the war on the spot if that's what you people decide you want."

He waited. Authari had the look of a man who'd just discovered his lady friend not only had a husband but that the fellow was twice his size and bad tempered to boot. He licked his lips, then said, "I'll take your word back with me, lord prince. Since you put it so, I expect we'll let the Sibyl and the god decide it, if that's their will."

"I hoped you'd see it that way," Gerin said, with irony that sailed past Authari. He sighed again. "Sup, drink, stay the night. I have to find my son and let him know what's happened."

"Grandfather dead?" Duren's face twisted in surprise. That startlement was all the more complete because, when Gerin tracked him down in a corridor back of the kitchen, death had been the last thing on his mind; exactly what he'd been about to do with a serving girl wasn't obvious, but that he'd been about to do something was.

"That's what I said," Gerin answered, and summarized what Authari had told him, finishing, "He lived a long life, and a pretty good one, taken all in all, and he died easy, as those things go. A man could do worse."

Duren nodded. Once over his initial surprise, he starting thinking soon enough to please his father. "I wish I'd known him better," he said.

"I always thought the same," Gerin said, "but he was never one to travel much, and I—I've had an active time, most of these years. And—" He hesitated, then brought it out: "And the matter of your mother clouded things between us."

He watched Duren's face fall into a set, still mask. That happened whenever the youth had to think of Elise, who'd given him birth and then abandoned him along with Gerin. He didn't remember her at all— for as long as his memory reached, Selatre had been his mother—but he knew of his past, and it pained him.

Then he made the mental connection he had to make: "With Grandfather dead, with my mother—gone—that leaves me heir to the holding."

"So it does," Gerin said. "What do you think about that?"

"I don't know what to think yet," Duren answered. "I hadn't thought to leave Fox Keep so soon." After a moment, he added, "I hadn't thought to leave Fox Keep at all."

"I always knew this was one of the things that might happen," his father said. "That it chose now to happen— complicates my life."

"It complicates my life, too," Duren exclaimed with justifiable indignation. "If I go down there—do you really think I can give orders to men so much older and stronger than I am?"

"You won't be a youth forever. You won't even be a youth for long, though I know it doesn't seem that way to you," the Fox said. "By the time you're eighteen at latest, you'll have a man's full strength. And take a look at Widin Simrin's son. He wasn't any older than you when he took over his vassal barony, and he's done a fine job of running it ever since."

"But he's your vassal," Duren said. "I wouldn't be. I'd be on my own." His eyes widened as he thought that through. "I'd have as much rank as you, Father, near enough. I wouldn't call myself prince or anything like that, but—"

Gerin nodded. "I understand what you're saying. You'd owe no one allegiance, not unless you wanted to. That's right. You could go to war with me if you chose to, and you'd break no oaths doing it."

"I wouldn't, Father!" Duren said. Then, proving he was indeed the Fox's son, he added, "Or rather, I don't see any reason to now."

"I didn't expect you to call out the chariots the moment you become a baron," Gerin said, chuckling. "I'd hope you wouldn't. And, even though you wouldn't be my vassal as Ricolf's heir, you're still my son, and Ricolf's chief vassals know that. It's one of the things that bother them: if they don't answer to you, they'll have to answer to me, and not in ways they fancy. That will help you for a while, and by then, Dyaus willing, they'll have the habit of obeying you."

"I can't lean on you forever," Duren said. "Sooner or later, likely sooner, I'll have to lead on my own."

"That's true." Duren's being able to see it made Gerin want to burst with pride. "When the time comes—and it'll come sooner than you think; it always does—I expect you'll be able to do it."

"What if—" Duren paused, then went on: "What if the Sibyl at Ikos says I'm not to rule Grandfather's holding?"

"Then you're not," Gerin answered. "That's all there is to it. You can try to twist a god's will, you can try to trick a god, but if you try to go dead against what a god says, you'll fail. If the Sibyl says Ricolf's holding is not for you, you know you have a place here."

"I don't even know that I want to try to run that holding," Duren muttered, perhaps more to himself than to his father.

"If you don't think you want it, if you don't think

you're ready, I won't set on you a burden you can't bear," the Fox assured him. "That's what we'll tell Authari, and he'll ride south and tell it to the rest of Ricolf's vassals."

"And the holding will be lost to us," Duren said. It didn't sound like a question, as it easily might have. It came out flat and harsh.

"Things aren't always lost forever," Gerin said. "My guess here is that once the vassals fought among themselves for a while, they'd welcome an overlord who wasn't a jumped-up equal but someone they could all follow without any jealousy."

Duren looked at him in blank incomprehension. Gerin smiled and put a hand on his son's shoulder. For Duren, half a year felt like a long time, and waiting a few years to let things sort themselves out was beyond his mental reach. Gerin didn't blame him. He'd been the same himself at the same age, as had everyone else who made it to and then past fourteen.

"I do want it," Duren declared. "If Biton says I have the right to rule that holding, I'll do the best I can there. One day, maybe—"

He didn't go on. He set his jaw, as if to say Gerin could not make him go on. Gerin didn't try. He could make a pretty good guess as to what was in his son's mind: one day he would die, too, and then Duren would inherit his broad holdings as well as Ricolf's single barony.

His son was right. That was what would happen. If the Gradi got their way, it was liable to happen before the year was out. Of course, if the Gradi got their way, Duren would be in no position to inherit anything but a grave.

Selatre said, "I wish I were coming with you." That wasn't serious complaint; if she'd made serious complaint about riding south with Gerin and Van and Duren, she would have gone. Wistfully, she went on, "I'd like to see how Biton restored his shrine after the earthquake laid it low."

"From all we've heard, it's just the same as it used to be," Gerin said, which was both true and in large measure beside the point: when it took divine intervention to bring back what had been destroyed, the restoration was on the face of it worth seeing.

"And it would be so interesting to go into the underground chamber of prophecy just as a person, not as a Sibyl—to see the prophetic trance from the outside instead of being a part of it."

"It's because you were the Sibyl that I want you to stay here," Gerin told her. "My vassals are more likely to listen to you because the god once spoke through you than they are to any of their own number. And a good thing, too, if you ask me, for you're more clever than any of them."

"More clever than Rihwin?" Selatre asked, mischief in her voice. Her gaze flicked out to the hallway beyond the library chamber where they sat quietly talking: there of all places in Fox Keep they were least likely to be disturbed. But Rihwin, formidably educated himself, was one who might come in to look at a scroll or codex.

Gerin glanced outside, too, before replying, "Much more clever than Rihwin, for you have the sense to know when cleverness for its own sake isn't the answer, and he's never yet figured that out."

"For which I thank you," his wife said. "I'd have been angry if you told me anything else, but I do thank you for what you did tell me."

"Van would say something like 'Honh!' about now," Gerin said.

"So he would," Selatre agreed. "He'll probably say it several times on the trip down to Ikos. He'll probably do several other things on the way down to Ikos, too, things where he'd be better off if Fand never heard of them."

"She won't hear about them from me, or from Van, either, I hope," Gerin said. "Only trouble is, that won't matter. Whether he'll tell her about them or not, she'll know what he's been doing, and they'll have a row when we get home. Or maybe she'll do something to keep herself amused—or to make him furious—while he's gone. Do you suppose you could keep her from trying something like that?"

"Me?" Selatre stared at him in horrified disbelief, then clutched his hand as if she were drowning in the Niffet and he a floating log. "Take me with you to Ikos after all, oh, please! Anything but trying to keep Fand from what she sets her mind on doing!" She laughed, and so did Gerin, but he knew she wasn't altogether joking. She went on, quite seriously, "If anyone can restrain Fand, it's Van, and the other way around. But neither has much hope of that out of the other's sight."

"Too true," Gerin said, and then again, "Too true. I've given up on it, for both of them."

"And you expect me to manage with her?" Selatre said. "I like that!"

Dagref poked his head into the library. "Manage what, Mama? And with who?"

"What I need to manage, and with the person I was talking about," she said.

"Why won't you tell me?" Dagref demanded. Any child would have let out that eternal complaint, but he went on, "Why shouldn't I know? Would I tell someone? Would it make that person angry?" He brightened. His string of questions had led him to an answer. "I'll bet it has something to do with Aunt Fand! She gets angry faster than anyone else I know. Why didn't you want to tell me that? I wouldn't tell your secret, whatever it is. It must have something to do with Uncle Van going away. Is that right?"

Gerin and Selatre looked at each other. It wasn't the first time Dagref had done that to them. His relentless pursuit of precision would take him a long way—unless he failed to notice it leading him into trouble. *He's nine now*, Gerin thought uneasily. *What will he be like as a man grown?* Only one answer occurred to him: *as he is now, only more so.* It was a vaguely—or perhaps not so vaguely—alarming notion.

He said, "No, son, we were talking about one of the cows down in the village, and what your mother should do if it has chickens."

"Cows don't have chickens," Dagref said indignantly. Then his face cleared. "Oh. "You're making a joke." He sounded like Gerin letting off some serf after a minor offense, and warning the wretch of how much trouble he'd be in if he ever did such a thing again.

"Yes, a joke," the Fox agreed. "Now go on out of here and let us finish talking about whatever it was." Knowing secrecy was a losing battle, he fought it anyhow.

Dagref left without any more disputation. That surprised Gerin for a moment. Then he realized his son, having won the argument, didn't need to stay and fight it through a second time. He rolled his eyes. "What are we going to do with that one?"

"Hope experience lends him sense to go with his wits," Selatre answered. "It often does, you know."

"Yes, leaving Rihwin out of the bargain." Gerin glanced warily toward the door, half expecting Dagref to reappear and ask, *Out of what bargain?*

Selatre's gaze had gone in the same direction, and probably for the same reason. When her eyes met Gerin's, they both started to laugh. But she sobered quickly. "If the Gradi or Adiatunnus attack us, I can't lead the men into battle," she said. "Who commands then?"

Gerin wished he hadn't just made his joke, because that question had only one answer. "Can't be anyone but Rihwin," he said. "He's the best of all of them here, especially if he has someone to check his enthusiasm. That's what you'll do, up till the fighting starts. Once it does . . . Well, when the fighting starts, everyone's plans, good and foolish alike, have a way of breaking down."

"I'll miss you," Selatre said. "I always worry when you're away from Fox Keep."

"Sometimes I have to go, that's all," Gerin said. "But I'll tell you this: with you here, I have all the reason I need and then some to want to come back again."

"Good," Selatre said.

The Fox rode south with a force of twenty chariots at his back. That wouldn't be as many as all of Ricolf's vassals could gather, but it was plenty to make him dangerous in a fight. Besides, if Ricolf's vassals didn't have factional squabbles of their own, that would be a miracle about which the minstrels would sing for years to come.

Instead of Raffo, Duren was driving the chariot in which Gerin and Van rode. He handled the reins with confidence but without undue arrogance; unlike some a good deal older than himself, he'd come to understand the importance of convincing the horses to do what he wanted rather than treating them like rowboats or other brainless tools.

As Fox Keep disappeared behind trees when the road jogged, Van let out a long, happy sigh. "Does my nose good to get away from the castle stink!" he said. "Yours is cleaner than most, Fox, but that only goes so far, especially with all the extra warriors packed in."

"I know," Gerin answered. "My nose is happier away

from the keep, too. But if we keep rattling along like this, my kidneys are liable to fall out."

"Pity you can't keep the Elabon Way repaired up to the way it used to be," Van said, "but I suppose I should be grateful there's any road at all."

Gerin shrugged. "I haven't the masons to keep it the way it was, or the artisans to build the deep strong bed that holds up to traffic and weather both. Cobbles and gravel keep it open in the rain and mud, even if they are hard on a man's insides and a horse's hooves."

"To say nothing of the wheels," Van added as they jounced over a couple of particularly large, particularly rough cobbles. "Good thing we have spare axle poles and some extra spokes in case we break 'em."

"This isn't even a particularly bad stretch," Gerin said. "Those places farther south where Balamung wrecked the roadway, those are the ones that haven't been the same since in spite of all the effort I've had the peasants put into them."

"You'd expect wizardry to smash a road worse—or faster, anyway—than ordinary wear and tear," Van said. A glint came into his eyes as he went on, "I wonder if you could set it right by wizardry, too."

"Maybe you could." The Fox refused to rise to the bait. "The gods know I wouldn't be madman enough to try."

His little army halted by a peasant village to spend the night. As the sun set, the serfs sacrificed several chickens, letting their blood run down into a small trench they'd dug in the dirt. The offering of blood, the torches flickering outside their huts, and the great bonfire the warriors made were enough to keep the keening of the night ghosts down to a level a man could bear.

Up in the sky, pale Nothos was a fat waxing crescent; Gerin was surprised to realize it had almost completed one of its slow cycles since he'd made his ruling on the rightful ownership of Swifty the hound. A lot had been crowded into that time.

Quick-moving Tiwaz, also a waxing crescent, hung a little to the east of Nothos. Ruddy Elleb, a nail-paring of a moon, soon followed the sun into the west. Golden Math would not rise till after midnight.

Inside the borders of his own holding, he posted only a couple of sentries for the night. Not all his men went straight to sleep, anyhow. Some of them tried their luck with the women, unattached and otherwise, of the village. Some of that luck was good, and some of it was bad. One thing Gerin's subjects had learned during the generation he ruled them: they did not have to give in for no better reason than that a warrior demanded it of them. He'd outlawed fighting men who forced women. His men knew what he expected of them, too, and by and large lived up to it.

When Duren made as if to go after a pretty girl who looked a couple of years older than he was, the Fox said, "Go ahead, but don't tell her who your father is."

"Why not?" Duren asked. "What quicker way to get her to say yes?"

"But will she have said it because you're you or because you're my son?" Gerin asked. He wondered if Duren cared, so long as the answer turned out to be the one he wanted. Probably not; he remembered how little he'd cared at the same age. "Try it," he urged his son. "See what happens."

"Maybe I will," Duren said. And maybe he did, but the Fox didn't find out one way or the other. Feeling no urge to chase after any of the peasant women, he lay down, wrapped himself in a blanket, and slept till the sun woke him the next morning.

The ride down to Ricolf's keep was more peaceful than the journey had been when he'd made it in his younger days. Now all the barons between his own holding and Ricolf's acknowledged him as their overlord, and had, for the most part, given up squabbling among themselves. Even what had been Bevon's barony—now held by his son Bevander, since his other sons had backed Adiatunnus against Gerin in their last clash—seemed to be producing more crops than brigands. *Progress*, he thought.

Because Ricolf had always formally remained free of Gerin's suzerainty, he had kept up the post between his land and Bevon's. His border guards saluted when the Fox and his fighting tail drew near. "Pass through," one of them said, standing aside with a spearshaft he had held across the road. "Authari said you would be coming after him."

"And so we are." Gerin set a hand on his son's shoulder. "And here is Duren, Ricolf's grandson, who, if Biton the farseeing agrees, will become your lord now that Ricolf—a brave man and a good one, if ever such there was—no longer lives in the world of men."

The border guards looked curiously at Duren. Nodding to them, he said, "If I can rule this holding half so well as Ricolf did, I will be pleased. I hope you will be pleased with me, too, and teach me what I need to learn."

Gerin hadn't told him what to say on first meeting Ricolf's men. He wanted to see how his son fared on his own. He would be on his own if he succeeded to the barony. The guardsmen seemed happy enough with what he'd said. One of them asked, "If you take the holding, will it be as vassal to the Fox here?" He pointed at Gerin.

Duren shook his head. "He hasn't asked that of me. Why would he? I'm his son. What kind of oath could I give to bind me to him tighter than that?"

"Well said," one of the border guards answered. He waved southward, deeper into the territory Ricolf had ruled. "Ride on, then, and may the gods make it all turn out for the best."

Once they'd passed beyond the border station, Gerin said, "You did fine there. You can give Authari and the rest of the petty barons the same answer. I don't see how they can fault you on it, either."

"Good," Duren answered over his shoulder. "I've been thinking about these things ever since Authari came to Fox Keep. I want to do them as best I can."

"You will, with that way of looking at them," Gerin told him. He studied his son's back as the chariot rattled along. Duren was starting to do his own thinking, not coming to the Fox for every answer. *He's becoming a man*, Gerin thought, bemused, but he took it for a good sign.

They came to the keep that had for so many years been Ricolf's as the sun was sliding down the western sky. Elleb had grown to a plump waxing crescent, while Nothos, at first quarter, hung like half a coin a little east of south. Tiwaz had swelled in the past three days to halfway between quarter and full, and was climbing toward the southeastern part of the sky.

"Who comes to this castle?" the watchman called, and Gerin felt a jar inside him at hearing Ricolf's name omitted from the challenge. Approaching Ricolf's keep gave him an odd feeling these days anyhow: old memories twisted and stirred and muttered in his ear like the night spirits, fighting to be understood once more in the world of the living. Here he had met Elise, here he had spirited her away south of the High Kirs, here on returning he had bedded her, here after beating Balamung he had returned and claimed her for his wife.

And she was gone now, and had been gone for most of the time since then, and taken a piece of his spirit with her when she went. And so, for all the happiness he'd found since with Selatre, coming here was like poking at a scar that, while it had healed on the surface, remained sore down below. It probably would be, so long as he lived.

But change came along with memory. He answered the watchman: "I am Gerin, called the Fox, come with my son Duren who is also the grandson of Ricolf the Red to discuss the succession to this holding with Authari Broken-Tooth and whichever of Ricolf's vassal barons he may have summoned hither."

"You are welcome here, lord Gerin," the sentry said. He could hardly have failed to know who the Fox was, but the forms had to be observed. With a rattle of chains, the drawbridge lowered so Gerin and his companions could cross over the moat and enter the keep. Unlike Gerin's, Ricolf's ditch had water in it, making it a better ward for the castle.

Ricolf's men stared down from the walls at Gerin and the small chariot army he'd brought with him. In the failing light, he had trouble reading their faces. Did they think him ally or usurper? Even if he could not tell now, he'd find out soon enough.

Authari came out of the great hall along with several other men who wore authority like a cloak. Authari bowed, well-mannered as usual. "I greet you, lord prince." His eyes swung to Duren. "And you as well, grandson of the lord who held my homage and fealty."

He conceded Duren nothing. Gerin had expected as much. Duren said, "Dyaus and the other gods grant you give me vassalage as good as my grandfather got from you."

Gerin admired his son's self-possession. It seemed to startle Authari, but he quickly rallied, saying, "That is what we have gathered here to decide." He gave his attention back to Gerin. "Lord prince, I present to you Hilmic Barrelstaves, Wacho Fidus' son, and Ratkis

Bronzecaster, who with me are—were—Ricolf's chiefest vassals."

Hilmic Barrelstaves was short and stocky, with bowed legs that had probably given him his ekename. A streak of white ran through his black hair, almost like a horse's blaze. The end of a scar that must have seamed his scalp just showed on his forehead. Gerin had seen cases like that before, where hair grew in pale along the length of a healed wound.

Wacho, by contrast, could have been a Trokmê from his looks; he was tall and blond and ruddy, with pale eyes above knobby cheekbones and a long, thin nose. Ratkis seemed an ordinary Elabonian till you noticed his hands, which were callused and scarred, probably from the craft from which he derived his sobriquet.

As with Authari, Gerin knew them, but not well. They greeted him as equal to equal, which was technically correct—till Ricolf had a successor they acknowledged, they were their own men—but struck the Fox as arrogant all the same. He let it go. Power still lay with him.

"Shall we start the wrangle now, or wait till after supper?" Authari asked once the greetings were done.

"No wrangle," Gerin answered. "Two things can happen. First, you can accept Duren as your baron straightaway—"

"We won't," Wacho said, and Hilmic nodded emphatic agreement. Neither Authari nor Ratkis backed Wacho by word or gesture. That disconcerted him; he choked down what he might have been about to add and instead asked, "What's the other thing?"

"We wait to see what the Sibyl at Ikos says," Gerin told him. "If Biton says Duren is to rule here, rule he will, and nothing you try to do about it will change things a bit. And if the god says he's not meant to be your baron, he'll go back to Fox Keep with me. Where's the wrangle in any of that? Or don't you agree to the terms

Authari and I settled on?" Without changing his voice in any easily describable way, he let Wacho know disagreeing with those terms would not be a good idea.

Ratkis spoke for the first time: "The terms are fair, lord prince. More than fair: you could have brought a real army with you, not a guard, and installed the lad in this keep by force. But sometimes, when Biton speaks through the Sibyl, what he means isn't clear till long afterwards. Life's not always simple. What do we do if it's complicated here?"

Gerin almost grabbed him by the hand and swore friendship with him for life for nothing more than recognizing that ambiguity could exist. To most men in the northlands, something was either good, in which case it was perfection, or bad, in which case it was abomination. The Fox supposed that made keeping track of things simple, but simplicity was not always a virtue.

"Here's what I have in mind," he said. "If anyone thinks the Sibyl's verse can have more than one meaning, even if interpreted with all possible goodwill, then we put it to the four of you on the one hand and Duren, Van, the lady Selatre, and me on the other. Whoever has the most backers among those eight will see his view prevail."

"And if the eight of us divide evenly?" Authari asked.

"The four of you against the four of us, you mean?" Gerin said.

"That seems likeliest," Authari answered.

The Fox was about to reply, but Duren spoke first, his voice for once man-deep, not cracking at all: "Then we go to war, and edged bronze will tell who has the better right."

"I was about to say the same thing," Gerin said, "but my son—Ricolf's grandson, I remind you once more—put it better than I could hope to do." He didn't add that he wanted a war with Ricolf's vassals about as much as he wanted an outbreak of pestilence in the village by Fox Keep.

"If we go to war, Aragis the Archer will—" Wacho began.

"No, Aragis the Archer won't," Gerin interrupted. "Oh, Aragis may choose to fight me over Ricolf's holding here, but he won't be doing it for you and he won't do you any good. I'll have beaten you before his men get this far north, I promise you that. A bear and a longtooth may quarrel over the carcass of a deer, but it doesn't matter to the deer any more, because it's already dead."

Hilmic Barrelstaves scowled at him. "I knew it was going to be like this. You come down here and threaten us—"

"By all the gods, I've gone out of my way *not* to threaten you," Gerin shouted, clapping a hand to his forehead. When he lost his temper, he usually did it for effect. Now he was perilously close to losing it in truth. "We could overrun this holding: Ratkis said as much. You know it, I know it, any half-witted one-eyed dog sniffing through rubbish down by the shore of the Orynian Ocean knows it, too. Instead of that, I proposed letting Biton decide. If that didn't satisfy you, I proposed a way to solve the difficulty. And if you won't heed the god and you won't heed men, sirrah, you deserve to have your thick head knocked in."

A silence rather like the one just after the crash of a thunderbolt filled the courtyard to Ricolf's castle. Authari chuckled nervously. "Well, if the god is kind, he'll give us a response that tells us what we want to know. Then we won't have to worry about any of the rest of this."

Gerin pounced on that. "So you do agree—all four of you do agree—to let Biton speak on this matter?"

One after another, Ricolf's vassals nodded, Authari first, Hilmic last, looking as if he hated to be moving his head up and down. Ratkis Bronzecaster said, "Aye, we agree. We'll take any oath you set to bind us to it, and you'll take ours to do the same."

"Let it be so," Gerin said at once. Of the four of them, Ratkis impressed him as a man of sense. Hilmic and Wacho spoke before they thought, if they thought at all. He wasn't sure what to make of Authari, which probably meant Authari would play both ends against the middle if he thought he saw a chance.

"Let it be so," Authari said now, "and let us sup. Perhaps this will look better after meat and bread."

"Almost anything looks better after meat and bread," Gerin said agreeably.

Ricolf had always set a good table, if not a fancy one, and his cooks carried on after his passing: along with beef and roast fowl, they set out plates of boiled crayfish, fried trout, and turtles baked in their shells. There was plenty of good chewy bread to eat along with the meat and soak up the juices, and scallions and cloves of fragrant garlic to spice up the food. For the hundredth, maybe the thousandth, time, Gerin missed pepper, though he could find no complaint with what was set before him.

His men and those who owed allegiance to Ricolf— or rather, to his chief vassals—crowded the hall. They got on well enough, even after the servants had refilled their drinking jacks a good many times. Some of Gerin's retainers and some of Ricolf's had fought side by side in old wars, after the werenight and against the monsters and in the four-cornered struggle that had wracked Bevon's barony for so long. If they had to battle one another, it would not be with any great enthusiasm.

That didn't mean they wouldn't battle one another. Parol Chickpea said, "If the lord prince gives the order, we'll squash you lads underfoot like a nest of cockroaches. I won't much care for that, but what can you do?"

"You can get beaten back to your own land where you belong," said the fellow sitting beside him: one of Ricolf's troopers, and one who, by his look and bearing, a man of sense would not annoy.

Parol was a lot of things, but seldom sensible. A monster had bitten off a large chunk of one of his buttocks; Gerin wondered if sitting lopsided for years had unbalanced his brain. Probably not, the Fox judged. Parol hadn't been bright before he developed a list.

"No one in this hall wants to go to war with anyone else here," Gerin said loudly, wishing Parol would keep his mouth shut. "If we wanted to go to war, we would have done it already. I always reckoned Ricolf a friend and his men allies. Father Dyaus grant that my men and those of this holding always stay friends and allies."

"Truth there," Ratkis Bronzecaster said, and raised his drinking jack in salute. Gerin was pleased to drink with him.

A buxom young serving girl did everything she could to attract Duren's notice but plop herself down in his lap. Duren did notice her, too. His eyes stuck to her the way little scraps of cloth would stick to amber after you rubbed it. But he did not get up and follow her, despite the glances she kept throwing over her shoulder.

"Good for you," Gerin told him. "If you're going to rule this holding, you don't want to get a reputation as a man who thinks with his spear first and his head later. You're a likely-looking lad; finding willing women shouldn't be any trouble for you. But this wench—who knows what she's after, making up so soon to the fellow who's likely to be her overlord?"

"That's what I was thinking," Duren answered. What else he was thinking, though, was also obvious from the way he kept watching the girl.

Wacho Fidus' son breathed ale fumes into Gerin's face. "So you will be going on to Ikos, eh, lord prince?"

"A man with a gift for the obvious," Gerin observed, which, as he'd expected, made Wacho stare at him in beery incomprehension. Sighing, he went on, "As a matter of fact, what point in going on to Ikos if you retainers of Ricolf's try to ignore what the god tells you if it's not to your liking? I don't want to do it, mind you, but we might as well just fight the war. You'd have no doubt of what you were supposed to do then, anyhow."

Wacho understood that well enough, and looked appalled. He said, "No such thing, lord prince. We were just talking about what to do if the Sibyl's verse turned out to be obsc—ob—hard to make head or tail of, that's all. If it's plain, we have no quarrel."

"By everything you and your three comrades have said and done, you'd do anything to show the Sibyl's verse was obscure, regardless of whether that's really so," Gerin said. "I don't know why I'm wasting my time with you."

He knew perfectly well why he was wasting his time with them: he didn't want to get into a little war down here, not when two bigger ones were building in the west and Aragis the Archer loomed, watching and waiting, in the south. But if he could push Ricolf's vassals into forgetting that, he'd do it without hesitation or compunction.

Still looking horrified, Wacho went off and collared Authari, Ratkis, and Hilmic. The four of them put their heads together, then came back over to the Fox. "See here," Authari said, his voice full of nervous bluster. "I thought we had a bargain to abide by what the Sibyl at Ikos said."

"So did I," Gerin answered. "But when I got down here, what I found you people meaning was that you would interpret Biton's words they way they suited you, no matter what he said."

"We never said any such thing," Hilmic Barrelstaves said indignantly.

"I didn't say you said it. I said you meant it," Gerin told him. " 'What do we do if we don't agree? What do we do if we don't agree?' You might as well have been crickets, all chirping the same note." He got up as if to stamp out of the great hall, as if to stamp out of Ricolf's keep altogether, in spite of the ghosts that turned the night to terror.

"Give us an oath," Ratkis said. "Give us an oath we can swear and we will swear it. Authari was talking about that with you, I know, and I said as much earlier myself. We want—I want—fair dealing here."

Him Gerin believed. He was less sure about the other three. But a strong enough oath would attract the notice of even the rather lackadaisical Elabonian gods if it was violated. "All right. Will you swear by Father Dyaus and farseeing Biton to accept the words of the Sibyl on their face if there is any possible way to do so. Will you also swear that, should you violate your oath, you pray you will have only sorrow and misfortune in this world and that your soul will not even wander the world by night, but will rest forever in the hottest of the five hells?"

Ricolf's four vassals looked at each other, then went off to put their heads together again. When they came back, Authari Broken-Tooth said, "That's a strong oath you require of us."

"That's the idea," Gerin said, exhaling through his nose. "What point to an oath you don't fear breaking?"

"Will *you* swear the same oath?" Wacho demanded.

By his tone, he expected the Fox to recoil in dismay from the very idea. But Gerin said, "Of course I will. I don't fear what Biton says. If Duren isn't fated to rule this holding, the god will make that plain. And if he is so fated, Biton will tell us that, too. So I will swear that oath. I'll swear it now, this instant. Join me?"

They went off once more. Gerin sipped his ale and watched them argue. It seemed to be Authari and Ratkis on one side, Wacho and Hilmic on the other. He couldn't hear them, but he would have been willing to guess which men were on which side.

At last, rather glumly, the barons returned. Speaking for them, Authari said, "Very well, lord prince. We will swear the oath with you. If we disagree in spite of it, we will settle the disagreements as you proposed. In short, we agree with all your proposals, straight down the line."

"No, we don't agree with them," Hilmic Barrelstaves said angrily. "But we'll go along with them. It's either that or fight you, and our chances there don't look good to us, not even if Aragis comes in on our side."

"You're right," Gerin said. "Your chances wouldn't have been good. Shall we swear now, before our men?"

Wacho and Hilmic looked as if they would have delayed if they could have found any good reason for doing so. But Ratkis Bronzecaster said, "It would be best so. That way, our retainers can have no doubt about what the agreement is."

"Exactly my thought," Gerin said. *It also makes it harder for you to go about breaking the oath later: your own men will call you on it if you do.*

When the two hesitant barons nodded at last, Duren said, "I will swear this oath, also. If this is to be my holding, it will be *mine*, so I should speak for myself in matters that touch on it."

"Good enough," Gerin said heartily, and Ricolf's vassals also made approving noises. Down deep, Gerin wondered how good it really was. Would his son, if he became lord here, suddenly start ignoring everything he said? Duren was of about the right age to do something like that. And his mother, from whom he drew half his blood, had always been one to follow her impulses to the hilt, whether it was running away with Gerin or running away from him a few years later. Was Elise's blood showing itself in Duren? And if it was, what could the Fox do about it?

He quickly answered that one: *nothing*. Forcing the issue by bringing Duren here had been his idea. Now he would have to face the consequences, whatever those turned out to be.

He got to his feet. So did Duren, and so, a moment later, did Ricolf's four leading vassals. Gerin looked at them, hoping one of their number—maybe Authari, who liked to hear himself talk—would announce to the expectantly waiting warriors his approval of what they had agreed upon. That would make it look as if the oath had been in large measure their idea, not his.

But Authari and his comrades stood mute, leaving it up to the Fox. He made the best of it he could: "We now seal by this oath we are about to swear to abide by the farseeing god's choice as to whether Duren should rule this holding, the oath setting out what we hope will happen to us in this world and the next if we go against any of its provisions. I will say the terms, and Ricolf's vassals and my son will repeat them after me, all of us committing ourselves to this course."

He waited for any objection from his men or from those who owed allegiance to Ricolf's vassals. When none came, he said, "I begin." He turned to Duren and to Ricolf's lordlets: "Say each phrase of the oath after me: 'By Dyaus All-Father and farseeing Biton I swear—' "

" 'By Dyaus All-Father and farseeing Biton I swear—' " Authari and Ratkis, Wacho and Hilmic, and Duren all echoed him. He listened carefully to make sure they did. If not everyone swore the same oath, people would be able to question its validity. That was the last thing he wanted.

He made the oath as comprehensive and strict as he could, so much so that Wacho and Hilmic and even Authari looked at him sidelong as provision after stern provision rolled off his tongue. Duren took the oath without hesitation. So did Ratkis Bronzecaster. The Fox thought Ratkis honest. If he wasn't, he was so shameless as to be deadly dangerous.

At last he could think of nothing more to bind Ricolf's vassals to their promises. "So may it be," he finished, and, with evident relief, they repeated the words after him: "So may it be." The oath had done what it could do. The rest would be up to the men who had followed Ricolf so long—and to the farseeing god.

Eight chariots rattled down the narrow track through the strange and haunted wood that grew around the little valley housing the hamlet of Ikos and Biton's shrine nearby. Gerin, Duren, and Van rode in one; their retainers filled three more; and Authari, Wacho, Ratkis, and Hilmic each headed one crew.

"I've never been to see the Sibyl, not in all my days," Hilmic Barrelstaves said, his voice unwontedly quiet as he peered this way and that into the wood. "Did I see a—? No, I couldn't have." He shook his head, denying the idea, whatever it had been, even to himself.

Gerin had been through that curious wood a good many times, but he was wary there, too. You were never quite sure what you saw or heard—or what saw and heard you. Sometimes you got the strong feeling you were better off not knowing.

Even Van spoke softly, as if not wanting to rouse whatever powers rested in uneasy sleep. "I think we'll make it to the town before sundown," he said. "Hard to be sure, when the leaves block the sunlight so—and when you're in this place any which way. Time feels—loose—here, so it's hard to judge how long you've really been traveling."

"This forest is as old as the world, I think," Gerin answered, "and now, it's a little, mm, disconnected from the rest of the world. It puts up with this road through it, but only just barely."

Duren drove on in silence. The horses were nervous, but he controlled them. Like Hilmic, he was making his first visit to Ikos, and he was as busy as Ricolf's vassal trying to look in every direction at once, and as wide-eyed at the things he was—and the things he wasn't—seeing.

To Gerin's relief, Van proved right: they emerged from the wood with some daylight left. The idea of having to camp in among those trees chilled the Fox. Who could say what kind of ghosts lived in this place? He did not want to find out, and was glad he would not have to.

"Rein in," he told his son, and Duren obediently brought the chariot to a stop. Gerin stared down into the valley at the white-marble splendor of Biton's shrine and the almost equally splendid wall of marble blocks surrounding its compound. "Will you look at that?" he said softly.

"Amazing," Van agreed, nodding. They'd both seen that shrine and that wall overthrown in the earthquake that had released the monsters from their age-long underground captivity and loosed them on the upper world. Van went on, "It looks the same as it always did."

"That it does," Gerin said. It would have been impossible for any men in the northlands to restore that temple, built as it was with the full resources of the Empire of Elabon in its glory days and all the talented artists and artisans the Empire provided. But Biton had rebuilt the shrine, and in an instant. Because of that, Gerin had wondered if it would be even more magnificent than it had been before. But no—at least from a distance, it merely seemed the same.

Ikos—the town, as opposed to the shrine—was different from what it had been. Biton had not restored the overthrown hostels and eateries as he had his own temple. There were fewer of them now than there had been before the quake; some then had been just hanging on, for traffic to the Sibyl's underground chamber had shrunk since the Empire of Elabon cut itself off from the northlands. The ones who had been suffering, evidently, had not rebuilt. By the quiet streets that wound between the surviving shelters, more would have been superfluous.

When the innkeepers saw eight cars bearing down on them at once, they fell with glad cries on the warriors those cars carried. Gerin remembered the outrageous prices he'd paid to rest his head in the days before the werenight. He and his companions got bigger rooms, with meals thrown in as part of the bargain, for less than half as much. Any business, these days, was better than none to the townsfolk.

"How do these people live when the inns are empty, the way they look to be most of the time?" Van asked in the taproom later that evening.

"They get rich, taking in one another's laundry," Gerin answered, deadpan.

Van started to nod, then stared sharply and let out a snort. "You want to watch that tongue of yours, Fox. One fine day you'll cut yourself with it." Gerin stuck out the member in question and stared down at it, cross-eyed. Van made as if to drench him with a jack of ale, but didn't do it. That relieved the Fox; his friend started tavern brawls for the sport of it.

Gerin and **Duren** shared a chamber. Van took the one next to theirs, and didn't want any of the rest of the Fox's followers in there with him. Even with the bargain rates they were getting, Gerin, who made money last till it wore out, fretted at the extra expense. But it quickly became obvious Van did not intend to sleep alone. He made advances to both serving girls who were bringing food from the kitchens, and soon had one of them sitting on his lap, giggling at the way his beard tickled while he nuzzled her neck.

The Fox sighed. One way or another, word of what Van was doing would get back to Fand, and that would start another of their fights. Gerin was sick of fights. How were you supposed to live your life in the middle of chaos? But some people reveled in such disorder.

Van was one of them. "I know what you're thinking, Captain," he said. "Your face gives you away. And do you know what? I don't care."

"That's what Rihwin said, when he danced his wife away," Gerin answered. Van wasn't listening to him. Van wasn't listening to anything save his drinking jack and the stiff lance he had in his breeches.

Duren looked hungrily at the serving girl. But then he took a long look around the taproom. A couple of other wenches were serving there, true. But all the men they were serving were both older and far more prominent than he. He took a sip from his jack of ale and then said, "My chances aren't good here tonight, are they?"

The Fox set a hand on his shoulder. "You're my son, sure enough," he said. "There're men twice your age—Dyaus, there're men four times your age—who'd never make that calculation, and who'd sulk or rage for days because they didn't have some doe-eyed girl helping 'em pull their breeches down."

Duren snorted. "That's foolish."

"Aye, so it is," Gerin answered. "Doesn't stop it from happening all the time—and women aren't immune to it, either, not even a little bit. People *are* foolish, son—haven't you noticed that yet?"

"Oh, maybe once or twice," Duren said, as dryly as

the Fox might have. Gerin stared at him, then started to laugh. If Duren did take over at what had been the holding of Ricolf the Red, Wacho, Hilmic, and Authari would never know what hit them. Ratkis Bronzecaster might, but the Fox had the feeling he'd be on Duren's side.

After a while, Gerin tipped his drinking jack over on its side and went upstairs carrying a candle, Duren trailing along behind him. Van and the serving maid had already gone up there; the noises from behind the outlander's door told without any possible doubt what they were doing. The amatory racket came through the wall, too. As Gerin used the candle to light a couple of lamps, Duren said, "How are we supposed to sleep with *that* going on?"

"I expect we'll manage," Gerin said. A moment later, a moan from the other side of the wall contradicted him. He thought about rapping on the timbers, but forbore; as any man was liable to do, Van grew testy if interrupted, and a testy Van was not something to contemplate without trepidation. "We'll manage," the Fox repeated, this time as much to convince himself as his son.

When the shutters were closed, they made the bedroom dark and hot and stuffy. Leaving them open let in fresh air, but also bugs and, come morning, daylight, which woke Gerin earlier than he would have liked.

He sat up and rubbed his eyes with something less than enthusiasm. He hadn't slept as well as he would have liked, and he had had a little more ale than he should have—not enough for a true hangover, but plenty to give him the edge of a headache behind his eyes and to make his mouth taste like something scraped off the dung heap.

To improve his mood yet further, a rhythmic pounding started in the chamber next door. That was enough to wake Duren, who stared at the wall. "I *was* asleep," he said, as if not quite believing it. He lowered his voice. "Is he at it still, Father?"

"Not still, the gods be thanked. Only again." Gerin raised an eyebrow. "If he's not down by breakfast, we'll rap on the door. Of course, if he's not down by breakfast, the serving girl won't be, either, so breakfast may be late."

Van did come down for breakfast, looking mightily contented with the world. After bread and honey and ale, he and Gerin and Duren, along with Ricolf's four leading vassals, walked down to Biton's shrine, a little south of the hamlet of Ikos.

At close range as from a distance, the shrine and its grounds seemed identical to the way they had been before the earthquake tumbled them and loosed the monsters on the northlands. There within the marble wall was the statue of the dying Trokmê; there not far away stood the twin gold-and-ivory statues of Ros the Fierce, conqueror of the northlands, and Oren the Builder, who had erected the temple to Biton in half-Sithonian, half-Elabonian style.

Both Ros and Oren seemed perfect and complete. Gerin scratched his head at that. After the temblor, he'd taken away the jewel-encrusted golden head of Oren when it rolled outside the bounds of Biton's sacred precinct, within which it was death to steal. The precious metal and gems had helped him greatly in the years since, and yet here they were, restored as they had been. The Fox shrugged. The ways and abilities of gods were beyond those of men.

Yet not even Biton, it seemed, had been able to bring back to life the guardsmen and eunuch priests who had served him. All those here now looked young (though more and more of the world looked young to Gerin these days), and no faces were familiar. The ritual, however, remained the same: before a suppliant went down below the temple to put a question to the Sibyl, money changed hands. Because Gerin was prince of the north, his offering was larger than any ordinary baron's would have been. That irked him, but he paid. You tried to constrain the gods, or their priests, at your peril.

When the plump leather sack he handed to a eunuch had been judged and found adequate, the priest said, "Enter lord Biton's shrine and pray for wisdom and enlightenment."

"Remember when you used to have to queue up even to get into the temple?" Van said to Gerin. "Not like that any more."

"But perhaps it shall be again one day," the eunuch said before Gerin could reply. "The fame of Biton's restored temple has spread widely through the northlands, but times are so unsettled, few make the journey despite its reputation: travel is less safe than it might be."

"I know," Gerin answered. "I've done everything I could do make it safer in the lands whose overlord I am, but it's not all it could be. That hurts trade, and costs money, too."

He and his companions followed the eunuch into Biton's shrine. As always on entering there, the ancient image of the farseeing god caught and held the Fox's eye, more than all the architectural splendor Oren had lavished on the building surrounding it. Given a choice, Oren surely would have discarded the image and replaced it with a modern piece from one of his stable of sculptors. That he hadn't discarded it suggested someone, whether a priest of Biton, the Sibyl at the time, or the god himself, had given the Elabonian Emperor no choice.

The statue, if it could be dignified by that word, was a pillar of black basalt, almost plain. The only marks suggesting it was more than a simple stele were an erect phallus jutting from its midsection and a pair of eyes scratched into the stone a hand's breadth or two below the top. Gerin studied those eyes. Just for an instant, they seemed brown and alive and human—or rather, divine. He blinked, and they were scratches on stone once more.

Along with his son, his friend, and Ricolf's vassals, he sat in the front pews of the temple and, peering down at the tiny tesserae of the floor mosaic, prayed that the farseeing god would give him the guidance he sought. When he raised his eyes, the eunuch priest said, "I shall conduct you to the Sibyl's chamber. If you will come with me—"

A black slit in the ground led to the countless caverns below Biton's shrine. Duren's eyes were large as, side by side with Gerin, he set foot on the stone steps that eased the suppliant's way on the beginning of the journey. Gerin's heart pounded, though he had been this way several times before. Behind him, Wacho and Hilmic muttered nervously.

He wondered whom Biton's priests had found for a Sibyl to replace Selatre. When the farseeing god restored his temple compound, he'd wanted to restore Selatre to her place as well. Gerin would not have—indeed, how could he have?—hindered that, but Selatre had begged Biton to let her stay in the new life she'd found, and the god, to the Fox's relief and joy, had done as she asked. Now Biton spoke through someone new.

The air in the caverns was fresh and cool and moist, with a hint of a breeze. Gerin, with his itch to learn, wished he knew how it circulated rather than merely that it did. The priest carried a torch, and others burned at intervals along the rock wall. The flickering light did strange, sometimes frightening things to the shadows the travelers along that ancient way cast.

Yet it also picked out sparkling bits of rock crystal set into the rough walls of the passage, some white, some orange, some red as blood. And, now and again, the torchlight showed ways branching off from the main track, some open, some walled up with brick and further warded by potent cantrips.

Gerin pointed to one of those walled-off passages. "Do the monsters still lurk back there, behind the spells that hold them at bay?"

"We believe so," the priest answered, his sexless voice quiet and troubled. "Those wards are, however, as the lord Biton made them. None of us has been past them to be certain—nor, I might add, have the monsters made any effort to return to the world of light."

"Those horrible things." Ratkis Bronzecaster made a hand sign to avert ill-luck. "They gave us no end of trouble when they were loose." *And do I get any credit for tricking the gods into taking them off the surface of the world?* Gerin thought. *Not likely*. But then Ratkis went on with a thought that hadn't occurred to him before: "I wonder if they have gods of their own down here."

Now Gerin's fingers twisted in the avert-evil sign. Some of the monsters—not all—might well be smart enough to conceive of gods, or to have whatever gods who already dwelt in these caves take notice of them: philosophers argued endlessly about how the link between gods and men (or even between gods and not-quite-men) came into being. The Fox was certain of one thing—he didn't want to meet whatever gods might dwell down here in this endless gloom.

"I wonder what Geroge and Tharma would think if we ever brought them down here," Duren said as he walked along the fairly smooth path uncounted generations of feet had worn in the stone.

"That's another good question," Gerin agreed. He started to add that he didn't want to answer it, but stopped and held his peace. If the monsters at Fox Keep did prove troublesome as they matured, he might have no choices left but to slay them or send them down here with their fellows.

The passage wound down and down through the living rock. Most times, that was just a semipoetic phrase to the Fox. Down in the midst of it, though, the rock of the cave walls did seem alive, as if it were dimly conscious not only of his presence but also of separating him from the monsters in the deeper, walled-off galleries.

And it would have twitched and writhed like a living thing in the earthquake that had freed the monsters. Gerin wondered what being underground here when the quake struck would have been like. He was glad he hadn't found out; he and Van had spoken with Selatre (whose name, of course, he had not then known) less than a day before the temblor shook the whole northlands.

A pool of brighter light ahead marked the entrance to the Sibyl's chamber. The priest asked, "Would you like me to withdraw so you can put your question to Biton's voice on earth in private?" Having him withdraw would have involved paying him more. When no one seemed ready to do that, he shrugged and led the suppliants into the chamber.

Torchlight shimmered from the Sibyl's throne, which looked as if it was carved from a single, impossibly immense black pearl. Clad in a simple white linen shift, the girl on the throne was plainly of the old northlands stock whose blood still ran strong around Ikos; by her looks, she might have been cousin to Selatre.

"What would you ask my lord Biton?" she asked. Her

voice, a rich contralto, made Gerin move her age up a few years: though maid-slim, she was probably on his side of twenty, not the other one.

He asked the question in exactly the words upon which he and Ricolf's vassals had agreed: "Should my son Duren succeed his grandfather Ricolf the Red as baron of the holding over which Ricolf held suzerainty till he died?"

The Sibyl listened intently—as well she might, for she was listening for her divine master as well as herself. The mantic fit hit her hard, as it had the predecessors of hers whom Gerin had seen on that black-pearl throne: Selatre, and before her an ancient crone who had been Biton's voice on earth for three generations of suppliants.

Eyes rolled back in her head to show only white, the Sibyl writhed and twitched. Her arms jerked and flailed, seemingly at random. Then she stiffened. Her lips parted. She spoke, not with her own voice, but with the firm, confident baritone Biton always used:

> *"The young man shall hold all the castles*
> *And all within shall be his vassals.*
> *But peril lurks, like dark in caves*
> *And missteps here fill many graves.*
> *Aye! Danger lurks in many shapes,*
> *O'ershadowing you like bunchèd grapes."*

V

Ricolf's vassals were being difficult. Gerin had been sure they would be difficult, from the instant the eunuch priest led him, his son, Van, and them out of the Sibyl's chamber. Now, back at the hostel in the village of Ikos, they, or at least three of them, openly bickered with the Fox.

"Didn't mean a thing," Wacho Fidus' son declared, thumping his balled fist down onto the table. "Not one single, solitary thing."

" 'The young man shall hold all the castles/ And all within shall be his vassals'?" Gerin quoted. "That means nothing to you. Are you deaf and blind as well as—" He broke off; he'd been about to say *stupid*. "We asked about Ricolf's holdings, and the god said he'd rule all the castles. What more do you want?" *A good dose of brains wouldn't hurt. You could take them by enema, so they'd be close to what you use for thinking now.*

"The god said 'all *the* castles,' " Authari Broken-Tooth declared. "The god said nothing about *Ricolf's* castles. Duren here is your heir, too. When you die, he stands to inherit your lands and the keeps on them."

Gerin exhaled through his nose. "That's clever, I must admit," he said tightly. "Are you sure you didn't study Sithonian hair-splitting—excuse me, philosophy—south of the High Kirs? The only problem is, the question wasn't about the keeps I control. It asked specifically about the holding of Ricolf the Red. When you take

146

the question and the answer together, there's only one conclusion you can reach."

"We seem to have found another one," Hilmic Barrelstaves said, tipping back his drinking jack and pouring the last swallow's worth of ale down his throat. He waved the jack around to show he wanted a refill.

"Aye, you've found another one," Gerin answered. "Is it one that will let you keep the oath you swore to Dyaus and Biton and Baivers" —he pointed to Hilmic's drinking jack— "and all the other gods?"

Wacho, Hilmic, and Authari appeared to take no notice of that. But Ratkis Bronzecaster, who'd said little, looked even more thoughtful than he already had. *Oathbreaker* wasn't a name anyone wanted to get for himself. It hurt you in this world and was liable to hurt you worse in the next.

Duren said, "From all I've heard and read of Biton's prophetic verse, the god never names names straight out."

"What do you know, lad?" Wacho said with a sneer.

"I know insolence when I hear it," Duren snapped. Physically, he was not a match for the bigger, older man, but his voice made Wacho sit up and take notice. Duren went on, "I know my letters, too, so I can learn things I don't see with my own eyes and hear with my own ears. Can you say the same?"

Before Wacho answered, Gerin put in, "I've been to the Sibyl several times now, over the years, and the next name I hear in one of those verses will be the first." Van nodded agreement.

Ratkis broke his silence: "That is so, or it has been for me, at any rate. It gives me one thing more to think about."

"You're not going to turn against us, are you?" Hilmic Barrelstaves demanded. "You'd be sorry for that—three against one would—"

"It wouldn't be three against one for long," Gerin broke in. Hilmic glared at him. He glared back, partly from anger, partly for effect. Then, musingly, he went on, "If your neighbors outside Ricolf's barony hear how you'd seek to go back on your sworn word, they might hit you from behind while you were fighting Ratkis, too, for fear you'd treat them the same way after you'd beaten him. And that doesn't begin to take into account what I'd do."

He carefully avoided saying exactly what he would do. Absent other troubles, he would have descended on Ricolf's holding with everything he had, to make sure it would be in Duren's hands before Aragis the Archer could so much as think of responding. Absent other troubles— He laughed bitterly. Other troubles were anything but absent.

Then Ratkis said, "I expect I can hold my own. If the Trokmê tide didn't swamp me, I don't suppose my neighbors will." He looked from Hilmic to Wacho to Authari Broken-Tooth. "They know I don't go out looking for mischief. Aye, they know that, so they do. And they know that if mischief comes looking for me, I mostly give it a set of lumps and send it on its way."

By the sour expressions on the faces of his fellow vassal barons, they did know that. Authari said, "Do you want to see us dragged into doing whatever Gerin the Fox here orders us to do?"

"Not so you'd notice," Ratkis answered. "But I can't say I'm dead keen on going against what a god says, either, and looks to me as if that's what the three of you have in mind."

Wacho Fidus' son and Hilmic shook their heads with vehemence that struck Gerin as overwrought. Smoothly, Authari said, "Not a bit of it, Ratkis—nothing of the sort. But we do have to be certain what the lord Biton means, don't we?"

"I think we're all of us clear enough on that," Van rumbled, and then drained his drinking jack. "If we weren't, some people wouldn't be trying so hard to get around the plain words."

"I resent that," Authari said, his versatile voice now hot with anger.

Van got to his feet and stared down at Authari. "You do, eh?" He set a hand on the hilt of his sword. "How much d'you resent it? Care to step onto the street and show me how much you resent it? What d'you suppose'll happen after that? D'you suppose your successor, whoever he is, will resent it, too?"

The taproom got very quiet. The warriors who'd accompanied Ricolf's vassals eyed those who'd come to Ikos with Gerin, and were eyed in return. And everyone waited to hear and see what Authari Broken-Tooth would do.

Gerin did not think Authari a coward; he'd never heard nor seen anything to give him that idea. But he did not blame Authari for licking his lips and keeping silent while he thought: Van was two hands' breadth taller, and likely weighed half again as much as he did.

"Well?" the outlander demanded. "Are you coming out?"

"I find—I find—I am not so angry as I was a moment before," Authari said. "Sometimes a man's temper can make him say things he wishes he had kept to himself."

To Gerin's relief, Van accepted that, and sat back down at once. "Well, you're right there, and no mistake," he said. "Even the Fox has done it, and he's more careful with his tongue than any man I've ever known."

Much of what Van called being careful was simply knowing when to keep his mouth shut. But Gerin knew not to say that, too. What he did say was, "Since you're not out of temper now, Authari, can you take a calmer look at the verses the god spoke through the Sibyl and admit the lines that talk about my son can have only one meaning?"

Authari looked resentful again, but carefully did not claim he was. Gerin's intellectual challenge was as hard for him to withstand as Van's physical challenge had been. At last, very much against his will, Ricolf's vassal admitted, "There may be some truth in what you say."

That made Hilmic and Wacho let out indignant bleats. "You've sold us, you traitor!" Wacho shouted, quickly red in the face with fury. "I ought to cut your heart out for this, or worse if I could think of it."

"I'd face *you* any day," Authari retorted. "I'd face the Fox, too. I don't fear him in the field, not when he has so many concerns besides me. But Biton? Who can fight against a god and hope to win? Since the farseeing one knows my heart, he knows I thought to oppose his will. But thought is not deed."

"You speak truth there," Gerin agreed. "Now, though, you will recognize Duren as your rightful overlord?"

"So I will," Authari said sourly, "when he is permanently installed in Ricolf's keep, and not a day sooner."

"That is fair," Gerin said.

"This was all your idea, and now you're running away from it?" Wacho bellowed. Hilmic Barrelstaves set a hand on his arm and whispered in his ear. Wacho calmed down, or seemed to. All the same, Gerin wouldn't have cared to be Authari right then. By himself, Authari was more powerful than either Wacho or Hilmic. Was he more powerful than both of them put together? Ratkis had said he could hold out against all three of Ricolf's other leading vassals, so presumably Authari could hold out against two of them. But that didn't mean he'd enjoy doing it.

And then Duren said, quietly but firmly, "When I succeed my grandfather, my vassals will not fight private wars against one another. Anyone who starts that kind of war will face me along with his foe."

Gerin had imposed that rule on his own vassals. For that matter, Ricolf had enforced it while he lived. A strong overlord could. All of Ricolf's leading vassals had assumed Duren, at least apart from Gerin, would not be a strong overlord. But Duren hadn't said anything about asking help from his father, nor had he sounded as if he thought he'd need it. By the looks on their faces, Authari, Hilmic, and Wacho were all having second thoughts.

So was Gerin. He'd done his best to train Duren up to be a leader one day. He hadn't realized he'd succeeded so well, or so fast. A boy turned into a man when he could fill a man's sandals. By that reckoning—his games among the serving women at Fox Keep to one side—Duren was a man now. Scratching his head, Gerin wondered exactly when that had happened, and why he hadn't noticed.

Ratkis Bronzecaster noticed. Speaking to Duren rather than Gerin, he asked, "When do you expect to take up the lordship of the holding that had been your grandfather's?"

"Not this season," Duren answered at once. "After my father has beaten Adiatunnus and the Gradi and no longer needs me by his side."

"Your father is lucky to have you for a son," Ratkis observed, with no irony Gerin could hear.

Duren shrugged. "What I am, he made me."

In some ways, that was true. In those ways, it might have been more true of Duren than of a good many youths, for, with his mother gone, Gerin had had more of his raising than he would have otherwise. But in other ways, as the Fox had just realized, Duren had outstripped his hopes. And so he said, "A father can only shape what's already in a son."

Ratkis nodded at that. "You're not wrong, lord prince. If a lad is a donkey, you can't make him into a horse you'd want pulling your chariot. But if he's already a horse, you can show him how to run." He turned to Duren. "When that time comes, you'll have no trouble from me, not unless you show you deserve it, which I don't think you will. And I say that to you for your sake, not on account of who your father is."

"I will try to be a lord who deserves good vassalage," Duren answered.

Ratkis nodded again, saying, "I think you may well do that." After a moment, Authari Broken-Tooth nodded, too. Hilmic and Wacho sat silent and unhappy. They'd been as difficult and obstructive as they could and, by all the signs, had nothing to show for it.

If only all my foes were so easy to handle, the Fox thought.

The drive back from the Sibyl's shrine to the Elabon Way showed the damage the monsters had done in their brief time above ground. The peasant villages that lay beyond the old, half-haunted wood west of Ikos were shadows of what they had been. In a way, that made the journey back to the main highway easier, for the peasants, who were their own masters, owing no overlord allegiance, had been apt to demonstrate their freedom by preying on passing travelers.

"Serves 'em right," Van said as they rode past another village where most of the huts were falling to ruin and a handful of frightened folk stared at the chariots with wide, hungry eyes. "They'd have knocked us over the head for our weapons and armor, so many good-byes to 'em."

"Land needs to be farmed," Gerin said, upset at the sight of saplings springing up in what had been wheatfields. "It shouldn't rest idle."

The state of the land was not the only worry on his mind, for he very much hoped he would find that his warriors had rested idle while he was consulting the Sibyl. Ricolf's vassals had men enough to crush his small force if they set their minds to it, and to seize or kill him as he returned to their holding, too. He vowed to take Wacho and Hilmic—and Authari, for luck—down to the underworld with him if their followers turned traitor.

But when he came upon those of his troopers he'd left behind, they and the men who had served Ricolf were getting on well. When they recognized him and his companions, they hurried toward them, loudly calling for news.

"We don't know what we're going to do," Wacho said, still unready to resign himself to recognizing Duren as his suzerain.

"No, that isn't so," Ratkis Bronzecaster said before Gerin—or Duren—could scream at Wacho. "Sounds like the god thinks the lad should come after his grandfather. But he won't take over Ricolf's keep quite yet."

"Why aren't we fighting the Fox, then?" one of the soldiers demanded. "His kin have no call taking over our holding."

"Biton thinks otherwise," Ratkis said; having made up his mind, he followed his decision to the hilt. With a nod to one of his comrades, he added, "Isn't that right, Authari?"

Authari Broken-Tooth looked as if he hated the other baron for putting him on the spot. "Aye," he answered, more slowly than he should have. He could hardly have been less enthusiastic had he been discussing his own imminent funeral obsequies.

But that *aye*, however reluctant, produced both acclamations for Duren and loud arguments. Gerin

glanced toward Hilmic Barrelstaves and Wacho Fidus'
son. Hilmic, sensibly, was keeping quiet. Wacho looked
as if he had no intention of doing anything of the sort.

Gerin caught his eye. Wacho glared truculent defiance
at him. He'd seen it done better. He shook his head, a
single tightly controlled movement. Wacho glared even
more fiercely. The Fox didn't glare back. Instead, he
looked away, a gesture of cool contempt that said Wacho
wasn't worth noticing and had better not make himself
worth noticing.

Had Wacho shouted, Gerin's men might have found
themselves in a bloody broil with the troopers who
followed Ricolf's vassals. But Wacho didn't shout. He
was big and full of bluster, but the Fox had managed
to get across a warning he could not mistake.

Gerin said, "Hear the words of farseeing Biton, as
spoken through his Sibyl at Ikos." He repeated the
prophetic verse just as the Sibyl had given it to him,
then went on, "Can any of you doubt that in this verse
the god shows Duren to be the rightful successor to
Ricolf the Red?"

His own men clapped and cheered; they were ready
to believe his interpretation. Three out of four of Ricolf's
leading vassals, though, had disputed it. What would
the common soldiers from Ricolf's holding do? They
owed Gerin no allegiance, but they did not stand to
lose so much as Authari and his colleagues, either: who
the overlord of the holding was mattered less to men
who had to take orders regardless of that overlord's name.

And, by ones and twos, they began to nod, accepting
that the verse meant what he said it did. They showed
no great enthusiasm, but they had no reason to show
great enthusiasm: Duren was an untried youth. But they
seemed willing to give him his chance.

Ricolf's vassal barons saw that, too. Ratkis took it in
stride. Whatever Authari thought, he kept to himself.

Wacho and Hilmic tried with indifferent success to hide dismay.

"I thank you," Duren said to the soldiers, doing his best to pitch his voice man-deep. "May we be at peace whenever we can, and may we win whenever we must go to war."

Van stuck an elbow in Gerin's ribs. "Have to be careful with that one," he said under his breath, pointing to the Fox's son. "Whatever he wants, he's liable to go out and grab it."

"Aye," Gerin said, also looking at Duren with some bemusement. His own nature was to wait and look around before acting, then strike hard. Duren was moving faster and, by the way things seemed, able to be gentler because of that.

For Ricolf's troopers were nodding at his words, accepting them more readily than they had Gerin's interpretation of the oracular response. Before the Fox could say anything, Duren went on, "I will not take up this holding from my grandfather now, for my father still has need of me. But when that need has passed, I will return here and accept the homage of my vassals."

Gerin wondered how the troopers would take that; it reminded them of Duren's link to him. By their anxious expressions, Hilmic and Wacho were wondering the same thing, and hoping the reminder would turn the warriors against Duren. It didn't. If anything, it made them think better of him. One comment rising above the general murmur of approval was, "If he looks out for his kinsfolk, he'll look out for us, too."

The Fox didn't know who'd said that, altogether without being asked. He would gladly have paid good gold to get one of Ricolf's men to come out with such a sentiment; getting it for free, and sincerely, was all the better.

Ratkis looked satisfied. Authari Broken-Tooth's

expression could have meant anything, though if it betokened delight, Gerin would have been very much surprised. What Hilmic's and Wacho's faces showed was at best dyspepsia, at worst stark dismay. The Fox knew they—and probably Authari, too—would be haranguing their retainers every day till Gerin got back to Ricolf's holding. How much good that haranguing would do them remained to be seen.

Then Ratkis got down from his chariot and went to one knee on the stone slabs of the road close by the car Duren was driving. Looking up at Duren, he said, "Lord, in token of your return, I will gladly give you homage and fealty now." He pressed the palms of his hands together and held them out before him.

At last, after seeing so much maturity from his son, Gerin found Duren at a loss. He tapped the youth on the shoulder and hissed, "Accept, quick!"

That got Duren moving. He'd seen Gerin accept new vassals often enough to know the ritual. Scrambling down from the chariot, he hurried over to stand in front of Ratkis Bronzecaster and set his hands on those of the older man.

Ratkis said, "I own myself to be your vassal, Duren son of Gerin the Fox, grandson of Ricolf the Red, and give you the whole of my faith against all men who might live or die."

"I, Duren, son of Gerin the Fox, grandson of Ricolf the Red, accept your homage, Ratkis Bronzecaster," Duren replied solemnly, "and pledge in my turn always to use you justly. In token of which, I raise you up now." He helped Ratkis to his feet and kissed him on the cheek.

"By Dyaus the father of all and Biton the farseeing one, I swear my fealty to you, lord Duren," Ratkis said, his voice loud and proud.

"By Dyaus and Biton," Duren said, "I accept your

oath and swear in turn to reward your loyalty with my own." He looked to Ricolf's other leading vassals. "Who else will give me this sign of good faith now?"

Authari Broken-Tooth went to one knee more smoothly than Ratkis had. He too gave Duren homage and then fealty. So far as Gerin could see, the ceremony was flawless in every regard, with no error of form to let Authari claim it was invalid. He was glad Authari had subordinated himself, but trusted the vassal baron no more on account of that.

Everyone looked at Hilmic and Wacho. Wacho's fair face turned red. "I'm not pledging anything to a lord who isn't here to give back what he pledges to me," he said loudly. Turning to Gerin, he went on, "I don't reject him out of hand, lord prince; don't take me wrong. But I won't give homage and swear fealty till he comes back here to stay, if I do it then. I'll have to see what he looks like when he's here for good." Hilmic Barrelstaves, perhaps encouraged that Wacho had spoken, nodded emphatic agreement.

Again, Duren handled matters before Gerin could speak: "That is your right. But when I do return, I'll bear in mind everything you've done since the day my grandfather died."

Neither Hilmic nor Wacho answered that. Several of Ricolf's men spoke up in approval, though, and even Wacho's driver looked back over his shoulder to say something quiet to him. Whatever it was, it made the vassal baron go redder yet and growl something pungent by way of reply.

Gerin caught Duren's eye and nodded for him to get back into the chariot. He didn't want to give his son orders now, not when the boy—no, the young man—had so impressed Ricolf's followers with his independence. Duren had impressed the Fox, too, a great deal. You never really knew whether someone could swim till he found himself in water over his head.

Duren jumped up into the car and took the reins from Van, who'd been holding them, saying, "When my duties farther north are done, I'll come back here. The gods willing, we'll have many years together." He flicked the reins. The horses trotted forward. The rest of Gerin's little army followed.

The Fox looked back over his shoulder. There in the roadway stood Authari Broken-Tooth, Ratkis Bronzecaster, Wacho Fidus' son, and Hilmic Barrelstaves. They were arguing furiously, their men crowding around them to support one or the other. Gerin liked that fine.

Half a day south of Fox Keep, Gerin spied a chariot heading his way. At first he thought it belonged to a messenger, heading down toward Ricolf's holding with news so urgent, it couldn't wait for his return. The only sort of news that urgent was bad news.

Then the driver of the car held up a shield painted in white and green stripes: a shield of truce. "Those are Trokmoi!" the Fox exclaimed. A few years earlier, he wouldn't have been able to recognize them as such at so long a distance, but his sight was lengthening as he got older. That made reading hard. He wondered if there was a magic to counter the flaw.

He had little time for such idle thoughts: a moment later, he recognized one of the Trokmoi in the car. So did Van, who named the fellow first: "That's Diviciacus, Adiatunnus' right hand."

"His right hand, aye, and maybe the thumb of the left," Gerin agreed. "Something's gone wrong for him, or he'd not have sent Diviciacus out to try to make it better—and probably to diddle me in the process, if he sees a chance."

The Trokmoi made out who Gerin was at about the

same time as he recognized Diviciacus. They waved and approached. Duren stopped the team. The rest of Gerin's men halted their chariots behind him.

"What can we be doing for you, now?" Gerin called in the Trokmê tongue.

"Will you just hear the sweet way he's after using our speech?" Diviciacus said, also in his language. He quickly switched to Elabonian: "Though I'd best be using yours for the business ahead to be sure there's not misunderstandings, the which wouldn't be good at all, at all." Even in Elabonian, he kept a woodsrunner's lilt in his voice.

"The years haven't treated you too badly," Gerin remarked as Diviciacus got out of his chariot. The Trokmê was thicker through the middle than he had been when he was younger, and white frosted his mustache and the red hair at his temples. He still looked like a dangerous man in a brawl, though—and in a duel of words.

"I'll say the same to your own self," he answered, and then astonished Gerin by dropping to one knee in the roadway, as Ratkis Bronzecaster had done for Duren. As the Trokmê clasped his hands together in front of him, he said, "Adiatunnus is fain to be after renewing vassalage to your honor, lord prince, that he is."

"By the gods," Gerin muttered. He stared at Diviciacus. "It took the gods to get me his allegiance the last time he gave it. I always thought—I always said—I'd need them again to get him to renew it. Before I accept it, I want to know what I'm getting . . . and why."

Still on that one knee, Diviciacus replied, "Himself said you'd say that, sure and he did." His shoulders moved back and then forward as he sighed. "He'd not do it, I tell you true, did he not find worse in these lands south o' the Niffet than you'd be giving him."

"Ah, the Gradi," Gerin said. "A light begins to dawn.

He wants my help against them, and reckons the only way he'll get it is to pretend to be a good little boy for as long as he needs to, and then to go back to his old ways."

Diviciacus assumed a hurt expression. He did it very well—but then, he'd had practice. "That's not a kind thing to be saying, not even a bit of it."

"Too bloody bad," Gerin told him. "The only debt I owe your chief is that I had my retainers gathered against him at Fox Keep when the Gradi raided us, and so I was able to throw them back without too much trouble."

"Would that we could say the same," Diviciacus answered gloomily. "They lit into us, that they did. I gather you're after hearing about their raid on us by boat, and that they did it in the aftermath of striking you."

"Yes, I heard of that," Gerin answered. "If they hadn't hit us and you, Adiatunnus and I would be at war now, I suppose, and you wouldn't have to come to me and swallow his pride for him."

Diviciacus winced. "Sure and you've an evil tongue in the head o' you, Fox. They say that in the olden times a bard could kill a man by no more than singing rude songs about him. I never would have believed it at all till I met you." He held up a hand; a gold bracelet glittered on his wrist. "Don't thank me, now. You've not yet heard what I'm about to tell you."

"Go on," Gerin said, concealing his amusement; he had been about to thank the Trokmê for noting the bite of his sarcasm. "What haven't I heard that you're about to tell me?"

"That the black-hearted omadhauns struck us again ten days ago, this time coming by land, and that they beat us again, too." Diviciacus bared his teeth in an agony of frustration. "And so, for fear of worse from them, Adiatunnus will fight alongside you, will fight under you, will fight however you choose, for the sake of having your men and your cars in the line with us. Whatever should befall after that, even if it's you turning into our master, it's bound to be better nor the Gradi ruling over us."

He shivered in almost superstitious dread. The Trokmoi who'd come in the chariot with him gestured to avert evil. The Gradi whom Gerin had captured took beating the woodsrunners for granted. Evidently the Trokmoi felt the same way about it. That worried Gerin. What sort of allies would the Trokmoi make if they broke and fled at the mere sight of their foes?

He asked Diviciacus that very question. "We fight bravely enough," the Trokmê insisted. "It's just that—summat always goes wrong, and curse me if I know why. Must not be so with you southrons, not if you beat the Gradi the once. With you along, we'll do better, too—I hope."

"So do I," Gerin told him. He mulled things over for a bit, then went on, "Come back to Fox Keep with me. This is too important to decide on the spur of the moment."

"However you like it, lord prince," Diviciacus answered. "Only the gods grant you don't take too long deciding, else it'll be too late for having the mind of you made up to matter."

When they started north up the Elabon Way toward Fox Keep, Gerin told Duren to steer his chariot up alongside the one in which Diviciacus rode. Over squeals and rattles, the Fox asked, "What will Adiatunnus say if my whole army comes into the land he holds as his own?"

"Belike he'll say, 'Och, the gods be praised!—them of Elabonians and Trokmoi both,' " Diviciacus answered. "More than half measures we need, for true."

"And what will he say—and what will your warriors

say—when I tell them to fight alongside my men and take orders from my barons?" the Fox pressed.

"Order 'em about just as you wish," Diviciacus said. "If there's even a one of 'em as says aught else but, 'Aye, lord Gerin,' take the head of the stupid spalpeen and be after hanging it over your gate."

"We don't do that," Gerin said absently. But that wasn't the point. Diviciacus knew perfectly well that Elabonians weren't in the habit of taking heads for trophies. What he meant was that Adiatunnus and his men were desperate enough to obey the Fox no matter what he said. Given Adiatunnus' pride in the strength he'd had till the Gradi struck him, that was desperate indeed. Unless . . . "What oath will you give that this isn't a trap, to lead me to a place where Adiatunnus can try to take me unawares?"

"The same frickful aith I gave your lady wife when she put me the same question," Diviciacus said: "By Taranis, Teutates, and Esus I swear, lord Gerin, lord prince, I've told you nobbut the truth."

If swearing by his three chief gods would not bind a Trokmê to the truth, nothing would. Gerin smiled a little when he heard Selatre had asked the same guarantee of Diviciacus: Biton didn't speak through her these days, but she saw plenty clear on her own. "Good enough," the Fox said.

"I pray it is; I pray you're right," Diviciacus told him. "The priests, they've been edgy of late, indeed and they have. It's as if, with the gods o' the Gradi so near 'em and all, our own gods have taken fear, if you know what I'm saying."

"I think perhaps I do," Gerin said after a moment's pause. The Gradi prisoners had also boasted of how much stronger their gods were than those of the woodsrunners, and again seemed to know whereof they spoke.

Diviciacus sent Gerin a keen look. "You know more of this whole business than you let on, I'm thinking." When Gerin didn't answer, the Trokmê went on, "Well, that was ever the way of you. Adiatunnus, he swears you stand behind him and listen when he's haranguing his men."

"With the way Adiatunnus bellows, I wouldn't need to be that close to overhear him," Gerin said. Diviciacus chuckled and nodded, acknowledging the hit. Gerin was careful not to deny possible occult means of knowledge. The more people thought he knew, the more cautious they'd be around him.

The one thing he wished as the chariot clattered northward was that he really knew half as much as friends and foes credited him with knowing.

"Are we ready?" Gerin looked back at the throng of chariots drawn up behind him on the meadow by Fox Keep. The question was purely rhetorical; they were as ready as they'd ever be. He waved his arm forward, tapping Duren on the shoulder as he did so. "Let's go!"

They hadn't gone far before Diviciacus' chariot came up beside Gerin's. "It's a fine thing you do here, Fox, indeed and it is," the Trokmê said. Then his face clouded. "Still and all, I'd be happier, that I would, were you bringing the whole of your host with you and not leaving a part of 'em behind at Castle Fox."

"I'm not doing this to make you happy," Gerin answered. "I'm not doing it to make Adiatunnus happier, either. I'm doing it to protect myself. If I leave Fox Keep bare and the Gradi come up the Niffet again" —he waved back toward the river— "the keep falls. I don't really want that to happen."

"And if your men and Adiatunnus' together aren't enough to be beating the Gradi, won't you feel the fool, now?" Diviciacus retorted.

"Those are the risks I weigh, and that's the chance I take," Gerin said. "If I could bring my whole army, and Adiatunnus', too, down the Niffet against the Gradi, I'd do that. I can't, though. The Gradi control the river, because they have boats beside which ours might as well be toys. And as long as that's true, I have to guard against their taking advantage of what they have. If you don't care for that, too bad."

"Och, I'd not like to live inside your head, indeed and I wouldn't," Diviciacus said. "You're after having eyes like a crayfish—on the end of stalks, peering every which way at once—and a mind like a balance scale, weighing this against that and that against this till you're after knowing everything or ever it has the chance to happen."

Gerin shook his head. "Only farseeing Biton has that kind of power. I wish I did, but I know I don't. Seeing ahead's not easy, even for a god."

"And how would you know that?" Diviciacus said.

"Because I watched Biton trying to pick out the thread of *the* future from among a host of might-bes," Gerin answered, which made the Trokmê shut up with a snap. Diviciacus knew that Gerin had made the monsters vanish from the face of the earth, but not how he'd done it or what had happened in the aftermath of the miracle.

They soon left the Elabon Way and rolled southwest down lesser roads. Serfs in the fields alongside the dirt tracks stood up from their endless labor to watch the army pass. One or two of them, every now and then, would wave. Whenever that happened, Gerin waved back.

Diviciacus stared at the serfs. "Are they daft?" he burst out after a while. "Are they stupid? Why aren't they running for the woods, aye, and taking the livestock with 'em, too?"

"Because they know my men won't plunder them," the Fox answered. "They know they can rely on that."

"Daft," Diviciacus repeated. "I'll not tell Adiatunnus, for himself wouldna credit it. He'd call me drunk or ensorceled, so he would."

"I had trouble making sense of it when I first came here, too," Van said sympathetically. "It still strikes me strange, but after a while you get used to it."

"For which ringing endorsement of my ideas I thank you very much," Gerin said, his voice dry as the dust the horses' hooves and chariot wheels raised from the road.

"Think nothing of it," Van said, dipping his head.

"Just what I do think of it, and not a bit more," Gerin said.

Both old friends laughed. Diviciacus listened and watched as if he couldn't believe what he was hearing and seeing. "If any of our Trokmoi, now, bespoke Adiatunnus so," he said, "the fool'd be eating from a new mouth slit in his throat, certain sure he would, soon as the words were out of his old one."

"Killing people who tell you you're a fool isn't always the best idea in the world," Gerin observed. "Every so often, they turn out to be right." Diviciacus rolled his eyes. That wasn't the way his chieftain handled matters, so, as far as he was concerned, it had to be wrong.

They came to the keep of Widin Simrin's son late the next day. Widin and Diviciacus greeted each other like old neighbors, which they were, and old friends, which they weren't. "Better you southrons for friends nor the Gradi," Diviciacus told him, and that seemed to suffice.

Widin had a good-sized garrison quartered at his keep: had Adiatunnus begun the war against Gerin rather than the other way round, those troopers would have done their best to slow the Trokmê advance and buy the Fox time to move down and deal with the woodsrunners. "So we'll really be on the same side as the Trokmoi?" Widin said to Gerin. "Who would have believed that at the start of the year?"

"Not I, I tell you for a fact, but yes, we will," Gerin replied. "The Trokmoi would rather work with us than with the Gradi, and from what I've seen of the Gradi, I'd rather work with the Trokmoi than with them, too."

"I haven't seen anything of them, lord prince," Widin said, "but if they're rugged enough to make the Trokmoi cozy up to us like this, they must be pretty nasty customers." He grinned wryly. "I won't be sorry to move out against the Gradi myself, I tell you that much. You go feeding a good-sized crew of warriors for a while and you start wondering whether anything'll be left for you to eat come winter."

"You don't sing me that song, Widin," Gerin told him. "I sing it to you." His vassal baron grinned and nodded, yielding the point. The Fox had been feeding a lot more warriors for a lot longer than Widin. The Fox had also made the most thoroughgoing preparations for feeding and housing a lot of warriors of any man in the northlands, save perhaps Aragis the Archer—and he would have bet against Aragis, too.

Ruefully, Widin said, "And now, of course, the whole army guests off me, even if it is for only the one night."

"I don't see you starving," Gerin observed, his voice mild.

"Oh, not now," Widin answered. "The apples are harvested, and the pears, and the plums. The animals are getting fat on the good grass. But come the later part of next winter, we'll wish we had what your gluttons will gobble up tonight."

"Well, I understand that," Gerin said. "The end of winter is a hard time of year for everyone. And Father Dyaus knows I'm happy to see you thinking ahead instead of just living in the now, the way so many do. But if we don't beat the Gradi, how much you have in your storerooms won't matter to anyone but them."

"Oh, I understand all that, lord prince," Widin assured him. "But since you take so much enjoyment complaining about every little thing, I wouldn't think you'd begrudge me the chance to do the same."

"Since I what?" The Fox glowered at his vassal, much as if he were serious. "I expect to hear that from Van or Rihwin, not from you."

"Can't trust anyone these days, can you?" Widin said, now doing a wicked impression of Gerin himself. The Fox threw his hands in the air and stalked off, conceding defeat.

By the extravagant way Widin fed the army that had descended on his castle, his plea of hunger to come had been a case of averting an evil omen, nothing more. As if to extract some sort of revenge on the lesser baron, Gerin ate until he could hardly waddle off to his blanket. He committed gluttony again the next morning, this time because he knew what sort of country lay ahead.

The land between Widin's holding and Adiatunnus' territory belonged to no one, even if it was formally under Gerin's suzerainty. The Fox and the Trokmê chieftain had been probing for advantage down there for years; even after giving Gerin homage and swearing fealty, Adiatunnus conducted himself like an independent lord.

Caught between two strong rivals, most of the peasants who had farmed that land in the days before the werenight were dead or fled now. Fields were going back to meadows, meadows to brush, and brush to saplings. Looking at some pines as tall as he was, Gerin thought, *This is how civilization dies.* When his army— or Adiatunnus'—wasn't crossing this country (on dirt roads also vanishing from disuse), it belonged more to wild beasts than to men. And it bordered his own holding. That was a profoundly depressing thought.

Adiatunnus had pushed his border station north and east, toward the edges of Gerin's land. More than once, Gerin had moved against the Trokmoi with an army, routing his enemy's guards and overturning the prevaricating boundary stones they would set up to support their claims. When he and his army came upon the Trokmê guards now, the red-mustachioed barbarians cheered and waved their long bronze swords in the air.

Laughter rumbled from Van. Turning to Gerin, he said, "There's something you've never seen before, I'll wager."

"Woodsrunners cheering me?" The Fox shook his head. "The only time I ever thought the Trokmoi would cheer me was after I died."

Diviciacus rode near enough to hear that. "We tried to arrange it, Fox dear, time and again we did," he said, "and we'd have cheered like madmen if we'd done it. But things being as they are—"

"Yes, things being as they are," Gerin agreed. Without the Trokmoi, he wouldn't have become baron of Fox Keep, wouldn't have set forth on the path that had made him prince of the north. The woodsrunners had ambushed his father and older brother, putting an end to his hopes of passing his days as student and scholar.

And, on returning from the City of Elabon to take up the barony, he'd sworn never to stop taking revenge on the barbarians for what they'd done to him and his. Over the years, he'd taken that revenge many times and in many ways. And now he found himself allied to the Trokmoi against a danger he and they both recognized as worse than either was to the other. Did that leave him forsworn?

He didn't think so. He hoped not. He hoped the spirits of his father and brother understood why he was doing what he was doing. He thought his brother would. Of his father, he was less certain. The Dagref after whom he'd named his first son by Selatre had not been the most flexible of men.

The Fox shrugged. Regardless of what his father would have thought, he'd chosen this course and would have to see it through. What came afterwards, he'd sort out afterwards.

He knew the way to the keep Adiatunnus had held as his own since the Trokmê invasion after the werenight. He'd been that way before, with soldiers at his back every time. He'd had to fight his way through Adiatunnus' holding then. The Trokmoi welcomed him and his men now.

Trokmoi were not the only folk still living on the land, of course. A good many Elabonian peasants remained, serfs toiling for tall, fair overlords now, not for barons of their own race. Whenever he rode past one of their villages, Gerin wondered how much that bothered them. He suspected they cared only how much of their crops their overlords, whoever those overlords were, exacted from them and how much those overlords interfered in the day-to-day routine of their lives.

He passed a couple of strongpoints he'd burned out in his last serious campaign against Adiatunnus, more than a decade before. One had been rebuilt, the other was still in ruins. Here and there in his holding, ruins remained from the werenight, well before that. The Trokmoi were moving at a pace not too far from his own.

When night fell, the Elabonians stopped at a village dominated by a stockaded building too large and strong to be a house, too small to be a castle. Several Trokmê warriors dwelt there with their wives and children, plainly to lord it over the Elabonian serfs who lived in the usual huts of wattle and daub. Had Gerin extended his dominions to the forests of the Trokmoi north of the River Niffet, he might have used a similar system, save with Elabonians controlling woodsrunners.

Golden Math, just past first quarter, floated high in the south when the sun set. Pale, slow-moving Nothos, full or a day past, rose in the east during evening twilight. Elleb, approaching third quarter, would not come up till nearly midnight, while Tiwaz was too close to the sun to be seen.

"I wonder what the Gradi call the moons," Gerin said, staring up at Math from his seat close to a fire outside the village.

"That I can't tell you, Captain," Van answered. He paused to use a thumbnail to pry at a piece of mutton stuck between two back teeth, then resumed: "I'm amazed at how much of their speech has come back to me, now that I've had to try using it again, but I never was much interested in finding out about the moons. Maybe if some Gradi lass had looked up at 'em while I was on top of her—but she'd have been thinking about other things, or I hope she would."

"You are impossible," Gerin said, "or at least bloody improbable."

"Thank you, Fox," his friend answered. Gerin gave up and wrapped himself in his blanket. He had plenty of sentries out. Even in the worst of times, the Trokmoi weren't likely to brave the ghosts for a night attack, and his men and theirs were supposed to be allies. Nevertheless, he hadn't got as old as he had by taking needless chances. Knowing he'd taken none here, he slept sound.

Warriors Gerin led had—once—reached the village around the keep Adiatunnus had taken for his own. They'd fought their way in among the houses there, but never had managed to force their way into the keep.

With both Trokmoi—men and women—and monsters opposing them, they'd lost men too fast to make the assault worthwhile even if it did succeed.

And now here they were, more than ten years later, coming up to Adiatunnus' fastness once more. This time, no monsters fought them; the monsters, all save Geroge and Tharma, were back in the trackless caverns under Biton's temple at Ikos. The Trokmoi—men and women—stood in the narrow, rutted streets of the village, shouting for the Elabonians till their voices grew raw and hoarse. The drawbridge to the keep was down, and Adiatunnus rode out from it to greet the Fox. The last time Gerin had come this far, the two of them had done their best to kill each other, and they'd both nearly succeeded.

"Rein in," Gerin told Duren. The Fox also held up a hand to halt the rest of his chariots. His son pulled back on the reins. The horses obediently came to a stop.

Adiatunnus halted his own car perhaps twenty feet from Gerin's. He got out of it and walked half the distance before going down on one knee in the roadway. The watching Trokmoi sighed.

Gerin jumped down from his chariot and hurried over to Adiatunnus. The Trokmê chieftain clasped his hands together, Gerin covered them with his own, and they went through the same rituals of homage and fealty in person as they had by proxy through Diviciacus.

Speaking the Trokmê tongue so his folk could follow, Adiatunnus said, "I want no misunderstanding, now. You are my lord, and I own it's so. What you're after ordering me and mine to do against the Gradi, that we'll do, and promptly, too. You'll find us no more trouble than any of your other vassals."

The Fox noted Adiatunnus' reservation—he would take orders against the Gradi, but hadn't said anything about other orders. Gerin decided not to make an issue of it. Maybe the alliance against the new invaders would lead to better things later, maybe it wouldn't. For now, he wouldn't argue that it was necessary.

Also speaking the woodsrunners' language, he said, "Glad we are to have your valiant warriors with us in the fight. We'll teach the Gradi they chose the wrong foes when they decided to trifle with us."

The Trokmoi yelled and cheered; Gerin doubted they'd ever given any Elabonian a greeting like the one he was getting. Most of his own men understood the Trokmê speech well enough to have followed what he was saying. They cheered, too.

Some of them, he saw, had their eyes on Trokmê women, many of whom were strikingly pretty and who had a reputation among the Elabonians for easiness. Gerin knew that reputation was not altogether deserved; it was just that Trokmê women, like their menfolk, said and acted on what they thought more readily than most Elabonians. But, as Fand had taught him, you tried going too far with them at your peril. He hoped no trouble would spring from that.

Adiatunnus waved back toward his keep, whose drawbridge remained down. "Come in, Fox, come in, and the men of you, too. I'll feast the lot of you till you're too full to futter, that I will." Maybe he'd been watching Gerin's troopers eyeing the Trokmê women, too.

"For my men, I thank you," Gerin said. Save for insults on the battlefield, this was the first time he'd exchanged words with Adiatunnus. The Trokmê chief was close to his own age, a couple of digits taller and a good deal thicker through the shoulders and through the belly, with a balding crown and long, drooping fair mustaches now going gray. He wore a linen tunic and baggy woolen trousers, both dyed in checks of bright and, to Gerin's eye, clashing colors.

He was studying the Fox with the same wary care Gerin gave him. Seeing Gerin's eye on him, he chuckled self-consciously and said, "I've always been after thinking you're so high" —he reached up as far as he could— "with fangs in your mouth and covered all over with fur or a viper's scales, I never could decide which. And here, to look at you, you're nobbut a man."

"And you likewise," Gerin answered. "You've given me enough trouble for any other ten I could name, though; I tell you that."

"For which I thank you," Adiatunnus said, preening a little. His eyes were an odd shade, halfway between gray and green, and quite sharp. Looking intently at Gerin, he went on, "Ah, but if one o' them ten you could name was Aragis the Archer, now, would you still be telling me the truth?"

"Not altogether," the Fox admitted, and Adiatunnus preened again, this time admiring his own cleverness. Gerin said, "If you won't let me flatter you now, how am I supposed to fool you later?"

Adiatunnus stared at him, then started to laugh. "Och, what a wonder y'are, Fox. I've been glad to have you for a neighbor betimes, that I have, for you've taught me more than a dozen duller men could have done."

"For which I suppose I thank you," Gerin said, at which Adiatunnus laughed again. The Trokmê was telling the truth there. Over the years, Gerin had noted, Adiatunnus, more than any other Trokmê chieftain, had learned from the Elabonians among whom he'd settled. He played far more sophisticated—and far more dangerous—political games than his fellow woodsrunners, most of whom still seemed hardly better than bandits after all these years.

The game he was playing now was designed to make him seem a good fellow to the Fox and his warriors, and to make them forget they were more likely to be his foes than his friends. When he wanted to use it, he had a huge voice. He used it now, bellowing in Elabonian, "Into the keep, the lot of you. The meat and bread want eating, the beer wants drinking, aye, and maybe the lasses want pinching, though you'll have to find that out your own selves."

Gerin tried to shout just as loudly: "Any man of mine who drinks so much today that he's not fit to travel tomorrow will answer to me, and I'll make him sorrier than his hangover ever did." That might also keep his men from getting so drunk they started fights, and from being too drunk to defend themselves if the Trokmoi did.

"The same goes for my warriors," Adiatunnus said in his speech and in Elabonian, "save only that they answer to me first and then the Fox, and they'll care for neither, indeed and they won't."

Roast meat was roast meat, though the Trokmoi cooked mutton with mint, not garlic. Some of the bread the serving women set before the warriors struck Gerin as odd: thick and chewy and studded with berries. It wasn't what he ate at home, but it was good. He wasn't so sure about the beer. It wasn't ale, nor anything like what he and other Elabonians brewed, coming almost black from the dipper and tasting thick and smoky in his mouth.

Adiatunnus drank it with every sign of enjoyment, so it evidently was as it was supposed to be. "Aye, we make the pale brew, too," the Trokmê chieftain said when Gerin asked him about it, "but I thought you might be interested in summat new, you having the name for that and all. You roast the malted barley a good deal longer here, you see, so it's nearly burnt, before you make it into the mash."

"I'll bet the first fellow who brewed this did it by accident, or because he was careless with his roasting,"

Gerin said. He took another pull and smacked his lips thoughtfully. "After you get used to it, it's—interesting, isn't it? A new way of doing things, as you say."

"When all this is done, I'll send a brewer to Fox Keep to show you the making of it," Adiatunnus promised.

"When all this is done, if you're able to send him and I'm able to receive him, I'll be glad to do that." Gerin drained his mug of beer. Getting up to fill it with another dipper of that dark brew seemed the most natural thing in the world, so he did.

Van had other ideas about what the most natural thing in the world might be. If he got any friendlier with that serving woman—a lively redhead who, Gerin thought, looked a lot like Fand—they'd be consummating their friendship on top of the table, or maybe down in the rushes on the floor.

Gerin peered around for Duren but didn't see him. He wondered whether his son had found a girl for himself or was just off visiting the latrine. When Duren didn't come back right away, the first guess seemed more likely.

"A fine-looking lad y'have there," Adiatunnus said, which made the Fox start a little; he wasn't used to anyone save Selatre or sometimes Van thinking along with him. Adiatunnus went on, "Am I after hearing the grandfather of him is a dead corp, the which puts him in line for that barony?"

"That's so," Gerin agreed. He eyed the Trokmê with genuine respect. "You have your ear to the ground, to have got the news so soon."

"The more you know, the more you can do summat about," Adiatunnus answered, a saying that might have come straight from the Fox's lips.

Gerin peered down into the black and apparently bottomless mug of beer. When he looked up again, Duren was coming back into the great hall, a smug look on his face. That eased Gerin's mind; after the boy had been kidnapped when he was small, the Fox wasn't easy about letting him out of his sight.

Turning to Adiatunnus, Gerin said, "It will be strange, riding alongside you instead of at you."

"It will that." Adiatunnus knocked back the black beer in his mug at a single gulp, then sat there slowly shaking his head. "Strange, aye. But you southrons, now, you've no fear of the Gradi, have you?"

"No more than I do of you," Gerin answered. "By the fight they made with us, they're brave and they're strong, but so are you Trokmoi—and so are we."

"I canna tell you what it is, Fox," Adiatunnus said, his features sagging in dismay, "but when we face 'em, summat always goes wrong for us. And when you get to the point where you expect to have a thing happen, why, happen it will."

"Yes, I've seen that," Gerin said. He remembered Kapich, his Gradi prisoner, sneering at the Trokmê gods. Whether that had anything to do with the woodsrunners' bad luck against the Gradi, he couldn't have said, but the notion wouldn't have surprised him.

Adiatunnus said, "When we go against the Gradi, now, how will you work it? Will you mix our men together like peas and beans in the soup pot, or do you aim to keep 'em apart, one group from the other?"

"I've been chewing on that very thing," Gerin said, noting with some relief that Adiatunnus really did seem to accept his command. "I'm leaning toward mixing: that way, it's less likely your warriors or mine will think the other bunch has run off and left 'em in the lurch. How do you feel about it?"

He asked for more than politeness' sake; Adiatunnus had proved himself no fool. The Trokmê said, "Strikes me as the better notion, too. If we're to have an army, it should *be* an army now, if you ken what I'm saying."

"I do." Gerin nodded. "My chief worry is that your men won't follow my commands as quickly as they might, either because they think I'm trying to put them in more danger or just out of Trokmê cussedness."

"As for the first, I trust it won't be so, else I'd never have bent the knee to you," Adiatunnus said. "You fight hard, Fox, but you fight fair. As for t'other, well, there are times when I wonder you Elabonians don't bore yourselves to death, so dull you seem to us."

"I've heard other Trokmoi say as much," Gerin admitted, "but, of course, they're wrong." He brought that out deadpan, to see what Adiatunnus would do with it.

The chieftain frowned, but then started to laugh. "Try as you will, lord prince—I should be saying that now, eh? being your vassal and all, I mean—you'll not get my goat so easy."

"Good," Gerin said. "So. You're flighty to us, and we're dull to you. What of the Gradi? You know them better than we do."

"Belike, and how I'm wishing we didna." This time, Adiatunnus' frown stayed, making his whole face seem longer. "They're—how do I say it?—they're serious about what they do, that they are. It's not your fault you're in their way, mind you, but y'are, and so they'll rob you or kill you or whatever they like. And if you have the gall to be offended, mind, then they'll get angry at you for trying to keep what's always been yours."

"Yes, that fits in with what I've seen," Gerin agreed. "They're very sure of themselves, too: they don't think we can stop them. That goddess of theirs, that Voldar—"

Adiatunnus twisted both hands into an apotropaic sign. "Dinna be saying that name in this place. A wicked she-devil, no mistake." He shivered, though the inside of the great hall was smoky and hot. "Wicked, aye, but

strong—strong. And the others—" His fingers writhed
again.

You fear her, eh? Gerin started to ask that aloud, but
held his tongue. Dabbling in magic had taught him how
much power lay in words; saying something could make
it real. Voldar undoubtedly knew—or could find out—
Adiatunnus' feelings about her, but putting words in
the air made it more likely the Trokmê chief would
draw her notice.

"Father Dyaus will prosper our enterprise," Gerin
said, and hoped the chief Elabonian god was paying
as much attention to him as Adiatunnus feared the
chief Gradi goddess was paying to *him*. Dyaus usually
seemed content to reign over those who worshiped
him without doing much to rule them. Gerin had always
taken that for granted. Only in facing the Gradi had
he come to realize it had drawbacks as well as
advantages.

He was distracted from such musings when a very
pretty Trokmê girl less than half Adiatunnus' age sat
down on the chieftain's lap. Adiatunnus was holding a
mug of black beer in one hand. The other closed over
her breast through her tunic. The public display of what
Gerin would have kept private didn't disturb her; indeed,
she seemed proud Adiatunnus acknowledged she'd
captured his affection, or at least his lust.

"And can I be finding you summat lively in the line
of women?" the Trokmê chieftain asked. His hand
opened and squeezed, opened and squeezed. "I'd not
want you to think me lacking in hospitality, now."

"I don't," Gerin assured him. "Good food and good
drink are plenty for me, and you've given me those.
As for the other, I'm happy enough with my wife not
to care to look anywhere else, though I thank you all
the same."

"And what a daft notion that is," Adiatunnus exclaimed.

"Not that you're happy, the which is as may be, but that your being happy back there would keep you from poking a wench here. What has the one to do with t'other? A friendly futter is worth the having, eh, no matter where you find it."

The Fox shrugged. "If that's how you want to live, I'm not going to say you shouldn't. It's your affair— and you can take that however you like. And since I'm happy enough to let other people do as they please, I'm even happier when they let me do the same."

"You're happy to drive a lesson home like a man splitting logs with an axe, too," Adiatunnus retorted. "But all right, have it as you will, since you're bound to, anyhow. And if you're not fain to have yourself a good time, I'll not be after making you do it. So there."

Gerin laughed out loud and raised his own mug in salute. Not many men could puncture him at arguments of that sort, but Adiatunnus had just done it. That said something about how sharp the Trokmê's wits were, not that Gerin hadn't already had a good notion of that. It also said Adiatunnus would make a useful ally— provided Gerin kept an eye on him.

The Trokmê's leman found something interesting to do with her hand, too. Gerin wondered with abstract curiosity whether Adiatunnus would suddenly need to change his trousers. Before that happened, the woodsrunner got up and slung the girl over his shoulder—no small display of strength—and carried her upstairs while she laughed.

Gerin turned to Duren and said, "I daresay you're learning some things here that you wouldn't see at Fox Keep."

"Oh, I don't know," his son answered, sounding very much like him. "Van and Fand do things like that sometimes."

"Mm, so they do," the Fox admitted. He thumped

Duren on the shoulder and started to laugh, then got to his feet. "Well, now you're going to see something you *have* seen before: I'm going to bed." Also laughing, his son went up with him.

Van scratched his head, then, in fashion most ungentlemanly, reached inside his breeches and scratched there, too. He squashed something between his thumbnails, look at it, wiped it on his trouser leg, and let out a long sigh. "I'm going to have to go over myself for nits," he said, and dug in the pouch at his belt for a fine-toothed wooden comb. As he started raking it through his beard and hissing as the thick, curly hairs got stuck, he shook a thick forefinger at Gerin. "And don't you twit me about these cursed lice and where I got 'em. I know where I got 'em, and I had fun doing it, too."

"Fine," Gerin said. "You can have fun explaining to Fand where you got 'em, too."

But Van refused to let that sally faze him. "There's too many ways to—ouch!—pick up lice for anybody to be sure which one I found."

That was true. Gerin, for his part, had fresh bedbug bites, courtesy of no one more intimate than whoever'd last slept in the bed Adiatunnus had given him and Duren. But he also knew that Fand, given a hundred possibilities, would always choose the one likely to lead to the wildest fight—and, this time, she'd be right.

The Fox didn't waste a lot of time brooding over it, though he did spend a moment hoping he wouldn't come down with lice himself. As he got grayer, the vermin and their eggs got harder to spot in his hair.

Getting the army ready to move soon made all such insectile worries seem of insectile size and importance. His own men were quickly ready to ride, whether on horseback or in their chariots. He'd never before watched the Trokmoi getting ready to move out on campaign—most of the campaigns on which they'd moved in these parts had been aimed at him. Now that he was watching them, he concluded they had to start days earlier than he would have to set out at the same time.

They bickered. They bungled. They got drunk instead of eating breakfast. They went off for a fast poke with a serving girl instead of eating breakfast. An Elabonian captain would have killed a couple of his men on the spot before he put up with insubordination the Trokmê leaders ignored.

When the woodsrunners had finally fought, they'd always done well against the Fox's troopers. He had to hope the same would hold now. The longer he watched them—and he had a good long while to watch them—the more forlorn that hope seemed.

Adiatunnus was everywhere at once, shouting, blustering, cursing, cajoling. The chieftain did get his fair measure of respect, but, as far as Gerin could see, matters moved no faster because of the racket he made. Gerin had to hope Adiatunnus wasn't making things slower, another hope that faded as the morning wore on.

Van muttered, "We'd have done better if the woodsrunners lined up with the Gradi, I'm thinking."

"I wouldn't argue," Gerin said mournfully, watching two Trokmoi draw swords and scream at each other before their friends pulled them apart.

The closest Adiatunnus came to acknowledging anything was wrong came when he said, "Och, you're ready a bit before us, looks like," and gave a breezy shrug to show how little that mattered to him. The Fox, ignoring the way his stomach churned, managed to nod.

At last, with the sun a little to the west of south, not

even the Trokmoi could delay any more. Their women calling last farewells, they rode west from Adiatunnus' keep along with Gerin's men. The Fox murmured a prayer to Dyaus that the campaign would end better than it had begun.

VI

Early omens were less than good. The army crossed the Venien River, which flowed into the Niffet, not far from where the Gradi had come down in their galleys and beaten the Trokmoi. Though the woodsrunners had burned the bodies of their comrades who had fallen, they still muttered among themselves as they passed the battlefield.

On the west side of the river—land that had been still in Elabonian hands, not under Adiatunnus' control—the hair prickled up on Gerin's arms for no reason he could see or feel. He kept quiet about it, doubting his own judgment, but after a while Van said, "The air feels—uncanny."

"That's it!" Gerin exclaimed, so vehemently that Duren started and the horses snorted indignantly. "Aye, that's it. Feels like the air in the old haunted woods around Ikos."

"So it does." Van frowned. "We've been out this way a time or two, and it never did before. What's toward, Fox? Your usual Elabonian gods, they don't make a habit of letting folk know they're around like this."

"You're right; they don't, and they certainly never have around here—you're right about that, too." Gerin scowled. What followed from his words did so as logically as the steps in a geometric proof from Sithonia. "I don't think we're feeling the power of Elabonian gods."

"Whose, then?" Van glanced around to make sure no Trokmoi could overhear him. "The woodsrunners' gods are too busy brawling amongst themselves to pay much heed to impressing people."

"I know," Gerin said. "Folk get the gods they deserve, don't they? So who's left? Not us, not the Trokmoi, not . . ." He let that hang in the air.

Van had been many places in his travels, but never to Sithonia. Yet he needed to be no logician to see what Gerin meant. "The Gradi," he said, his voice as sour as week-old milk.

"Can't think of anyone else it could be," the Fox said unhappily. He waved, trying to put into words what he felt. "We're heading toward high summer now, but doesn't the air taste more the way it would at the start of spring, when winter's just loosed its grip? And the sun." He pointed up to it. "The light's . . . watery somehow. It shouldn't be, not at this season of the year."

"That it shouldn't," Van said. "I've lived here long enough to know you're right as can be, Captain." He shook his fist toward the west, toward the Orynian Ocean. "Those cursed Gradi gods are settling in here, making themselves at home, growing like toadstools after a rain."

"My thought exactly," Gerin said. "Voldar and the rest of them, they must be strong to do . . . whatever they're doing. Dyaus and the Elabonian pantheon, they wouldn't interfere with the sun." He didn't say, *They couldn't interfere with the sun*, though that was in his mind, too. He didn't know whether it was so or not. The Elabonian gods were so lax about manifesting themselves in the material world, he honestly didn't know the full range of their power.

He didn't know the full range of Voldar's power, either, or the powers of the other Gradi gods and goddesses. He had the ominous feeling he was going to find out. This would have been a fine mild day, had it come a little before the vernal equinox. Drawing near the summer solstice, though . . .

Over his shoulder, Duren said, "I wish we could find out what the weather's like back on the east side of the Venien. That would tell us more about whether what we're worrying about is real or we're shying at shadows."

Gerin smiled. "There are times when I wish I could send Dagref down to the City of Elabon to learn all the things he can't learn here in the northlands. Maybe you should go, too, for that's reasoned like a scholar."

"Aye, so it is," Van rumbled, "but there's more going on here than scholarship or whatever you call it. It's not just the weather, lad. It's what I feel in the hair on the nape of my neck, and I'm not talking about lice." He set a hand on the flared neckpiece of his helmet.

"What do we do about it?" Duren said, yielding the point.

"Fight it," Van declared. As usual, the world looked simple to him.

Gerin wished the world looked simple to him, too. Here, though, he saw no better answer than the one his friend had proposed.

By the time they camped, that first night west of the Venien, the Trokmoi were all edgy, looking over their shoulders and muttering to themselves over anything or nothing. The presence of the more stolid Elabonians seemed to steady them, as Gerin—and Adiatunnus—had hoped it would.

They were still in land under Gerin's suzerainty, but not land where his control was as firm as it was closer to Fox Keep. The serfs hereabouts had not seen enough of him and his armies to have any confidence in their goodwill. They probably had seen enough of Trokmê raiders to have no confidence in them whatever. At first sight of a large force heading their way, they fled into the woods.

The warriors took—even Gerin did not like to think of it as stealing—enough chickens and sheep to sacrifice to keep the night ghosts quiet. Other than that, they did not harm the villages or the fields around them. They built great bonfires not only to hold the ghosts at bay but also to give themselves warning if the Gradi were close enough to dare a night attack.

To reduce the risk of that as much as he could, Gerin set scouts out all around the campsite, each small group with a fowl to offer so the ghosts would not trouble them in spite of their being away from the fires. Adiatunnus watched that with interest and attention; the Fox got the idea the Trokmê was storing the notion to use against him one of these years.

Swift-moving Tiwaz had come round close to first quarter. Math was almost full, while Nothos, though four days past, still had only a bit of his eastern edge abraded by darkness. Out where the light of the bonfires grew dim, men had three separate shadows, each pointing in a different direction.

Except to go out to stand sentry or to answer calls of nature, though, few men, either Elabonians or Trokmoi, strayed far from the fireside. The warriors either rolled up in their blankets or sat around talking, often with folk not of their own kin. Most of them understood and could speak at least some of the language of their hereditary foes, and most relished the chance to swap tales with the men they usually met with weapons, not words.

Drungo Drago's son turned to Van and said, "Give us a tale, why don't you?"

Instantly, all the Elabonians began clamoring for a tale from the outlander, too. He'd seen and done things none of them, Gerin included, could match, and he told a good story, too. Seeing how enthusiastic the Elabonians were to hear him, the Trokmoi started shouting, too.

"Well, all right," Van said at last. "I thought I'd sooner sleep, and I thought a lot of you would sooner sleep, too, but who knows? Maybe I'll put you to sleep and then get some myself. You'd like that, hey?"

Somebody threw a hard-baked biscuit at him. He caught it out of the air and went on without missing a beat: "Well, I've yarned a good deal about creatures of one kind or another I've seen, and those tales haven't had too many people flinging their suppers my way, so maybe I'll give you one of them just to stay safe. How does that sound?"

No one said no. Several warriors said yes, loudly and enthusiastically. Van nodded. "All right, then," he said. "South and east of the City of Elabon, way south of the High Kirs, the coast of the Bay of Parvela runs southeast between Kizzuwatna, which is far away from here and hot as you please, to Mabalal, which is even farther, even hotter, and muggy to boot." He looked around. The night, like the day, was cooler than it should have been. "Feels good to think about something hot right now, doesn't it?"

His listeners nodded. Gerin wished he could put into a jar whatever his friend used to draw an audience into a story. Even if it wasn't sorcery, it was magic of a sort.

Van went on, "Some of you, now, some of you may have heard I had to get out of Mabalal in a kind of a hurry once upon a time." He got more nods, from a few of the Trokmoi and a lot of the Elabonians. He grinned; his teeth flashed white in the firelight. "By the gods, some of you have heard a whole raft of different reasons why I had to get out of Mabalal in a hurry. Now does that mean I get into a pack of trouble or I tell a pack of lies?"

"Both, most likely," Drungo said. He wasn't a match for Van in size or strength or speed, but he was a large, strong man, and confident of his prowess. Even so, he made sure he was grinning, too.

The outlander, busy shaping his story, didn't take it for a challenge, as he might have in his younger days. He just said, "Well, I was there, and I'm the only one here who was, so nobody'll prove anything on me, and that's a fact. Anyway, there I was, sailing away from Mabalal up toward Kizzuwatna, getting away from whatever I was getting away from, and we put in at this miserable little port called Sirte.

"There's only two reasons anybody would ever put in at Sirte. One is, you can fill your waterskins there. The water you get is harsh, and it can give you a flux of the bowels if you're not used to it, but the spring never fails. And the other is that, a ways inland, there's a grove of myrrh trees in a valley that some more springs water. If you can get the myrrh, which is a sticky resin that grows on the trees, you'll sell it for a goodly price."

"It's one of the incenses they burn at Ikos, isn't it?" Gerin put in.

"That it is, Fox." Van nodded. "When we got to Sirte, maybe half of dozen of us—ne'er-do-wells every one, you'd say—we decided to see if we couldn't get hold of some of this myrrh for our own selves, and strike out inland to see what we could do with it. I don't know about the others, but me, I was sick of being cooped up on a ship.

"The folk at Sirte spoke some of the language of Mabalal, and so did we. When they got the drift of what we wanted to do, they told us to watch out for snakes on the way to the myrrh trees. We'd just come out of Mabalal, now, so we thought we knew something of snakes—I've told stories about the serpents there, I expect."

"I liked the yarn about the snake with the stone in its head that was supposed to make you turn invisible, but didn't," Parol Chickpea said.

"For which I do thank you, friend," Van said. "Aye, we thought we knew something of snakes, that we did, so when the folk of Sirte warned us of the kinds they had out there in their desert—the chersidos and the cenchris and the seps and the prester and the dipsas and the scytale and I don't know what all other sorts they named—we just nodded our heads and said 'Yes, yes' when they told us about the different kinds of venom the serpents had. We figured they were spinning tales to frighten us and make us stay away from the myrrh."

The outlander shook his head. The firelight deepened the lines that carved his face and exaggerated his expression of rue. "Only goes to show what we knew, or rather, what we didn't. We bought waterskins and filled 'em and trudged out into the desert toward the myrrh trees, which were about a day and a half's travel inland from Sirte. The local folk shook their heads watching us go, as if they didn't expect to see us ever again, which, truth to tell, they probably didn't. To this day, if they remember us, they probably think we all perished in the desert. Lucky we are that we didn't— or some of us didn't, too."

"I suppose the people of Sirte went back and forth to the myrrh trees every so often," Gerin said. "If they looked for the snakes to get you, wouldn't they have expected to find your bodies along whatever trail there was?"

"That's a good question, Captain, and before I trod that trail I would have thought the same thing," Van said, "that is, if I'd believed them about the snakes, which I can't say I did. Like I told you, my notion was that they were just trying to scare us and keep us from going after the myrrh. I mean . . . well, hear me out and you'll see.

"We'd been walking along for a bit when all of a sudden something reared up out of the sand and gravel and hit me a lick right here." The outlander tapped his left greave, not far below the knee. "If I hadn't been wearing it, there's an awful lot of stories I wouldn't have told since, and that's the truth.

"I took a whack at the snake with my sword, and off flew its head. But we'd stirred up more than one, it turned out. Maybe the second was mate to the first. I won't ever know that. I killed it, too, but not till after it bit one of my friends.

"It wasn't a very big snake, and we hoped it wasn't any of the kinds the locals had warned us about, but it turned out to be a seps, and oh" —Van covered his eyes with a hand— "how I wish it hadn't been."

"How do you know it was, if it was only a little snake you killed?" someone asked.

"By the action of the venom," Van answered. "The seps bit my friend—well, actually, he was a robber and a thief, but we were traveling together—just above the ankle. Half an hour later, the gods beshrew me if I lie, there was nothing left of him but a little puddle of greenish fluid."

"What?" that same somebody exclaimed. "A snakebite doesn't do that."

"I thought the same thing," Van said, "but I was wrong. The natives at Sirte had told us the seps' venom made you disappear, and they knew what they were talking about. The fellow's flesh got clear around the bite, so you could see the bone through it, and then it just melted away, and the bone with it." He shuddered dramatically. "I never saw a man dissolve before and, if the gods are kind, I'll never see it again. How he screamed as he watched himself vanish—till he couldn't scream any more, of course. The rest of us, we pushed on in a hurry, let me tell you, and by the time we got out of there, like I say, he was nothing more than a little, stinking puddle the hot sun was already drying up.

"You can't blame us for not sticking around the spot where anything that horrible happened, but running away so fast turned out to be a mistake, too, for we didn't watch where we were putting our feet as carefully as we should have, and one of us stepped right on a prester.

"The thing looked like the vipers they have here, more or less, but when it came writhing out of the sand, it was the color of melted copper. It sank its teeth into poor Nasid—that was his name; it comes back to me even after all these years—then dove back into the sandbank and disappeared before anybody could do anything to it.

"And poor Nasid! Instead of melting, he started to swell, like rising bread dough but a hundred times as fast. His skin turned as fiery red as the prester's. He looked like there was a storm inside him, puffing him out every which way at once.

"Here's how fast he blew out: he was wearing trousers and a tunic with buttons, almost Trokmê-style, and the buttons flew right off the tunic, so hard that the one that hit me gave me this little scar over my eye, right here." The outlander pointed to a mark on his much-battered hide.

Gerin admired that touch. If Van's stories weren't true, they should have been, for he adorned them with a wealth of circumstantial detail. "What happened then?" the Fox asked.

"What do you mean?" Van returned. "To Nasid? He exploded, and there was no more left of him than of the other poor devil. To the rest of us? We ran. We probably should have run back to Sirte, but we went on toward the myrrh instead, and actually got to it with nobody else dying on the way. Then we headed up toward the Shanda country, but my other three friends— friends? ha!—tried to kill me for my share of the myrrh, and I left them as dead as anybody a snake bit."

"And what would the moral o' the tale be?" Adiatunnus asked. "A fine one it is, but it should have a moral."

"You want a moral, eh?" Van said. "I'll give you one. What this story shows is, some things are more trouble than they're worth."

The Trokmê chieftain laughed and nodded. "It does that. And a truth worth remembering it is, too." He glanced up at the moons. "And if you'd gone on much longer, the story'd have been more trouble nor it was worth, with us having to get up in the morning and all. But you didna, for which I thank you." He laid a blanket on the ground and wrapped himself in it.

Gerin couldn't resist a parting shot: "Even if you do get up in the morning, will you be moving before afternoon?" Adiatunnus made a point of ignoring him. Chuckling, the Fox also swaddled himself in a blanket and was soon asleep.

Maybe sleeping in the open was what the Trokmoi needed. Maybe they were starting to remember what being on campaign was all about. Whatever the reason, they moved reasonably fast when the sun came up the next morning. Gerin had been looking forward to screaming at them to hurry. Disappointed, he gnawed dry sausage and made sure he was ready to get going so they couldn't twit him.

The farther west they traveled, the more heavily the unnatural coolth lay on the land. Gerin eyed the fields with curiosity and concern mixed. "They'll not have much of a crop this year," he observed.

"Aye, the wheat's well behind where it ought to be,"

Van agreed. "They look like they had to plant late to start with, and they won't make up for lost time, not with weather like this they won't." His shiver held only a little exaggeration for dramatic effect.

"Pity you couldn't have brought one of those prester snakes along with you from Sirte—is that the name of the place?" Gerin said. Van nodded. The Fox went on, "Sounds like just what we'd need to heat up . . . a certain goddess I'd be better off not naming."

Van chuckled and nodded. "Aye, a prester would heat her up if anything would. The thing of it is, would anything?"

"I don't know and I don't care," Gerin answered. "If we beat the Gradi and drive them away, it doesn't matter, anyhow. Without men and women to worship her, that goddess won't gain a foothold here."

He didn't know whether not naming Voldar would do any good. But he'd been of the opinion that Adiatunnus knew more about the Gradi than he did, and the Trokmê chief had given him no reason to change his mind. If Adiatunnus thought saying Voldar's name would draw her notice, the Fox was willing to refrain.

He wished, though, that he could draw the notice of the local barons by speaking their names. Many of them seemed to have abandoned their keeps, though the Gradi didn't seem to be garrisoning those keeps, either. Some of the serf villages looked deserted, too. Again, Gerin saw the delicate fabric of civilization tearing.

He sent scouts out farther ahead and to either side than he was used to doing. He also maintained a substantial rearguard: the Gradi, with their ability to travel down rivers, were liable to try to set troops behind him and pin him between two forces. He would have thought about doing that had he been in their place, anyhow.

As his army advanced through country that lay ever

deeper in the frigid embrace of the Gradi gods, he wished he could come to grips with the Gradi themselves. He began to worry when he encountered none of them, and started complaining shortly thereafter.

When he did, Van fixed him with a gaze that might have belonged on a battlefield itself and said, "We'll come across them soon enough, and when we do, you'll be wishing just as loud you'd never set eyes on them." Since that was undoubtedly true, the Fox maintained what he thought was a prudent silence. Van's snicker said it might have been less prudent than he'd hoped.

And then, a couple of days later, the army did come upon a troop of Gradi; the invaders were happily plundering a peasant village. They'd killed a couple of men, and a line of them were having sport with a woman they'd caught. They seemed utterly astonished to find foes so far into territory they obviously thought of as theirs. As some of them were literally caught with their breeches down, they put up a fight less ferocious than they might have otherwise, and several made no effort to slay themselves rather than submitting to capture.

Gerin ordered the men who'd been holding down the peasant woman and the one who'd been on top of her bound and handed over to the surviving serfs. "Do as you like with them," he said. "I'm sure you'll think of something interesting."

The peasants' eyes glowed. "Let's get a fire going," one of them said.

"Aye, and we'll boil some water over it," another added enthusiastically.

"Will we want sharp knives—or dull ones?" somebody asked.

"Both," said the woman who'd been raped. "I claim first cut, and I know just where I'm going to make it, too." She stared at the crotch of one of the Gradi with an interest anything but lewd. Gerin couldn't tell whether any of the bound Gradi understood Elabonian. They might not know what was in store for them. He shrugged. If they didn't, they'd find out soon enough.

One of the other northerners did speak the language of the land they'd invaded. "I not tell you anything," he said when Gerin started to question him.

"Fine," the Fox said. He turned to the warriors holding the captives. "Take him where he can watch the serfs at work. If he doesn't come back talkier after that, we'll give him to them, too."

"Come on, you," one of the Elabonians said. They frogmarched the Gradi away. Before long, the Fox heard hoarse screams rising up from inside the village. When the guards brought the Gradi back, his face was paler than it had been. The guards looked grim, too.

"Hello again," Gerin said briskly. He looked thoughtful, a look he'd had occasion to practice over the years. "Do you suppose your goddess would be interested in keeping you around for the afterlife if you end up dead with some interesting parts missing? Do you suppose you'd enjoy the afterlife as much if you didn't have them? Do you want to find out the answers to those questions right away?"

The Gradi licked his lips. He didn't answer right away; maybe he was taking stock of his own spirit. Dying in battle, even slaying yourself to avoid capture, seemed easy if you measured them against mutilation that would be long agony in this world and might ruin you for the next.

Gerin smiled. "Are you more in the mood to talk now than you were a little while ago? For your sake, you'd better be."

"How I know I talk, then you do things to me anyway?" the Gradi asked.

"How do you know you can trust me, you mean? That's simple—you don't. Nothing complicated there,

eh? But I tell you now that I won't do all those interesting
things to you if you do talk. You can believe me or not,
as you choose."

The Gradi sighed. "I talk. What you want?"

"For starters, tell me your name," Gerin said.

"I am Eistr."

"Eistr." Gerin found a stick and wrote the name in
Elabonian characters in the soft ground at his feet. "Now
that I know it and have captured it here, I can work
magic against it—and against you—if I find out you
lie."

Eistr looked appalled. Gerin had hoped he would.
Nothing the Fox had seen made him think the Gradi
knew the use of writing. Literacy was thin enough among
Elabonians, and almost nonexistent among the Trokmoi,
who, when they did write, used the characters of their
southern neighbors. Ignorance added to Eistr's fear.
And the truth was that Gerin, if sufficiently ired, might
even have been able to use name magic against him,
though it wasn't anything the Fox really wanted to try.

"You ask. I tell," the Gradi said. "I tell true, swear
by Voldar's breasts."

Gerin had no idea how strong an oath that was, but
decided not to press it. He said, "Where did your band
come from? How many more of you are back there?"

Eistr pointed back toward the west. "Is keep, two
days' walk from here. Is by a river. We have maybe ten
tens when I there. Is maybe more now. Is maybe not
more, too."

The Fox thought that over. It struck him as a likely
way to get his army to walk into a trap without leaving
Eistr forsworn. Gerin said, "Why don't you know how
many men of yours are likely to be in this keep now?"

"We use for—how you say?—for middle place. Some
go out to fight, some come in to fight, some stay to
mind thralls," Eistr said. "Is now many, is now not."

"Ah." That did make a certain amount of sense. "Is your band supposed to be back at this base at any set time, or do you come and go as you please?"

"As we please. We are Gradi. We are free. The goddess Voldar rules us, no man." Pride rang in Eistr's voice.

"You may be surprised," the Fox said dryly. Eistr's cold, gray eyes stared at him without comprehension. Gerin turned to the guards. "Take him away. We'll find out what some of the others can tell us."

He got pretty much the same story from the rest of the Gradi who spoke Elabonian. Then he had to figure out what to do with them. Killing them out of hand would have meant having the same thing happen to any of his men the Gradi captured. Holding them prisoner would have made him detach men from his own force to guard them, which he didn't think he could afford to do. In the end, he decided to strip them naked and turn them loose.

"But these thralls, they catch us, they kill us," Eistr protested, he being the most articulate of the Gradi. He glanced nervously toward the peasant village.

"You know, maybe you should have thought about that before you started robbing and raping and killing them," Gerin said.

"But they *ours*. We do with them how we like," Eistr answered. "Voldar has said, so must be true." The other Gradi who followed Elabonian nodded agreement to that.

"Voldar isn't the only goddess—or god—in this land, and people here have more sway on their own than you're used to," the Fox said. As if to add emphasis to his words, another scream came from one of the raiders he'd given over to the serfs. He blinked in surprise; he'd thought those Gradi surely dead by now. The peasants had more patience and ingenuity than he'd given them credit for. He finished, "Now you're going to find out what it's like being rabbits instead of wolves. If you live, you'll learn something from it."

"And if you don't live, you'll learn summat from that, too," Van added with ghoulish glee.

When ordered to strip bare, one of the captured Gradi, though weaponless, threw himself at Elabonians and Trokmoi and fought so fiercely, he made them kill him. The rest looked much less fearsome without jerkins and helms and heavy leather boots. They ran for the woods, white buttocks flashing in the sun.

"They have no tools for making fire," Gerin observed, "nor weapons to hunt beasts for sacrifices to the night ghosts. They'll have a thin time of it when the sun goes down." He smiled unpleasantly. "Good."

He gave the helms and shields and axes he'd taken from the Gradi to the men of the peasant village. He didn't know how much good they would do folk untrained to war, but was certain they couldn't hurt. Some of the villagers were still busy with the captive Gradi. He did his best not to look at what was left of the arrogant raiders.

He did say, "When you're done there, find someplace to be rid of the bodies so the Gradi never find them. For that matter, if you get word we've lost, you probably ought to think about running for your lives."

"You won't lose, lord prince," one of the serfs exclaimed. "You *can't*."

Gerin wished he shared the fellow's touching optimism.

The Fox pushed the pace as his force of chariotry approached the keep the Gradi were holding. He didn't want any of the men he'd released deciding to act heroic and getting there ahead of his warriors to warn the garrison. Taking a keep was hard enough without having the foe alerted in advance.

One thing: the Gradi seemed to have no idea he and his troopers were anywhere nearby. To make sure they didn't, on his approach he sent out dismounted scouts, who, if they were seen, were likely to be taken for either Gradi or for Elabonian peasants. The scouts came back with word that, sure enough, the Gradi did hold the keep, but that they had the drawbridge down and were keeping no watch worth mentioning.

"Why don't we just march up on foot and tramp right in, then?" the Fox said. "With luck, they won't notice we aren't who we're supposed to be till it's too late to raise the drawbridge against us."

"What, and leave the cars behind?" Adiatunnus demanded.

"We can't fight with them inside the keep anyhow, can we?" Gerin said. The Trokmê chieftain scratched his head, then shrugged, plainly not having looked at it that way. Gerin said, "They've got us here faster than we could have come on foot, and we're not worn out from walking, either. They've served their purpose, but you can't use the same tool for every job."

"Ah, well," Adiatunnus said. "I told you I'd follow against the Gradi where you led, and if you'll be after leading with the feet of you, I'll walk in your footsteps, that I will." His eyes, though, said something more like, *And if this goes wrong, I'll blame you for it, that I will.*

That was the chance you took in any battle, though: if you lost, you got the blame, assuming you lived. Actually, you could get the blame if you died, too, but then you had other things to worry about.

The Fox told off approximately equal numbers of Elabonians and Trokmoi to stay behind with the horses. As for the rest, he put those who in looks and equipment most closely resembled the Gradi at the head of the column, to confuse the warriors in the keep for as long as he could. Being dark haired himself, with gear of the plainest, he marched along at the fore.

Van, who with his blond hair and fancy cuirass resembled almost anything in the world more than a Gradi, was relegated to the rear, to his loud disgust. He complained so long and so bitterly, Gerin finally snapped, "I'm getting better obedience out of the Trokmoi than I am from you."

"Oh, I'll do it, Fox," the outlander said with a mournful sigh, "but you can drop me into the hottest of your five hells if you think you'll make me like it."

"So long as it gets done," Gerin said. He wished he'd been able to find an excuse to hold Duren back at the rear. If both of them fell, all his hopes would fall, too—not, again, that he'd be in a position to do anything about it.

He led the column of warriors on a looping track to bring them up to the keep from the south, figuring the Gradi were less likely to take alarm if he and his men didn't come into view from straight out of the east. "We'll get as close to the keep as we can," he said, "and then charge home. If enough of us can get inside, they'll be very unhappy."

"And if not enough can," somebody—he didn't see who—said, "we will." Since that was undoubtedly true, he wasted no time arguing about it.

His first view of the keep confirmed the scouts' reports and his own hopes. The Gradi had only a handful of men up on the walls. Several more were passing time outside, a couple going at each other with axe and shield, three or four more standing around watching.

When the Gradi caught sight of the oncoming column, the first thing they did was raise a loud, wordless cheer. "Yell back!" the Fox hissed to his own men, who did. A shout was a shout in any language.

One of the Gradi perfecting his axework was the first

to notice that Gerin and his followers were not what they appeared to be. By then, though, they were less than a hundred yards from the drawbridge. The sharp-eyed Gradi let out a shout that, though still without words, was of altogether different tone from those his countrymen had been exchanging with Gerin's masquerading warriors. He rushed at the Elabonians and Trokmoi, the sun glinting off the bronze head of his axe.

Several archers shot him. He fell before he got close to the attackers. "Run!" Gerin shouted, giving up the pretense. "We seize the gateway, we get inside, and we clean them out."

Yelling for all they were worth, his men and Adiatunnus' dashed for the drawbridge. The Fox wasn't the first man onto it—some of the young bravos ran faster—but he wasn't far behind. He wondered if the Gradi were going to raise it with warriors on it and inside the keep.

They didn't, as they hadn't tried raising it before their enemies reached it. When he stormed into the keep, Gerin realized the raiders from the north hadn't kept any sort of gate crew on the winches that would have moved the bridge up or down. Maybe they hadn't seen the need. Maybe castles in their own cold homeland had gates that worked differently. Whatever the reason, they made his work easier for him.

As soon as he and his men got inside the keep's outer wall, the fight was as good as won. The Gradi would have done better to throw down their axes and beg for mercy. Not all of them even had axes, or helms, or leather jerkins. They'd been expecting no attack. Had they yielded, they would have lived.

With few exceptions, they would not yield. Instead, they hurled themselves at the Elabonians and Trokmoi with loud cries of "Voldar!" As had a couple of their warriors back at the peasant village, many of them, armed with nothing more than belt knives and stools and whatever they could snatch up, fought so fiercely, they made their foes slay them.

And they slew their foes, too. Outnumbered, outmatched, they still did a lot of damage. One of them, swinging a bench from the great hall, leveled a whole row of Elabonians, as if he were scything down wheat. A couple of the warriors who went down didn't get up again, either: he'd managed to split their skulls.

His next flailing swipe with the bench almost took Gerin out with it. The Fox had to skip back in a hurry to keep from getting his ribs stove in. But a bench was an unhandy thing with which to make a backhand stroke. Gerin stepped forward, thrust his sword into the Gradi's belly, twisted to make sure the stroke killed, and jerked the blade free. The Gradi toppled, clutching himself and howling.

Adiatunnus shouted in his own language: "Into the castle, now! We'll not be letting 'em use it for refuge against us!"

Had the Gradi thought to do that, they might have given Gerin's army a hard fight. Many of them tried to get into the great hall to lay hold of their weapons and then return to the fight out in the courtyard. When Elabonians and Trokmoi got in with them, the chance of using the castle as a citadel disappeared.

And when the fighting raged in the great hall as well as outside, the servants in the kitchen—Elabonians all—joined Gerin's warriors, throwing themselves at the Gradi with kitchen knives and cleavers and spits and two-tined serving forks. They had no armor, they had no skill at fighting, some of them were women, but they had hatred and to spare. In the tight quarters, in the chaos, that let them bring down more than one of the men who had oppressed them, though more of their number fell making the effort.

After the great hall of the castle was forced, the battle became a hunt for any Gradi who still lived. The tall, pale, dark-haired men would find shelter and then spring out, selling their lives dear as they could. Before the sun went down, almost all of them were dead.

The castle servants helped there. They knew every hiding place in the keep, and led Gerin's men to them one by one. The Gradi, deprived of surprise, wreaked a smaller toll than they might have otherwise.

"We won," Adiatunnus said, looking around at the carnage with dazed, almost disbelieving eyes. "Who'd have thought we could lay into those omadhauns and beat 'em, the way they've pounded us like drums?"

"They're only men," Gerin said. From inside the castle, screams rose. The kitchen servants were having their revenge on some of the Gradi who yet lived. The air was thick with the smell of roasting meat. Gerin decided he didn't want to know what sort of meat was being roasted.

He went to do what he could to help the wounded, sewing up gashes and setting broken bones. A physician down in the City of Elabon would no doubt have laughed at his efforts. Here in the northlands, he came as close to being a physician as anyone, and closer than most.

A skinny young woman came up to him with bread and beef ribs and ale. He took some, but said, "Here, you eat the rest. You look as if you need it more than I do." The very idea of a scrawny kitchen helper struck him as strange.

So did the amazed way the woman stared. She started to cry. "The Gradi, they'd beat us or worse if we ate of what we made for them." She didn't talk for a while after that, instead cramming her mouth full of bread and beef. Then she asked, "Do you want me? I don't have anything else I can give you for setting us free."

"No, that's all right," Gerin answered. The young

woman—young enough, easily, to be his daughter—
didn't look as if it was all right. She looked as if she
wanted to punch him in the eye. *So much for gratitude*,
he thought, a thought that frequently crossed his mind
when he was dealing with human beings. The woman
went off and approached a Trokmê. Gerin thought it
likely that, if she wanted to thank him that particular
way, he'd let her.

He was about to send a runner to order the chariots
up to spend the night with the rest of the army when
they came up without orders, a driver sometimes leading
another team or two behind the car in which he stood.
"Figured we wouldn't break surprise now, and you might
be able to use us," said Utreiz Embron's son, the warrior
he'd left in charge of the chariotry.

"Nicely reasoned," Gerin said with an approving nod.
He'd thought well of Utreiz for years. The man thought
straight and kept his eyes on what was important all
the time. He was no swashbuckler, but he got the job
done, and done well. He was, in fact, rather like a small-
scale model of the Fox.

"I expected you'd have things well in hand," he said
now. "If they'd gone wrong, you'd have been yelling
for us a long time ago."

"That's likely so," Gerin agreed. He went on in a
thoughtful tone of voice: "You know, Utreiz, this land
is going to need reordering if we ever drive the Gradi
out of it. I think you'd be a good man to install as a
vassal baron."

"Thank you, lord prince," Utreiz said. "I'd be lying
if I said I didn't hope you'd tell me something like that."
Gerin wondered if he ought to be annoyed Utreiz had
anticipated him. He shook his head: no, not when he'd
thought for years that the fellow's mind worked like
his.

He looked around to make sure his men up on the

wall of the captured keep were more alert than the Gradi had been. He didn't know how close their next large band was, and didn't want to throw away the victory he'd won over them.

The harried Elabonian servitors at the keep assumed the Fox would want to sleep in the room the Gradi commander had used, and led him up to it when he said he was tired. One whiff inside convinced him he didn't want to do that. Even by the loose standards of the Elabonian northlands, the Gradi were not outstandingly clean of person. He wondered whether that came from living in such a cold climate.

No matter where it came from, it made him go on down into the great hall and roll himself in a blanket there with his men. The racket in the hall was still loud, as warriors drank and refought the battle over and over again. The Fox didn't care. After he'd learned to fall asleep with newborn infants in the same room, nothing his men could do fazed him.

He was not a man who dreamed much or often remembered the dreams he had. When he found himself walking along a snowy path through a white-draped forest of pines, he thought at first he was awake. Then he realized he wasn't cold and decided it had to be a dream, even though he hardly ever remembered having such a clear one. When he understood he was dreaming, he expected to wake up at once, as often happens when a dream is seen for what it is.

But he stayed asleep and kept walking down the path. He tried to force himself awake, but discovered he couldn't. Fear trickled through him then. Once, years before, the Trokmê wizard Balamung had seized his spirit and made it see what the wizard would have it see. He hadn't been able to fight his way from that dream till Balamung released him. Now—

Now, suddenly, the pines gave way. The path opened out into a snow-covered clearing dazzlingly white even under a leaden sky. And in the middle of that clearing stood a comely naked woman with long dark hair, twice as tall as the Fox, who held in her right hand an axe of Gradi style.

"Voldar," Gerin whispered. In the silence of his mind, he thanked his own gods that the Gradi goddess had chosen to meet him in a dream rather than manifesting herself in the material world. He was in enough danger here in this place that was not a true place.

She looked at him—through him—with eyes pale as ice, eyes in which cold fire flickered. And he, abruptly, *was* cold, chilled in the heart, chilled from the inside out. Her lips moved. "You meddle in what does not concern you," she said. He did not think the words were Elabonian, but he understood them anyhow. That left him awed but unsurprised. Gods—and, he supposed, goddesses—had their own ways in such matters.

"The northlands are my land, the land of my people, the land of my gods," he answered, bold as he dared. "Of course what happens here concerns me."

That divinely chilling gaze pierced him again. Voldar tossed her head in fine contempt. Her hair whipped out behind her, flying back as if in a breeze—but there was no breeze, or none Gerin could sense. In face and form, the Gradi goddess was stunningly beautiful, more perfect than any being the Fox had imagined, but even had she been his size, he would have known no stir of desire for her. Whatever her purpose, love had nothing to do with it.

She said, "Obey me now and you may yet survive. Give over your vain resistance and you will be able to live out your full span most honored among all those not lucky enough to be born of the blood of my folk."

Did that mean the people who worshiped her or the

people she'd invented? Gerin had never thought he'd have the chance to ask a god that philosophical riddle, and, with the moment here, discovered having the chance and having the nerve were two different things.

He said, "I'll take my chances. I may end up dead, but that strikes me as better than living under your people—and under you. Or I may end up alive and free. Till the time comes, you never know—and we Elabonians have gods, too."

Voldar tossed her head again. "Are you sure? If you do, where are they? Drunk? Asleep? Dead? I have hardly noticed them, I tell you that. The Trokmoi have gods—aye, gods who flee before me. But you folk here? Who would know? I think you pray to emptiness."

Gerin knew he could not afford to give full heed to anything she told him. She had her own interest, and fooling him and dismaying him were to her advantage. But what she said about the Trokmê gods paralleled all too well what had happened in the material world for him to dismiss it out of hand. And what she said about Dyaus and the rest of the Elabonian pantheon put him in mind of his own thoughts . . . and his own worries. He wondered how much of the dream he would remember when he woke.

"I'll take the chance," he said. "The Trokmoi brought their gods south of the Niffet when they crossed over it some years back, and those gods do live in this land now, but they haven't run off the gods we Elabonians follow. The Trokmoi haven't conquered us, either, you'll notice, as they surely would have if our gods were as weak as you say."

"As I also told you, it's the Trokmê gods who are weak," Voldar answered. But she did not sound so grimly self-assured as she had before; maybe he'd given her a response she hadn't expected. She gathered herself before resuming, "In any case, my people and I are not puny and foolish, as are the Trokmoi and their gods. We do not come here to visit or to share. We come to *take*."

As far as Gerin was concerned, the Trokmoi had come for the same reason. But the Gradi and Voldar and the rest of their gods were much more serious, much more methodical about it than the woodsrunners.

Voldar went on, "I tell you this: if you stand against us, you and your line shall surely fail, and it will be as if you had never been. Be warned, and choose accordingly."

For a moment, Gerin knew stark despair. Voldar had struck keenly at his deepest secret fear. Almost, he was tempted to give in. But then he remembered Biton's verses promising Ricolf's barony to Duren. Had the farseeing god been lying to him? He had trouble believing that. He wondered if Voldar had so much as sensed Biton's presence in the land, the Sibyl's shrine being far from anywhere the Gradi had reached and Biton himself being only superficially Elabonian. He did not ask. The more ignorant the Gradi and their gods remained of the northlands, the better off their opponents would be.

He also wondered whether Voldar had yet encountered whatever older, utterly un-Elabonian powers dwelt *under* the Sibyl's shrine, the powers controlling the monsters. Then he wondered if there were any such powers. So much he didn't know, even after a busy lifetime in the world.

"What is your answer?" Voldar demanded when he did not speak.

"Who can say whether what you tell me is the same as what will be?" he replied. "I guess I'll take my chances fighting on."

"Fool!" Voldar screamed. She stabbed out a finger at him. Cold smote, sharp and harsh as any spear thrust.

He clutched at his chest, as if pierced—and woke up, panting, his heart pounding with fear, in the great hall of the keep he and his army had just seized.

Adiatunnus was lying a few feet away. No sooner had Gerin's eyes flown open in the gloom of guttering torches than the Trokmê chieftain gave a great cry—"The hag! The horrible hag!"—in his own language and sat bolt upright, his pale eyes wide and staring.

Several warriors muttered and stirred. A couple of men woke up at Adiatunnus' shout and complained before rolling over and going back to sleep. Adiatunnus gaped wildly, now this way, now that, as if he did not know where he was.

"Did you just visit a certain goddess in your dreams?" Gerin called quietly. He still didn't know whether mentioning Voldar by name would help make her notice him, but, after what he'd just seen, he didn't want to find out, either.

"Och, I did that," Adiatunnus answered, his voice shaky. He needed a moment to realize why Gerin was likely to be asking the question, a telling measure of how shaken he was. His gaze sharpened, showing his wits beginning to work once more. "And you, Fox? The same?"

"The same," Gerin agreed. "She—whoever she was" —no, he'd take no chances— "tried to frighten me out of going on with the campaign. What happened to you?"

"Just the look of her turned the marrow in me to ice for fair," Adiatunnus said, shivering. "Humliest wench I'm ever after seeing, and that's nobbut the truth. And the blood running from the jaws of her, it came from some good Trokmê god, I'm thinking, puir fellow."

"Ugly? Blood? That's not how she showed herself to me," Gerin said, more intrigued than surprised. Gods were gods, after all; of course they could manifest themselves in more than one way. "She was beautiful but terrible, fear and cold and awe all mixed together. What I thought was, *No wonder she's chief among all the Gradi gods.*"

"We saw her different, that we did," Adiatunnus said with another shudder. "I wonder which was her true seeming, or if either one was. We'll never ken, I'm thinking. However you saw here, though, what did the two of you have to say to each other?"

As best he could, Gerin recounted his conversation with the Gradi goddess, finishing, "When I told her I wouldn't give up, she—I don't know—flung a freeze at me. I thought my heart and all my blood would turn to ice, but before that happened, I woke up. What befell you?"

"You said her nay?" Adiatunnus asked in wondering tones. "You said her nay, and she didn't destroy you?"

"Of course she destroyed me," Gerin answered irritably. "Look—here you are, talking with my blasted corpse."

Adiatunnus stared, then frowned, then, after a long moment, started to laugh. "Fox, it's many a time and oft I've wished to see the dead corp of you, blasted or any way you choose. The now, though, I'll own to being glad you're still here to give me more in the line of troubles."

"I thank you for that in the same spirit you meant it," Gerin said, squeezing another chuckle out of Adiatunnus. The Fox went on, "What did . . . she . . . say or do to make you wake up with such a howl?"

"Why, she showed me the ruin of everything I'd labored for all these years, if I was to go on with the war against her people," the Trokmê answered.

"And you believed her?" Gerin said. "Just like that?"

"So I did," Adiatunnus said with yet another chuckle. "What I want to know is, why you didna."

"Because I assumed she was lying to me, to put me

in fear and make me lose heart," Gerin said. "If I were a Gradi god, it's what I'd do. You Trokmoi are a tricksy folk—have you no trickster gods?"

"Aye, we do that," Adiatunnus admitted. "But the goddess in my dream, now, she's not that sort, not from all the tales of her I ken, any road. And the Gradi, they're not that sort, either. They come and they take and they kill and they go, with hardly even a smile to say they're enjoying the work."

That last phrase drew a snort from the Fox, who said, "Well, from what I've seen, you're right about the Gradi. You may even be right about . . . that goddess. Maybe she wouldn't lie for the sport of it, the way a woodsrunner would." He relished Adiatunnus' glare, a sign the chieftain's spirit was recovering. "But would she lie to help her own folk? Of course she would. This side of Biton, can you think of a god who wouldn't?"

Adiatunnus pondered that. Slowly, he nodded. "Summat to what you say, lord prince." He used Gerin's title in a tone half grudging, half admiring. "You've got sand in you, that you do. You aim just to keep on after the Gradi as if you'd never dreamt your dream, do you now?"

"We've beaten them once, you and I together," Gerin said. "I've beaten them another time, all by my lonesome. Till they show me they can beat me, why should I pull back?"

"Sure and you have a way to make it all sound so simple, so easy," Adiatunnus said. "But they're after beating us a whole raft o' times—us Trokmoi, I mean. When that happens" —he sighed— "the only thing you can think of is that it'll happen again, try as you will to stop it."

"Which is why you made common cause with us," Gerin observed.

"Truth there," Adiatunnus said.

"Then let me take the lead, since you gave it to me, and don't trouble your head with dreams, even dreams with goddesses in them," the Fox said.

"Dinna fash yoursel'. Dinna fash yoursel'." Adiatunnus made his voice high and squeaky, as if he were a mother shouting at a little boy. "Easy to say. Not so easy to do, not when you're in the middle o' the dream."

There was truth in that, too. But Gerin asked, "Are you dreaming now?"

"No," the Trokmê chieftain said at once. But then he looked around the dim-lit great hall. "Or no is what I think, the now. But how can you be sure?"

"Good question," Gerin said. "If I had a good answer, I'd give it to you. I'll tell you this much: I don't think I'm dreaming, either." He pulled his blanket up around him; the rough wool scratched at his neck. "With any luck, though, I will be soon." He closed his eyes. He heard Adiatunnus laugh softly and, a little later, heard his snores join those filling the hall. A little later than that, he stopped hearing anything.

When the Fox's army rode west from the captured keep the next morning, they rode toward dark gray clouds piled high on the horizon and scudding rapidly toward them on a startlingly nippy breeze. "Wouldn't know we were at the summer season, would you?" Gerin said, shivering a little as that wind slid under his armor and chilled his hide.

Duren looked back over his shoulder at his father. "If I didn't know what season it was, I'd guess those clouds held snow in them, not rain."

"I wish they did," Van said, peering ahead with a frown. "Snow'd leave the road hard. Rain like the rain those clouds look to have in 'em'll turn these dirt tracks into hub-deep soup." He turned from Duren to Gerin. "Your Elabonian Emperors were no fools when they made their fine highways. Hard on a horse's hooves, aye, but you can move along 'em and bite the thumb at the worst of the weather."

"I won't say you're wrong, because I think you're right." Gerin studied those fast-moving clouds and shook his head. "I've never seen weather so ugly this late in the year."

Even as he spoke, the wind freshened further. It smelled of rain, of damp dust somewhere not far away. A moment later, the first drop hit him in the face. More rain followed, the wind blowing it almost horizontally through the air. Rain in summer should have been pleasant, breaking the humidity and leaving the air mild and sweet when it was gone. This rain, once arrived, chilled to the marrow and gave no sign it would ever leave.

A few of the warriors had brought rain capes with them, of oiled cloth or leather. For once, Gerin found himself imperfectly forethoughtful and getting ever more perfectly wet. The horses splashed through the thickening ooze of the roadway and began to kick up muck instead of dust. The chariot wheels churned up a muddy wake as the car rolled west.

Gerin's world contracted; the rain brought down dim curtains that hid the middle distance and even the near. He could see the couple of teams and chariots closest to him, no more. Every Gradi in the world might have been gathered a bowshot and a half off to one side of the road, and he would never have known it. After a while, he stopped worrying; had the Gradi been there, they wouldn't have known about him, either.

Water dripped from Van's eyebrows and trickled through his beard. "This is no natural storm, Fox," he boomed, raising his voice to make himself heard through wailing wind and drumming drops.

"I fear you're right," Gerin said. "It puts me in mind

of the one Balamung the wizard raised against us before he led the Trokmoi across the Niffet." He remembered the gleaming, sorcerous bridge over the river as if it had been yesterday, though more than a third of his life had passed since then.

Van nodded. The motion shook more water from his beard. "And if a wizard could do what Balamung did, how hard a grip can gods take on the weather?"

"A good question," Gerin answered, and then said no more for some time. A lot of people had been coming up with good questions lately. At last, he added, "It's such a good one, I wish you hadn't asked it."

As if to give point to what the outlander had said, a lightning bolt crashed down and smashed a tree somewhere not far away. Gerin saw the blue-purple glare and heard the crash, but could not see the tree through the driving rain.

As the rain went on, the army traveled more and more slowly. The Fox had trouble being sure they were still traveling west. He had trouble being sure they were still on the road; the only way to tell it from the fields through which it went was that the mud seemed deeper and more clinging in the roadway.

Days were long at this season of the year, but the clouds were so thick and black, they disguised the coming of night almost till true darkness arrived. The army, caught away from a keep and even away from a peasant village, made a hasty, miserable camp. The only offering they could give the ghosts was blood sausage from their rations. Starting fires was out of the question. So was hunting.

Gerin set his jaw against the discontented, disappointed wails of the night spirits and did his best to ignore them, as he would have tried to ignore the first twinges of a tooth beginning to rot in his head. He squelched around the unhappy encampment. There were tents enough for only about a third of his men. He shouted and cajoled troopers into packing those tents as tight as serfs stuffed barley into storage jars. That helped, but it wasn't enough. Nothing would have been enough, not in that rain.

He got the men who could not be stuffed into tents to rig what shelters they could with blankets and with the chariots they'd been riding. Such would have done against the usual warm summer rain. Against this— "Half of us will be down with chest fever in a couple of days," he said, shivering. "I wouldn't be surprised if we got sleet."

"I'd sooner fight the Gradi than the weather, any day," Van said. "Against the Gradi, you can hit back." Glumly, Gerin nodded.

Adiatunnus called, "Fox, where are you the now? With the murk so thick and all, I'm liable to fall in a puddle and drown myself or ever I find you."

"Here," Gerin answered through the hiss of the rain. He spoke again a moment later, to guide the Trokmê chieftain to the blanket under which he huddled. Adiatunnus sat down beside him with a series of soft splashes.

"Lord prince, can we go on in—and against—this?" the woodsrunner asked.

"I aim to try," Gerin answered.

"But what's the use?" Adiatunnus wailed. "If we go on, we'll drown for fair, unless you're after reckoning death from sinking in the muck a different thing nor drowning."

"There's a question over which I suspect the philosophers have never vexed themselves," Gerin said, thereby amusing himself but not the Trokmê. He went on, "And what if we give up and the sun comes out before noon tomorrow? This is a bad storm, aye, but not so bad as all that." That he'd been saying just the opposite to Van a little while before fazed him not at all; he wanted to keep Adiatunnus' spirits as high as he could.

That proved not to be very high. With a sigh, the chieftain said, "One way or another, they'll overmaster us. If they canna be doing it by force of arms, that goddess and the rest will manage. We're better for having you here, Fox, but is better good enough? I doubt it, that I do."

Gerin fell back to the last ditch: "Do you remember your oath?"

"Och, that I do." Adiatunnus sighed again. "While you go on, lord prince, I'll go with you, indeed and I will. So I swore. But whether I think 'twill do any good— there's another story." He splashed away, leaving Gerin without any good reply.

Spurred largely by the Fox's shouts and curses, the Elabonians and Trokmoi did fare west again after dark gave way to a grudging, halfhearted morning twilight. Riding straight into the teeth of the rain only made things worse. So did the miserable breakfasts the troopers choked down, the slow pace the mud forced, and the out-of-season cold of the rain.

Toward midmorning, little bits of ice began to sting the soldiers' faces. "Not so bad as all that, you say?" Adiatunnus shouted through the slush after his chariot plowed forward to come up level with Gerin's. Again, the Fox found none of his usual sharp comebacks.

A little later, the army came up to a peasant village. The serfs were frantic. "The crops will die in the fields!" they screamed, as if Gerin could do something about that. "We'll starve come winter if we don't drown first— or freeze to death. Ice in summer!"

"Everything will be all right," Gerin said. He wondered if even the most naive serf would believe him.

As he and his men slogged on, he looked back enviously at the thatch-roofed huts in which the peasants huddled. They would undoubtedly keep drier than his army. Had the village been large rather than small, he would have been tempted to turn the serfs out of their homes and appropriate the shelters for his men. He was glad he didn't have to worry about that.

The farther west he and his troopers went, the worse the weather got. Somewhere, the Gradi were waiting. He hoped they were as wet and miserable as his own men.

Duren said, "At this rate, we could drive straight into the Orynian Ocean and we'd never know it. I don't see how we could get any wetter than we are now."

"Oceans taste of salt, lad," Van said. "I've been on 'em and in 'em, so I know. Past that, though, you're right. I keep expecting to see fish swim by me. Haven't yet, so maybe this is still land."

Whatever it was, it was dreadful going. Some small streams had climbed out of their banks, their water pouring in brown sheets across fields already sodden from the downpour. As had that first lot across which the army had come, serfs huddled in their villages, looking out with glum astonishment on the ruin of the year's crops. Gerin shuddered to think what winter would be like. The peasants were liable to end up eating grass and bark and one another. Uprisings started after years like this, among men who had nothing left to lose.

Toward evening (or so the Fox thought; by then, he seemed to have been traveling forever), the army did come across some Gradi: a double handful of the invaders were trudging, or rather squelching, across a field, oiled-leather rain capes over their heads. "There they are!" Gerin shouted. "The men whose gods are making this campaign so horrid. What do you say we pay those gods back for the grief they've given us?"

Afterwards, he didn't know whether to be glad or sorry he'd put it that way. The Gradi, spying his forces coming out of the rain at about the same time as he saw them, started running clumsily toward some trees bordering the edge of the field. The ground was mucky, but not quite so impossible as some he'd been through. That meant chariots could outdistance men afoot. His troopers cut the Gradi off from escape, then jumped down and slaughtered them, one after another. The water standing in the field was puddled here and there with red till the rain eventually diluted it and washed it away.

The fight itself wasn't what disturbed Gerin. But the savage glee both Elabonians and Trokmoi had taken in massacring the Gradi gave him pause, even though— and perhaps especially because—he'd encouraged them to do just that. Putting the best face he could on it, he told Adiatunnus, "There—you see? Every time we come on them, we beat them."

"Truth that," Adiatunnus said. "The warriors, we can beat them, sure and we can." He didn't sound happy about it, continuing, "And what good does that do us, I ask you? When the gods and goddesses are all after pissing out of the heavens down onto us, what good does killing men do?"

"If we hadn't shown we could do that, the Gradi gods and goddesses wouldn't have joined the fight against us," Gerin said.

"Are you saying that'd be better, now, or worse?" Adiatunnus asked, and splashed off before the Fox could reply.

The ghosts did not trouble the army that night, not with the fallen Gradi nearby to give them their boon of blood. But rain and sleet kept pelting down, which made the encampment as wretched as it had been the night before. Gerin wondered if Voldar would appear to him when he slept (if he slept, wet and cold as he was), but he remembered nothing after finally dropping off.

Dawn was the same misnomer it had been since the storm began. The Fox got the army moving more by refusing to believe it would not move than any other way. Exhausted, dripping men hitched exhausted, dripping horses to chariots and did their best to keep moving west against the Gradi.

Gerin would have relished a big fight that day. It would have been a focus for the anger that filled his men. But how could you fight back against a gray sky that kept pouring rain and ice on your head? You couldn't, which was precisely the problem.

"You won't make 'em go tomorrow," Van said as they slowly slogged on. "Damn me to the five hells if I know how you made 'em go today."

"They're more afraid of me than of the Gradi gods and goddesses right now," the Fox said. "They know what I can do, and they still aren't sure about them."

But by the next day it wasn't just streams out of their banks, it was rivers. And rain and sleet turned to hail and then to snow. Gerin shook a fist at the heavens, wishing he had a bow that could reach beyond them. Wishing was futile, as usual.

Shivering, teeth chattering, he gave in. "We go back," he said.

VII

Back on the eastern side of the Venien River, in territory Adiatunnus controlled, the weather was cool and rainy. No one there seemed willing to believe the tales the returning warriors told of what they had endured trying to penetrate to the heart of the Gradi power.

"Only thing I can think of," Gerin said, standing close to the fire roaring in the hearth at Adiatunnus' great hall, "is that Voldar and the rest don't hold full sway this far east. Not yet, anyhow."

Adiatunnus' long face grew even more dolorous than it had been of late when he heard the Fox name the Gradi goddess. Gerin didn't care. Defiance burned like fever in him. Maybe it was making him delirious, as fever sometimes did. He didn't care about that, either. He wanted to hit back at the Gradi any way he could, and at their deities, too.

"How will you keep 'em from stretching their sway, though?" Adiatunnus demanded. He too stood close by the fire, as if he couldn't get warm enough. The Fox understood that, for he felt the same way. "You're nobbut a man, lord prince, and a man who fights a god— or even a goddess—he loses afore he begins."

"Of course he does," Gerin answered, "if he's stupid enough to make the fight straight on. Gods are stronger than men, and they see farther than men, too. That doesn't mean they're smarter than men, though."

"And how smart d'you need to be to step on a

cockroach, now?" Adiatunnus returned. "That's what you are to the gods, Fox: lord Gerin the Bug, prince of cockroaches."

"No doubt," Gerin said, annoying Adiatunnus by refusing to be annoyed himself. "But if I can get other gods angry at the ones the Gradi follow, and if I can steer them in the right direction—" Listening to himself, he could gauge how desperate he was. Playing with vipers—even the ones Van had described—was a safer business than getting involved with the gods. But if he didn't get divine aid of his own, the Gradi and their grim deities would swallow up the whole of the northlands. He felt it in his bones.

"And which gods will you summon, now?" Adiatunnus sounded both anxious and worried. "Our own, now, they willna face the ones the Gradi follow. So we've seen, to our sorrow. Is it any different with your Elabonian powers?"

"I don't know," Gerin said. That wasn't all he didn't know: he was wondering if he could make Father Dyaus pay any real attention to the affairs of the material world at all. The head of the Elabonian pantheon had swallowed up the savor of any number of fat-wrapped thighbones over the years; could he now give value for value? Gerin had taken his power for granted till he saw how Voldar supported the Gradi. Ever since, and especially since the storm, he'd wondered . . . and worried.

" 'I don't know' isn't much to rest the hopes o' the land on," Adiatunnus said.

"If I thought you were wrong, I would say so," Gerin answered. "As a matter of fact, I don't intend to summon an Elabonian god to deal with the goddess and the gods the Gradi follow. There's a foreign god with whom I've dealt before . . ."

He stopped. Adiatunnus noticed him stopping. "Tell

me more," the Trokmê urged. "What foreign spirit is it, now? What powers has he got?"

"Mavrix is the Sithonian god of wine and poetry and fertility and beauty," the Fox answered. "Along with Biton, he's also the god who drove the monsters back underground after the earthquake."

"A mighty god indeed," Adiatunnus said, looking impressed. "I was talking with one of those monsters, that I was, figuring ways to smash you to powder, Fox, when he softly and silently vanished away, leaving nobbut the rank smell of him behind to show he'd been no dream."

"So Diviciacus told me," Gerin said. "That was when you swore vassalage to me the first time." Adiatunnus nodded, not a bit abashed. He'd been frightened into swearing submission then, just as he had now because of the Gradi. If the danger went away, he was liable to try to reclaim his freedom of action once more, as he had a decade earlier.

What the Fox didn't tell him was that he faced the prospect of summoning Mavrix to his aid with the same enthusiasm he would have given the notion of having an arrowhead cut out of his shoulder: both were painful necessities, with the emphasis on *painful*. Mavrix and he had never got on well. He hadn't persuaded the Sithonian god to get rid of the monsters so much as he'd tricked him into doing it. Mavrix would just as soon have got rid of him instead—maybe sooner.

He'd survived Mavrix once, he'd tricked him once. Could he do it again? He'd said a man could be more clever than a god. Now he was going to have his chance to prove it . . . if he could.

Adiatunnus found another interesting question to ask: "Is your Sithonian god truly strong enough to beat back . . . that goddess?" He wouldn't name Voldar. "She's no mere monster, monster though she seems."

"I don't know that, either," Gerin told him. "All I can do is try to find out." He held up a hand. "And I know what your next question is going to be: what will we do if Mavrix turns out not to be strong enough?"

He didn't answer the question. He made a production out of not answering it. Finally, Adiatunnus prodded him: "Well, what will we do then?"

"Jump off a cliff, I suppose," the Fox said. "I haven't got any better ideas right now. Have you?"

To his surprise, the Trokmê chieftain spoke up, asking, "Will you be taking all your southrons back to your own holding the now?"

"I hadn't thought about doing anything else with them," Gerin admitted. "I didn't think you'd want them on your land—they are Elabonians, after all—and I didn't think you'd want to keep feeding them any longer than you had to. Why? Am I wrong?"

Adiatunnus hesitated, but at last, looking shamefaced, said, "I wouldn't mind your leaving a couple of hundred behind for the sake of watching the line of the Venien and fighting alongside us should the Gradi be after trying to force it. Indeed, I ask that, Fox, as your vassal I do."

"You mean it," Gerin said in slow wonder. His expression unhappier than ever, Adiatunnus nodded. The Fox scratched his head. "Why, after spending so many years trying to kill every Elabonian you could find?"

"Because if it's us by our lonesome and the Gradi coming over the river and all, we'll lose," Adiatunnus answered bleakly. "Summat'll go wrong, same as it always does when the shindy's 'twixt us and the Gradi. You southrons, though, you can stand up to 'em. With my own eyes I saw it. And so—"

Gerin slapped him on the shoulder. "For that, I'll leave men behind. A lord protects his vassals, or else he doesn't stay their lord long—or deserve to. Would it suit you if I left Widin Simrin's son to command my men?"

"We're all your men now, Fox—however little we like it," Adiatunnus said with a wry grin. "Aye, Widin pleases to lead the Elabonians. I know his worth—I should, the trouble he's given me. But will he follow my lead when it's a matter of southrons and Trokmoi together?"

"Without me here?" Gerin rubbed his chin. "That seems fair. There'll be more of your men here than mine." He wondered if Adiatunnus really wanted him to leave a good chunk of his army behind so the woodsrunners could fall on it. He didn't believe that, though, not after their aborted campaign against the Gradi. Any man who feared him more than Voldar was a fool, and Adiatunnus didn't qualify there.

The Trokmê said, "I hope your foreign god knows too little of these Gradi to be in fear of 'em."

Mavrix was, or could be, a great coward. The Fox didn't tell that to Adiatunnus.

"There it is." Gerin breathed a great sigh of relief. Fox Keep still stood; the land around it hadn't been disturbed since the last Gradi raid. He thought he would have heard of any catastrophe as he traveled through his own holding, but you could never be sure. Sometimes the only way you found news was by stumbling over it.

The lookout in the watchtower was alert. Gerin heard, thin in the distance, the horn call he blew to alert the garrison to the approach of the army. Armed men popped up on the palisade with commendable speed.

"Ride out ahead," the Fox said, tapping Duren on the shoulder. "We'll let them know we came through in one piece." He'd hoped to be coming back in triumph. That hadn't happened. He'd feared coming back in defeat, perhaps with a force of fierce Gradi in pursuit. That hadn't happened, either. Had he won, then, or had he lost? If he didn't know himself, how was he supposed to tell anybody else?

Someone up on the wall shouted, "It's the Fox!" The warriors cheered. They didn't know what he'd done, any more than he knew what had gone on here. As he had been after the earthquake that toppled Biton's shrine, he was on the outermost ripple of spreading news.

"All well, lord prince?" Rihwin the Fox called down to him.

"All well—enough," Gerin answered. "And you? And the keep? And the holding? How has the weather been?"

"You go off to war and you ask about the weather?" Rihwin demanded. When Gerin only nodded, the southern noble who'd chosen to come to the northlands spread his hands in confusion. At last, pierced by his overlord's stare, he answered, "Weather's not been bad. On the cool side, and more rain than I remember most summers, but not bad. Why? How was the weather farther west?"

"Well, let's see—how do I put it?" Gerin mused. "If it weren't for the sleet's getting me prepared, I would have liked the hail even less than I did." That drew all the incredulous comments he'd thought it would. He waved impatiently. "Let down the drawbridge and we'll tell you what went on."

The drawbridge lowered. Duren drove the chariot into the keep. The rest of the force followed. Questions rained down on them: "Did we beat the Gradi?" "Did the Gradi beat us?" "Is Adiatunnus ally or traitor?" "Will we go back out on campaign again this season?"

Gerin answered abstractedly, for Selatre was waiting for him in the courtyard with their children. Seeing her and them reminded Gerin he had indeed come home. Seeing her also reminded him she'd been the intimate of a god, even if Biton was in many ways Mavrix's opposite. He wanted to talk with her before summoning—or trying to summon; you never could tell with gods—the Sithonian deity.

Before he could talk with his wife, though, he had to keep on answering questions and to deal with what seemed like everything that had happened at Fox Keep while he was away on campaign. Not for the first time, he wondered how anything important ever got done when people had to wade through so many trivia first.

At last, those who'd stayed behind stopped asking questions, at least of him. He'd settled arguments, handed down judgments, put off handing down others till he found out more, confirmed almost everything Rihwin and Selatre had done in his name while he was gone, and, somewhere along the way, acquired a couple of juicy beef ribs and a jack of ale. He ate gratefully: having your mouth full was a good excuse for not saying anything for a while.

When he finally did get the chance to speak of what he intended to do, Selatre nodded gravely. "A risky course, but one I think we have to take if the danger from the Gradi and their gods is as great as you say," was her verdict.

"Exactly what I thought," the Fox said, which was pleasing but not surprising; over the past eleven years, he'd come to see that his mind and Selatre's worked in ways very much alike—and ways that, as time went on, grew more alike as they went on living and planning together.

Rihwin the Fox was all excitement. "A chance to work with gods!" he burbled. "A chance to match wits with the immortals, to manipulate forces far stronger than we even dream of being, to—"

"—Get killed in nasty ways or have other unpleasant things happen to us," Gerin finished for him. "Or don't you remember why you can't work magic any more?

You were trying to manipulate Mavrix then, too, as I recall."

Rihwin had the integrity to look embarrassed. All he'd done—a small thing, really—was ask Mavrix to turn some wine that had soured into vinegar back into something worth drinking once more. But the Sithonian god, already piqued at Gerin for reasons of his own, had not only not fixed the wine but had robbed Rihwin of his sorcerous talent to keep from being bothered by him any more in the future. If you went through rapids in a canoe and came out the other side alive and unhurt, you hadn't manipulated them, you'd just survived. You forgot the difference at your peril.

"Why should Mavrix concern himself with Voldar and the other Gradi gods?" Selatre asked. "What are they doing that he'll particularly loathe?"

"For one thing, they're making the part of the northlands the Gradi have seized as cold and bleak as the Gradi homeland," Gerin answered, glad to marshal arguments for his wife so he'd have them ready when he had to give them to the god. "For another, they'll kill or torment those who don't bow down to them. Sithonians and their gods are fond of freedom; one of the things they don't like about us Elabonians is that we give our rulers too loose a rein."

"Voldar doesn't sound as if she likes the idea of wine," Rihwin remarked.

"Yes, I think you're right about that," Gerin said. "It would be more useful, though, if we could get wine in the northlands these days. The winters are too hard to let the vines live even now. If the Gradi and their gods settle down to stay, even the summers will be too cold." He shivered, remembering the unnatural freezing storm through which he'd tried to lead his army.

Rihwin's mobile features assumed a comically exaggerated expression of longing. "How I miss the sweet grape!" he cried, sighing long and deep like a minstrel with a song of unrequited love.

"You miss finding a great deal of trouble because you miss the sweet grape," Selatre pointed out.

Now Rihwin looked indignant, an expression perhaps not altogether assumed. "My lady," he said with a low bow, "I regret to have to offer the opinion that your judgments have been clouded by overlong association with that lout there." He pointed to his fellow Fox.

"Heh," Gerin said. "She's right, Rihwin, and you know it bloody well. Oh, you can drink yourself stupid with ale as easily as you can with wine, but you never got Baivers' dander up at you. Whenever you touch wine, you seem to bump up against Mavrix, and when you bump up against the lord of the sweet grape, horrible things happen."

"They aren't *always* horrible," Rihwin insisted. "Without Mavrix, we might never have been rid of the monsters."

"True," Gerin admitted, "but *getting* rid of them wasn't your doing, and the odds were all too good we'd end up getting rid of ourselves instead." He paused. "And speaking of monsters, how have Geroge and Tharma been?"

"Except for eating as much apiece as any three people I could name, they've been fine," Rihwin answered, and Selatre nodded agreement. "If your vassals and your serfs gave as little trouble, your holding would be easier to run."

"Back to Mavrix," Selatre said firmly. Even more than Gerin, she had a knack for holding to the essential.

"Aye, back to Mavrix," Rihwin said. "How, lord prince, do you purpose summoning him without wine?"

"Books, grain, seed, fruits—a naked peasant girl, if that's what it takes," Gerin replied. "I'll aim at his aspects as patron of the arts and fertility god, not the ones that pertain to wine." He shrugged. "Wine would probably be a stronger summons, but we do what we can with what we have." He took that for granted; he'd been making do, improvising, ever since he became baron of Fox Keep. He knew he couldn't keep juggling forever, but he hadn't dropped too many important things, not yet, anyhow.

Rihwin pursed his lips and looked thoughtful. Mavrix hadn't robbed him of his magical knowledge, merely the ability to use it. "You may well encounter success by this means," he said. "It may even be that the aspect of Mavrix you summon thus will be less flighty by nature than that which has to do with the grape. Or, of course, it may not." The last sentence and the shrug with which he accompanied it said he'd been associating with Gerin for a long time, too.

"When will you summon the god?" Selatre asked.

"As soon as may be," Gerin told her. "The Gradi and their gods are pushing hard. If we don't do something to push them back soon, I worry about what they— and Voldar—will do to us next."

"Surely your blow against them gained something," Rihwin said.

"A little, no doubt," Gerin said. "A fortress and a few villages cleared of them—but we couldn't keep those. And when we tried to press on, the storms I have to think their deities raised stopped us cold—literally. Much as I wish I could, I can't claim a victory there."

"And so you shall bring to bear the power of the god," Rihwin declared.

"So I shall," Gerin agreed. "The next intriguing question is whether I'll bring it to bear against the Gradi . . . or against me."

Had the world wagged exactly as the Fox wanted, he would have undertaken the conjuration that afternoon. But more than the minutiae of running his holding made him wait for a couple of days. Much as he liked to deal with problems by attacking them head-on, he also knew that attacking them without full understanding was liable to be worse than ignoring them altogether. And so he spent most of those next two days closeted in the library above the great hall, reading every scrap about Mavrix he had in his book-hoard.

He had less than he would have wanted. That was true of his store on every subject where he had any scrolls or codices at all. Books were too rare and precious for any man, even with an insatiable itch to know and the resources first of a barony and then of a principality behind him, to have as many as he would have liked.

In her time at Fox Keep, Selatre had made the library as much her domain as it was his. She had once enjoyed a knowledge of a different sort from that contained in books, knowledge that came to her direct from Biton. Since she'd lost that, she'd made up for it in every other way she could. She helped Gerin in his studies, finding even the most obscure mentions of Mavrix and passing them to him.

The more he read, the more he hoped: the Sithonian god's hatred of ugliness was one of his most salient characteristics. That had been one of the hooks the Fox had used to get Mavrix to drive the monsters back into their dark caverns, but the more he read, the more he worried, too. Mavrix was among the flightiest of gods. He would do whatever he did and then go off and do something else altogether. One thing Voldar seemed to have was implacable purpose.

Gerin rolled up the last scroll. "I don't know if this is going to work," he told Selatre, "but then, I don't know what choice I have, either. A man will pick a bad course when all the others look worse."

"It will be all right," Selatre said.

He shrugged by way of reply. She didn't know that, and had no rational basis for believing it. Neither did he. After a moment, though, he admitted to himself that hearing it from her made him feel better.

As was his way, Gerin carefully assembled everything he thought he would need and everything he thought he might need before he tried to summon Mavrix. He sent Rihwin to the peasant village to bring back a girl who would be enticing enough naked to tempt the fertility god if that proved necessary. Rihwin's experience with the peasant women was wider than his own. Moreover, by having his friend pick the girl, he made sure he would not have Selatre asking how he knew what she looked like without clothes.

Though the woman, whose name was Fulda, wore a long, woad-dyed linen tunic when Rihwin led her up to the keep, Gerin had to admit she did look likely to shape well in the role if required. By the half-amused, half-tart sniff Selatre let out, she thought the same.

The little shack where Gerin tried magic when he got up the nerve to try magic was set well away from Castle Fox. It was also set well away from the palisade, the stables, and everything else in Fox Keep. If something went wrong—and Gerin's conjurations, like those of any half-trained mage, had a way of going wrong—he wanted the destruction to be as limited as possible.

When he, Rihwin, Selatre, and Fulda went out to the shack, the rest of the people packing Fox Keep made a point of keeping their distance, and of not looking at the ramshackle building, either. Nothing had gone too hideously wrong over the years, but everyone got the idea that meddling with Gerin while he worked at his magic—or, for that matter, meddling with him when he worked at anything—was less than a good idea.

He began to chant from the Sithonian epic of

Lekapenos. He'd had the verses literally beaten into him by his teachers, and so did not need the scroll he held to be sure he had the words right. He held it nonetheless, to remind Mavrix of another reason he was being summoned.

On a rickety table, he set out wheat (not barley; Mavrix had nothing but scorn for Baivers), ripe and candied fruit, and several eggs from the castle henhouse. "Do you want me to strip off now, lord prince?" Fulda asked, reaching up to the neck of her tunic.

"Let's wait and see if we can bring the god here some other way first," Gerin answered, to Rihwin's evident disappointment. One of Selatre's eyebrows rose for a moment. Gerin didn't know exactly what that meant. He didn't much want to find out, either.

He used his rusty Sithonian for as much of the invocation as he could, wanting to make Mavrix feel as much at home as he could in the northlands. Despite repeated beseechings, though, the god declined to appear. Gerin wondered if that wasn't just as well, but went on anyhow.

"Fulda," Selatre said, and nodded.

The peasant woman pulled the tunic off over her head. One glance told Gerin she was as lushly made as he'd guessed. Past that one glance, he didn't look at her. If he made a mistake with his invocation, whether her body was beautiful or not wouldn't matter. Rihwin's eyes lit up. Gerin suspected he would try to see Fulda naked under other circumstances as soon as he could. That thought appeared in his mind, but vanished a moment later: Mavrix still showed no sign of coming forth.

Gerin wondered if the Sithonian god now refused to have anything to do with him at all. He also wondered whether he should have brought a pretty boy into the shack instead of Fulda. Mavrix's tastes sometimes veered in that direction.

Stubbornly, he kept on working as many variants of the spell as he could imagine. A man without his perseverance—or a man in less desperate straits—would have quit a long time before. The Fox realized he wouldn't be able to go on much longer, either, not without making an error that would at least invalidate everything he'd already done and at most . . . he didn't want to think about all the unpleasant things that might happen then.

As he was about to give up, the inside of the shack seemed all at once to grow vastly larger, though its exterior dimensions had not changed in any way. Gerin had felt that happen before. The hair prickled up on the back of his neck. Here was Mavrix, so now he had what he'd thought he wanted. How much would he regret seeing his prayers granted?

"You are the noisiest little man," the god said, his deep, honeyed voice sounding somewhere in the middle of Gerin's head rather than in his ears. The Fox was not sure whether Mavrix spoke Sithonian or Elabonian; he took meaning directly, at a level more basic than words.

Gerin spoke Sithonian, in the hope of making Mavrix better inclined toward him. "I thank you, lord of the sweet grape, lord of fertility, lord of wisdom and wit, for deigning to hear me."

"Deigning to hear you?" Mavrix's eyebrows rose almost all the way to his hairline. His handsome features, had they been human, would have been impossibly mobile. But he was not human, even if his rosebud mouth would have made any boy-lover quiver with lascivious delight. His eyes were all black, fathomless, deep beyond deep, warning of power and terror far beyond any to which a mere human could aspire. "Deigning to hear you?" he repeated. "You were doing your best to deafen me, not so?"

"I would not have troubled you were I not deep in trouble myself," Gerin answered, which was no less than truth: even as he spoke, he wondered whether his proposed cure was worse than the Gradi disease.

"And why should I care a fig for your troubles, lord Gerin, prince of the north?" In Mavrix's mouth, the Fox's titles were poisonously sweet. "Why should I not rejoice, in fact?"

"Because I did not make them, for one," Gerin answered. "And, for another, because the gods who did make them now purpose turning the northlands into a cold and dreary country where next to nothing will grow, and where for months at a time all will be covered by ice and snow." Hearing his own accidental rhyme, he wished he'd thought to include metre as well; Mavrix appreciated such artful touches.

"That sounds—distasteful," the Sithonian god admitted. "But, I ask you again, why should I care? These barbarous northlands are scarcely part of my normal purview, you know. You Elabonians are quite bad enough" —the fringes on his fawnskin tunic fluttered as he shivered to show what he thought of Elabonians— "and the woodsrunning savages now infesting the land worse. If something dreadful befalls the lot of you— so what?"

"The Gradi are worse, and so are their gods," Gerin said, stubborn still. "You may not think much of Dyaus, and I have no notion what you think of Taranis, Teutatis, and Esus, but you have your place and they have theirs, and you don't try to drive them off, nor they you."

He didn't mention Baivers, some of whose aspects were close enough to those of Mavrix to make them compete with rather than complementing each other. He especially didn't mention Biton, whose quarrel with Mavrix had led to banishing the monsters infesting the northlands back to their gloomy caverns. If the god remembered those quarrels, he would remind Gerin of them. If he didn't, Gerin wasn't going to remind him.

Mavrix sniffed. "I have never impinged upon these Gradi gods, nor they on me. For all I know, you lie for your own reasons. Humans are like that." He sniffed again, in fine contempt.

But he wasn't so smart as he thought he was, because, while suspicious of Gerin's arguments, he didn't notice the logical flaws and omissions in them. If you were sly enough and quick enough and lucky enough, you could guide him like a man leading a barely broken horse. You'd never be sure he'd go in the direction you wanted him to take, but if you made all the other choices look worse, you had a chance.

Mavrix, though, was no horse, but a god, with a god's abilities and strength. Gerin said, "If you doubt me, look into my mind. See for yourself my dealings with the Gradi and with Voldar. With your divine wisdom, you will know whether I lie or not."

"I do not need your permission, little man; I can do that any time I choose," Mavrix said. A moment later, he added, "I do think better of you—a bit better—for the invitation."

And then, all at once, Gerin's world turned inside out. It did not feel as if Mavrix entered his mind, but more as if his mind suddenly became a small fragment of the god's. He'd expected Mavrix to grub for facts like a man opening drawers in a cabinet. Instead, the power of the god's intellect simply poured through him, as if he were air and Mavrix rain. The search was far quicker, far more thorough, and far more awesome than he'd expected.

When Mavrix spoke to him again, it was almost as if he listened to, almost as if he were a part of, the god's thoughts, which echoed all through his own mind: "What you say is true. These Gradi are indeed nasty and vicious men, and their gods nasty and vicious deities. That they should infest their own homeland is quite bad enough, that they should seek to spread to this relatively temperate and tolerant district intolerable. And, being intolerable, it shall not be tolerated. I commence."

Mavrix set out on a journey across the plane the gods customarily inhabited, a plane that impinged on the mundane world of men and crops and weather but was not really a part of it. He had not released the Fox's mind from its place, if that was the right word, as part of his own, and so Gerin, willy-nilly, accompanied him on his travels.

Afterwards, Gerin was never quite sure how far to trust his sensory impressions. Eyes and ears and skin were not made to take in the essence of the divine plane, nor was he really along in the flesh, but only as a sort of fleabite, or at most a wart, on Mavrix's psyche. Did the god truly drink his way through an ocean of wine? Did he really fornicate his way through . . . ? If he did, why on earth—or not on earth—would Fulda have drawn the least part of his notice? Even the dim part-understanding of what might have just happened left the Fox's sensorium spinning.

Then the going got more difficult (*not harder*, Gerin thought, being unable at the moment to imagine anything harder than . . .). Gerin felt Mavrix's surprise, discomfort, and displeasure as if they were his own. They were, in fact, his own, and more than his own.

Pettishly, Mavrix snapped, "I should never have let you entice me into this predicament." The Sithonian god did not take well to discomfort of any sort, that being a negation of everything he stood for. In the little mental cyst inside Mavrix' mind that remained his own, Gerin had all he could do to keep from bursting into laughter that would surely anger the god. Enticing

Mavrix was just what he'd hoped to do. And Mavrix would have to endure more unpleasantness if he reversed his metaphysical route . . . wouldn't he?

Gerin wondered about that. For all he knew, Mavrix could break free of where he was and be somewhere else without bothering to traverse the space in between. And even if he couldn't do that, the combination of overwhelming wine and even more overwhelming satiety might be plenty to counteract whatever lack of pleasure the god knew now.

And then, without warning, Mavrix found himself in a place, or a sort of a place, Gerin recognized from his dreams: the chilly forest to which Voldar had summoned him during his dream. "How bleak," Mavrix murmured, moving along a track in it.

This is the domain of the Gradi gods, Gerin thought, not knowing whether Mavrix was paying any attention to his small separate fragment of consciousness.

"Really?" the god replied as he came to a snow-filled clearing. "And here all the while I thought I was back in my native Sithonia. The grapes and olives are looking particularly fine this time of year, aren't they?"

Had Gerin been there corporeally, he would have turned red. Having Mavrix flay him with sarcasm wasn't what he'd had in mind when he summoned the god. Of course, when you did summon a god, what you got wasn't always what you had in mind, for gods had minds of their own.

He tried to pitch his thoughts so they would carry to Mavrix, forming them as much like speech as he could: "Voldar summoned me to this place in a dream."

"A nightmare, it must have been," the Sithonian god replied. Maybe he shuddered, maybe he didn't: Gerin's view of this plane shook back and forth. Mavrix went on, "Why any self-respecting deity would choose to inhabit—or I might better say, infest—such a place when so many better are there for the taking must remain eternally beyond me."

"We like it here."

Had that actually been a voice, it would have been deep and rumbling, like an outsized version of Van's. Gerin didn't truly hear it; it was more as if an earthquake with meanings attached had shaken the center of his mind. A great form reared up out of the snow. Gerin sensed it as being half man, half great white bear, now the one predominating, now the other.

"This ugly thing cannot possibly be Voldar," Mavrix said with a distinct sniff in his voice. Sniff or not, Gerin thought he was right: the Gradi god, whether in human or ursine form, was emphatically male. Mavrix directed his attention toward the god rather than the Fox. "Who or what are you, ugly thing?"

Given a choice, Gerin would not have antagonized anything as ferocious looking as that white, looming apparition. He was not given a choice; that was one of the risks you took in dealing with gods. The half-bear, half-man shape roared and bellowed out its reply: "I am Lavtrig, mighty hunter. Who are you, little mincing, puling wretch, to come spreading the stink of perfume over this, the home of the grand gods?"

"Grand compared to what?" Mavrix said. He waved his left hand, the one in which he carried his thyrsus, an ivy-tipped wand more powerful than any spear would have been in the hands of a mere man. "Stand aside, before I rid the plane of the gods of an odious presence. I have no quarrel with underlings, not unless they seek to trouble their betters. Since, in your case, anything this side of a horse turd would be an improvement, I suggest you leave off the business of troubling altogether."

Lavtrig roared with rage and rushed forward. He had more claws and teeth and thews than Gerin cared to contemplate. The Fox had hoped Mavrix would fight the Gradi gods. He hadn't intended to get stuck, absolutely helpless, in the middle of such a fight. Mavrix didn't care what he intended.

Wand notwithstanding, the Sithonian god's semblance was as nothing when measured against Lavtrig's fearsome aspect. But, as Gerin should have realized, appearances among gods were apt to be even more deceiving than among mankind. When Lavtrig's hideous jaws closed, they closed on nothingness. But when Mavrix tapped the Gradi god with his thyrsus, the howl of pain he evoked might have been heard in distant Mabalal, by the deities there if not by the men.

"Run along now, noisy thing," Mavrix said. "If you force me to become truly vexed, the barbarians who worship you will have to invent something else more hideous than themselves, for you will be gone for good."

Lavtrig bellowed again, this time more with rage than with pain, and tried to keep fighting. He scratched, he clawed, he snapped—all to no effect. Sighing, Mavrix lashed out with a sandal-shod foot. Lavtrig spun through the air—if the gods' plane had air—and crashed against a pine. Its burden of snow fell on him. He writhed once or twice, feebly, but did not get up to resume the struggle.

Mavrix let him lie and strode on. "Could you really have destroyed him?" Gerin asked.

"Oh, are you still here?" the Sithonian god said, as if he'd forgotten all about the Fox. "A god can do anything he imagines he can do." The answer did not strike Gerin as altogether responsive, but he could hardly have been in a worse position to demand more detail from Mavrix.

The god he had summoned to his aid strode down a path through more snow-covered trees. If Mavrix was cold, he did not show it. Once, as if to amuse himself, he pointed his thyrsus at one of the pines. Clumps of

bright flowers sprang into being at the base of its trunk.
Gerin wondered if they continued to exist after Mavrix
stopped paying attention to them.

Golden-eyed wolves stared out of the woods at Mavrix:
wolves as big as bears, as big as horses, divine wolves,
the primeval savage essence of wolf concentrated in
their bodies as a cook might concentrate a sauce by
boiling away all excess. When Gerin felt their terrible
eyes on him, he wanted to quail and run, even though
he knew he was not there in body. Wolves like that
could—would—gulp down his very soul.

Mavrix pulled out a set of reed pipes and blew music
such as had never been heard in the grim realm of the
Gradi gods, not in all the ages since they shaped the
place to their own satisfaction. It was the music of
summer and joy and love, the music of wine and hot
nights and desire. Had he been able to, Gerin would
have wept with the sorrow of knowing that, try as he
might, he would never be fully able to remember or
reproduce what he heard.

And the wolves! All at once, utterly without warning,
they lost their ferocity and came rushing through the
snow at Mavrix, not to rend him but to frisk at his
heels like so many friendly puppies. They yipped. They
leaped. They played foolish games with one another.
They paired off and mated. They did everything but
guard the road, as the Gradi gods had plainly intended
them to do.

Amusement seeped from Mavrix's mind to Gerin's.
"Perhaps we should throw cold water on some of them,"
the Sithonian god said. "Plenty of cold water here."

"Oh, I don't know," Gerin replied. "Why not let them
enjoy themselves? I have the feeling this is the first
time they've ever been able to."

"That is nothing less than the truth," Mavrix said,
and then, "I own that I responded to your summons

with resentment, but now I am glad I did. These Gradi gods need to be dealt with. They have no notion of fun." He spoke as the Fox did when passing sentence on some particularly vicious robber.

Gerin wondered if the Sithonian god could instill levity into whatever Voldar used for a heart. If he could, that would be a bigger miracle than any he had yet worked.

But Mavrix had not yet won through to confront the chief goddess of the Gradi. When he stepped out into a clearing, Gerin wondered if Voldar would await him there. But it was not Voldar. It was not anything anthropomorphic at all, but a whirling column of rain and mist and ice and snow, stretching up as far as the eye could see.

From the middle of the column, a voice spoke: "Get you gone. This is not your place. Get you gone."

At Mavrix's feet, the wolves whined and whimpered, as if realizing they'd betrayed themselves with a stranger and were going to be made to regret it by the powers that were their proper masters. Mavrix, however, spoke lightly, mockingly, as was his way. "What have we here? The divine washtub for this miserable place? Or is it but the chamber pot?"

"I am Stribog," the voice declared. "I say you shall not pass. Take your jests and japes somewhere we do not yet touch, then await us there, for one day, rest assured, we shall overwhelm it and quench them."

"Ah—right the second time," Mavrix said cheerfully, perhaps to Gerin, perhaps to Stribog. "It is the chamber pot."

He moved out into the clearing. Stribog did not attack as Lavtrig had. Instead, the Gradi god hurled all the vile weather he had inside him straight at Mavrix. Gerin's soul felt frozen. Here, he saw, was the god who had raised the summer storms against him and his army. Those, though, had been storms of the world, even if divinely raised. This was the very stuff of the gods, used by one to fight another.

And Mavrix noticed this onslaught, where he had been impervious to Lavtrig's. The chill and wet Stribog raised struck at his spirit. He grunted and said, "Now see— someone's gone and spilled it. We'll just have to set it to rights once more."

The wolves fled back to their gloomy haunts. With Mavrix's attention not on them, they forgot the dimmest notion of happiness. Too, they were soaked to their metaphysical skins. Stribog had indeed poured a bucket of cold water on them, a bucket big as the world.

Mavrix lashed out with his wand, as he had against Lavtrig. It must have hurt, too, for Stribog bellowed in pain and rage. But the Gradi god was a more diffuse entity than Lavtrig; he had no central place to strike that would do him lasting damage. And his rain and ice, his winds and lightnings, hurt Mavrix, too. The Sithonian god's anguish washed through Gerin, who knew that, had his spirit been there alone, he would swiftly have been destroyed.

When Mavrix tried to go forward against the storm that was Stribog, he found himself unable. The Gradi god's laughter boomed like thunder. "Here you will perish, you who try to trouble Gradihome!" he cried. "Here you will drown; here you will rest forevermore."

"Oh, be still, arrogant windbag," Mavrix said irritably, and for a moment Stribog *was* still, the storm silent. Even as it resumed, Mavrix went on, "Not just an arrogant windbag, but a stupid one, too. If you water a fertility god, you promote—"

"Growth!" Gerin's mind exclaimed.

"There, you see?" Mavrix told him. "You have more wit to you than this blowhard. Not much of a compliment, I fear, but you may have it if you want it."

And with that, he began to grow, to soak up all the stormstuff Stribog flung at him and make it his own instead of letting it remain a weapon belonging to the Gradi god. The pain he felt at Stribog's attacks vanished, or rather was transmuted into a satisfaction somewhere between that of a good meal and that which follows the act of love.

Stribog realized too late that he was no longer doing Mavrix any harm. He boomed like thunder again, but this time in alarm. Where before he had reached as high as the eye—or whatever sense passed for vision here—could see and Mavrix seemed small beside him, their relative sizes reversed with startling speed. Now, from his place in the Sithonian god's consciousness, Gerin peered down on a small, furious, futile whirlwind that churned up the snow around Mavrix's ankles.

Mavrix stooped and seized the whirlwind. He flung it away: whither, the Fox had no idea. Maybe Mavrix didn't, either, for he said, "I hope the alepot tempest lands among the Kizzuwatnan gods or some others who properly appreciate heat."

He was, without warning, the apparent size he had been before his fight with Stribog began. He reached up and adjusted the wreath of grape leaves around his forehead to the proper jaunty angle. The landscape of Gradihome seemed undisturbed by the divine tempest that had lashed it; Gerin wished the land of the material world recovered from rain so readily.

"Onward," Mavrix said, and onward they went. But the Sithonian god, despite his triumph, seemed wearier and less sure of himself than he had been. If defeating Lavtrig was like climbing a flight of stairs, besting Stribog had been more like climbing a mountain. If the next challenge proved correspondingly harder still . . . Gerin did his best not to think about that, for fear Mavrix would sense it and be moved either to anger or to despair.

The god came to a clearing in the snowy woods. Gerin waited to see what sort of Gradi god would confront Mavrix there, but the clearing seemed empty. More snow-covered pines stood at the far edge of the open space, perhaps a bowshot away, perhaps a bit more.

"Well," Mavrix said brightly, "variety in the landscape after all. Who would have thought it?" He brought his pipes to his lips and began to play a cheerful tune as he strolled across the rolling ground.

Had Gerin had his normal, physical eyes, he would have blinked. Something strange had happened, but he wasn't sure what. The god came to a clearing in the snowy woods. Gerin waited to see what sort of Gradi god would confront Mavrix there, but the clearing seemed empty. More snow-covered pines stood at the far edge of the open space, perhaps a bowshot away, perhaps a bit more.

"Well," Mavrix said brightly, "variety in the landscape after all. Who would have thought it?" He brought his pipes to his lips and began to play a cheerful tune as he strolled across the rolling ground.

That sensation of needing to blink repeated itself in the Fox's mind. There was the clearing . . . the same clearing. When Gerin realized that, he recovered at least a part of what he and Mavrix had just been through.

"Well," Mavrix said brightly, "variety in the landscape after all. Who would have thought it?" He brought his pipes to his lips.

Before he could begin to play, Gerin said, "Wait!"

"What do you mean, wait?" the Sithonian god demanded irritably. "I aim to celebrate coming across something different for a change." And then Mavrix, as Gerin had before him, hesitated and went back over what had gone on. "Have I—done this before?" he asked, now sounding hesitant rather than irritable.

"I—think so," Gerin answered, still far from sure himself.

"I am in your debt, little man," Mavrix said. "I wonder how many times I would have done that before I twigged to it myself. I wonder if I would ever have twigged to it myself if I didn't have you riding along like a flea on my bum. It would have been a beastly boring way to spend eternity, I can tell you that."

Gerin wondered if the only reason he hadn't been completely caught in the trap was its being set for gods, not mere men. He had spoken before of mankind's occasional advantages in dealing with vastly more powerful beings, but hadn't expected his littleness to become one: he'd slipped through the spaces in a net intended to catch bigger fish.

In tones more cautious than Mavrix usually used, he asked, "Who is out there in the clearing?"

Nothing answered: "I am Nothing," it said, voice utterly without color or emotion.

"Trust these stupid Gradi to worship Nothing," Mavrix muttered.

"Why not?" Nothing returned. "Soon or late, all fails. In the end, everything fails. I am what is left. I deserve worship, for I am most powerful of all."

"You're not even the most powerful god in your pantheon," Gerin jeered, trying to ruffle that uncanny calm. "Voldar rules the Gradi, not you."

"For now," Nothing said imperturbably.

"Stand aside, Nothing, or know nothingness," Mavrix said. From caution, he had swung back to anger.

"Wait," Gerin said again. If finding a way to hurt Stribog had been hard, how could the Sithonian god harm Nothing? Hoping he was pitching his thoughts in such a way as to let Mavrix but not Nothing hear them, he suggested, "Don't fight—distract. You're a fertility god—you can make all sorts of interesting . . . somethings, can't you?"

Mavrix's mirth filled him, as strong sweet wine might have had he been there in the flesh. "Somethings," the god said, and then, changing the timbre of his thoughts so he addressed not the Fox but the thing—or the no-thing—in the clearing: "Nothing!"

"Aye?" the Gradi god said, polite but perfectly indifferent.

Mavrix held out his hands. He breathed on them, and a flock of bright-colored singing birds appeared, one after another. "Do you see these?" he asked as he waved his hands and the birds began to fly around the clearing.

"I see them," Nothing replied. "In a little while, in a littlest while, they will cease to be. Then they will be mine."

"That's so," Mavrix agreed, "but they're mine now. And so is this." He sent a deer bounding across the open space. Gerin hoped the wolves of Gradihome wouldn't notice it. "And so are these." Flowers sprang up in the clearing, made with a purpose now instead of merely for a game. "And so is this." An amphora of wine appeared. "And so are these." Four preternaturally beautiful women and a like number of handsome and well-endowed men sprang into being. They enjoyed the wine and then began to enjoy one another. They had no more inhibitions than they did clothes.

Gerin wondered if they were figments of the Sithonian god's imagination or if Mavrix had plucked them from some warmer, more hospitable clime. He didn't ask, not wanting to bump the god's metaphysical elbow.

"They're all mine!" Mavrix shouted. "They're all doing things, right there before you."

"For now," Nothing said.

"Yes, for now," Mavrix said. "And the things they do now will cause other things to be done and to be born, and those will cause still others, and the ripples that spread from those will—"

"Eventually come to Nothing," Nothing said, but with—perhaps?—the slightest hesitation as Mavrix's creations cavorted in the clearing.

Speaking in a sort of mental whisper, Mavrix said to Gerin, "If it's not distracted now, it never will be. I am going into the clearing. If I end up here again and that space before us is empty—we are apt to be here . . . indefinitely."

Gerin's small sensorium, carried pickaback on the god's vastly larger one, crossed the clearing in a hurry. He could even look back as Mavrix regained the path that led ever deeper into Gradihome. All at once, the Sithonian god's creations vanished as if they had never been.

"That was petty of old Nothing," Mavrix said, a chuckle in his voice. "As it told us, they would have been its sooner or later. Ah, well—some deities simply have no patience." Then Mavrix suddenly seemed less sure of himself. "Or do you think Nothing will pursue me through this frigid wilderness?"

"If I had to guess, I'd say no," Gerin answered. "The Gradi gods seem to be testing you, each in his own place. Lavtrig and Stribog stayed behind once you'd bested them. I think Nothing will, too."

"You had better be right," Mavrix said. "And if I have to test and best every single puerile godlet the Gradi own—or the other way round—I shall grow quite testy myself, Fox. Bear that in mind."

"Oh, I shall," Gerin assured him. "I shall." Mavrix was more powerful than he; he knew that full well. But he had seen the progression in the actions of the Gradi gods where Mavrix was uncertain about it. Did that prove him divinely clever? If it did, he was clever enough to know he shouldn't let himself get carried away by the idea.

He did not think Mavrix had stepped up the pace, but the next clearing appeared very quickly. Mavrix went out into it with almost defiant stride, as if expecting Nothing to sow confusion in his mind once more.

But the god—or rather, goddess—standing in the open space had a definite physical aspect. "Gerin the Fox, the Elabonian," Voldar said. "You have proved more troublesome than I reckoned on, and your ally stronger." Her smile struck the Fox as imperfectly inviting. "Whether he is strong enough remains to be seen."

Her aspect was not quite as Gerin had seen her in the dream she'd induced him to have. She seemed partway toward the hag image with which she'd so horrified Adiatunnus—now and again, by starts and flickers, her hair would gray, her skin wrinkle, her teeth grow broken and crooked, her breasts lose their eternally youthful firmness and sag downward against her chest and the top of her belly. Sometimes her whole body seemed squat, slightly misshapen—and sometimes not. Gerin had no idea what her true seeming was, or if indeed she had but one true seeming.

Mavrix spoke with some indignation: "Well! I like that: a goddess greeting a mortal before a god. But I'm not surprised, not with what I've seen of manners here in Gradihome. Go ahead—ignore me."

"Nothing tried that," Voldar said. "It failed. That means I must deal with you—and when I have, you'll wish you'd been ignored. But I spoke to the mortal first because, without him, you would not be here—and would not have caused so much damage to the lesser gods around me."

"I greeted them in the spirit with which they greeted me," Mavrix replied. "Is it my fault if their spirits could not bear up under the force of my greeting?"

"Yes," Voldar said in the deadly cold voice Gerin remembered from his dream. "You should have been driven from Gradihome wailing, or been swallowed by Nothing for all eternity."

"I'd be delighted to leave this cold, ugly place," the Sithonian god said, "and I will, in an instant, once you vow you'll make no more of the material world into as close a copy of it as you can engender. God may not lie to god in such vows: so it has been, so it is, so shall it be."

"I could lie to you," Voldar said, "but I shall not. Gradihome in the world grows. So it is, so shall it be."

"No," Mavrix said. "It shall not be. There is too much cold and ugliness and sterility in the material world as it is now. I shall not permit you to increase their grip on it."

"You cannot stop it," Voldar said. "You have not the power for that, nor have you the roots in the land of which you speak that would let you draw upon its strength, as we even now are beginning to do."

"It is not your land, either," Mavrix said. "And if I have not the strength, how do I come to stand before you now?"

"You come before me, as I said before, on account of the guile of the mortal whose consciousness you carry with you," Voldar answered, "and I should not be surprised if his cunning helped you pass and overcome my fellows."

"Well! I like that!" Mavrix drew himself up straight, the picture of affronted dignity. "First speak to the mortal ahead of me, then count him as more clever. I shall take vengeance for the slight."

Gerin felt rather like a mouse that had the misfortune to find itself in the middle of a clearing where a bear and a longtooth clashed. Whichever won might not even matter to him, because they were liable to crush him without so much as knowing he was there.

And yet the fight did not begin at once. Voldar was

plainly given pause because Mavrix had managed to reach her, and Mavrix in turn seemed thoughtful at facing the goddess who lorded it over the formidable foes he had already beaten.

Suddenly, his voice grew sweet, persuasive, tempting: "Why do we have to quarrel at all, Gradi goddess? You can be pleasing to the eye when it suits you; I sense as much. Why not lie with me in love? Once you know what proper pleasure is, you'll feel less attracted toward death and doom and ice." He began to play on his pipes, a tune a shepherd might have used to lure a goose girl to a secluded meadow on a warm summer evening.

But Voldar was no goose girl, and Gradihome knew nothing of warmth. "You cannot seduce me from my purpose, foreign god. May your lust curdle and freeze; may your ardor wither."

"I *am* ardor," Mavrix said, "nothing else but, and I kindle it in others. I would try even in you, to teach you somewhat of the ways of existence about which, it would seem, you now know nothing."

"I told you, I am not your receptacle." Voldar's voice grew sharp. "Leave Gradihome now and you will suffer nothing further. If you stay, you will learn the consequences of your folly."

"I *am* folly," Mavrix said, in the same tone of voice he had used to declare himself ardor. Gerin thought he meant the one as much as the other. Ardor, to his way of thinking, certainly engendered folly. Maybe that was what the god had had in mind.

"You are a fool, that certainly." Voldar spoke as Gerin might have while chiding a vassal for something stupid he'd done. "Very well. If you will be a fool, you will pay for it." Raising her great axe, she advanced on Mavrix.

All the Sithonian tales of the fertility god named him an arrant coward. The Fox had seen some of that himself.

He more than half expected Mavrix to run away from that determined, menacing advance. Instead, though, Mavrix jeered, "Are you truly a battleaxe, Voldar, or just after my spear?" That part of him leaped, leaving Voldar in no possible doubt of his meaning.

She snarled something Gerin didn't understand, which was probably just as well. Then she swung the axe with a stroke any of the warriors who worshiped her would have been proud to claim as his own. Gerin wondered what would have happened had that blow landed as she intended. His best guess was that the Sithonian pantheon would have wanted a new deity.

But the blow did not land. Mavrix's phallus was not all that had leaped. He used his wand to bat the axehead aside. The thyrsus looked as if it would break at such usage, but looks, when it came to gods and their implements, were apt to be deceiving.

Voldar evidently had been deceived. She shouted in fury at finding herself thwarted. "There, there," Mavrix said in syrupy, soothing tones, and reach out to pat her— not at all consolingly—on her bare backside. Gerin couldn't tell whether his arm had got long to let him do that, or whether he'd shifted his position in some way allowed to gods but not men and then returned in an instant to where he had been.

However he'd done it, it made Voldar even angrier than she had been already. Her next cut with that axe would have left Mavrix metaphorically spearless. Again, he used the wand to turn aside the stroke, though Gerin, perched there on the edge of his consciousness, felt the effort that had required. Mavrix was not a god of war, where Voldar seemed to exist for no other purpose than conquest and subjugation.

"Are you going to be able to hold out against her?" he asked the Sithonian god. The question had immediate practical import for him. If Voldar beat Mavrix, would his own spirit be trapped here in Gradihome? He was hard-pressed to imagine a gloomier fate.

"We'll find out, won't we?" Mavrix answered, not the most reassuring reply the Fox could have got.

He quickly became convinced Mavrix was overmatched. The Sithonian god was indeed no killer; he sought to provoke Voldar, to infuriate her, to drive her to distraction. She, by contrast, was grimly intent on harming him—on destroying him, if she could.

The longer they struggled, the more Gerin grew concerned she could do exactly as she intended. This was not a struggle of the same sort as Mavrix had had with the other Gradi gods. It put the Fox more in mind of some of the desperate fights he'd had on the battlefield, ferocious brawls with anything past the notion of bare survival forgotten. Voldar and Mavrix hammered and pounded and cursed each other, the curses landing as heavily and painfully as kicks and buffets.

When Mavrix squeezed her, Voldar would for a moment weaken and lean toward him as if intending an embrace: the struggle was, in some ways, a spectacularly violent attempt at a seduction. But Voldar never really came close to yielding, however much Gerin wished and hoped she would. She had her own purposes, which were not those of Mavrix.

And when she gained the upper hand for the time being, the Fox felt Mavrix's nature changing into something harder and colder than seemed fitting for the Sithonian god. Voldar, he realized, was trying to bend Mavrix to her will no less than he her to his. Those stretches came more and more often as the battle progressed. Gerin wondered if Mavrix realized as much himself, and if he should warn the god.

Suddenly Mavrix gave a great cry—not of pain but of rejection—and broke away from Voldar. The disengagement was not like that between two struggling humans. One instant, he was locked in the fight with the Gradi goddess, the next he stood at the edge of the clearing in which she had awaited him.

"No," he said hoarsely. "You shall not make me into something you can rule." He understood the stakes, then. "I will not allow it. I do not allow it."

"If you stay here, I shall," Voldar said. "This is Gradihome, and Gradihome is mine." She strode toward the Sithonian fertility god, implacable purpose on her face and in every line of her body.

Mavrix broke and fled. Voldar's harsh, mocking laughter rang in his ears as he dashed away, snow flying up under his sandal-clad feet. "Be careful," Gerin shouted in his metaphysical ear. "Don't fall into Nothing's lair again."

Mavrix swerved aside, off the path. The fierce wolves of the home of the Gradi gods came coursing after him, but fawned like friendly pups once more when they drew near: so much of his power, at least, he still retained. And then he was on the path again, and running faster than ever. "I thank you for reminding me of the trap," he said, "though I do not thank you for involving me in this misadventure in the first place."

"I was trying to save what was mine," Gerin answered. *And I've failed,* he thought, wondering if he could keep that from Mavrix. *That means I have to try something else, and I don't know what.*

"I am not rooted in your northern land well enough to be as effective as I might have been fighting for Sithonia if the Gradi gods were coming there, which the power above all deities prevent," Mavrix said. "You would do better seeking out the powers in and under your own soil, those who have most to lose if enslaved or expelled by Voldar and her vicious crew."

He had been vicious himself; neither Stribog nor Lavtrig cared to try conclusions with him a second time.

Soon he was out of the realm of the Gradi gods. Gerin, meanwhile, wondered which Elabonian deities Mavrix meant. Biton, perhaps, but anyone else? He put the question to the god who carried his spirit.

"No, not that wretched farseeing twit," Mavrix said scornfully. "He'll be useless to you here, I guarantee it. Voldar would chew him up and spit him out while he was still looking every which way. He and Nothing might get on well, though; with luck, they'd bore each other out of existence."

He sounded very sure of himself, which alarmed Gerin. If Biton was not the answer against the Gradi gods, who was? "Who in the northlands can hope to stand against them?" the Fox persisted.

"I've told you everything I know, and more than you deserve," Mavrix answered, petulant now. "This is not my country. I keep saying as much: this is not my land. I don't keep track of every fribbling, stodgy godlet infesting it, nor would I want to. Since you were foolish enough to choose to be born here, I leave all that up to you."

"But—" Gerin began.

"Oh, be still till you have flesh to make noise with," Mavrix said, and Gerin perforce *was* still. The god went on, "Here we are, returned to this dank, chilly, unpleasant hovel you inhabit. If only you knew the sunshine of Sithonia, the wine, the sea (not all gray and frigid like the nasty ocean splashing your soil, but blue and bright and beautiful), the gleam of polished marble and sandstone yellow as butter, as gold— But you do not, poor deprived thing, and maybe for the best, for you might slay yourself in despair at your lack. Since you are trapped here, I return you now to the really quite ordinary body from which I abstracted you."

All at once, Gerin was seeing with his own eyes, hearing with his own ears, moving his head, his hands, his legs. There before him stood Mavrix. There too stood Selatre and Rihwin and Fulda, who remained lushly nude. "How long were we gone?" the Fox asked. As Mavrix had said, in his own flesh he could speak again.

"Gone?" Selatre and Rihwin spoke the word together. "You've been here all along," Gerin's wife went on. "Where did you go? What did you do?" She turned to Mavrix. "Lord of the sweet grape, are the Gradi gods vanquished?"

"No," Mavrix said. The simple denial brought a gasp of dismay from Rihwin. Mavrix continued, "I did what I could. It was not enough. I can do no more, and so I depart this unpleasant clime." Like mist under the sun, he began to fade.

Gerin had been with him, and knew he had been beaten. Selatre and Rihwin recognized he meant what he said. But Fulda, like so many people Gerin knew, had unquestioned and unquestioning faith in those above her. Hearing a god admit failure was more than she could bear. She cried, "Do you leave us with nothing, then?"

Mavrix resolidified. You could not tell which way his uniformly dark eyes were turned, but, by the direction in which his head pointed, he was probably looking at her. "So you want me to leave you with something, do you?" he said, and laughed. "Very well. I shall."

Fulda gasped. At first Gerin thought it was surprise, but after a moment he realized it was something else entirely. Fulda's eyes closed. Her back arched. Her nipples went stiff and erect. She gasped again, and shuddered all over.

"There," Mavrix said, sounding smug and self-satisfied, or possibly just satisfied: despite what he'd done on the plane of the gods, he hadn't disdained Fulda after all. On the contrary, for he continued, "I've left you something. In three fourths of a year, you'll find out exactly what, and that, I have no doubt, will prove interesting for all concerned. But now . . ." He faded again, this time till he disappeared. The shack in which Gerin attempted to perpetrate magic abruptly seemed to resume its normal cramped dimensions, which convinced the Fox Mavrix was truly gone.

Fulda opened her eyes, but she wasn't looking at the inside of the shack. "Oh," she said, shivering once more. Then she too realized Mavrix had vanished. "Oh," she repeated, this time in disappointment. She reached for her tunic and put it back on. Selatre being there, Gerin made a point of not watching her.

He looked instead to his wife and to Rihwin. They plainly shared his thought. "The god didn't—" Rihwin said.

"The god wouldn't—" Selatre echoed.

"Didn't what?" Fulda asked. "Wouldn't what?"

"Unless we're all daft, you're going to have a baby," Gerin told her. "Quite a baby." She yelped. No, she hadn't understood. The Fox sighed. "One more thing to worry about," he said.

VIII

Selatre shook her head. "I fear the lord of the sweet grape was right in what he told you," she said to Gerin. "Biton is principally concerned with the valley that holds his shrine and the enchanted wood beyond it. The chief reason he involved himself in the broader affairs of the northlands when the monsters burst out is that they sprang from his valley, or from below it."

"Oh, a pestilence!" the Fox said. "You're supposed to tell me what I want to hear, not what you think is true."

Selatre stared at him. Then, warily, she started to laugh. "You are joking, aren't you?" Only when he nodded did she relax, a little.

"When you start telling me things for no better reason than you think they'll please me——" Gerin stopped. "I don't need to go on with that, because you know better, the gods be praised." The phrase tasted sour in his mouth. "The gods who are awake and listening to me, anyhow."

"I don't know whether Mavrix is listening to you, but no one could doubt he's awake," Selatre answered. "I went into the village yesterday. Fulda's courses should have started. They haven't. She says she hasn't lain with any of the men there since her last flowing. I believe her. That leaves——"

"Divine ecstasy?" Gerin suggested, not quite so sardonically as he would have liked.

But Selatre's face was serious as she nodded. "Just

257

so. We were talking about that. It was, I think, different from the ecstasy Biton gave me . . . but then, he and Mavrix are very different gods. And when next spring comes—"

"We'll have a little demigod on our hands," Gerin said. "If, of course, the Gradi haven't overrun us by then. If they have, they'll be the ones worrying about a little demigod. It would almost be worthwhile losing, just to find out what they do about that. Almost, I say."

"We still don't know how to keep that from happening," Selatre said.

"Don't remind me," Gerin told her. "For all I can tell, what Mavrix was really saying was to give up, because none of the gods on or under the ground of the northlands whom I know are likely to have the power to stop the Gradi gods, or even to care about doing it."

"No, I don't think so," Selatre said. "You're letting yourself be too gloomy. After all the trouble you've had with Mavrix, if you had no hope he'd come right out and say as much. He'd probably gloat about it, as a matter of fact."

Gerin chewed on that and found himself nodding. "Yes, that's just what he'd do. He doesn't love the Gradi gods or what they stand for, so he was willing to go against them, but he doesn't love me, either. I've seen that over the years, and no mistake about it."

Downstairs, in the great hall, a hideous commotion erupted. Selatre raised an eyebrow. "I've heard a lot of strange noises down there, but hardly anything like this. Who's killing whom, and why are they torturing them before they finally let them die?"

That was an exaggeration of the quality of the racket, but not a large one. "I'll go down there and tell whoever it is to stuff a pair of drawers in his gob," Gerin said. "If I have to, I'll smash a couple of heads together. That generally shuts people up."

Down he went, left hand on the hilt of his sword. He didn't know what he'd find when he got downstairs— an argument just this side of a brawl was his best guess. What he did discover was in a way more reassuring, in another way more alarming: Van and Geroge and Tharma sitting around beside an enormous jar of ale that had probably been full when they started it and now was certainly almost empty.

What Gerin and Selatre and probably everyone else in Fox Keep had mistaken for strife was the outlander and the two monsters trying to sing. The result sounded more nearly catastrophic than musical. But that was not what made Gerin snap, "What do you think you're doing?" at Van.

"Oh, hullo, Fox," Van said with a broad, foolish grin. "Trying to see if I can hold more ale than these walking fur rugs here. I thought so when I started, but I'm not so sure any more."

"Lord prince," Geroge rumbled. He grinned, too, displaying his formidable teeth. The Fox didn't doubt the grin was meant as friendly, but it raised his hackles all the same. Geroge was at least as strong as Van. He usually behaved himself very well, but who could say how he'd act with a bellyful of ale sloshing around inside him? More to the point, if he decided to behave monstrously, how much damage would he do before he could be controlled or killed?

Like everyone else at Fox Keep, he and Tharma drank ale every day, with their meals and when they were thirsty. But they didn't drink—or they hadn't drunk— for the sake of getting drunk, not till now they hadn't. It was not a habit Gerin wanted to encourage in them.

He glared at Van, wishing his friend had shown better sense. As usual for such wishes, this one came too late. With what he thought was commendable restraint, he said, "Looking into the bottom of a jack of ale is one thing. Looking into the bottom of a jar of ale is something else again. You'll be clearer on the difference come morning," he added with malice aforethought.

"Likely tell you're right." Van scowled. "And likely tell I'll have Fand screeching at me, too, making me wish my poor aching head would fall off." He held his poor, not yet aching head in his hands.

If the prospect of hangovers daunted Geroge and Tharma, they didn't show it. "Oh, I bless lord Baivers, yes I do, for making me feel so fine," Geroge howled. He spilled what he probably intended as a little ale on the table for a libation. He wasn't moving so smoothly as he had been, though, and ended up emptying most of his jack of ale. He didn't care about the mess; he cared about the missing ale. He got up, went over to the jar, and dug with the dipper. He didn't get much back for his effort. Peering down into the jar, he howled again, this time in desolation. When words came back to him, he said, "It's all gone! How did that happen?"

Van laughed then, morose though he'd been a moment before. So did Tharma; she laughed so hard, she fell off her bench and rolled in the rushes before slowly climbing back to her feet. And Gerin said, "Do you think you might have had something to do with it?"

"Who, me?" Geroge's narrow little eyes went as wide as they could when that idea worked its way into his fuddled wits: it plainly hadn't occurred to him. "Well, maybe I did."

He laughed, too, in big, snarling chuckles that would have sent any sensible watchdog running for its life, tail between its legs. Like Tharma, he was turning out to be a good-natured drunk, for which Gerin thanked not only Baivers but every god he could think of this side of Voldar. A nasty, sullen drunken monster was about the last thing Gerin wanted to contemplate. If

Geroge rampaged out of control, how was anyone supposed to stop him without spearing him or filling him full of arrows?

The Fox stuck two fingers in the puddle of ale Geroge had spilled on the table. He sucked the brew off one of them, then flicked a golden drop from the other in a libation of his own. "I bless you, Baivers," he said out loud, and silently appended, *because your bounty turns monsters friendly and foolish, not vicious and savage*. Considering what they were, that was no small boon from the god.

Van with a hangover was a shuddering horror. But Van had had a great many hangovers in his time. He drank a tiny bit more ale come morning, nibbled at a heel of bread, and did his best to stay away from bright sunlight and loud noises (though Fand didn't make that latter easy) until his poor abused body had the chance to recover.

Geroge and Tharma felt every bit as bad, if not worse, and had no idea what to do about it. Some forms of virginity were more enjoyable to lose than others. They moaned they were dying, and flinched from the harsh din of their own voices. Gerin did very little to make them more comfortable. The less they enjoyed the aftermath of their debauch, the less likely they were to repeat it.

Having been moderate the day before, he didn't flinch from leaving the shade of the great hall for the bright sunlight that streamed down into the courtyard. As soon as he went out there, he began to sweat; it was a fine, hot summer's day.

He wondered if that meant Stribog hadn't recovered from the drubbing Mavrix gave him. He also wondered what the weather was like west of the Venien, in lands where the Gradi held sway. If Stribog really was out of commission, the peasants might bring in some kind of crop even there. *Have to try to find out*, he thought. The more he learned about what the Gradi and their gods could do, the better his own chances of figuring out what to do about them.

He climbed up onto the palisade. Everything looked normal enough, as far as the eye could see: the trouble was, the eye couldn't see far enough. But here, peasants labored in the fields, cattle and sheep grazed on the meadows, pigs foraged for whatever they could find. In the peasant village near the keep, smoke came out the smoke holes in a couple of roofs as women simmered soup or stew for the evening meal.

What was Fulda doing there? Cooking? Weaving? Brewing? Weeding? Whatever she was doing, her courses hadn't come. She was pregnant, sure enough, and without a human partner. Why had Mavrix chosen to spawn a demigod in the northlands? What sort of demigod would the child be?

Time would answer those questions, provided Gerin remained alive to see the answers. Actually, time would answer those questions whether he remained alive or not, but he preferred not to dwell on that.

He didn't have to dwell on it for long. The lookout in the watchtower above the castle winded his horn and cried, "A chariot approaching, lord prince, out of the west!" Gerin peered southwest, in the direction of Adiatunnus' lands. For years, that was the direction from which trouble had come, out of the west. Then the lookout amplified his earlier words: "A chariot along the path by the Niffet."

Gerin whirled. When he thought about the Niffet these days, he thought of war galleys full of Gradi with axes, every one of the raiders bellowing Voldar's name. Much to his relief, he saw no galleys. For a little while, he saw no chariot, either. His watchtower was the tallest around, precisely to afford the sentries up there the widest possible view.

No, there it was, coming out from behind a grove of plum trees. The horsemen were trotting along at a pace that, while not the quickest, covered the most ground if you held it for a long time. Somebody up on the palisade next to Gerin said, "From out of Schild Stoutstaff's holding, maybe."

"That would be my guess," Gerin agreed. "Now we have to find out what sort of news he's bringing."

When the chariot came up to the keep, the fellow in the car named himself Aripert Aribert's son, one of Schild's vassal barons, though not a man the Fox knew well. Since there was only the one car, Gerin's warriors did not hesitate to lower the drawbridge and let him into the keep.

Once in the courtyard, he jumped down from the car and looked all around, calling, "The Fox! Where is the Fox?" He didn't know Gerin by sight, either. He was about thirty-five, stocky, with sharp features and a quick, jerky way of moving.

"I'm the Fox." Gerin had made his way down from the palisade. "What's gone so wrong in Schild's barony that you had to rush here and tell me about it?"

"You have the right of it, lord prince," Aripert said, pacing back and forth. He evidently couldn't stand to hold still more than a few breaths at a time. He cracked his knuckles, one after another, till they all popped, and hardly seemed aware he was doing it. "The wild men from out of the west, the Gradi, ships full of them landed in Schild's holding. His keep held against them, and those of his vassals, too, but they burned villages and killed serfs and trampled crops and stole livestock and we're all going to be hungry this winter on account of it." He stared at Gerin, as if convinced it was the Fox's fault.

"We haven't been sitting idle, Aripert," Gerin said. Aripert gnawed dead skin at the edge of his thumbnail. Gerin wondered if he had a wife. Living with such constant fidgeting would have driven him mad. But that was not what mattered at the moment. He went on, "Your own overlord has fought against the Gradi at my side."

"So what?" Aripert said, swatting at something that might have been a gnat and might have been a figment of his imagination. "It didn't do me any good. It didn't do Schild's holding any good."

"That's not so," Gerin said. "It might have been worse for you—it might have been much worse—if we hadn't. If you don't believe me, send a messenger down to Adiatunnus and ask him."

Aripert scratched his head, tugged at his ear, and plucked a hair out of his beard. Spinning it between thumb and forefinger, he answered, "All right, maybe it would have been worse. I don't know. It was cursed bad, I tell you." He started pacing again. "How are you going to keep those bastards off the Niffet? That's what I want to know." He yanked out his knife and cleaned his nails with it.

Just watching him made Gerin tired. "I don't know how we can keep the Gradi off the Niffet," he said. "They make better ships than we do. Best we can hope for is to beat them once they get off their ships to fight. But they can pick the spots where they do that."

"Not good enough." Aripert stuck one of his newly clean fingernails deep into his ear, stared with interest at what he dug out, and wiped his hand on his breeches. "Not good enough, not even close. We have to keep them from doing that."

"Fine," Gerin said, which surprised the newcomer into several heartbeats of immobility. The Fox fixed him with a sour stare. "How?"

Aripert opened his mouth, closed it, licked his lips, noisily sucked in air, licked his lips again, and finally said, "You're the prince of the north. I'm not. You're supposed to tell that to me."

Gerin laughed. Aripert glared. Gerin glared back, and kept on laughing. "If I had a cow for everyone who's said that to me since spring," he said, "I'd eat beef the rest of my life."

That left Aripert unimpressed. "If the prince of the north doesn't have the answers, who does?" he demanded.

"Maybe no one," Gerin said, which made the vassal baron's eyes open very wide. As Aripert was scuffing the ground with one foot, the Fox thought, *Maybe Voldar.* He wouldn't say that out loud, and wished it hadn't crossed his mind. What he did say was, "You'll have to put more watchers along the river, to keep an eye out for Gradi galleys and give the alarm when they spot them. Then you can decide whether you want to show yourself in force enough to keep them from wanting to land or hole up in your keep."

Aripert started pacing again, then hopped up in the air suddenly enough to startle the Fox. Even before his feet hit the ground again, he was talking: "Well, that's something, lord prince, so it is. If these cursed Gradi come and go on the Niffet as they please, the way you say, we will have to keep a tighter watch for 'em, do those kinds of things."

"If they land, try to burn their boats," Gerin said. "They guard them, but it would be worth doing if you could. If they're stranded in our country, we can hunt them down the way we would any dangerous wild beasts."

"Aye, lord prince—sense in your words." Aripert's jaws worked, as if literally chewing up and swallowing Gerin's advice.

"Had you done any of these things before the Gradi raided you?" Gerin asked. Aripert shook his head. He gnawed some more at the skin of his thumb, looking contrite. Now the Fox glared in good earnest. "Why not?" he shouted. "You know what the Gradi did to us here this spring. By the five hells, why did you think you were immune?"

"It wasn't that so much, lord prince," Aripert said, shifting from foot to foot and twisting his body back and forth as if he were dancing. "We didn't know what to do, so we didn't do anything much. If they come back, we'll give them a better fight for your wise words."

"How much wisdom does it take to see this?" Gerin held a hand out in front of his face. "How much wisdom does it take to feel this?" He wanted to hit Aripert over the head with a rock, with luck letting in some light and fresh air, but contented himself with squeezing the minor baron's arm. "You don't need to go to the Sibyl's shrine at Ikos for advice like what I've given you. You don't need to come to me, either. All you need to do is sit down on your fundament and ask yourself a few simple questions. *Are the Gradi likely to come here? If they do, how will they come? If that's what they do, how can I best pour sand in their soup? How will they try to stop me? How can I keep them from doing that?* It's not hard, Aripert. Any man can do it, if he will." He knew he sounded as if he were pleading. He couldn't help it. He *was* pleading.

Aripert Aribert's son scratched his head. He sighed, long and deep. "What am I supposed to say, lord prince?"

"You're not supposed to say any one thing," Gerin answered, quietly now. "You're not supposed to do any one thing. You're just supposed to think for yourself."

Aripert scratched his head again. He scratched his neck. He scratched his forearm, and the back of his hand. Watching him made Gerin itch. He started scratching his own head. Aripert said, "When a serf asks me something, I don't tell him to figure it out for himself. I give him an order, and I make certain sure he follows it."

"Sometimes that works fine." Gerin was always ready to talk about the art—or maybe *magic* was a better word—of ruling. "Sometimes it keeps him from getting a different idea, one as good as yours or maybe better. And sometimes, unless you're a god—maybe even if you're a god—you're going to be flat-out wrong. If the serf blindly goes ahead and does what you tell him, you've done him wrong. Of course, sometimes he'll know you're wrong and go ahead and do what you tell him anyhow, for spite or anger or to show you up for a fool. That's why I give fewer orders like that than I used to."

"By the way you talk, you want every man doing so much for himself, there'd be no need for barons—or for a prince," Aripert added pointedly.

"If every man were as smart as every other man and if everybody got along with everyone else, that would be fine," Gerin said. "But some men can't think, and, worse, some who can won't. And some people are quarrelsome and some want what their neighbors have but don't want to work the way the neighbors did. I don't think lords will disappear from the landscape tomorrow, nor even the day after."

"Heh," Aripert said. He sketched a salute. "All right, lord prince, I'll try not to be one of those people who can think but won't. Thinking about watchers along the river is a good place to start. Beacon fires, maybe." He plucked at his beard, then tugged at an earlobe.

"A string of beacon fires would be a good thing to have," the Fox agreed. "If you do set 'em up, I'll put a watcher next to Schild's land to relay news here to Fox Keep."

"Well, that's fine, lord prince. One thing I can't do for myself is make men out of thin air. Can you spare me some soldiers to come leap on the Gradi if they do land again?"

"Not a one," Gerin answered firmly. "But if you want to arm your serfs against them, I won't say a word. Peasants don't usually make the best soldiers—the gods know that's so—but if they have weapons, they'll do the Gradi some damage, anyhow."

"But if they learn to fight, they'll do us nobles damage down the road, too," Aripert protested.

"Which has the greater weight, what may happen down the road if you do arm them or what's almost sure to happen now if you don't?" Gerin asked. Aripert bit his lip, stamped his foot, and finally nodded. He was thinking, even if he didn't like the answers he was getting; Gerin gave him credit for it. The Fox said, "Here, spend the night with us. We'll feed you; you can drink some ale with us, if any turns out to be left in the cellar."

"Uh, thank you, lord prince." Aripert sounded a little unsure of himself, as if he couldn't decide whether Gerin was joking. Since Gerin couldn't decide, either, no reason for Aripert to be able to.

Geroge came out of the great hall, braving the vicious sunlight for a chance to breathe fresh air instead of the smoke inside the castle. The Fox's men, knowing the monster's delicate condition, prudently left him alone. He might have been good-natured most of the time, but anyone feeling the aftereffects from a day's binge was liable to be on the testy side. If you were huge, hairy, and armed with teeth like a wolf's, no one wanted to find out whether you were feeling testy or not.

"Father Dyaus!" Aripert yelled, grabbing for his sword. "It's one of those horrible things! I thought they were all gone."

Gerin seized Aripert's arm and kept him from getting

the length of edged bronze out of the scabbard. Geroge swung his intimidating gaze toward Aripert. "Well!" he said, with almost as much condescension as Mavrix could have loaded into the word. "Some people don't insult strangers just for the fun of it, or so the Fox tells me, anyhow." His long, narrow nostrils were ideally suited to sniffing.

For once, Aripert stood completely motionless. He stared at the monster. By the look on his face, he would have sooner expected one of the logs on the palisade to say something to him than Geroge. "If you'll look closely, you'll notice he is wearing breeches," Gerin said. "We're friends."

"Friends," Aripert repeated through frozen lips. "You have some . . . unusual friends, lord prince."

Gerin set a hand on his shoulder. "Oh, I don't know. You're not so unusual as all that, are you?"

Geroge got the point of the gibe before Aripert did. The monster started to throw back his head and roar laughter. One or the other or both of those must have hurt, for he stopped with a grimace that showed off his formidable dental equipment. Aripert started to draw his sword again, but checked himself before Gerin had to stop him.

The Fox introduced the monster to the vassal baron, then explained for Aripert's benefit: "He was deep in the ale pot yesterday, the very first time, and he's feeling it now."

"Oh." Aripert stuck out a finger at Gerin. "Now I understand why you were wondering if you had any ale left. Must take up a bit to fill up one his size."

"Not one," Geroge said. "Three: me, Tharma, and Van of the Strong Arm."

Aripert didn't know who Tharma was, but he knew about Van. He let out an awed whistle. Gerin said, "There, you see? You can think, after all."

"What I think is, I'd like to have seen that," Aripert said. "From a safe distance, I mean. When you see a Gradi galley out on the Niffet, it's pretty, too, but you don't want it getting any closer."

"A good deal of truth there," Gerin said. "If we weather the storm, we'll have to see about making galleys of our own. But that's for later, in the great by-and-by. For now, come into the hall and we'll start feeding you. And you can watch Geroge and Tharma be very moderate tonight, unless I miss my guess." He turned to the monster. "How about it, Geroge? Feel like having your head pound like a drum again tomorrow morning?"

Geroge held up both hands in a gesture of genuine horror. "Oh, no, lord prince! Doing that once was plenty for me."

"He's not stupid," Aripert said, hopping into the air in surprise. He belied his own words, speaking as if Geroge wasn't there or couldn't understand even when giving a compliment. But then he went on, "Plenty of ordinary men who don't think getting drunk once is enough. Plenty of ordinary men who don't think getting drunk once in a day is enough, come to that."

"Aye," the Fox agreed mournfully. "We both know too many like that. Everyone knows too many like that. Well, come on. We'll see if we can make you happy without having you sleep in the rushes under the table when you're done."

Aripert Aribert's son rode out of Fox Keep the next morning, every bit as fidgety as he had been when he rode in. Gerin dared hope he would put some of that restless energy to work watching for the Gradi and resisting them if they struck Schild's holding again.

A few days later, he got word from a trader who had come out of the forests north of the Niffet with a load of fine beeswax and amber that the Gradi had also raided that side of the river. The trader, a lean, weathered, balding man named Cedoal the Honest (a sobriquet the Fox would have bet he'd invented himself), said, "I didn't see the bastards my own self, lord prince; you got to understand that. But I did see the woodsrunners who were running from 'em. They like to swamp the village where I was at, and every one of 'em had worse tales to tell than the next."

That was logically impossible, but Gerin didn't press the merchant about it. Instead, he tried to figure out exactly when the raid had taken place. He wished he had Aripert back, to nail down the exact day. As best he could tell, though, both raids had probably been by the same band. Figuring out where Cedoal had been in relation to Schild's holding wasn't easy, either. The Fox thought the Gradi had hit Schild first and then raided the Trokmoi on the way west, but knew he couldn't be sure.

And then, a few days after that, Gradi galleys came rowing up the Niffet toward Fox Keep. Fires from Schild's holding warned of them, so Aripert had not only thought but also acted. "We'll smash them, Father!" Duren cried as he drove the chariot with Gerin and Van out toward the river. The Fox had decided to meet the raiders on the bank, not wanting them to ravage fields and assail the peasant village again.

But the Gradi did not land. Instead, sails taking advantage of the wind from the west and oars working with drilled precision, they propelled their galleys past Fox Keep and on up the Niffet. Gerin and a good many Elabonians shot arrows at them, but most of the shafts fell short: the Niffet was a broad stream, and a ship closer to the northern bank than the southern all but immune to archery.

Van normally disdained the bow in war. Seeing that the Gradi were not going to stop and fight, though, he grabbed the strongest bow any of Gerin's comrades carried: it belonged to Drungo Drago's son. Drungo had put a couple of arrows close to the galley. He growled when Van took the bow from him, but stared, slack-jawed, as the outlander bent it till the wood creaked and threatened to snap, then let fly.

One of the Gradi who weren't rowing—by that, a captain of some sort—went down. The Elabonians raised a cheer. Drungo bowed to Van. "I thought I put everything into that bow it would take," he said. "I was wrong."

"Not bad for a lucky shot, was it?" Van said, laughing. He proceeded to empty Drungo's quiver at the galleys, and made a couple of more hits. Neither was as spectacular as that first had been. Whatever Van did, he had a flair for the dramatic.

Gerin watched in some consternation as the Gradi kept sailing east up the Niffet. "What are they doing?" he demanded, perhaps of the Elabonian gods—who, as usual, did not answer. "I thought they meant to close with me and find out once for all who would rule the northlands."

"What else could they want?" Duren demanded. "Till they've beaten you, they haven't really accomplished anything."

"Oh, I don't know, lad." As he often did, Van had a ruthlessly pragmatic way of looking at things. "If they plunder other people, they bring home loot and slaves with less risk and cost to themselves. And we won't be able to rest easy, not with them farther up the river than we are. For all we know, they may try and hit us on their way back toward the ocean."

"Let's make life difficult for them," Gerin said. He hadn't thought of setting up a chain of watchfires east of Fox Keep, not imagining the Gradi would go on past his holding. But that didn't mean he couldn't send riders east to warn the petty barons along the banks of the Niffet the raiders were coming.

Watching the cars rattle off down the road, Van said, "I wonder if they'll get there ahead of the galleys. Horses tire out same as men do, and the Gradi have the wind working for them, though they are rowing against the current, and that's not easy."

"It's in the hands of the gods," Gerin said, and then wished he hadn't: the Gradi gods were too greedy by half to suit him. More consolingly, he added, "I've done everything I can."

"I wish we could move the whole army after them," Duren said.

"That we can't do," Gerin answered. "If we did, they'd let us stay with them for a while, and then they'd turn around right in the middle of the Niffet, take down their sails, and use oars and current to rush back here. They'd swoop down on the keep before we could get here, and that," he added with what he thought of as praiseworthy understatement, "would be very bad."

"Aye, you're right, Fox," Van said. "I'm all for charging straight ahead most times, but not now. If we run away from what's most important to us, we end up losing it, sure as sure."

"Well, we haven't lost it this time, the gods be praised." Gerin didn't know whether that was irony in his voice or the hope that, if the Elabonian gods repeatedly heard themselves addressed, they would pay more attention to this corner of the world.

He waved. The army rode back from the banks of the Niffet toward Fox Keep. The men on the palisade raised a cheer. So did the serfs who lived in the village near the keep. Some of them came out of the fields and huts to congratulate the warriors on keeping the Gradi from landing. Gerin didn't know whether those congratulations were truly in order, or whether the Gradi had intended to bypass his holding from the beginning. If the peasants were so eager to approve of him, though, he was willing to let them.

Among the serfs came Fulda. Her fellows regarded her with more than a little awe. So did a good many of the warriors; she hadn't been shy about spreading the story of what had happened inside the shack that served as Gerin's magical laboratory. The proof of how the other peasants in the village felt was that they'd been doing a lot of her work for her since her encounter with Mavrix.

The Fox had never doubted she was pregnant by the Sithonian god, and, if he had, those doubts would have perished. Not only had her courses failed to come, but she glowed in a way that was similar to the glow other pregnant women got, but so magnified that Gerin would almost have taken oath she didn't need a lamp by night.

That wasn't so; incurably curious, he'd gone over to the peasant village one night to find out. But he did note that the night ghosts, perhaps sensing the demigod in her belly, stayed far away from the village, and that even those whose wails could be heard at a distance seemed less cold and fierce than was their wont.

"Lord prince," Fulda said now. She still treated him with respect, perhaps from lifelong habit, perhaps because he was married to Selatre, who had also known intimacy with a god, even if intimacy of a different sort from hers.

"How are you feeling today?" he asked her. He knew he sounded cautious. How else could he sound when, though she was still one of his serfs, the god who had impregnated her might be listening?

"I'm well, thank you," she said. Her smile, like everything else about her, was radiant. One of the advantages of having a god for the father of her child, it seemed, was immunity to morning sickness.

"Good," Gerin said. "That's good." No, he hadn't figured out how to react to Fulda. She was a good-looking young woman, certainly, but not very bright. And yet Mavrix had chosen to sire a child on her. The Fox shrugged. A fertility god no doubt cared for beauty more than wit. After all, that had been the point in having her there in the first place.

Rihwin the Fox, mounted on a horse, came up to Fulda. Gerin suspected Rihwin would sooner have mounted her. She smiled up at him in a way that suggested she might have been interested in the same thing.

"Rihwin, are you trying to make Mavrix angry at you again?" Gerin asked.

"Who, me?" his fellow Fox asked, looking innocent so convincingly as to be altogether unconvincing. "Why should Mavrix be angry at me for conversing with this charming lady when I, in a manner of speaking, introduced the two of them? And why, furthermore, should he be angry with me if I do rather more than converse with her? He could never doubt the paternity of the child to be born, and I would raise it as one of my own. He might even be grateful to me."

Rihwin, as far as Gerin could see, was thinking with his lance, not his head. Gerin sighed. Rihwin would do whatever he would do, and would probably end up paying the penalty for it. He did pay those penalties without complaint; Gerin gave him that much. As far as Gerin was concerned, not putting yourself in a position where you would have to pay them would have been wiser yet, but he'd learned Rihwin, like a lot of people, didn't think that way.

"Be careful," he said to Rihwin. Rihwin nodded, almost as if he would heed. Gerin sighed again.

"Lord prince?" Carlun Vepin's son still spoke hesitantly whenever he needed to address Gerin. The Fox might have made him steward, but he had the ingrained habits of a serf—and knowing he thrived by Gerin's sufferance couldn't have made matters any easier. But, hesitantly or not, he went on, "Lord prince, I do need to speak to you for a moment."

"Here I am," Gerin said, agreeably enough. "What's troubling you?"

Carlun looked around the great hall. Several warriors sat here and there along the benches, some drinking ale, one gnawing the roasted leg of a fowl, three or four more rolling dice. Lowering his voice, Carlun said, "Lord prince, may I speak with you in private?"

"I suppose so," Gerin said. "Shall we walk down toward the village, then? That should do the job."

Carlun agreed at once. Whenever he got out of Fox Keep these days, he seemed a flower spreading itself in the bright sunshine. And the sunshine remained bright and hot. The drubbing Mavrix had given Stribog did keep the Gradi god from meddling with the weather.

"Here we are," Gerin said. "I asked you once, so I'll ask you twice: what's troubling you?"

"Lord prince, how long will Fox Keep be full of warriors?" Carlun asked. "How much longer will they stay here?"

"How long?" The Fox frowned. "Till we've beaten the Gradi, or till they've beaten us, whichever happens first. Why?"

"Because, lord prince, they are eating us—eating you—out of house and home," Carlun answered. "If you hadn't been so prudent about storing up food, your larder would long since have been bare. As things are, this will be a hungry, thirsty winter even without your vassals here."

"What do you suggest I do, then?" Gerin asked. "Shall I send everyone home, with the Gradi still on the Niffet east of here? Shall I surrender to the Gradi? Is that better than letting them make me poor instead of prosperous?"

Carlun licked his lips. "That's not, uh, what I had in mind, lord prince. But you do need to know that even the supplies you have stored up won't last forever."

"Oh, I know that all too well," Gerin said. "Every time I go down into the cellars and see another storage jar opened or another jar gone, it gives me something new to worry about, and I have plenty of things already, thanks."

"Every time you go down into the cellars—" Carlun repeated. He stared at the Fox. "Lord prince, I didn't know you did that. As far as I could see, lords know only about taking, not about saving and watching."

"That's because you've looked at things with the eyes of a serf," Gerin answered. *It's also because I look further ahead than most lords*, he thought, but he didn't say that out loud. What he did say was, "I have to manage this entire holding the way you ran first your house and then the village. Here, I'll tell you what I have left down there—" He started reeling off jars of ale, of wheat, of barley, of rye, of beans, of peas, of salted beef and mutton, of smoked pork, so many hams, so many sausages, so many hung joints of beef, and on and on till Carlun's eyes all but popped from his head.

"Lord prince," the peasant-turned-steward whispered when the Fox was finally through, "I couldn't have done that without checking the latest records, nor come close to it, but I think from what I do remember of those records, your memory is as near perfect as makes no difference."

"I would have made a splendid scholar," Gerin said, "since I have a jackdaw's memory for useless bits of this and that. Every now and again, it comes in handy in the world where I find myself."

"Lord prince, if you remember all these things, why

did you put me in the place where you put me?" Carlun asked. "Not that I'm not grateful mind, when I think what you could have done, but you don't need me. You could do the job yourself."

"Of course I could," Gerin said, with confidence so automatic he didn't notice it himself. "But with you doing it, I don't have to. And so I don't, not really. If we do run low, you're the one who's going to make sure we lay in more supplies from . . . somewhere. And if you do a bad job at it, I'll throw you out on your ear."

"Oh, I've known that all along, lord prince," Carlun said. Both men smiled, although they both knew Gerin hadn't been joking: he expected no less from those around him than he did from himself. Carlun's smile faded first. He asked, "How am I to pay for whatever I have to bring in?"

"You have my leave to spend my gold and silver," Gerin answered. "I wouldn't have brought you here if I didn't intend to let you do that. I do expect you to spend as little of it as you can."

Carlun bowed his head. "I wouldn't think of doing anything else." He grinned wryly. "I wouldn't dare do anything else."

"No, eh?" Gerin hadn't said one word about checking on Carlun. He didn't intend to say one word about checking on Carlun. He did, however, intend to check on him. If Carlun couldn't figure that out for himself, the Fox had made a mistake in promoting him rather than sending him off to some other village. And if Carlun tried cheating, he'd find he'd made a mistake himself.

They were almost out to the village where he had been headman not long before. Abruptly, he spun on his heel and started walking back toward Fox Keep again, much faster than he'd left it. "I don't want to go back to the hut that used to be mine," he said. "I don't even want to see it, not up close. Do you understand that, lord prince?"

"Maybe I do," the Fox said. "Is it that you don't want to be reminded of how you started out—and of how you could end up?"

Carlun jerked as if Gerin had stuck him with the pin from a fibula. "Did you work magic to see that, lord prince?"

"No," Gerin answered, and immediately wished he'd said *yes*—if Carlun thought his magic better than it was, he might be more tempted to walk the straight and narrow. But, having answered honestly, he went on, "Seeing that one wasn't hard. When you were headman, you had to know what the rest of the people in the village were thinking, didn't you?" When Carlun nodded, the Fox finished, "I've had to do that for my holding, and for much longer than you needed to do it. I've seen a lot, I've remembered a lot, and I can put all that together. Do you follow me?"

A lot of men—some of them his vassal barons—wouldn't have. They remembered little and learned less, going through life, or so it seemed to Gerin, more than half-blind. But Carlun, whether honest and reliable or not, was anything but stupid. "You may not be casting a spell," he said, "but that doesn't mean it isn't magic."

Since Gerin had had the same thought about the craft of ruling men as recently as Aripert's arrival at Fox Keep, he glanced toward Carlun with considerable respect. As they came back to the keep, he said, "I have your gracious permission to keep the garrison here a while longer, eh?"

"Of course, lord prince," Carlun said, sounding on the lordly side himself. When Gerin gave him a sharp look, his burst of bravado collapsed and he added, "Not that you need it, mind you."

"There is that," Gerin agreed, happy Carlun knew his place after all.

Dagref, Clotild, and Blestar were playing with Maeva and Kor. Gerin watched the game with faint bemusement. Dagref was not only oldest but sharpest witted. A lot of the time, he couldn't be bothered playing with his sibs; his mind, though not his body or spirit, was nearly that of an adult. When he did join them and Van's children, the role he saw for himself was halfway between overseer and god: he invented not just rules but a whole imaginary world, and put himself and them through their paces in it.

"No, Maeva!" he shouted. "I told you. Don't you remember? The bark of that tree" —a stick— "is poisonous."

"No, it's not," Maeva said. To prove her point, she picked up the stick and whacked Dagref with it. "There. You see?" But for the high pitch of her voice, that self-satisfied directness might have come straight from Van. "Didn't hurt me a bit."

"You're not playing right," Dagref said angrily: by his tone, he could imagine no felony more heinous.

"Be careful, son," Gerin muttered under his breath. Dagref was older, but Maeva, girl or no girl, was both stronger and more agile. If Dagref forced a confrontation, he'd lose. If he wanted to get his way here, he'd have to figure out how to do it without getting into a fight.

Just then, Geroge and Tharma came out of the great hall. All the children greeted them with glad cries. The brewing quarrel between Dagref and Maeva was forgotten. The two monsters, though now approaching adulthood, had always been part of the children's games at Fox Keep. They were bigger and stronger than any of the others, which more than balanced their also being duller. Had they been bad-tempered, their strength would have made them terrors. Since they weren't, they became companions all the more desirable.

"What game are you playing?" Tharma asked Dagref.

"Well," he said importantly, "Clotild here is a wizard, and she's turned Kor into a longtooth" —a role well suited for one of Kor's fierce, blustery temper— "and we're all seeking ways to get him back his own shape. Maeva seems to be immune to poisons, and so—" He went on laying out the framework of the world that existed only inside his own head. Gerin noted he'd incorporated Maeva's recalcitrance into the structure of the game.

Geroge laughed, loud and boisterously—so loud and boisterously, Gerin's ears quivered in suspicion. Geroge sounded as if he'd been dipping deep into the ale jar again, in spite of earlier promises. He said, "That's a *good* game!" His voice quivered with enthusiasm. "Let's make the longtooth fly and see what happens then."

He picked up Kor and threw him high in the air— so high, he had time to circle under the little boy before he came down. The circling was wobbly—yes, he'd been drinking more than he should have.

Gerin started toward him on the dead run, but Geroge plucked Kor out of the air neat as you please. Tharma grabbed Blestar and threw him even higher. Even more than it had when Kor soared, Gerin's heart leaped into his mouth. He breathed out a harsh sigh of relief as his little son came down safe.

He and Kor both squealed with glee at their flights. The Fox was less amused. "This game is over," he said in a voice filled with as much doom as he could manage.

That evidently wasn't enough. Barons and Trokmê chieftains quailed before him. His own children, along with Van's and with Geroge and Tharma, protested loudly and bitterly. He held his ground. "We were fine," Clotild said, stamping her foot. "I wanted to go next. No one got hurt."

"No, not this time. But you were lucky, because someone might have," Gerin answered. He'd long since found out that arguments based on *might have* were for all practical purposes useless with children. So it proved here. But when he got a whiff of Geroge's breath, he had another, better argument. "Baivers and barley!" he exclaimed, wrinkling his nose. "You didn't just dive into the ale jar, you went swimming around in there."

Geroge looked as shamefaced as a tiddly monster could. The result would have made anyone who didn't know him flee in terror, but Gerin recognized the display of fangs as placatory, not hostile. "I'm sorry," Geroge said with a growl that also sounded more fearsome than it was. "I don't know what came over me. But I feel so good with the ale inside." He punctuated that with an enormous belch. Gerin's children and Van's dissolved in gales of laughter.

The Fox felt like laughing, too, but didn't let his face show it. He rounded on Tharma. "I thought you had better sense than he did," he said accusingly.

"I'm sorry," she answered, hanging her homely head. "But he started drinking the ale, and I—"

"If he decided to jump off the palisade and break his fool neck, would you do it, too, just because he did it?" Gerin had trotted that one out so many times for his own children, it sprang forth of its own accord now. He'd used it on Geroge and Tharma a few times, too, generally to good effect. Today, though, Tharma looked back at him. "It wasn't like that," she protested. "It was like, like . . . something was pushing at us to drink the ale."

"Probably the same sort of thing that pushes at me when I feel like getting into the candied fruit or the honey cakes," Dagref said, sounding far more dubious than someone his age had any business doing. *What will he be like when he grows up?* Gerin thought uneasily. His eldest by Selatre would be a man to reckon with . . . if nobody murdered him young.

"It wasn't like that," Tharma said. "It really was . . . I could almost feel something pushing me toward the jar." Geroge's big head jerked up and down, up and down as he nodded agreement.

Gerin started to shout at both of them for being not just liars but stubborn liars to boot. He stopped, though, before the words passed his lips. Mavrix had used Rihwin as an instrument in a way much like this, prodding him to get drunk on wine and afford the Sithonian god an easy conduit into the northlands. But this wasn't Mavrix, who had nothing to do with ale. It was . . .

"Baivers." Gerin's mouth shaped the name of the god in silent astonishment. Baivers was as Elabonian a deity as any. And, up till now, the Elabonian gods had been uniformly quiet, even when Voldar and her Gradi cohorts added their weight to the invaders' power.

Up till now . . . Gerin wondered if he was a drowning man grabbing at straws as he tried to stay afloat. The affection Geroge and Tharma suddenly felt for ale might have nothing whatever to do with Baivers, might, in fact, have nothing to do with anything save an increasingly well-developed thirst, of the sort that turned ordinary men into drunks with no divine intervention whatever.

"Well," the Fox said, more to himself than to the monsters, much more to himself than to the still-disappointed children, "if you're going to grab at straws, by Dyaus—and by Baivers—*grab* at them. Don't let them slip through your hands."

"What *are* you talking about, Father?" Dagref, as usual, sounded highly insulted when Gerin said something he didn't follow.

"Never mind," Gerin said absently, which insulted

his son all the more. To compound his crime, he took no notice of Dagref's annoyance. Instead, he seized Geroge's arm in one hand and Tharma's in the other. "Come back to the great hall with me, you two. You're going to drink some more ale."

Geroge greeted that pronouncement with a roar of delight. Tharma said, "You're not going to make us drink till we hurt the next day, are you?" That made Geroge thoughtful; the memory of his first hangover was after all still painfully vivid in him, too.

Had Gerin been able to get away with not answering that, he would have done it. He didn't think he could, and the prospect of enraging two monsters, each bigger and stronger than he, was disquieting at best. He said, "I don't know. I want to find out why you like ale so much lately. I want to see if a god is meddling with your fate."

He wished Baivers' meddling weren't so subtle he had trouble telling if it was even there. Till the Gradi came, he had enjoyed being free from interference at the hands of the Elabonian gods. Now, just when he really would have relished interference, he wasn't sure whether he had any or not.

In the great hall, Carlun Vepin's son sat at a corner table, well away from the four or five warriors in the chamber. The steward was quietly nursing a mug of ale. When Gerin called for another jar to be brought up from the cellar, Carlun's face expressed ostentatious disapproval. Gerin was just as ostentatious about ignoring him.

Geroge smacked his lips as he guzzled ale. The Fox studied him in the same way he might have studied some curious new beast that had wandered in from the forest. "How do I find out why you've got so fond of ale?" he murmured.

"Because it tastes good? Because it makes me feel good?" Geroge suggested.

"But you've been drinking it since you were tiny," the Fox said. Imagining Geroge as tiny wasn't easy now. Gerin persisted nonetheless: "It made you feel good then, too, didn't it?"

"Not as good as I feel now," the monster said enthusiastically. Beside him, Tharma nodded, also with great vigor. She drained her jack of ale, then filled it again. Carlun tried to catch Gerin's eye. Gerin didn't let him.

"Does it feel better because you're drinking more now," Gerin asked, "or is there something over and above that, too?"

Both monsters gave the question serious consideration. Gerin admired them for that, the more so considering how much ale they'd already drunk. A lot of ordinary people he knew wouldn't have looked so hard for an answer. At last, Tharma said, "I think it's made us feel better than we did since the time we drank and drank with Van."

"Didn't feel so good afterwards, though," Geroge said, making a horrible face at the memory. As if to help himself forget, he drank deep.

Gerin, meanwhile, called down curses on his friend's head. But that wasn't fair, either; a god might have been nudging Van into getting the monsters drunk that day. For that matter, Gerin thought he was acting as a free agent now, but he was honest enough to admit he didn't know for certain whether he really was one. How much did being prince of fleas mean when a dog started scratching?

That thought led nowhere, though. Whether he was truly his own man or nothing more than a tool of the gods, he had to act as if he were free and independent. Not even a god could restore to you an opportunity you'd missed yesterday.

He studied Geroge and Tharma. They weren't paying

much attention to him, or to anything but their ale. When he was down below Biton's shrine at Ikos, he'd wondered whether the monsters had gods of their own. Now that thought came back to him. If they had gods, what did those gods think of two of their number's being left aboveground when Biton and Mavrix had returned all the others to their gloomy haunts? Even more to the point, what did they think about the Gradi?

He shook his head. Here he was, building castles in the air—or rather, castles under the ground. He didn't know for a fact that the monsters had any gods at all. Geroge and Tharma gave the Elabonian deities the same absentminded reverence he did himself. Why not? That was what they'd learned from him.

How was he supposed to find out if they had gods of their own? Asking them didn't seem likely to give him his answer. Whom to ask, then? Biton would probably know, but, even if he did, he'd cloak whatever reply he gave to the Fox in such ambiguity, it wouldn't come clear till it was too late to do him any good.

Who else might know? He thought of Mavrix, and wished he hadn't. Disaster felt very close whenever he dealt with the Sithonian fertility god—and Mavrix had already shown he despised the monsters, which meant he was certain to despise their gods, too.

Then he realized Baivers might know. The god of barley and brewing was intimately connected to the earth, and so were the monsters. If Gerin invoked him, Baivers would be a logical deity to ask. *If* Gerin invoked him—if he *could* invoke him—the Elabonian gods seemed so uninterested in the world, though, that it might not be possible.

The Fox had resolved to try when the lookout in the watchtower winded his horn and cried, "The Gradi! The Gradi are coming down the river!"

Baivers forgotten, Gerin rushed out of the great hall.

Men on the palisade were pointing east. The sentry had got it right, then: these were the Gradi who had gone up the Niffet to see what damage they could do beyond Gerin's holding, not a new band coming to join them. That was something, if not much.

"We'll greet them as we did before: on the riverbank," the Fox ordered. "If they want to try to land here in the face of that, let them, and may they have joy of it."

Ahead of the rest, he sent out Rihwin the Fox and the other adventurous sorts who rode horses. They had their animals ready for action faster than teams could be hitched to chariots. He also sent out a fair number of men on foot: the more resistance the Gradi faced at the water's edge, the less likely they were to try to land.

By the time Van, Duren, and he were rattling across the meadow toward the Niffet, the raiders' war galleys were already passing Fox Keep. The Gradi shouted unintelligible insults across the water, but stayed near the Trokmê bank of the river and showed no desire to clash with foes so obviously ready to receive them.

"Cowards!" Gerin's men yelled. "Spineless dogs! Eunuchs! White-livered wretches!" The Gradi probably could make no more sense of their pleasantries than they could of those coming from the raiders.

Duren said, "The gods be praised, we frightened them away."

"Here, for now, yes," Gerin said. "But what did they do, farther upstream? Whatever it is, they've come faster than the news of it." When he was younger, fits of gloom had threatened to overwhelm him. They came on him less often these days, but he felt the edge of one now. "They can do as they like, and we have to respond to it. With them controlling the river, they can pick and choose where to make their fights. Where we seem strong, they leave us alone. Where we're weak, they strike. And when we try to hit back over land, their gods make even moving against them the next thing to impossible."

"Have to light our beacons, to warn Aripert and the rest of Schild's vassals still in his holding," Van said.

"Right," Gerin answered, with a grateful glance at his friend. The outlander had shown him something simple and practical he could do that would help his cause. He shouted orders. A couple of Rihwin's riders went galloping back to the keep for torches with which to light the watchfires.

Before long, the first fire was blazing, glowing red and sending a great pillar of smoke into the sky. Gerin peered west. His own watchers quickly spotted the warning fire and started another to pass the word into Schild's holding. And, soon enough, another column of smoke rose, this one small and thin in the distance. The Fox nodded somber approval. Either Aripert Aribert's son or another of Schild's vassals—but someone, at any rate—was alert. The Gradi might land again in Schild's holding, but he did not think they would be delighted with their reception.

"We've done something worthwhile there," he said, and both Van and Duren nodded.

Hagop son of Hovan was a man who put Gerin in mind of Widin Simrin's son: a baron who'd taken over his holding as a youngster but who had matured into a good enough overlord for it. He acknowledged the Fox his suzerain, paid him his feudal dues, and sent men to fight on his behalf. Had all Gerin's vassals been so tractable, he would have had an easier time of it by far.

Now, though, he was a man in despair. "Lord prince," he cried as he got down from his chariot, "the Gradi dealt me a heavy blow, and it fell on me all the harder because so many came here to fight the raiders along with you. I never dreamed they could sail up the Niffet and strike my holding." His swarthy, big-nosed face was still haggard with shock.

"I didn't dream of it, either," Gerin answered. "That's the only excuse I can make for not setting up watchfires running east from here. Using oars and sails both, the Gradi outran the news of their coming. I did send out riders to try to warn you and the others upstream. I'm sorry they didn't get there in time."

"So am I," Hagop said bitterly. "They got there half a day after the Gradi did. I give them credit; they fought at my side, and a couple of them were wounded. They're still back at my keep. But the damage is done, lord prince, and we'll be a long time getting over it."

What he meant was, *You are my lord, and your duty is to keep such things from happening to me. You failed me.* That he was too polite to come out and scream what he meant, as so many of Gerin's vassals would have done, made the Fox feel worse, not better.

Gerin said, "They're bad enemies, worse than the Trokmoi and" —he looked around to make sure Geroge and Tharma were out of earshot— "worse than the monsters, too. I have a couple of things I intend to try to see if I can't get the upper hand on them, but it hasn't happened yet. I'm sorry."

Hagop's dour countenance immediately became more confident. "If you think you can overcome them, lord prince, I am sure it will be so in the end."

I wish I were, Gerin thought. Explaining exactly how worried he was, though, struck him as less than wise. The more you seemed to believe in yourself, the more your vassals would believe in you . . . till you let them down. Hagop, luckily, didn't seem to think he'd been let down for good—not yet, anyhow.

Hagop asked, "How long do you intend keeping my vassals under your direct command, lord prince? I tell you true, I would not be sorry to see them back in my holding to stand off the Gradi, should the raiders come again."

"I aim to hold them here through the summer, while we can move against the Gradi," Gerin answered. To his great relief, Hagop accepted that with no more than another frown. If Gerin's leading vassals started pulling *their* vassals out from under him, he wouldn't be able to accomplish anything against the invaders.

In short order, he realized, he wouldn't be prince of the north any more, either. He'd be one petty baron among many, with no more power and no more reach than any of the rest. And the Gradi would eat up the northlands a barony or two at a time, and after a while a new, cold, dismal Gradihome would arise here. Voldar would be very happy, no doubt. So would the Gradi. The Elabonians, even the Trokmoi, would have less reason to rejoice.

"Not that I want to jog your elbow—" Hagop began, an opening almost invariably a lie. So it proved here, for he continued, "—but whatever you're going to set in motion against the Gradi, the gods grant you start it soon. The busier they are answering us, the less chance they'll have to make us answer them."

That was inarguably true. It also marched with Gerin's own thoughts. He said, "I intend to start as soon as I can. I still have some more sorcerous research to undertake before I can begin, though."

As he'd hoped, mentioning magic impressed Hagop. His vassal said, "Lord prince, if you know a spell for turning the lot of those buggers into toads, that would be a great thing."

"So it would," Gerin agreed. He didn't say anything past that. If Hagop wanted to conclude he did have such a spell, that was Hagop's concern. By the awestruck look on Hagop's face, he wanted to conclude just that.

"I hope your spell succeeds," he breathed.

"So do I," the Fox replied. He still hadn't said that the spell was one for the batrachifaction of the Gradi. He always hoped his spells succeeded, and knew such hope was always urgently necessary. Repeatedly finding himself in deep trouble had made him try spells a half-trained, lightly talented wizard had no business undertaking. Here he was in deep trouble again, and about to go into sorcery over his head once more, too.

"How soon can you do the—what did you call it?—the research, that was the word you used?" Hagop asked.

"I have to go through the volumes in my library. It will be a couple of days," Gerin told him. "I don't care for much companionship when I incant, but if you'd like to stay and see the results of the magic, you're more than welcome."

Most of his vassals would have accepted at once. Hagop shook his head. "I thank you, lord prince, but no. I shall go back to my holding after tonight. My people need me there. They need more than me, but I am willing to believe—for now—you need my vassals more. I trust you will use them wisely."

"I hope so." Gerin bowed to Hagop. "I'm lucky to have you for a vassal; your serfs are lucky to have you for a lord."

"They do not think so right now," Hagop answered. "If your research and your spell go as you would have them go, that may yet prove so, though. The gods grant you do it well, and that you do it soon." He plainly meant, *What are you waiting for?*

Gerin went up to the library. He had the feeling Hagop was right—every moment he delayed invited disaster. But if he was going to summon Baivers, to dicker with the god to aid him against the Gradi and Voldar, he wanted to learn everything he could about him before he started.

When you'd worshiped a god all your life, you took him for granted. Gerin poured Baivers a libation whenever he drank ale, as did every other Elabonian in the northlands and down in whatever was left of the Empire of Elabon south of the High Kirs. In return, Baivers made the barley flourish and made it ferment into ale. He was very reliable about that. Beyond it, he wasn't often a pushy god, of the sort who frequently stuck his nose into human affairs.

What the Fox wanted to find out from his scrolls and codices was how to make Baivers pushy, how to make him want to intervene in the northlands. As he began working the handles of a scroll, he shook his head. What he really wanted to find was whether there was any way to make Baivers pushy. If Baivers was resolutely confined to his one power, what point in summoning him?

Baivers was the son of Father Dyaus and a daughter of the earth goddess. Gerin knew that, of course, as he knew most of the other bits and pieces of lore he dug out about the god of barley. But they weren't things he commonly thought about; reading of them was a quicker way to call them to mind than rummaging through his memory, good though that was.

Selatre came in, saw what he was doing, and pulled out another two scrolls and a codex for him. "These talk about the god, too," she said, and then, cautiously, "Have you found anything that will help you?"

"Not as much as I'd like," he said, his voice edgy with discontent. "By most of this, and by most of everything I've seen, once barley turns to ale, Baivers is content." He paced back and forth. "I don't want him content. I want him angry. I want him furious. He's a power of the earth, and Mavrix half told me a power of the earth was my best hope against Voldar and the Gradi gods."

"Is he the right one?" Selatre asked. "Many powers rest in the earth."

"I know. But Mavrix wouldn't have been shy about naming most of them. He despises Baivers. He wouldn't come out and say, 'I failed, but this god I detest might succeed.' He wouldn't *say* it, but I think it's what he meant."

After considering that, Selatre gravely nodded. "Yes, that rings true. Mavrix reminds me of a child who can't admit he isn't always the best at something and, even when it's plain he isn't, won't give the one who really is his due."

"The trouble is, you can't take a god, turn him over your knee, and spank that kind of foolishness out of him." Gerin let out a long, weary sigh. "But oh, Father Dyaus, how I wish you could."

IX

Geroge and Tharma stared fearfully at the interior of the shack where Gerin worked—or tried to work—magic. As he had with his own children and Van's, the Fox had warned them of the dire consequences they would suffer if they ever so much as set a toe inside. The monsters had taken him more seriously than the children had; he'd never had to punish either of them.

"It's all right," he said now, for about the fourth time. "You're here with me, so that's different." Constant repetition eventually eased the monsters' worries. Gerin wondered if it should have. The mischief they might have raised coming in by themselves was as nothing next to the disaster of a spell gone awry.

"What do we need to do?" Geroge asked.

"Well, for starters, you get to drink some ale," Gerin answered. That made both monsters visibly cheerier. Gerin used a knife to cut the pitch sealing the stopper of a fresh jar. He dipped out large jacks for Geroge and Tharma, and half a jack's worth for himself. Normally, he would no sooner have tried magic after drinking ale than he would have tried leaping off the palisade headfirst, but when the god whose aid he sought was also the deity who turned malted barley to ale, what he would normally do took second place to that special concern.

He filled the monsters' jacks after they emptied them, thanking all the gods—Baivers in particular—they didn't grow rowdy or fierce as they took on ale. He sipped at

294

his own jack, too. He wanted to feel the ale ever so slightly, but not so much that it interfered with the passes and chants he would have to make.

Selatre spread seed barley and unthreshed ears of the grain on the worktable in the shack. She stayed sober. If the conjuration went very wrong, she would try to set it right. Gerin did not think that would be the problem. Getting Baivers to respond at all would be the hard part.

"We begin," the Fox said. Selatre stood quiet, watchfully waiting. Geroge and Tharma watched, too, their deep-set eyes wide with wonder as Gerin began to chant, begging the boon of Baivers' presence. He praised the god for barley, not just transformed as ale, but also as porridge and even as bread, though barley flour refused to rise as high as that ground from wheat: *a little hypocrisy in a good cause never hurt anyone*, he thought.

When he began his song in praise of ale, he made sure he set it to the tune of a drinking song he knew Van had taught to Geroge and Tharma. He gestured, and the monsters, quick on the uptake for their kind, began to sing. Their voices were unlovely, but he hoped that would not matter: unlike Mavrix, Baivers was not a snob in such matters.

Once started, the monsters didn't stop singing. That suited Gerin fine. If they didn't attract the god's attention, nothing would. That nothing would, however, remained dismayingly possible. As he generally did when dismayed, the Fox carried on as if success were assured.

He discovered that changing from the chant in the tune of the drinking song to a new one was harder than he'd expected, because having Geroge and Tharma braying out the one tune made him struggle to keep the other. Some of the ancillary spells he was using required quick and difficult passes from the right hand, too. For most wizards, that would have made matters simpler. The left-handed Fox found it a nuisance.

"Come forth!" he cried at last. "Come forth, great Baivers, lord of barley, lord of ale! Come forth, come forth, come forth!"

Nothing happened. He turned away from the barley on the worktable, convinced he had failed. What was the point to trying to summon the Elabonian gods? They might have all gone off on holiday, leaving their portion of the world to look after itself. But now other gods were looking—hungrily—at that portion of the world. Did they know? Did they care? Evidently not.

And then, as he was about to tell—to shout at— Geroge and Tharma to cease their wretched din, the inside of the shack seemed to . . . enlarge. The monsters fell silent, quite of their own accord. "It is the god," Selatre said quietly: she, of all people, recognized the presence of the divine when she felt it.

Gerin bowed very low. "Lord Baivers," he said. "You honor me by hearing my summons."

"You have summoned others before me, not least that wine-bibbing mountebank from Sithonia," Baivers answered. As with Mavrix, Gerin heard the god's voice in his mind, not with his ears. The rustic accent came through anyhow.

"Lord Baivers, who comes first is less important than who comes last, for that says where help was truly found," Gerin said.

"Aye, likely tell," Baivers said, like a sour old farmer who hadn't believed anyone's tales about anything since his wife told him she was going out to gather herbs in the woods and he found her in bed with the village headman. Grudgingly, though, he nodded to the Fox. "Well, I'm here. Say your say."

"Thank you." Gerin knew he sounded more sincere than most people giving thanks. Most people, though, didn't get the chance to thank gods, not in person.

Baivers nodded again. If a god could look like an old farmer, he did. His hair wasn't hair, but ears of ripe barley, a pale yellow. His craggy face was tired and weathered, as if, like the crop whose lord he was, he spent his whole lifetime in the sun and open air. Only when you looked in his eyes, which were the color of fresh new green barley shoots poking up out of the ground after the first rains of spring, did you get the sense of divine vitality still strong under that unprepossessing semblance.

What he looked like, Gerin thought, was a part of the land. That raised hope in the Fox: not only did it hold echoes of what Mavrix had said to him, but it also made him think Baivers truly belonged in the northlands, that the long Elabonian presence here had made him as much a god of this terrain as he was around the City of Elabon, as much a god here as one longer established like Biton.

With that in mind, Gerin asked, "Do you want the Gradi and their gods seizing this land that has been Elabonian for so long, that has given you so much barley and so many libations—so much reverence, not to put too fine a point on it?"

"Do I want that?" Baivers spoke in mild surprise, as if the question had not occurred to him in such a form. "Do I want it? No, I don't want it. The Gradi and their gods feed on blood and oats." He spoke with somber scorn. "Their land is too poor, too cold, their souls too meager, too cold, for my grain."

Geroge and Tharma had stopped singing their hymn when Baivers appeared. They'd stared in awe at the god. Now Geroge burst out, "If you don't want these nasty Gradi around, why haven't you done anything about them and their gods?"

"Why haven't I done anything?" Again, the question

seemed to startle Baivers. With some bitterness, Gerin found that unsurprising: the idea of actually doing anything appeared to be one that was alien to the entire Elabonian pantheon. Baivers turned his green, green gaze on Geroge. "A voice from below the roots," he murmured, more to himself than to any of the mortals with him. "There are powers below the roots."

"What are you talking about?" Geroge demanded. "I don't understand what you're saying."

Gerin had often heard that complaint from Dagref. When he and Selatre would talk about adult matters, the oldest child they'd had together would listen, following as far as his own experience let him, and would keep on trying to follow past that point, trying to make his parents slow down and let him know what they meant.

Baivers' murmurs perplexed the Fox, too, but he thought he had some notion of what was in the god's mind. Groping for words, he asked, "Lord Baivers, are the powers below the roots connected to those who make a habit of living down there?" To show what he meant, he pointed to Geroge and Tharma.

"Of course," Baivers answered, once more sounding surprised. "Where there are no folk there are no powers."

"Ah," Gerin said. That answered one question he'd long had: at least in the eyes of the god, the monsters were people. From the day they'd emerged from the caverns below Biton's shrine, Gerin had wondered. He'd phrased his question carefully, to avoid both saying they were and saying they weren't. He found another question: "Will that power—?"

"Those powers," Baivers corrected, sounding finicky and precise.

"Those powers, then. Will they fight for us against the Gradi?"

Still finicky, the god replied, "They will fight. It is

why they exist: to fight. Against the Gradi? Who can say for certain. For us?" Those sprout-green eyes swung to Gerin. "Why do you think you and I are 'we'?"

"Why?" Gerin said in some alarm. "You just said you didn't like the Gradi or their gods. If they take the northlands, you get no more libations here, no more worship. I'm only a mortal, lord Baivers, I know that, but as mortals go, I'm strong. If you can help me fend off the Gradi gods, I think I can beat the Gradi themselves."

"Could be so," Baivers said. "Could be nonsense, too. But what I think and what I do, they're not the same. My power is over growing and brewing—you know that. I'm not a god of blood, a god of war."

"But you can fight—I know you can." Gerin came up with one of the bits of lore he'd culled from the scrolls up in his library: "When that demon sent the barley blight, you didn't just fight him and beat him, you made him swallow his own tail and eat himself up."

Selatre silently clapped her hands.

"Well, of course I did," Baivers said. "He was causing my crop all kinds of trouble. He had it coming, he did, and I gave it to him." For a moment, he seemed a formidable deity indeed.

"The Gradi are the same," Gerin insisted. "If they win here, there won't be any barley, because they'll make the northlands too cold for it to grow. Do you want that to happen?"

"Do I want it to happen? Of course I don't want it to happen. It would sadden me," Baivers answered. "But if the grain won't grow, then it won't and that's all there is to it. It's not the same, it's not close to the same, as murdering it in the shoot, the way that demon did. He'll never find his way back to this world, never once."

The distinction Baivers drew was so fine it meant nothing to the Fox, but it plainly did to the god. Gerin kicked at the dirt floor of the shack. He'd feared that, even if Baivers did appear for him, the god would keep on doing what the gods of the Elabonian pantheon did most of the time: nothing. He'd needed an angry Baivers, a furious Baivers, and what he found was a regretful but resigned Baivers, which did him no good.

How to find a furious Baivers? Even as the question formed in his mind, so did an answer. He tried to find another, because he didn't like that one. But nothing else occurred to him. And, when he was about to enrage a god, he didn't think prayer would do him any good.

His laugh was loud and scornful. George and Tharma stared at him. So did Selatre, in dismay: she knew more about gods, or about gods more directly, than Gerin. And so did Baivers. "Don't like your tone, young fellow," he said sharply.

"Why should I care?" Gerin retorted. "I've spilled a lot of ale to you over the years, and what has it got me? Not bloody much, that's plain. I should have paid more heed to Mavrix. He has a long memory for foes, but he has a long memory for friends, too, and that's more than I can say about you. He was right about what he told me—he certainly was."

"The Sithonian?" Baivers snorted. "The next time he's right'll be the first."

"Oh, no!" Jeering at a god was something of which Gerin would never have dreamt were his need less great. If he overdid it, he was liable to be destroyed by a deity he might have brought to his side. But if he didn't do it, he was all too sure he *would* be destroyed by the Gradi and their gods. And so jeer he did: "Mavrix said you were useless, said you'd always been useless, said you'd always be useless, too. And he's right, looks as if to me."

"Useless? Mavrix talks about useless?" Baivers threw back his head and laughed; his barley hair rustled. "The

Sithonian, who can't play the pipes, who manures himself whenever he's in trouble" —that wasn't fair or true, but Gerin had long since noted gods were no more fair and probably less truthful than human beings— "who buggers pretty boys and calls himself a fertility god? He thinks *I'm* useless? I'll show him!"

As the Fox knew, buggering pretty boys was not all Mavrix did to amuse himself. He feared Baivers' tirade would draw the notice of the Sithonian god. He'd wanted Biton and Mavrix together; they'd spurred each other on against the monsters. He didn't want Baivers and Mavrix together, lest they go after each other instead of the Gradi.

But he had to keep Baivers roused. And so he kept on jeering: "You might as well be from the law courts of the City of Elabon, not the fields where the barley grows. All you care about is the detail of the law" —he was being unfair himself; that charge applied more justly to his son Dagref than to Baivers— "if you'd fight that demon but not the Gradi gods. The barley is gone, whether killed in the shoot or never planted. Yes, Mavrix was right—useless is the word."

For a moment, he glanced over to Selatre. Her face was white as milk; she knew, probably better than he, all the different risks he was running. *If I get through this, I'll never traffic with gods again,* he told himself, though he knew that was a lie. If he got through this, he'd have to try to find some way to enlist whatever gods the monsters had against the Gradi. That was likely to make dealing with Baivers seem a stroll on the meadow by comparison.

Then Tharma spoke to the god of barley and brewing: "Please don't let the barley go away from here. We like your ale."

"Call me useless?" Baivers said to Gerin. "Mavrix said it and so you believe it? I'll show you useless, I will.

Powers of the earth, powers under the earth, we're stronger than you think, little man. Loose us against the invaders and—" The Fox had hoped he'd prophesy victory. He didn't, instead finishing, "—and we'll give 'em all the fight in us."

Gerin wished he knew how much that was. Relieved he hadn't been turned into an insect pest or something else small and obnoxious, he dared one more question, no longer mocking: "Lord Baivers, can you bring Father Dyaus into the fight, too?"

Baivers looked astonished, then sad. "I wish I could," he said. "We'd win certain sure then. But Dyaus, he's—gone round to the far side of the hill, you might say, and I don't know what it'd take to call him back."

"You know, lord Baivers—or maybe you don't know, if I don't say it—we Elabonians have the feeling sometimes that all our gods have gone round to the far side of the hill," Gerin said.

"We're pleased enough with the way things are here, or we have been, anyhow," Baivers answered. "When a thing is to your liking, you don't need to meddle with it, and you don't want to, either, for fear you'll make it worse." Gerin nodded at that, for he thought the same way himself. Baivers suddenly grunted, a most ungodlike sound. "Could be that's why Elabonians latch onto Sithonian gods sometimes, I suppose. They're born meddlers, every one of them. And Mavrix worse than the others," he added with a growl.

He was angry, all right. Now Gerin could but hope he would stay angry till the monsters' gods joined the cause—if they joined it. The Fox asked, "Once I go down under Ikos, how will I summon you back to the world?"

"You found a way once," Baivers said. "Likely tell you can find a way twice." And with that, he vanished as abruptly as Mavrix had, but without—Gerin devoutly hoped—leaving any progeny behind.

As they did whenever a god departed, the walls of the shack seemed to close in around Gerin. He sighed, long and deep, then turned to Geroge and Tharma. "I thank you both. You did very well there."

"You're going down to Ikos," Selatre said: statement, not question. Gerin nodded to her in the same sort of agreement he'd given Baivers not long before. His wife went on, "And you're going to take Geroge and Tharma with you."

After a good many years together with Selatre, the Fox knew how well she thought along with him. "Aye, I am," he said. "I see no other choice. If I'm going to treat with the powers under the ground, I can't think of better intermediaries than the two of them. Can you?"

"No," Selatre answered. "And you're going to take someone else along, too."

"Duren, do you mean?" Gerin said. "That's a good notion. We'll pass through the holding that was Ricolf's and will be his. Might as well let the barons there have another look at him."

"Take Duren if you like, but I didn't mean him," Selatre said. "I meant me."

Dagref and Clotild had at last given up their nightly struggle against sleep. Blestar had drifted off some time before; he fought sleep, too, but had fewer resources than his older sister and brother. Gerin and Selatre generally relished the time when their children were asleep, for it gave them their best chance to make love. Now it gave them the chance to argue without having to explain everything to Dagref as they went along.

Gerin's argument was simple: "I need you here," he said.

"You'll need me more there," Selatre said, almost as if she were still the Sibyl at Ikos. "How will you manage to get down to the underground passage that leads to the monsters' caves? You won't be going down there to ask farseeing Biton any question, which is the only reason for those who aren't priests—or the Sibyl—to enter that passage."

"Carlun hasn't told me the whole treasury is empty," Gerin answered, "so I expect I can bribe my way down there if I can't talk the priests into letting me go. Eunuchs love gold. Why shouldn't they? It's all they *can* love."

"Yes, I suppose you may be able to talk your way or pay your way down there—if you go by yourself," Selatre said. "But you're going with Geroge and Tharma. Do you think the priests and temple guards will be glad to see monsters after it took a miracle from the god to restore his shrine?"

"All right, the bribe will have to be bigger," Gerin said. He had seldom been wrong in counting on the greed of his fellow man.

But Selatre shook her head. "That won't work," she said positively. "Oh, you may be able to spread enough gold around to let you take the monsters down under the temple. If anyone else were trying, I'd say no, but you've shown you have a gift for such things." She set a hand on his arm to let him know she didn't disapprove. But then she went on, "All right, now you have Geroge and Tharma under the temple. You want to meet the rest of the monsters and their gods. What do you do then?"

"What I have to do," the Fox replied. "I break through the wall—"

"You break through the charms and spells that keep the monsters from breaking through in the other direction," Selatre interrupted.

"Well, yes, I would have to, because . . ." Gerin's voice trailed away. He saw, all too clearly, the point Selatre was making.

She drove it home anyhow: "There isn't enough gold in all the northlands—there isn't enough gold in all the world—to pay the bribes you'd need for the priests to let you do that. You know it as well as I do." Her voice brooked no denial; she understood him too well to believe for an instant that he didn't know it as well as she did.

He used the only weapon he had left: "Why would your being there make the priests see things any different?"

"Because Biton spoke through me," she said. "I'm Sibyl no more, and by my own choice, and glad of it" —she shifted in the bed, getting up on one elbow so she could look at their sleeping children— "but the god has spoken through me, and the priests cannot help but know it. If I tell them this must be done, they are far more likely to listen to me than they are to you."

Gerin mulled that over. "You're very annoying when you make good sense," he said at last.

"Oh? Why is that?" Selatre asked.

"Because it means you're right and I'm wrong, and I'm going to have to change my plans," he told her. "I don't usually have to do that, but I will this time."

"A lot of people won't change their plans even when they're wrong," Selatre said. "I'm glad you're not one of them."

"A lot of people are fools," Gerin said. "If they weren't, how do you think I'd have done as well as I have for as long as I have? Of course" —he took Selatre in his arms— "it doesn't hurt to find other people who aren't fools."

"Who, me?" she said, just before he kissed her.

Gerin looked back over his shoulder as Fox Keep disappeared when the road jogged behind a stand of trees. "I haven't felt so nervous about leaving the place behind since I went south to the City of Elabon," he said. "That's a long time ago now."

Beside him on the seat in the wagon, Selatre nodded. "I didn't think then that I would be the one to replace Biton's Sibyl when at last the god called her to himself. And I certainly never imagined everything that would happen afterward." For a moment, fondly, she let the palm of her hand rest on his leg, a little above the knee.

The wagon was not the only unusual part of the procession of chariots making the journey south along the Elabon Way. In the chariot Duren drove stood Geroge and Tharma, exclaiming at every new thing they saw. Their travels hadn't taken them far from Fox Keep till now. They would be going a good ways now—farther from home than most serfs traveled in all their lives. But for them, this was in a way a return to the very root of their race.

With Gerin driving the wagon and Duren sharing a chariot with the monsters who had been his friends since childhood, Van rode with Raffo Redblade as his driver and Drungo Drago's son his companion in the car. The three of them probably made a fighting team more to be feared than Van, Gerin, and Duren: Raffo was in the prime of life, and Drungo the only warrior among the Fox's followers who came close to Van for strength.

Another dozen chariots rode with those two. That gave Gerin enough of a fighting tail to overawe bandits and make petty barons think twice about trying to end his career prematurely. If Ricolf's former vassals joined together and fell on him, his force would not be enough to withstand them, but he thought Ratkis Bronzecaster would be an ally there. In any case, he had to go through the holding that had belonged to Ricolf, for the path to Ikos branched off the Elabon Way not far south of it.

Selatre enjoyed the unwinding countryside as much as did Geroge and Tharma, and for the same reason. She'd not traveled far from Fox Keep since Gerin and Van saved her from the monsters and brought her there more than a decade earlier. Before then, her only journey had been from the village where she grew up to Ikos to become Biton's voice on earth. Everything she saw seemed fresh and new to her.

"You have no idea how lucky you are, being a man," she told Gerin. "If you want to go somewhere, you up and go, and you don't have to worry about it. How long has it been since I've been farther from the keep than the village close by?"

"I don't know," the Fox answered, "but the reason I leave the keep most often is that unfriendly strangers—or unfriendly neighbors—are trying to take what's mine, and so I have the great privilege of giving them the chance to ventilate my carcass in ways the gods didn't intend. That may be luck, but I'm not nearly sure it's good luck."

Had he said that to Elise, she would have got angry at him. Had Van said it to Fand, she not only would have got angry, she might have tried ventilating the outlander's carcass in ways the gods didn't intend. Selatre said, "I hadn't thought of it that way." A little later, she added, "The balance may be more nearly fair than it seemed when I've stayed behind. Not that it is, mind you—but more nearly."

"I love you," Gerin said, which left her looking puzzled but pleased.

When they camped that night, the ghosts were quieter than the Fox was used to, although the offering he and his men had given them—the blood of a couple of chickens bought from a roadside village—wasn't much for as many men as they had.

"It was like this when we were bringing your lady

from Ikos up to Castle Fox, too," Van said to Gerin. "I
remember. She calms the night spirits, that she does."

"That's true," Gerin said. "It was like this then." He
scratched his head. On the earlier journey, Selatre was
still a maiden, and barely removed from serving as
Biton's voice on earth, her only debarment being that
the Fox had had to touch her to save her from the
monsters unleashed in the earthquake. That was a long
time ago now, and four children ago, too, though only
three still lived. If Selatre still had the effect on the
ghosts that she'd had then, it meant . . . what? That
Biton still spoke through her? If he did, he'd given
no sign of it, not in all those years. That he still paid
attention to her?

When Gerin wondered about that out loud, Selatre
shook her head. "If the farseeing one still watched over
me, I would know," she said. But then her face clouded—
or perhaps it was just a trick of the light, the fires
blending with golden Math's nearly round disk, a couple
of days from full, pale Nothos' smaller gibbous fragment
of a circle east of it, and Elleb's slim young crescent.
"I think I would know it."

"When you were Sibyl, could you feel the god's
presence?" Gerin asked.

"I took it so much for granted, I never needed to
feel it," she answered, and then looked thoughtful. "Am
I taking his absence so much for granted now, I'm not
feeling it, either?" She laughed. "You've started me
wondering."

"We'll find out," the Fox said, and Selatre nodded.
She had come along because of how useful she might
be at Ikos, and she could be more useful than she'd
dreamt if Biton did still pay attention to her and to
what she did. Gerin hoped the god was paying attention.
As he'd said, he'd find out before long.

❖   ❖   ❖

The guards at the border between Bevander's holding and the one that had been Ricolf's looked to their weapons when Gerin and his companions bore down on them. Not so long before, they would have had those weapons ready to hand, for years of civil war among Bevander, his three brothers, and his father had wracked the holding north of them. Bevander had won with the Fox's help, and brought quiet to a stretch of land that had known only turmoil for too long.

"Who seeks to enter this holding?" the chief guard called, which kept him from having to worry about whether to name it *the former holding of Ricolf the Red* or *the holding of Duren Gerin's son* or to give it some other name altogether. Gerin approved of playing safe when you had the chance.

He named himself and Duren. That made the guards stir. Before they could say anything, he went on, "We make no claims on this holding now. All we are doing here today is passing through on the way to Ikos."

"But, lord prince," the leader of the guards said, "no one at the castle of—once of—Ricolf the Red will be ready to receive you. We had no word you were planning to come south."

That had not been accidental. "It's all right," the Fox answered easily. "As I said, we're only passing through. No need for anyone to go to any special pains over us." He knew that would fluster the guards more than anything else he could say, but no help for it.

One of the troopers spotted Geroge and Tharma. "Those things!" he exclaimed. "I thought we were rid of those things for good."

The monsters had drawn horrified looks ever since they left the vicinity of Fox Keep, where people were used to them. Gerin had warned them that would happen, in case the reactions of strangers coming to the keep hadn't been warning enough. Now Geroge said, "I am not a thing. Are you a thing?" The guard stared at him. The last thing he'd expect was for Geroge to talk.

Gerin didn't feel like discussing the monsters—or anything else—with the guards. Looking down his nose at their leader, he said, "Do we have your generous permission to pass through?"

They would pass through with or without the border guard's generous permission, and his face said he knew it. Ignoring Gerin's sardonic tone, he replied, "Aye, pass through in peace, and may you learn what you need at Ikos."

Duren spoke up: "Thank you. Give me your name, for I value good vassalage."

That pulled the guard up straighter. "Young lord, I'm Orbrin Darvan's son, and pleased to make your acquaintance." Now he waved the chariots and wagon through with a flourish.

At Van's order, Raffo steered his chariot up near Gerin's wagon. Van said, "I like that. The vassal barons will have a hard time raising any strife against your son if their men feel the way those guards do."

"You're right," the Fox replied, "and Duren handled him just right, too. I don't think we'll have any trouble on the way south, as a matter of fact—not least because Authari and the other leading vassals won't find out we've been here till we're already gone. What worries me is the trip back from Ikos. They'll have had time by then to ready whatever they aim to try."

"Aye, likely so," the outlander said. "Well, we deal with that when we come to it. Can't do anything else." Gerin could only nod; he'd been thinking the same thing himself.

Seeing the keep of Ricolf the Red, as he did late that afternoon, always made him feel strange, what with all the memories it brought to the surface. Seeing that keep with Selatre by his side felt stranger still. When he'd brought her up from Ikos, Ricolf had seen more between them than he had; he'd put the older man's remarks down to the short temper of a former father-in-law. But now Selatre was his wife of many years, and Ricolf gone from men. Things changed.

He found out how much they had changed when a lookout called the challenge: "Who comes to the castle to be Duren Gerin's son's?"

Gerin had been going to answer that challenge. When he heard how it was framed, he waved to his son instead. Duren said, "Duren Gerin's son comes to his own castle, not yet to live in it, but for a night's shelter."

That brought the drawbridge down in a hurry. The warriors who'd lowered it looked much less happy when they saw Geroge and Tharma in the chariot with Duren, but by then it was too late. Between them, Duren and Gerin managed to convince the soldiers the monsters were, if not harmless, at least unlikely to run wild unless provoked. A good look at their teeth gave an incentive against provoking them.

A lame old fellow name Ricrod Gondal's son was serving as steward for the castle in the absence of a lord in residence. He settled Gerin and his comrades in the great hall and fed them barley porridge, roast duck, and ale. When Gerin poured a libation, he wondered if Baivers would manifest himself in the hall. The god did nothing, though, as Elabonian gods were all too wont to do.

Ghosts crowded the hall for Gerin—not the night spirits, pacified by blood and held at a distance by fire, but ghosts from his own past: Rihwin, drunk and dancing obscenely; Wolfar of the Axe, an Elabonian as savage as any Gradi; Ricolf the Red himself, solid, steady, reliable; and Elise, of whom he still could not think without pangs of regret.

He glanced over to Selatre. She had no ghosts here, and could not sense his. She was the present, the reality, and better than he'd known in days gone by. He understood that. Understanding it, though, did not make his ghosts vanish. They would be with him till he died.

"Lord," Ricrod said, "what brings you back to this keep, your business in the north being unfinished?"

Gerin started to answer, but realized Ricrod had not directed the question at him. The steward had not said *lord prince*, and the Fox was not lord here. Duren was. He replied, "I'm bound for Ikos, with my father and my companions. If the gods are kind, it will help end the business in the north."

The gods Gerin sought under the Sibyl's shrine were unlikely to be kind. The less kind they were, in fact, the more likely they were to be useful to his cause. Ricrod, though, nodded and said, "I hope farseeing Biton gives you an answer you can unriddle fast enough for it to do you some good."

"I hope we can use what we learn, too," Duren said. He had not said a word about Biton. He'd let Ricrod draw his own conclusions, then encouraged him to believe they were right, all without telling a lie as he did it. Gerin was impressed. He couldn't have handled it any more neatly himself.

Selatre had seen the same thing. That night, in the chamber the steward had given them, she said to Gerin, "He'll do well here. He handles himself like a man: more so here, away from Fox Keep, where he's your son first. He's ready to rule."

"Yes, I think so, too," Gerin answered, "and so do . . . some of the vassal barons here. If we win, if Duren comes down here to take up his grandfather's barony, it will feel very strange at Fox Keep, not having him around. I'll have to start training up Dagref, see how he shapes."

Selatre laughed quietly. "It won't be a matter of his not knowing enough to lead men. The question will be whether they want to follow him or to wring his neck."

"That is one of the questions," the Fox agreed, laughing. Then he fell into a thoughtful silence. If Dagref did shape as a leader of men, was Gerin to leave his title to his son by Selatre and have Duren, as baron of one small holding, overshadowed by his younger half brother? Or was he to name Duren his heir in all matters and leave Dagref frustrated and resentful? Either path could lead to war between them.

Best way to solve the problem, Gerin thought, *is not to die*. The gray spreading in his beard warned him that solution, however desirable, wasn't practical—and that didn't consider unfriendly weapons at all. *Plenty of trouble around already*, the Fox reminded himself. *No need to borrow more*. No telling how Dagref would shape. If he couldn't lead and Duren could, nothing Gerin did for him would matter after the Fox was gone.

Selatre stirred on the rather lumpy bed. She'd always cared for Duren as if he were one of her own, and she'd never yet pushed for her children at his expense. But she couldn't be blind to the ties of blood, either. One of these days, she and Gerin would have to hash it out. This was not going to be the day, though. Like Gerin, she recognized that waiting sometimes solved problems better than arguing about them.

"We'll see," Selatre said at last, and then, as if fearing even that might have been too much, she added, "It's not that we don't have plenty of other things to see about first."

"Oh, is that why we're here and on our way to Ikos?" Gerin said. "And all the time I thought we were traveling for the fun of it." Selatre snorted and poked him in the ribs. Before long, lumpy mattress or no, they both fell asleep.

❖   ❖   ❖

Gerin almost missed the standing stone carved with the winged eye that marked the track leading from the Elabon Way east to the town of Ikos and the shrine of Biton it served. He cursed under his breath; every time he wanted to go to the shrine, he had to worry about getting lost along the way.

As before, the country between the highway and the forest surrounding the valley of Ikos left him dismayed. People would be a long time making up for the devastation first from the earthquake and then the monsters. The survivors who still struggled to make a go of farming were sadly overworked; he would have had more sympathy yet for them had they not been in the habit of sometimes robbing travelers before misfortune had smote. When they saw Geroge and Tharma, they fled for the shelter of the woods by their fields. They knew all they cared to of monsters.

One of the things Gerin had not thought about was how the enchanted forest around Ikos would react to the presence of the monsters. The Fox rarely missed important details, which made his discomfiture when he did all the more acute. Geroge and Tharma stared about with interest when, along with Gerin and Selatre and their companions, they plunged into the cool greenness of the track through that forest and under the leafy canopies of its trees.

The forest seemed to stare, too, and then to exclaim in outrage. Ten years before, the monsters must have worked outrages untold under those trees. And the trees seemed to remember, as did all the other strange creatures living in the forest, creatures a traveler who stayed on the path never saw but whose presence he often sensed, like a prickling at the back of his neck. Gerin felt more than a prickling now. He felt as if the whole forest full of all of those mysterious creatures, whatever they were, were about to fall on him and his companions—and that, when they were done, nothing whatever would be left to show he'd been rash enough to come this way.

Beside him, Selatre quivered. He wondered what she was feeling. Before he could ask—saying anything, here and now, took a distinct effort of will—she spoke, and loudly: "By farseeing Biton, I swear we all" —she stressed the last word— "come in peace, meaning no harm to this wood or to any in it."

Her words were not swallowed among the thick gray-brown boles of the trees, as others had been before them. Instead, they seemed to echo and reecho, somehow spreading farther from the path than they had any natural business doing. After that, the feeling of menace vanished, far more suddenly than it had grown.

"Thank you for winning the argument about whether you should come," Gerin said.

Selatre seemed as pleased and surprised as he was. "That worked—very well, didn't it?" she said in a small voice. Unlike the words of her oath, the reply did not ripple outward from the wagon.

When the Fox and his companions emerged from the strange and ancient wood, Geroge and Tharma both sighed with relief. "I didn't like that place," Geroge said, "not after the first little bit. It made me feel all funny inside."

"That place makes everyone feel funny inside," Gerin said. Then he glanced over to Selatre. "Almost everyone."

"And you wonder why Dagref has a way of pitching a fit if everything isn't exactly right," she said. The Fox maintained a dignified silence, knowing any other response would only leave him vulnerable to more truths from his wife. But Selatre was looking down into the valley of Ikos from the high ground on which they had paused. "The shrine, I see, looks as it always did—the god promised it would, so of course it must—but how sad and shrunken the town seems."

"I thought that when I came here to ask you what had become of Duren, all these years ago," Gerin answered. "Ikos started to wither when it couldn't draw questioners from south of the High Kirs. The earthquake and the fires it started made things worse, though; I wouldn't argue with that."

As they had earlier in the year, the innkeepers of Ikos greeted Gerin and his comrades with joy pure and unalloyed, save perhaps by greed. When it seemed as if that greed were about to keep their rates altogether extortionate, Van scowled at them and said, "We could just camp out in the open. We've got hard bread and smoked sausage, and in the god's valley fires should be enough to hold the ghosts at bay." Reason suddenly reentered the conversation, and Gerin got his men settled and horses stabled for about what he'd expected to pay, or perhaps even a bit less.

"So strange," Selatre said, over and over. "When you come back to a place you knew well, you expect it to be as it was when you left it. Seeing Ikos like this . . ." She shook her head.

A temple guardsman, a grizzled veteran, sat drinking ale in the taproom of the inn Gerin had chosen for himself and Selatre, and for Duren and Van, Geroge and Tharma. When the fellow saw the monsters, he coughed and choked and grabbed for his sword. Gerin had just managed to calm him down when he took a longer look at Selatre. Instead of choking again, he went white. "Lady," he blurted, "you're dead! Farseeing Biton has a new voice now."

"Farseeing Biton has a new voice," Selatre agreed. "As for the other, Clell, I thought you were dead, too, and glad I am to be wrong."

"Some few of us did live," Clell answered. "When we saw how many monsters came boiling up out from under the shrine, we went up into the woods, and skulked there like bandits, you might say, till the day all the monsters disappeared. Almost all the monsters," he amended, casting a dubious eye toward Geroge and Tharma.

"You went up into *those* woods?" Gerin pointed back at the haunted forest through which he'd just passed. He leaned forward, intense curiosity on his face. "You couldn't have stayed on—you couldn't have stayed near—the road that runs through them. What is it like, in there away from the road?"

"It's not *like* anything." The temple guard shivered. His eyes went wide and faraway. "I never would have done it—none of us would have done it—if it hadn't been a choice between that and the monsters. We lived, most of us, so I guess we did right, but . . ." His voice trailed off.

Gerin would have probed harder at him, but Selatre had another question: "Did you chance to see the temple restored when Biton worked his miracle and undid the damage from the earthquake?"

"Lady, I did," Clell replied, and his eyes went wider yet. "I was at the edge of the wood, hunting a—well, one of the creatures that dwells in it: a bird, you might say, for lack of a better word. As I drew my bow to shoot at it, it fluttered away. I glanced down, sadly, toward the ruins of the great shrine—"

"I never saw that, for which I thank the farseeing god," Selatre broke in. "When the earthquake hit, I was in a faint after the last oracle he gave me."

"I remember, lady." Clell paused to drink ale. "But anyhow, there I was, figuring I'd go hungry a while longer, and all of a sudden, the air started to quiver. I was afraid it was another earthquake, or the start of one, even though the ground wasn't shaking. And I looked down at the wreck of what had been the temple, and it was quivering, too. It was like it was coming alive. And then, in the blink of an eye, it was back, exactly the way it had been before. The monsters were gone, too, though we needed longer to be sure of that. But I haven't seen one since, till now."

"I'd have paid gold—a lot of gold—to see that with my own eyes," Gerin said. But, since he'd caused Biton to help Mavrix get rid of the monsters and the god had rebuilt the temple in that same sequence of events, he supposed he was entitled to some small part of the credit for it.

Clell said, "Most amazing thing I've seen in all my born days . . . except maybe some of the creatures and trees in the woods. I wondered if I dared try killing them, but when your belly drives you, you take the chance. And some were good eating, and some weren't, but I managed not to starve to death till farseeing Biton stretched out his hand."

"Good," Gerin said. "I'm as surprised—and as glad—as my wife to learn any of the old guards lived after the monsters came up from under the shrine."

"As your—wife, lord prince?" Clell stared, first at Gerin, then at Selatre. "We had heard somewhat of this—at Ikos, we hear a deal of news, though not so much as in the old days—but hearing and crediting are two different things. When you think what the god requires of his Sibyls—"

"I am Sibyl no more, as you must know," Selatre told him. "And I am now mother of three living children, all begot in the regular way. And it is by my choice; Biton would have taken me back when he restored the shrine, but I asked him if I might stay where I was, and he allowed it."

"Not all this news ever reached Ikos," Clell said, and

Gerin believed him, for Selatre seldom spoke of what had passed between her and Biton after the monsters were banished back to their gloomy underground haunts. The guardsman took another pull at his ale, then said, "If my asking does not offend, what question will you put to the farseeing god when you go below the shrine to meet his Sibyl? The Sibyl he has now, I should say."

"We're not here to ask farseeing Biton anything," Gerin replied. Clell was no priest, but was a servant of Biton's all the same. Gauging his reactions would give the Fox an idea of how the priests would respond. "We're here to treat with whatever gods or powers the monsters reverence. The monsters aren't gone, you know—they're just back where they were before the earthquake."

"You're joking," Clell said. Gerin and Selatre both shook their heads. The guardsman delivered another snap judgment: "You're mad."

"We don't think so," Selatre said.

She who had been the Sibyl at Ikos spoke with a certainty close to that which she had used when Biton spoke through her. Gerin had noted that several times since he'd decided to come here and to bring her with him. He did not know what it meant. He did not know for certain it meant anything. He did not even know whether to be awed or frightened or both at once.

Selatre's tone inspired respect in Clell, but no agreement. "They'll never let you do that," he said, sounding very certain himself. "They have the monsters walled and warded off so they can never break free again, and if you think I'm sorry about that, you're bloody daft."

"The wards are to keep the monsters from getting out," Gerin countered. "They aren't intended to stop anyone from going in to them."

"Of course they aren't," Clell said. "Nobody in his

right mind would want to do such an idiot thing. Why d'you want to do such an idiot thing, anyhow?"

"Because Baivers lord of barley has told me their gods, with him, offer the northlands the best hope against the Gradi and their gods," the Fox answered. "I don't know whether that best hope is a good one, but I have to find out."

He wondered whether Clell had even heard of the Gradi incursion. As the guard had said, Ikos wasn't the center for news it had been in years gone by. Clell did turn out to know; he said, "If that's true, lord prince, it may change things, but I wouldn't bet anything I didn't care to lose on it."

"I'm betting everything I have on it," Gerin answered: "my holding, my family, my life. The way things are now, I don't think I have any other choice. Do you?"

Clell didn't answer, not directly. What he did say was, "You poor bastard." After a moment's reflection, Gerin decided that fit the situation well enough.

Van rode with Gerin and Selatre in the wagon as they approached Biton's shrine. Beside them came Duren, Geroge, and Tharma in the chariot Gerin's son drove. The rest of the warriors stayed back in the town of Ikos. Gerin had not brought enough men to fight his way into the temple precinct. If Biton opposed him, he did not think he could have brought enough men to fight his way into the temple precinct.

"It all looks just as I remember it," Selatre said, "but then it would, wouldn't it? I thank the farseeing god for not letting me see it all tumbled into ruin."

No one else waited ahead of them to hear what the Sibyl would say. Selatre was used to that, her term as Biton's voice having begun after the Empire of Elabon blocked the last remaining pass through the High Kirs into the northlands. To Gerin, it still felt strange, unnatural. He remembered Ikos full to bursting, with folk from all over the Empire—and from beyond it as well—coming to consult the oracle.

The temple guardsmen stared in horror and what looked like a good deal of fear at the two monsters who rode with Duren. But the guards did not attack; Gerin's guess was that word of Geroge and Tharma had already reached them, most likely from Clell but also, perhaps, from the innkeeper who ran the hostel where they'd stayed or from anyone who worked with or for him.

"We do come in peace," the Fox called, holding up his right hand to show it was empty. The two monsters imitated the gesture.

"You had better," said a soldier whose gilded helmet proclaimed him a captain. "You'll be sorry if you don't. If we don't take care of that, the farseeing god will."

Gerin didn't mention that he hadn't come down to the shrine to talk to Biton, but to the powers that dwelt below it. He did say, "I'd like to speak with one of Biton's priests, to talk over what we need to do on our visit."

"All right," the guard captain said. He pointed to Geroge and Tharma. "You want to take them underground, you're going to have to see one of the priests first. Unless you do, it won't happen, and that's flat." He hadn't called the monsters *things*, though, which Gerin took for a better sign than most he'd had lately. One of the guards in a helmet not only ungilded but also unpolished hurried off to find a priest.

He returned a little later with one of Biton's eunuch servants. The plump, beardless priest bowed and said, "You may call me Lamissio. How may I, serving Biton, also serve you?"

The Fox nodded at that; Lamissio made his priorities plain. Gerin also approved of his taking no outward notice of Geroge and Tharma, who, by his bearing, might have been a couple of troopers rather than a couple of monsters. Thus encouraged, Gerin explained to the priest exactly what he had in mind.

Lamissio heard him out, which raised his hopes further. But then the eunuch shook his head, the soft, flabby flesh of his jowls wobbling as he did so. "This cannot be," he said. "Item: those not affiliated with the temple are not allowed below it, save only to consult with the Sibyl in her subterranean chamber."

"But—" Gerin began.

"I heard you out in full, lord prince," Lamissio said. "Have the courtesy to extend me the same privilege." Challenged so, Gerin had no choice but to bow his head in acquiescence. The eunuch ticked off successive points on his stubby fingers: "Item: creatures of the kind of these two" —he pointed to Geroge and Tharma— "are not permitted within the holy precinct for any reason whatsoever."

"We're no more 'creatures' than you are," Tharma said.

If her speaking surprised Lamissio, he did not show it. "That is true," he said gravely, "but you are no less creatures than I am, either." While Tharma pondered that, Lamissio went on, "Item: any meddling with the wards restraining creatures of the kind of these two is forbidden on pain of death, even were the other two difficulties abated."

By that, Gerin concluded, he meant he might have been bribed into letting the monsters into the temple precinct and even into the underground passages below the shrine, but that he would not let the Fox try to meet with their kin no matter what. "Are you sure you won't be reasonable?" he asked. "The temple would benefit from this—"

"The temple would be endangered," Lamissio countered. "That is unacceptable. We were lucky enough when farseeing Biton restored the shrine with one miracle; we may not rely on his giving us two."

He had a point. But Gerin had a point of his own: "If we don't treat with the powers that may dwell with the monsters down below Biton's shrine, all the northlands will need a miracle to restore them."

"This grieves me," the eunuch said. "What happens beyond the shrine, though, and especially what happens beyond this valley, is not my concern. I have to look to my own first."

"Look to your own long enough and you'll soon be looking at Gradi swarming out of the woods," Gerin said.

"I doubt that," Lamissio replied with great confidence: confidence that, considering those woods, might well have been justified.

Gerin corrected himself: "Swarming down the path, I should say. And, before too long, swarming up from the south where the woods don't protect you."

"I do not think this likely," Lamissio said. Did he sound smug? Yes, he did, the Fox decided.

"Why not?" Van demanded. "Did they take your brains along with your balls?"

"You will speak to the servant of farseeing Biton with the respect his position deserves," Lamissio said, his voice cold as a winter night in Gradihome.

"I'm not speaking to your position," Van retorted. "I'm speaking to *you*. If you talk like an idiot, I'm going to let you know it."

Lamissio gestured to the temple guards. They hefted their weapons and made as if to surround Gerin and his comrades.

"Stop that." The command came not from the Fox, not from the outlander, but from Selatre. It was not loud, but most authoritative. And the temple guards stopped.

"What is the meaning of this?" Lamissio demanded. "Who are you, woman, to—" He checked himself, looking cautious. "Wait. You are she who was once the voice of Biton on earth."

"That's right," Selatre said, and added, with a certain relish, "I trust you will treat me with the respect my position deserves."

That was probably a mistake. Gerin knew he wouldn't have said it, at any rate. Flicking a priest on his dignity was only likely to make him angry. And, angrily, Lamissio said, "And what position is that, you who have polluted yourself by contact with a whole man?"

"Be careful with your mouth, priest," Gerin warned.

But Selatre held up her hand. "I will tell you what my position is. When Biton remade this shrine after the earthquake cast it down, he purposed restoring me to the Sibyl's throne. That is simple truth. If you like, you may inquire of the Sibyl that is. Through her, the farseeing god will tell you the same. If Biton was satisfied enough to want to retain me as his instrument, though I was then no longer untouched, no longer even maiden, who are you, priest, to question me?"

Lamissio licked his lips. "But you are not Sibyl now," he said: more a question than a contradiction, for it was obvious Selatre intended to permit no contradiction.

"No, I am not Sibyl now," she agreed. "But by my choice I am not Sibyl, not by Biton's, though the farseeing god was generous enough not to force me back into a place I had outgrown."

"If you are not Sibyl, and it is by your own choice, why should we pay you any heed?" the priest asked.

"Because even though I am Sibyl no more, the god spoke truth through me," Selatre answered. "Has the god spoken through you, Lamissio?"

The eunuch priest did not answer. The temple guardsmen muttered among themselves. They made no further move to surround the chariot and wagon. A couple of them, in fact, stepped back toward where they had been.

Gerin said, "Can we talk about this like a couple of reasonable men?"

Only after the words left his mouth did he realize the answer could be something other than *yes, of course*. Himself reasonable to the core, he had come to see over the years how unreasonable so many people were, though their lack of reason struck him as being unreasonable in and of itself. And priests, by the very nature of their calling, were more apt to incline toward what they saw as following their god's dictates than toward thinking out what was best for them to do.

And how am I different? he asked himself while waiting for Lamissio's reply. *Why am I here, if not at the advice of a god, to recruit other gods to oppose still other gods?* But there was a difference; Lamissio not only accepted that Biton was more powerful than he, but made that fact the cornerstone of his being. Gerin accepted the gods' superior strength—he could scarcely have done otherwise—but did everything he could to exploit their rivalries and blind spots to build as much freedom for himself as he could.

Slowly, Lamissio said, "I shall do this, lord prince, not for your sake—for you are a mere man—but for the sake of the lady to whom you are wed, through whose lips the words of the god once sounded."

"Thank you," the Fox answered, and said no more. The priest's reasons were his own. So long as they gave Gerin what he wanted, or a chance to get what he wanted, he would not make an issue of them.

Selatre accepted Lamissio's acquiescence as no more than her due. She also accepted it without the slightest hint of I-told-you-so aimed at Gerin. The Fox took that for granted till Van whispered behind his hand, "If Fand

ever got me out of a scrape like that, d'you think she'd
let me forget it? Not bloody likely!"

No doubt the outlander was right. Fand came first
with Fand, first, last, and always. Selatre put the good
of the principality ahead of her own self-importance
without a second thought. *I'm lucky*, Gerin thought,
not for the first time.

Hoping to benefit his own cause, he asked Lamissio,
"Shall we move the discussion to the forecourt of the
temple?" He pointed to the opening in the marble wall
surrounding the temple precinct.

But the eunuch priest shook his head. "As I told you,
it is not permitted that creatures of their kind" —he
pointed once more to Geroge and Tharma— "enter
the holy grounds."

"That's foolish," Geroge said. "If what we've heard
is true, there are lots of creatures like Tharma and me
right under your silly temple. How are you keeping
them out? And if you can't keep them out, why fuss
over us?"

Lamissio opened his mouth, then shut it again without
saying anything. Geroge might not have been reasonable,
but a lifetime lived with Gerin had shown him how to
reason. For a monster, he was clever; even for a human
being, he wouldn't have been stupid. And he had a child's
directness to him.

"I had not thought of it like that," the priest admitted,
winning Gerin's respect as he did so. "We do not think—
we do not like to think—of the monsters still under
Biton's shrine. We have walled them away with bricks
and with magic charms, and we have walled them away
with forgetfulness, too."

"Letting these two come onto the temple grounds
would be a way of remembering, then," Gerin said.
"And if it displeases Biton, the god has ways of making
that known without going through priests or guards."

The Fox knew that was true; Biton smote with a loathsome and fatal curse those who tried to steal his treasures from within the sacred precinct. Asking Geroge and Tharma to pass inside that marble wall put them in some danger, but Gerin could not believe Biton would reckon them a worse threat to the northlands than the Gradi and their gods.

"You would have made a formidable priest, lord prince," Lamissio said.

"Maybe," Gerin said, though he aimed to profit himself first and the gods only afterwards and as he had to. He also contemplated with something less than eager enthusiasm the mutilation Lamissio had suffered so he could serve Biton and the Sibyl.

Selatre said, "Will you let us—will you let all of us—enter the temple precinct, Lamissio? No one will seek to harm or steal anything inside."

"Very well," the priest said, which made several of the guardsmen give him surprised stares. He went on, "As you say, and as I find impossible to deny, Biton has the power to punish these monsters, should that prove his will."

"Of course he does," Gerin said reassuringly. "He banished them underground, didn't he?" What he said was true. What he didn't say was that banishing the monsters back to haunts in which they'd dwelt for ages was different from destroying a couple of them. If Lamissio couldn't figure that out for himself, that was his lookout.

A couple of temple guards came up to take charge of the wagon and the chariot in which Gerin and his companions had approached the shrine of the farseeing god. Lamissio led Gerin and Selatre, Van and Duren, and Geroge and Tharma inside the gleaming white wall delimiting the temple precinct.

No hideous blight fell on the two monsters. Gerin

breathed a silent sigh of relief at that. Selatre breathed something, too: "All the same. It's all the same." Unlike Gerin and Van, she had no memory of its ever being different.

Like them, and like Duren, too, she had seen the treasures displayed outside the temple. Past a glance to make sure they were the same, too, she concentrated on the business at hand. To Geroge and Tharma, though, the statues of painted marble and of gold and ivory, the bronze pots on golden tripods, the stacked ingots of gold, were all new and marvelous.

"Pretty," Tharma said in a voice halfway between a growl and a croon. For the first time, a couple of the temple guards smiled at her.

Having talked Lamissio into letting the monsters into the temple precinct, Gerin hoped for further success. "The sooner we can go down under the shrine, the sooner we'll be able to start driving the Gradi and their gods out of the northlands," he said, a sentence with enough unexamined assumptions in it to give a Sithonian logician a bad case of dyspepsia.

It made Lamissio dyspeptic, too. "This cannot be," he declared. "I said as much before; were you not listening? We do not allow visitors below the shrine, save on their journey to the Sibyl, and we most of all do not allow the wards holding the monsters at bay to be tampered with, lest those monsters flood out into the world at large, as they did a decade ago."

"Aye, that's a risk," Van rumbled, "but the cursed Gradi are already loose in the world at large. They may not have sharp teeth like Geroge and Tharma here, but I don't want 'em for neighbors."

"I know nothing of the Gradi, and care to learn nothing," the priest replied. "I know the monsters required Biton's personal intervention to be bundled back into their caves once more. And I know the destruction they worked here and in the town and all through this valley, and I will not see its like repeated." As far as he was concerned, the temple, the town of Ikos, and the valley in which they lay might have been the whole world. If they stayed safe, he cared nothing for what happened in the rest of the northlands.

Duren saw that as plainly as Gerin. "Think past the valley!" he told Lamissio. A glance at the eunuch's face told Gerin the plea was in vain. Lamissio's mental horizon had no stretch in it.

What to do, then? The Fox couldn't take Lamissio aside and try to bribe him into cooperation, though he had planned to do just that. The temple guardsmen were obviously as leery as the priest about loosing the monsters once more. And, for all Gerin knew, their fear was liable to be justified. He was far from sure of his own course, despite Baivers' urging. All he knew for certain was that, so long as he could find a blow to strike against the Gradi and Voldar, he would try with everything in him to strike it, and would worry later about what came afterwards.

But he could not storm the temple, not if Biton did not care to permit it. If Lamissio remained inflexible, he was thwarted. And Lamissio could have been no more inflexible had he been carved from basalt like Biton's ancient image in the temple.

Dejected, the Fox turned to go, to try to figure out what other ploys he could find against the Gradi. "Wait," Selatre said suddenly, in a voice not quite her own. Gerin turned toward her. Her eyes were wide and staring, and looked straight through him. When she spoke again, it was in the powerful baritone Gerin had heard before, the voice Biton used in speaking through his Sibyls:

> "Let the travelers go below
> That they may learn what powers show.

The land is wide, the powers deep—
Shall they now a bargain keep?
Through Sibyl past I speak out now
To say to learn this I allow."

X

When the god abandoned possession of Selatre, she staggered as if stunned. Gerin put an arm around her, steadying her and keeping her from falling. She looked around in surprise. "Did I say something?" she asked. "What did I say?"

"That was the farseeing god," one of the temple guardsmen said, his voice clotted with awe. "No one else—the lord Biton."

"Biton?" Selatre's eyes opened very wide. "Did the lord Biton speak through me?" She seemed to be taking mental stock. "It might be so. I feel the way I did when—after—" She stopped in confusion. "But he couldn't have."

"He did," Gerin said. He let his hand tighten for a moment. "We all heard it." His companions and the guards nodded. He repeated the verses that had come from her mouth, adding, "Not much doubt about what they mean, either."

He was looking straight at Lamissio. Of all those present when the mantic fit hit Selatre, only Biton's priest doubted it was genuine. "How could the farseeing god speak through a vessel he himself discarded?" Lamissio said. "How could he speak through a woman not a maiden?"

But the guard who had first acknowledged that Biton was speaking through Selatre answered. "Gods make rules, and gods break rules, too. That's what makes them gods. And the prince of the north has the right of it here, too. No way to mistake the meaning of the oracular response."

Not all the response was clear. Gerin saw that, even if no one else did. Biton had given him leave to go down under the shrine and bargain with whatever powers were associated with the monsters. He had not said those powers would keep any bargain once made.

Van took a step toward Lamissio, plainly intending to force his cooperation if he could get it no other way. Gerin started to step away from Selatre to block the outlander. Before he could, Duren did. Their eyes met for a moment. The Fox knew he and his son were seeing the same thing: that if even the guardsmen recognized that Biton had, rules or no rules, filled Selatre for a moment, the priest could not help but give way.

And so it proved. Muttering something ungracious under his breath, Lamissio said, "Very well, it shall be as you say—and pray the farseeing god will permit no disasters to spring from it." Then his dour front tottered and collapsed, as the temple behind him had during the earthquake a decade before. "The god has expanded my notion of the possible," he murmured, which struck Gerin as far from the worst way to phrase it.

Van had let Duren hold him away from Lamissio, but he hadn't been happy about it. Now he growled, "You expand my notion of time wasting. Take us down there, and quit dawdling about it."

"It shall be as you say," Lamissio answered. "In the face of the words of the god I serve, how could it be otherwise? But there shall be one more brief delay." Van growled again, this time dangerously. Lamissio held up a plump hand. "The Sibyl has already taken her place in the chamber below the shrine. I shall send one of my colleagues down there to bring her forth. Should the worst befall and the monsters break loose once more, would you have her trapped in that chamber, with them between her and safety?"

That left Van with nothing to say. His gesture might have meant, *Get on with it*. The priest went into the shrine. Gerin, meanwhile, turned to the temple guardsmen. "You'd better be ready at the mouth of the underground opening. If we don't come up and the monsters do, your best bet is to try to hold them below ground. If they spread over the land again—" He didn't go on. He didn't need to go on.

Time seemed to crawl by very slowly. How long did a priest need to go down to the Sibyl and come back with her? At last, after what seemed much too long a time, a eunuch came out with the maid who have given Gerin and Duren the oracular response earlier in the year.

She and Selatre stared at each other. Gerin saw the shock of recognition run through both of them as each knew the other for what she was. The Sibyl nodded to Selatre, then let the eunuch lead her away. Lamissio came out of Biton's shrine and beckoned the Fox and his companions forward.

As she walked up to the temple, Selatre said, more to herself than to anyone else, "I never dreamt I would come here. And oh!—I never dreamt the god would speak to me, speak through me, again. Amazing." Her face glowed, as if a lamp had been lighted inside her.

Walking along with her, Gerin quietly worried. She had forsaken the god for him, but now that Biton had returned to her, would she still care about the merely human? The only way to find out was to wait and see. That would not be easy. Any other choice, though, looked worse.

Geroge and Tharma exclaimed in wonder at the magnificent ornamentation within Biton's shrine. Lamissio stood waiting near the black basalt cult statue with the jutting phallus, and near the rift in the ground through which supplicants descended to the Sibyl's cave—or, as now, to a journey and a fate apt to be blacker than any found there.

"I think our usual rituals no longer apply," the eunuch priest said. "We are not going into the depths of the earth to see the Sibyl, nor even to treat with the farseeing god in any way. All we can pray for now is our own safety."

"You don't have to come with us, Lamissio," Gerin said. "You're liable to be safer if you don't, in fact."

But the priest shook his head. "I am in my place. The god has permitted this. I leave my fate with him."

Gerin bowed, honoring his courage. "Come, then," he said.

As he strode toward the rift in the ground opening onto the hidden ways that ran deep underground, he glanced at the cult statue of Biton. For a moment, the eyes scratched into the living rock came alive: the god, he thought, was looking out at him. Then, as they had before on other visits to the shrine, Biton's eyes faded back into the hard, black stone.

Or they faced into the stone for him, at any rate. Selatre murmured, "Thank you, farseeing one," as she drew near the image, and seemed to speak more intimately than she would have to basalt alone.

Lamissio picked up a torch and lighted it at one of those near the entrance to the caves. Then, long robe flapping about his ankles, he walked down the stone steps that led into the cavern. Gerin took a deep breath and followed.

Sunlight vanished quickly, at the first turn of the path. After that, the torch Lamissio carried and those stuck in sconces set into the wall gave the only light. Geroge and Tharma whooped with glee at the way their shadows swooped and fluttered in the moving, flickering light.

"Keep an eye on them," Van muttered to Gerin.

"I am," the Fox answered, also under his breath. Caves and the underground were the monsters' native haunts, or at least the haunts of their kind. If their blood called to them, this was where they were liable to revert to the bloodthirsty ways of which the aboveground world had seen all too much eleven years before. For now, they showed no sign of any such reversion, only fascination with a place whose like they'd never seen.

Some passages in the tunnel that led to the Sibyl's cave were walled off because they held more treasures than Biton's priests displayed outside the shrine. Some were walled off because they held the monsters at bay. Magical wards set before them reinforced brick and mortar.

One of those walls was made of bricks in the shape of loaves of bread, a marker of very ancient brickwork indeed. Actually, the Fox reminded himself, the wall was no older than any other part of the shrine and underground caverns, having been restored by Biton after the earthquake. But, so far as he could tell, the farseeing god's restoration had been as perfect here as elsewhere, so the wall might as well have been—in effect, was—as ancient as it looked.

"Wait," he called to Lamissio, who had gone a few steps down toward the Sibyl's chamber. His voice echoed oddly along the winding corridor. The priest came back. The torch he carried gave the only light, as those in the brackets ahead of the wall and beyond it had burned out. With a deep breath like the one he had drawn when he entered the caverns, Gerin said, "I think this is the place."

"Very well: this is the place," Lamissio said. His round, pale face was far and away the brightest thing visible. "What now?"

"I don't quite know," Gerin answered. Some of the magical wards lay on the stone floor in front of the wall. Others hung from cords or lengths of sinew set into the rock above it. Methodically, the Fox kicked away the ones on the floor and knocked down those hanging in front of the wall.

The wall itself remained, solid and strong despite the oddly shaped bricks. "What now?" Van asked, as Lamissio had. He hefted his spear. The bronze-shod butt would make a fair prybar, but was not really the right tool with which to go knocking down a wall. "Shall we shout up to the guardsmen for some picks?"

"I don't know," Gerin said again.

"I don't think we'll need to do that," Selatre said in a small, strained voice.

Lamissio gasped. The torchlight showed his face even paler than it had been. All at once, Gerin realized they would not have to break down the wall. What waited on the other side knew the wards were down, and was coming to see what had happened, and what it could make of what had happened.

The torch Lamissio held flared and then went out, plunging the corridor into perfect darkness.

Because he was effectively blinded, Gerin was never sure afterwards how much of what followed took place down below Biton's shrine and how much in the peculiar space the gods could travel but mortals most often could not. Wherever the place was, it didn't strike him as pleasant.

He felt himself weighed, measured, tested in the silent black. After what might have been a moment and might have been some much longer time, the monsters' powers—he got the idea more than one of them was communicating with him—inserted a question into his mind. It was a simple question, one he himself might have asked under the same circumstances: "What are you doing here?"

"Seeking aid against the gods of the Gradi," he answered.

Another pause followed. "What are the Gradi? Who are their gods?"

Marshaling his thoughts in the midst of this blackness was hard. It was as if he had trouble remembering what vision meant, how it was used. As best he could, though, he pictured everything he knew not only about the Gradi but also about Voldar and the rest of their gods.

"They are only another band of you dirt-walking things," some of the powers that dwelt in darkness said scornfully. But now the Fox heard other voices, too, these saying, "For dirtwalkers, they seem strong and fierce."

"They are warlike," Gerin said. "They will even kill themselves to keep from being captured."

"Captured? What is captured?" The monsters' powers did not understand that. The monsters did not fight for booty or for slaves. What they were after was prey. When the Fox mentally explained as best he could, they seemed partly amused, partly horrified. The voices in the dark spoke all together now: "These Gradi are right. You kill or you are killed. Otherwise, you do not fight."

"Not everyone up on the surface would agree with you," Gerin said. "Like everything else, enmity has degrees."

"No!" The voices of the unseen powers dinned in his head, shrieking out their denial. They must have dinned in everyone else's head, too, for with his ears rather than his mind he heard Lamissio whimpering in fright. Frightened as he was himself, he could hardly blame Biton's servant.

But he kept up a bold front, saying, "I speak the truth. If I did not speak the truth, I would have slain Geroge and Tharma here when they came into my hands, for their kind was and had been the enemy of my people."

That made the voices divide again. Some of them said, "You should have slain them," while others said, "Good you left them alive." After that division, the voices snarled at one another. Gerin could not understand all or even much of that; he got the idea they were disagreeing among themselves. He hoped they were. Getting help from even some of them would be better than nothing.

Some of the voices seemed to fall silent after a while. Others said, in ragged chorus, "This he and she you have with you, they are a strangeness, not all of our kind, not all of yours. Yes, a strangeness."

"Proving we don't have to be foes, your kind and mine," Gerin said. He didn't know if it proved any such thing. Raising Geroge and Tharma, he'd had every possible advantage on his side. He'd got them as infants; they were clever as monsters went, which let them perform more like human beings than many of their fellows could have done; and there had been no other monsters around to distract them and perhaps lead them away from mankind.

"Why should we join you and your god of dirt-plants against the Gradi things?" the voices demanded.

The answer Gerin had braced himself to give—*to keep yourselves from being overrun*—did not seem good enough to offer here. He stood silent for a dangerously long time, trying to come up with a response that might satisfy these ferocious powers. He felt them gathering around him, ready to snuff out his life as they had snuffed out Lamissio's torch.

And then Van said, "Why? I'll tell you why, you bloodthirsty things! The Gradi and their gods are just about as nasty as you are, that's why. That's what the Fox has been telling you all along, if only you'd listen.

Where else are you going to find such good fighting?"

A spell of silence followed. Gerin wondered whether Van should have kept quiet. If the monsters' powers joined forces with the Gradi gods, they could easily wrest control of the northlands from the Elabonians and Trokmoi and their deities. He'd never thought he would reckon the Trokmoi as standing on the side of civilization, but he had new standards of comparison these days.

At last, the voices spoke again: "This is so. Foes worth fighting are a boon worth having. We will bargain for the chance to measure ourselves against them, for the chance to meet them with teeth and claws."

"A bargain," Duren murmured. Gerin was pleased, too, but less than he might have been. It was a bargain, aye, but one Biton had not promised these subterranean powers would keep. The monsters loosed on the northlands once more would be a problem as bad as the Gradi.

But the Gradi were a certainty—they were loose in the northlands now. The monsters were only a possibility. Gerin said, "Very well. Here are the terms of the bargain I propose: we will leave this breach in the wards open until I return to Fox Keep and summon Baivers once more. Then you and he will fight the Gradi gods, doing your best to defeat them."

He waited for the monsters' powers to demand access to the surface in exchange for their help. With the breach in the wards down, they could hardly be deprived of it—not by him, at any rate, although Biton might have something to say in that regard. If the powers dwelling down here were on good terms with him, though, he dared hope the monsters might not prove so vicious as they had on their first eruption from the caves.

None of those sometimes agreeing, sometimes arguing

voices said anything about that. Instead, speaking all together, they rumbled, "It is a bargain."

Gerin stared, though in complete darkness that had no point. Maybe Van had had the right of it after all, and the powers here wanted nothing more than a good brawl. Still, with Biton's verses fresh in his memory, he asked, "How shall we seal this bargain, so we know both sides can be sure it is good?"

That brought on more silence, the silence, Gerin judged, of surprise. When the monsters' gods answered, it was again in chorus: "Bargains have only one seal, the seal of blood and bone."

"Now wait a minute," Gerin said in some alarm. If he agreed to that without defining its limits, the underground powers were free to seize and rend him or any and all of his companions.

But he was too late. Somewhere in the darkness close by, a harsh, hoarse scream rang out. "The seal of blood and bone," the powers repeated. "What we agreed, we will do. It is sealed."

"My tooth!" someone groaned: Geroge, the Fox realized after a moment. "They tore out my tooth."

"Blood and bone," the subterranean gods said yet again. "That one is blood of our blood, but he is bone of your bone, for you raised him and his sister. That we take from him is fitting. And while we take, we also give."

Something was pressed into Gerin's hand, which closed around it. All at once, Lamissio's torch began to burn once more. The Fox looked down. He discovered he was holding the last two joints of a hairy, clawed finger, the blood from which stained his own hand. He almost threw the severed digit away with a cry of disgust, but in the end tucked it into a pouch on his belt instead, as security that the underground gods would live up to the bargain they had made.

That done, he went to see Geroge, who had both hands clutched to his muzzle. The monster's blood ran between his fingers and dripped to the floor. "Let me look at you," Gerin told him, and gently separated Geroge's hands. "Come on, open your mouth."

Moaning, Geroge obeyed. Sure enough, only a bloody socket showed where his right top fang had been. "It hurts," he said—almost unintelligibly, because he kept his mouth wide open all the time so the Fox could see.

"I'm sure it does," Gerin said, patting him on the shoulder. "When we get back to the inn, you can have all the ale you like. That will help dull the pain. And after we get back to Fox Keep and you're healed, I'll get you a new fang, all of gold, and have it fixed with wires to the teeth on either side. It won't be as good as the one you gave to the gods here, but it should be better than nothing."

"A gold tooth?" Tharma said, plainly trying to picture that in her mind. She nodded approval. "You'll look fine with a gold tooth, Geroge. You'll look splendid."

"Do you think so?" he asked. He was trying to adjust to the idea, too. Suddenly, absurdly, he began to preen. "Well, maybe I will."

Gerin turned to Lamissio. "Take us up now. We're done here." He pointed to the magical wards he'd disturbed. "And leave those down. You may be able to trap the monsters' gods down below if you restore them, but I know the northlands will have bad luck if you do, and I don't think the shrine and the valley would long be better for it, either."

"Lord prince, there I think you have nothing but reason," the eunuch priest answered. "It shall be as you say, I promise. And now, again as you say, let us return to the realm of light." He propelled his bulky frame up the path at a better pace than the Fox had thought he had in him.

Temple guards crowded Biton's shrine. They peered down anxiously into the rift in the earth leading down into the caves. When Lamissio called to them, their exclamations of relief were loud and voluble. "No monsters at your heels?" the captain in the gilded helm asked.

"Only the two who accompanied us," the priest replied. "The underground gods tore a tooth from one, which he bore bravely." It was, so far as Gerin could remember, the first good thing he'd had to say about Geroge and Tharma.

"Let us by, if you please," Gerin said, and the guards did step aside, though they kept watching the cave's mouth as if fearing surprise attack. The Fox did not suppose he could blame them for that.

More guards—and a bewildered suppliant—crowded the precinct outside the shrine itself. Lamissio asked, "Lord prince, with the wards down, do you think it safe for the Sibyl to return to her chamber and deliver the words of the god to those who come seeking them?"

Gerin shrugged. "Ask Biton. If he doesn't know, what point in worshipping him?"

"A point," Lamissio said. "A distinct point." He stopped at the entranceway set into the white marble fence around the temple precinct. "One of the more . . . unusual mornings in my years of service to the god."

" 'Unusual.' That's a word as good as any, and better than most. I do thank you for your help there," Gerin said, politely failing to mention that Lamissio had needed to have his god order him to help before he got moving and did it.

On the way back to the village, Selatre said, "Biton spoke through me again—he spoke through me." She said it several times, as if trying to convince herself. Gerin kept quiet. If Biton had spoken through her once now, would he do it again . . . and again? If he did, would

Selatre decide she preferred him to the Fox? And if she did that, what could he do about it? Nothing, as he knew perfectly well. If you fought a god straight out, you lost.

Why are you worrying? he asked himself, but here, for once, he knew the answer. *When a woman you've loved runs off with a horseleech, you're less inclined to take the world on trust than you used to be.*

Alongside having Biton speak through her, Selatre had a gift for fathoming Gerin's silences. After a while, she said, "You don't need to fear for me on account of Biton. I know where I want to be, and why," and set a hand on his arm. He set his own hand on hers for a moment, then walked on.

When he and his companions got back into the town of Ikos, the warriors he'd brought with him crowded round, wanting to know every detail of their visit to the Sibyl's shrine. They made much of Geroge and the courage with which he bore the loss of his fang. "Wouldn't want one of my teeth yanked out like that," Drungo Drago's son declared, "and they aren't near as big as yours."

As Gerin had promised, he let the monster have all the ale he could drink. Geroge grew boisterous in a friendly sort of way, made hideous attempts at singing, and eventually fell asleep at the table. Van and Drungo, who had also both had a good deal of ale, carried him upstairs to bed.

When Gerin and Selatre went up to their own chambers a little later, she barred the door, something he usually did. Then, quickly and with obvious determination, she got out of her clothes. "Come to bed," she said, and come to bed he did. Most times, making love solved nothing; it just meant you didn't think about things for a while. Drifting toward sleep afterwards, Gerin was glad to have found an exception to the rule.

✧   ✧   ✧

The Fox and his comrades entered with imperfect enthusiasm the holding that had belonged to Ricolf. Gerin would have been happiest scooting through that holding, seeing no one, and getting back to lands where he was suzerain. As he had discovered a good many times in life—Selatre being the splendid exception— what made him happiest was not commonly what he got.

A good-sized force of chariotry, quite a bit larger than his own, waited for him not far south of Ricolf's keep. At its head was Authari Broken-Tooth. Gerin nodded, unsurprised. "We have no quarrel with you and yours, Authari," he called when he recognized the baron who had been Ricolf's leading vassal. "Get out of our way and let us pass."

"I think not," Authari answered.

"Don't be foolish," the Fox told him. "Remember the oath you and your fellow barons swore."

"Like chicken or fish, oaths go stale quickly," Authari said.

What with the indolence of the Elabonian gods, Authari had a point, however much Gerin wished he didn't. But the Elabonian gods weren't the only ones loose in the land these days. Gerin pointed to the west, where thick gray clouds, nothing like those usually seen in summer, were building up. He feared Stribog had at last recovered from what Mavrix had done to him. "If you get rid of me, the only ones who will thank you are the Gradi and their gods."

"I'll take that chance, too," Authari said easily. "With you out of the way, I can afford to worry about them next."

"No," Duren said, not to that last comment, but to everything Authari had said: one comprehensive word of rejection. "Even if your men win a fight here, you will not follow my grandfather as baron to this holding."

"Oh? Why is that, pup?" Authari asked, still with mild amusement.

"Because all the men here will make straight for *your* car, Authari," Duren answered. "Your men may win, as I say, but you will not live to enjoy it."

The mild smile slipped from Authari's face. He did not have enough warriors with him to make it certain that Gerin's men could not live up to the threat. He could not hang back from the fighting, either, not unless he wanted his own soldiers to turn on him as soon as it was over.

"Stand aside and let us go," Gerin told him. At the same time, he sent his son an admiring glance. He couldn't have come up with—and hadn't come up with—a better way to throw Authari off-balance.

Off-balance the baron certainly was. Had he ordered a hard charge the moment he spotted Gerin's little force, he could have crushed them before they'd hit on that way of fighting back. But he'd hesitated, as he had the earlier time when the Fox and Duren entered his territory. Now he licked his lips, trying to make a choice that would have come naturally to a more ruthless man.

Van pointed to the west, too, but not to the building clouds. "Whose friends are those, I wonder?" he said: chariots were heading cross-country toward the Elabon Way, and toward the brewing trouble on it.

"Wacho has his holding in that direction," Gerin said. "So does Ratkis Bronzecaster, I think." He smiled over at Authari. "Isn't that interesting?"

Authari didn't answer. He didn't smile, either. He set his jaw and looked grim—but, again, not grim enough to order combat before the newcomers, whoever they were, arrived. If they were Wacho's men, he'd roll over Gerin's small band all the more easily. If they weren't . . .

They weren't. Heading up enough chariots to

counterbalance Authari's force, Ratkis approached the standoff. He waved to Gerin. "I didn't hear from Ricrod you'd passed through till day before yesterday," he said. "I thought it would be good to see you on your way back."

"I think it's good to see you," Gerin said. He smiled again at Authari. "Don't you think it's good to see him, too?"

"I can think of people I'd rather have seen," Authari growled. He clapped his driver on the shoulder. The fellow flicked the reins. The horses strode a couple of paces forward. Gerin grabbed for his bow. Then the driver swung the team into a turn. They started rolling away. Authari shouted angrily to his men. They followed.

"Hello, there," Gerin said to Ratkis. "If you'd turned out to be Wacho, I'd have been very embarrassed."

Ratkis shook his head. "I doubt it, lord prince. Hard to embarrass a dead man."

"A point. A distinct point," Gerin said, as Lamissio had earlier. He looked westward, wondering if he would see Wacho and his warriors riding up—*like Wacho to be late*, he thought. No new army was coming. But the clouds piled there were getting thicker and darker and spreading over more of the sky. That probably did mean Stribog was feeling chipper again, and probably also meant the Gradi and their gods were ready for another push against the Trokmoi and the Elabonians.

Ratkis said, "An oath is an oath. Once you've sworn it, you can't go forgetting it." He held up a hand. "No, I take that back. You can, but you'd better not. The gods don't like it."

He had more faith in the gods than Gerin did, which probably meant he had less knowledge about their present condition. The more fervent believers the Elabonian gods had, the likelier they were to take a more active part in the world. A year earlier, Gerin would have thought that a disaster. At the moment, it looked distinctly attractive.

Ratkis said, "Shall we ride with you a little ways?"

"I wouldn't mind that," Gerin allowed. Together, the two groups passed by the keep that had been Ricolf's without stopping. Not fully trusting Ricrod any more, Gerin preferred to shelter in a peasant village for the night.

The sun was sinking into that thick bank of building clouds when the Fox spotted a fair-sized force of chariotry approaching the Elabon Way from the east. Whoever was leading that force—Hildic was a good bet, he thought—saw the size of his contingent, too, and turned around and rode back in the direction from which he'd come.

"Another scavenger out to see what dead meat he could find," Ratkis remarked, and leaned out over the rail of his chariot to spit down onto the paving stone of the Elabon Way.

"You're probably right," Gerin said. "No, you're certainly right. We've gone past Wacho's keep, and he doesn't live east of the road, anyhow. Besides, I didn't get the idea that Wacho picked up news in a hurry, or was likely to figure out what to do about it if he did hear something."

"Right on both counts, lord prince," Ratkis said with a chuckle. He rode on in silence for a little while, then asked, "Why are you watching me out of the corner of your eye?"

Gerin's cheeks heated. "You weren't supposed to notice," he muttered. That wasn't answer enough, though, and he knew it. He sighed. "You have more men here than I do, Ratkis. I want to make sure you're not going to try to get me all cozy and then jump on me like a starving longtooth."

"I thought that was it," Ratkis answered. "But, like I

said, I swore an oath to your son, so you've got nothing to worry about there."

"Duren will be lucky to have you for a vassal," Gerin said. He did not tell Ricolf's former vassal that he always worried, whether he seemed to need to or not. If Ratkis got to know him better, he'd find that out for himself.

Here, though, for once, he did not need to worry. By the time they made camp, he was close to lands that recognized his suzerainty. And all Ratkis' men did that night was drink ale along with his and leer at the good-looking young women of the peasant village where they lay over. After fear going down below the shrine at Ikos to call on the underground powers, after more fear on the road earlier in the day, with still more fear ahead, the Fox treasured that small stretch of peace of mind. He wondered when—or if—he would find another.

Cold rain drummed down on the canvas cover of the wagon and soaked Gerin as he drove up to Fox Keep. The wind out of the west had a bite. It wasn't the blizzard Stribog and the other Gradi gods had blown up against the army he and Adiatunnus led against them, but it didn't feel like an ordinary summer storm, either. He scowled. Some rain now was fine, normal. Too much rain and he'd have a disaster on his hands even if the Gradi stayed at home.

He and his comrades had to come close to the keep and shout up to the men on the walls so those warriors could recognize their voices before the drawbridge came down with a wet, squelching slap. "Welcome back, lord prince," Rihwin the Fox called as Gerin came in. "Sorry we were so slow, but we couldn't be sure you weren't Gradi trying a sneak in the rain."

"I'm not angry," Gerin said. "The opposite, in fact." Any small bits of caution Rihwin showed were to be encouraged, nurtured, praised, in the hope they would grow. The longer Gerin knew Rihwin, the less likely that was: he knew as much, but had never been a man to give up easily.

"What luck had you, lord prince?" Rihwin asked.

"Geroge and Tharma's kind have gods," Gerin answered, which produced startled exclamations from several men who heard him. "They say they'll fight alongside Baivers and us. We'll know more tomorrow."

"Why tomorrow?" Rihwin said.

"Because that's when I intend to get magicking again," Gerin said. Rihwin gaped at him. He ignored that, continuing, "I'd do it today, but after we get the horses stabled, I'm going to have to spend the rest of the day readying what I'll need and studying the spells I intend to try." Rihwin was still gaping. Gerin condescended to notice him: "Aye, Rihwin, for once I'm as headlong as you. This storm tells me we have no time to waste. It's too much like what we saw west of the Venien. The Gradi are all too likely to use it as a cloak to hide whatever they intend to do till they're set to do it."

"Whatever you say, lord prince," Rihwin assured him, though his fellow Fox still looked somewhat dazed. Gerin had no time to worry about that, either. He jumped down from the wagon, then had to grab at it when he slipped in the mud. Once his own footing was secure, he handed Selatre down.

Their children came running out of the keep to greet them. Gerin hugged Dagref, Clotild, and Blestar in turn. So did Selatre, but then she said, "Now get back indoors this instant, before you catch cold." That led to noisy protests from all three children, and what looked suspiciously like deliberate falls in the mud by Dagref and Blestar. Dagref declared his innocence before the world when Selatre shouted at him; Blestar, as yet unpracticed in deceit, merely got up and ran, dripping, into the castle.

Shaking his head, Gerin went into the castle, too. He'd been wet for a good long while already, and enjoyed changing into a dry tunic and trousers. He knew the spell that had brought Baivers to him, but reviewed it in the library all the same. A mistake might mean the god's failure to appear, which might mean the northlands' going under.

Selatre poked her head into the library, saw him busy, and slipped away. When she came back, she set sausage, bread, and a jack of ale at his elbow. He'd eaten the food and almost emptied the jack before he noticed they were there and thought back on how they'd arrived. When he studied, he studied hard.

As far as Baivers was concerned, he was ready. Bringing forth the monsters' gods was a different business altogether. He had no invocation specifically intended to do that; whatever dealings with those powers mankind had had till now were designed to keep them under control and far away, not to bring them forth. Considering his meeting with them, he understood that down to the ground—and down under it, too.

Desperation, though, drove him to turn the usual way of doing things on its head. He got parchment and quill and ink and began adapting the spells of repulsion into ones that would draw the monsters. The spells he was crafting had not been refined by trial and error— others' error, corrected by mages who had observed . . . and survived . . . their colleagues' failure. That increased his risk in another way, and he knew it: if his own creations had flaws, the only way he would find out about it was the hardest way possible.

He looked up at the timbers of the ceiling. "If I had a choice, I wouldn't be doing this," he told them. They didn't answer. He suspected that was because they already knew.

✧   ✧   ✧

Along with Selatre and Duren, Van, and Geroge and Tharma, Gerin squelched through the mud of the courtyard toward the shack that doubled as his sorcerous laboratory. Cold rain still fell, stubbornly, steadily, out of a leaden sky, as if it had looked around, decided it liked the country, and settled in to stay.

Gerin patted his chest. He was carrying inside his undertunic the spells he'd written, to make sure—or as sure as he could—the rain didn't land on them and soak them into illegibility. The roof of the shack leaked. Normally, he didn't worry about such things. Today, they were liable to matter.

He'd been out there before, getting everything ready for the conjurations he would attempt: barley, ale, and porridge for summoning Baivers, and other things for summoning the monsters' gods. One of the other things, a billy goat, bleated as he and his comrades came in. He'd tied it to a post, with a rope so short it couldn't chew itself free. Its gaze was fixed on the barley on the worktable, which it could see and smell but could not reach.

"Sorry, old fellow," he told the goat. It bleated again, indignantly. He ignored it, pouring ale for himself and for Geroge and Tharma. After they'd drunk it, he got to work summoning Baivers. "Come forth!" he called when the spell was done. "Come forth, lord Baivers, come forth, come forth, come forth!"

For a moment, he wondered if he would have the same difficulty making the god notice him as he'd known the time before. But then the shack seemed to get bigger inside without enlarging on the outside: the sure mark of a god's presence. "I am here," Baivers said, and the stalks of barley that did duty for his hair rustled softly. His green, green eyes took in the interior of the shack. They rested on the billy goat: none too kindly, Gerin thought, for a goat could wreak havoc in the fields. "You have all in readiness to summon the other powers, the powers from under the ground?"

"Lord Baivers, I hope I do," Gerin answered, a statement true on several different levels.

"Begin, then," Baivers said. "We have little time to lose. The Gradi gods are reaching out, greedy as grasshoppers. Can you feel them?"

"Yes," Gerin said. He reached under his tunic and drew out the spells he had hastily devised. He started to shield the parchment from drips from the roof with his hand, then realized it hadn't leaked since Baivers came forth: an unexpected advantage of the god's presence.

Now he wished he'd drunk no ale. A slip in the spells summoning Baivers might well not have been fatal. A slip in the spells he was trying now surely would be. Geroge and Tharma watched him, their deep-set eyes wide, as he incanted. What were they thinking? They'd said little on the way up from Ikos by which he could judge how they'd taken their first meeting with the gods who ruled their own kind.

He shook his head, though the motion had nothing to do with the magic he was working. Even the monsters' gods had said Geroge and Tharma were neither fully of their kind nor of mankind. He wondered how those gods would have responded to his overtures had he slain the two monsters as cubs, as he'd been sorely tempted to do. He was glad he didn't have to find out.

Maybe that relief helped steady him. Whatever the reason, he managed to get through the chants and intricate passes of the spells unscathed. Nothing in those hastily adapted chants had either loosed the monsters' gods on the northlands or provoked them to eat them up. He reckoned that a triumph. The powers, though, still remained unsummoned.

"Let the blood bring them hither," he said, at the

same time thinking, *Now we find out what sort of fool I am, meddling with things beyond my power*. He knelt beside the billy goat. Up till his last trip out to the shack, he'd intended to slit its throat with a bronze knife. Since then, he'd had what he hoped was a better idea. From a pouch on his belt, he drew the severed finger of the monster the powers had given him in exchange for taking Geroge's fang. The finger had not decayed to any discernible extent, which made him think some power still lingered in it.

He used the claw to tear the goat's flesh. Though it did not feel unusually sharp to him, it might have been the keenest dagger he'd ever handled. Blood fountained from the goat's throat and drowned the animal's terrified, anguished bleat. "Let the blood bring them hither!" Gerin cried again, as it made a great red steaming pool that slowly began to sink into the ground.

The interior of the shack seemed to . . . expand again. For a moment, it seemed to go dark, too. Gerin wondered if the monsters' gods could stand the light of day. But then that light returned, and for the first time he saw the gods he had summoned.

As mankind's gods mostly partook of and modified the manlike shape, so the monsters' powers resembled the mortal creatures whose patrons they were. They too modified the basic pattern. One of them glowed. One had eyes bigger and rounder than an owl's, another great, batlike ears. One seemed nothing but muscle and fur and fangs and talons: if he didn't do duty as a war god, the Fox would have been mightily surprised.

"Blood brings us," they said all together, their voices dinning in his mind. "We have kept the bargain. Now it is for you to keep it as well. Show us the way to battle and slaughter."

"I'll do that," Gerin told them. Fighting *was* all they wanted, he realized; had he set them against Biton or against the Elabonian gods, they would have entered that fray with as much ferocity as this one. He shivered. If this fight should be won, he'd do what he could either to restore those wards under Biton's shrine or to form some arrangement between the monsters' gods and those who lived on the surface of the earth.

This is the way to the Gradi gods: he cast his thought toward Baivers. As Mavrix had, the Elabonian god picked up his mind and carried it along with his own over a plane of being no mortal could reach without divine aid. From his place as a small cyst on Baivers' vaster consciousness, the Fox sensed the underground powers following where the god of ale and barley led.

The route felt different this time: no sea of wine, no equally turbulent sea of sensuality. Gerin wondered if he was perceiving the same "places" through a different god's sensorium, or if Baivers had simply chosen a different path. Amber waves of grain were certainly more sedate than wine and polymorphous fornication.

Whatever the truth, whatever the route, in the end they reached the snow-covered forest of conifers to which Mavrix had brought him. "Too bleak for barley," Baivers said, in a tone of condemnation and abhorrence. "This is what they want to make my land into, is it?" The monsters' gods said nothing at all. They stared, hungrily, every which way at once, as if looking for rivals to massacre.

A path led through the woods, as it had before. Baivers started down it, the underground powers at his heels. The wolves of the divine Gradihome stared out from the trees at the strange gods who dared walk it. A couple of monsters sprang at the wolves. Maybe that was blood on the snow when they were done, maybe ichor. It looked like blood to Gerin.

"Who comes to Gradihome?" As he had during

Gerin's visit with Mavrix, the fierce god named Lavtrig stood in a clearing as Voldar's first sentinel against attack.

Baivers pointed a finger. Through the snow under Lavtrig's feet burst shoots of green. The Gradi god stared at them in something like horror. Mavrix had joked by setting flowers blooming in this grim land. Baivers used fertility as a weapon.

Lavtrig thundered toward him, stamping the shoots flat as he came. He raised a great club, plainly intending to smash the Elabonian god out of existence. Baivers pointed at the club. It turned into leaves and blew away on a sudden warm breeze. Lavtrig roared with rage. He drew from a sheath a bronze sword with a gleaming edge. Over metal Baivers had no power.

The monsters' god that was all thews and claws and teeth sprang out from the pack and onto Lavtrig. Lavtrig smote him. He smote back. "Good battle!" he shouted joyously.

Gerin sent a thought toward Baivers: "Shall the rest of us go on? He seems to have found what he wanted."

Go on they did; Lavtrig, though not defeated, was far too busy to block their path. More wolves stared out at Baivers and the underground powers as they pushed along the path. The wolves, though, no longer stayed to fight, but fled through the pine woods, wailing the alarm in all directions.

"They summon the rest of the Gradi gods," Baivers said.

He sounded worried to Gerin. If the monsters' gods shared his concern, they gave no sign of it. "We want those gods," they said in ragged chorus. "We will chew their flesh; we will gnaw their bones."

When they reached the next clearing, there stood Stribog, the father of all storms. He shouted in what might have been wrath and might have been fear at having his place in Gradihome assailed once more. Giving his foes no chance to enter the clearing, he flung a blast of chilly rain into their faces.

Baivers spread his arms wide. "I thank you for your gift of water," he told the Gradi god, "and shall turn it into blessed barley."

Stribog shouted again, this time in obvious fury. "Go back!" he roared wetly. "You and your band are doomed. Flee while you may." The rain changed to sleet, then to hail that pounded the unwelcome visitors like bullets from a sling.

The monsters' god who glowed stepped forward from among his fellows. That glow had been pale and wan; Gerin had associated it with the pallid gleam of fireflies and molds and certain mushrooms. All at once, though, its nature changed. It grew red as fire, red as the vents through which lava spilled out of some mountains and over the land. The glow grew hot as fire, too.

"Light," the other underground powers crooned. "Precious light!" To them, Gerin realized, any source of illumination, whether from decay or an underground vent for molten rock, was precious and potent.

Their light-bearing god sent a blast of fiery heat back at Stribog, melting hail, sizzling sleet into steam, sending the snow under the weather god's liquid feet boiling up as steam. Stribog roared in anger and pain and fought back with whips of winter. He rushed forward to bluster at the monsters' god, making steam rise up from his shining skin as snow and ice threatened to douse his flame. The underground power in turn redoubled his own effort.

Again, Gerin said, "The rest of us can push on, I think," and again Baivers and the monsters' gods did push ahead through the clearing. Like Lavtrig before him, Stribog was far too busy to prevent their passage. As they found the next path, the Fox warned, "Up ahead is the clearing where Nothing dwells. Watch out for him—he's dangerous."

Baivers, sensibly, stopped at the edge of the next clearing. Gerin let out a tiny mental sigh. He didn't know if he would be able to tell whether Nothing had been playing his tricks this time. He'd managed when Mavrix came this way, but who could guess whether the Gradi god was able to learn new tricks?

His old ones were quite bad enough. A couple of the underground powers, maybe filled with contempt for Baivers' cowardice, maybe just looking for a fight wherever they could find one, sprang out into the clearing with ferocious roars, staring all about them in search of a foe.

They sprang out, they roared . . . and they were gone.

It was not merely that they vanished. It was as if they had never been. Gerin needed a distinct mental effort to recall that they had been part of the ravening pack of gods accompanying Baivers here.

As for Baivers, he said, "You were right, mortal. This power is not to be despised."

"Mavrix didn't beat him," Gerin answered. "He managed to distract him, and that proved enough to get him by."

"Mavrix is full of distractions," Baivers answered. "Distraction is all he's good for. Sometimes I think distraction is all he is."

Behind the Elabonian deity, the monsters' gods were milling around and muttering among themselves. After a moment, one of them, in the shape of a monster but perfectly, light-drinkingly black, stepped past Baivers and out to the very edge of the clearing. "Nothing!" he called in a voice that sounded as if it was echoing and reechoing down the corridors of a cave.

"I am here," Nothing answered, his own voice quiet and flat. "I am everywhere, but I am here most of all."

"Give me back my comrades," the monsters' god said.

"It cannot be," Nothing said.

"Give them back, or you shall not be," the monsters' god warned.

"It cannot be," Nothing repeated.

"It can," the underground power answered, "for I am Darkness." He raised his hands, and the clearing was plunged into blackness as absolute as that Gerin had known when the monsters' gods met his summons below Biton's shrine. Darkness went on, "No one will know whether you are here or not, Nothing. No one will care. When you cannot be found, no one will miss you."

"Or you," Nothing returned, and for a moment black shifted to gray, or rather to the shade of complete and utter neutrality for which gray is the closest earthly approximation.

"I think we'd best move on, while they're busy figuring out which of them is less than the other," Gerin said.

"That's the right way, sure enough," Baivers said, and the rough chorus of the monsters' gods muttered agreement. They advanced into the clearing in which their comrades had ceased to be—into it and through it. As best Gerin could tell with his limited senses, Baivers did not need light to know where he was going.

On the far side of the clearing, light returned. Baivers seemed to glance through Gerin's mind. "Only this Voldar to go, eh?" the god of barley asked.

"I think so," the Fox answered. "After Mavrix got past Nothing, she was the last deity he met. She beat him, but we have more strength with us now."

"We will devour her and gnaw her bones," the monsters' gods chorused. Gerin remembered some of the things the monsters had done while they roamed above ground. If their gods did things like that here . . . he would, he supposed, be glad. And then he would worry about how to make sure the monsters didn't come boiling up onto the surface of the world once more . *If I can make sure of that*, he thought.

Whatever the answer was, he could worry about it later. The fight with Voldar was the immediate concern: immediate indeed, for the path opened out just then into the clearing where the queen of the Gradi gods stood waiting.

That clearing, Gerin thought, was larger than it had been when Voldar summoned him in the dream, larger than when he had come here with Mavrix. That jolted him far less than it would have back in the merely material world; the stuff of the gods had change as part of its very nature.

And it needed to be changeable, for Voldar did not stand alone here: the clearing had grown to accommodate what looked to be the rest of the Gradi pantheon. Most of the gods looked, not surprisingly, like Gradi—tall, fair, gray-eyed, with dark hair and grim expressions. Voldar led them, taller than any, grimmer than any, beauty and terror and rage all commingled.

She started to shout something to the divinities she headed. Before she could, though, Baivers outshouted her: "You frosters! You freezemakers! You bloodspillers! You blighters!" In the little encysted space in Baivers' mind where Gerin sheltered, he had all he could do not to giggle. Down in the City of Elabon, a few languid, affected young men had used *blighters* as a name for those of whom they did not approve. Imagining Baivers in their company was deliciously absurd. The god of barley, though, meant his insult literally.

Voldar did shout then, a belling contralto that sent shivers up and down the spine from which the Fox was divorced at that moment: "It's the local grass god, all puffed up with himself. And he's brought the kennel with him. We whip them back home, and then we go on about our business."

"Blighters!" Baivers bellowed again, and rushed forward. Voldar loped toward him, as deadly graceful as a longtooth. He picked her up; she let out a most ungodlike squawk of startlement as he slammed her down to the snowy ground. Inside Baivers, Gerin was cheering wildly. He'd wanted the god of barley angry, and now he'd got what he wanted. Not at his finest had Mavrix given Voldar such an overthrow.

But she was on her feet in an instant—feet around which little shoots of barley began to show, pushing their way up through the eternal snow of the divine Gradihome. Voldar hewed at those shoots with her axe. Each one she cut bled real blood, and at each stroke Baivers groaned as if she were cutting him down.

"Forward!" Voldar shouted to her divine companions. "Let's get them, and get them now. We'll—"

She got no further than that. Her cropping the growing barley had hurt Baivers, but had not quenched his determination—very much the reverse. He grabbed the axe handle. Voldar screeched in rage. Gerin felt a harsh tingling run up Baivers' arms, as if he'd grabbed hold of a lightning bolt. Baivers wrestled the axe from Voldar and threw it far—maybe infinitely far—away.

Gerin had hoped a good part of Voldar's power dwelt in that axe, and that without it she would be diminished. If she was, she gave no outward sign of it. She dealt Baivers a buffet that would have caved in the skull of an ordinary mortal.

The only ordinary mortal in that clearing, though, was Gerin, and he wasn't there in the flesh. A lot of flesh was flying, and fur, and divine ichor, from both the underground powers and the Gradi gods. The Fox couldn't help thinking Sithonian deities would have handled the battle with more elegance and panache. Any elegance or panache would have been more than was on display at the moment. Neither the monsters' gods nor those of the Gradi had much in the way of subtlety. They found the nearest foe and went at him, much as monsters and Gradi would have done had they collided in the northlands.

One of the Gradi gods burst into flame. The underground power he was fighting screeched. Another of the monsters' gods, though, tackled the Gradi god and rolled with him in the snow, after which his fire was extinguished for a while. And the subterranean god who had been burned healed with supernatural speed.

An underground power sprang on Voldar, claw raking cuts along her haunch. She screamed in mingled pain and fury and kicked out behind her like an angry horse. The monsters' god flew through the air and smashed headfirst into the trunk of a fir. He did not get up right away. He did not get up at all. Gerin wondered if he would ever get up again.

A Gradi god to whom the Fox had not been introduced tried to freeze Baivers where he stood, blowing an icy blast at him as if from the side of some snow-covered northern mountain. However hostile his intent, his power did not measure up to it. In response, Baivers pointed a finger at him. All the hair on his arms, on his face, on his head, turned to growing barley. He wailed and clawed at himself, but remained green and growing.

"How *dare* you interfere with our plans?" Voldar demanded of Baivers.

"Who's interfering in whose part of the world?" the god of barley retorted. "You leave my earth alone, maybe I'll think of leaving you alone. And maybe not, too. You deserve what you're getting, all the trouble you've caused there 'twixt the Niffet and the Kirs."

"Not half so much as we *will* cause," Voldar snarled. "We'll take revenge for eons, see if we don't."

She broke off then, with a howl of outrage, for one of the monsters' gods, one who beside her was like a small dog beside a man, bit her in the ankle. Gerin admired the courage of the underground power, and wished he'd had the chance to meet more of the monsters' gods in anything but the most perfunctory way before leading them into this fight.

The monsters' god was small, but held power not to be despised. Voldar's leg did not work as it should have after he sank his teeth into her. She beat on him with all her strength, but he would not let go his hold. "What are you, you savage worm?" she cried.

Speaking mind to mind, the underground power did not have to leave off biting her to reply, "I am Death."

Excitement rippled through Gerin when he caught that answer. Even Voldar might have trouble against such a foe. Were gods truly immortal? Would he find out now? Something that might have been alarm in her voice, Voldar shrilly cried, "Smerts! To me!"

Seeing Smerts, the Fox realized he—no, she, for the emaciated frame carried shrunken breasts—was Death's Gradi equivalent. Where Voldar had been unable to free herself from the underground power's onslaught, Smerts tore the fierce little god away from the queen of the Gradi pantheon. "You are mine," Smerts crooned in a fierce, hungry whisper.

"No," the monsters' Death said, just as hungrily, "you are mine." And he bit the hand that held him. Smerts squeezed him with her other hand. Gerin wondered what would happen if they slew each other. Would that bring immortality into the world?

Whether or not Voldar was immortal, she was imbued with enormous vitality. As soon as Smerts had plucked Death from her, she regained full use of that leg, and used it to smash in the ribs of an underground power who had torn a Gradi god almost in two.

The kicked power stumbled backward, groaning, and knocked Death out of Smerts' hands. Smerts seized the new underground power, while Death clamped his teeth into the first Gradi god he could reach. Gerin wished he had a body with which to groan. Mortality's power in the world would continue to hold sway.

He risked a question of Baivers: "Are we winning?"

"Don't know," the Elabonian god replied. He looked around the field, which meant Gerin perforce looked around the field, too. What he saw was what he'd seen since the brawl began: chaos loosed in the divine Gradihome. "Don't know if we're winning," Baivers repeated, "but I don't reckon we're losing, neither."

That was as much as Gerin had hoped for when he led the underground powers here. It seemed to be plenty to satisfy the monsters' gods, too. Some of the Gradi gods knocked down or uprooted trees with their bare hands and swung them, like enormous spearshafts, at their foes. That distressed the monsters' gods, who were unused to trees in all ways, and especially as weapons.

But Baivers knew about trees. Some of the power he used to make barley spring to life also worked on them. Their branches and roots turned unnaturally lively, grappling with the Gradi gods who tried to wield the trunks. And while the trees discommoded the Gradi gods, the underground powers sprang on them, rending and tearing.

Before the monsters' gods reached the divine Gradihome, their grim and savage intensity, their bloodthirsty devotion to slaughter, had alarmed the Fox, who wondered whether they weren't apt to be a worse bargain for the northlands than Voldar and her companions. He had thought the underground powers would only have grown more ferocious once they joined battle with the Gradi gods.

So far as he could tell, that wasn't happening. The clearing was filled not just with quasiphysical screams and shouts and groans, but also with the thoughts and feelings of the battling gods, sometimes as weapons, sometimes merely there. Gerin did not catch the same rage now from the monsters' gods as he'd felt when they were coming toward this fight. What he did get from them was so surprising, he had to pause and consider before he was willing to admit, even to himself, that he fully grasped it.

"They're enjoying themselves!" he told Baivers, almost indignantly. "They're like a serf village on a holiday, when they've got a couple of pigs roasting over the fire and plenty of your good ale and no work to do. They're having the time of their lives."

"They wanted battle," Baivers answered. "You've given 'em what they wanted, and then some. Bet they'll like you real well when this here is done."

Gerin didn't know whether that prospect was more appealing—if the underground powers felt well disposed toward him, they might be inclined to control the monsters' depredations—or appalling. What he did know was that the Gradi gods were not enjoying themselves. He had the feeling from previous encounters with them that they seldom enjoyed themselves, at least by any standards with which he was familiar.

What they felt now was anger, of a peculiar sort: the anger of those who see plans they had reckoned certain of success suddenly falling to pieces all around them. In his little space inside Baivers' sensorium, the Fox exulted. The Gradi and their gods had reckoned the northlands ripe for conquest and transformation. Now they were finding it wasn't so, and not caring for the discovery.

Here came Smerts, looking more deathly than ever. She seized Baivers as she had seized the death god among the underground powers. As she had with him, she crooned, "You are mine."

Baivers groaned. Dwelling inside him—dwelling, in

effect, as part of him—Gerin felt vitality flowing out of him and into Smerts. It was like watching ale leak out of a cracked jar—the level went down, down, down, steadily, inexorably. That gave the Fox an idea. "Feed Smerts more life than she can hold all at once," he thought at Baivers. "You're a god of growing things—make her grow lively if you can."

"If I can," Baivers said doubtfully. He seemed to quiver, gathering himself. Then—it was as if a lightning bolt passed from him to Smerts.

The Gradi goddess gasped. Her eyes opened very wide. The stringy white stood out straight on her skull. Was it the Fox's imagination, or did she all at once look less skeletal than she had?

"You can't do that," she gasped at Baivers. "You can't." But her voice was not the harsh croak it had been a moment before. It was smoother, richer: almost the voice of a being concerned with something other than extinction.

Gerin still wondered if he was more hopeful than he should have been, if he was letting that hope color what his senses (always unreliable on this plane anyhow) told him. No: Baivers sensed Smerts' weakness, too. "Yes I can," he said, fresh confidence in his own voice.

Watching Smerts, Gerin watched years peel away and emaciation flesh out. Contemplating his own middle-aged carcass back in the merely material world, he wished Baivers would put him through a similar course. It soon proved too much for the Gradi goddess. She broke free of Baivers and fled. At each stride, she seemed to age a few years, and was soon back to what she had been, but she did not challenge the god of barley again.

"I thank you," Baivers said to Gerin. "That was right sly. Worst thing for a lot of folks is too much of what they tell you they want." He strode toward Voldar, shouting to her, "You, there! We weren't done, the two of us!"

She whirled to face him. "No, we weren't," she said. Gerin wondered about the wisdom of confronting the queen of the Gradi pantheon so directly. Before he could more than begin to frame that thought, though, Voldar's pale gaze pierced the encystment within Baivers where his own small spirit sheltered. "You!" she cried, and she was not speaking to the Elabonian god.

"Yes, me," Gerin answered, as steadfastly as he could. "I told you that you weren't welcome in the northlands, and that I'd do everything I could to stop you."

Voldar's eyes flashed pale fire. "I never dreamt one mortal could cause so much trouble." Her wave encompassed the chaos all around, chaos with no resolution anywhere near at hand. Then she stabbed out a finger at the Fox. "And I say you may not come to the Gradihome of the gods." Her voice rose to a shrill shriek: "Begone!"

Darkness.

Gerin opened his eyes. He was in the shack again. "Did we win?" Van asked.

XI

Gerin cast a wary eye up to the sky. The day was hot and fair; the sun blazed down like a ball of molten bronze in the middle of a blue enamel bowl. The cold, nasty rain that had plagued the last part of the ride up from Ikos was gone, vanished more suddenly than a natural storm had any business disappearing.

Wiping his forehead with a sleeve, he said, "Unless I miss my guess, Stribog is either still fighting one of the monsters' gods or else laid up from having fought him."

"Been four days now since you and Baivers and all the underground powers went to fight Voldar and her chums," Van said. "Still no notion of how the fight turned out?"

"Not even the slightest," Gerin answered. "Every day since, I've tried to summon Baivers, I've tried to summon the monsters' gods, but I get no answer. Maybe they've been destroyed, but I don't think so. If they had been, the Gradi would be swarming up the Niffet in their war galleys, and we haven't seen a single fire beacon. The weather's too fine to make me think the Gradi gods won, too."

"What then?" Van asked.

"My best guess is that they're still fighting up there, out there, on that plane where the gods can go and we mostly can't," the Fox said. "Neither side looked to have any sort of edge when Voldar booted me off my perch on Baivers' shoulder, you might say."

"A fight that doesn't stop." Van sighed wistfully. "Must be a fine thing to be a god, to never need to eat or sleep, to heal up as fast as you're hurt, to war for as long as you like, for years on end, maybe." He let out a snort of laughter. "But then, I know a bit about warring for years on end. I ought to, married to Fand like I am."

He looked indignant when Gerin didn't chuckle at that. "Warring for years on end," Gerin said. He nodded, more to himself than to Van. "It could be so." He hoped it was so. If the Gradi were locked in battle with the underground powers and with Baivers for years, they'd have neither the time nor the ability to help their human followers. He smacked one fist into the other palm. "We have to hit the Gradi while their gods are busy—can't waste a moment. The more we drive those cursed raiders back, the harder the time they'll have recovering, even if their gods do end up beating the ones I turned loose on them."

Van stared at him. "You sound like you're heading out on campaign this very day."

"Tomorrow will have to do, I think," the Fox said reluctantly. "But I'm going to send out a messenger this instant to let Adiatunnus know we're on our way. We're going across the Venien again, and this time we're not coming back till we've beaten the Gradi."

"You've said that before," Van answered. "It didn't work out."

"I wish you hadn't reminded me," Gerin said, which made the outlander chuckle and bow as if he'd just been thanked for doing a favor. Slowly, Gerin went on, "If we can't beat them on the land they've stolen while their gods are busy, though . . . I don't think we'll be able to beat them at all. What we'll have to do in that case is not go after them any more, but hunker down in our keeps, fight them as hard as we can for as long as we can when they come to us, and probably end by going down fighting."

"There are worse ways to end," Van said. "I don't think I'd want to get old and creaky and have a fit so one side of my body doesn't want to work and spend my last days gumming gruel on account of I can't chew and I can hardly swallow. Next to that, an axe that splits my skull is kind."

"I wasn't thinking so much of my end," Gerin said. "I don't want to watch everything I've spent my life building fall to pieces, though, and see my children made into serfs for the Gradi."

"If the Gradi win, you won't see any of that, for they'll surely kill you," Van said, and the Fox could hardly disagree. "Still and all, I follow what you're saying," the outlander continued. "I tell you true, there are times I'm glad I don't try to look so far ahead as you do."

"We're all different," Gerin said with a shrug, "and we're all still free. Now we'll find out how long we get to stay that way."

In times gone by, the guards at the eastern border of Adiatunnus' holding would have fled at the approach of the Elabonian army Gerin led—either fled or, with mad Trokmê courage, tried to sell their lives dear. Now, instead, they let out whoops of delight. Their voices broke as they cried out: they had hardly more than Duren's years, with only light down on their faces.

"What word from the Venien?" Gerin called to them in their own language.

" 'Twas said the Gradi were after moving men up toward that stream," one of the youths replied. "How any man could be sure, though, with the bad weather we've been having and all, is past me, indeed and it is."

"What's the weather like on the other side of the river

these days?" the Fox asked, remembering the summer blizzard that had done more to defeat him than the axes of the Gradi.

Both the young sentries shrugged. "Been warmer here o' late," said the one who hadn't spoken before. "And you're only a day and a little bit behind the chariot you sent out, the which, I've no doubt, our chief will be right glad to see."

"And even gladder to see the whole lot of you," the other youngster added. "Adiatunnus is after gathering all the men he may, to hold the Gradi back, that being the reason the two of us get to do a soldier's job so soon."

"Do well. Do as well as you can," Gerin told them. "But we don't aim to hold back the Gradi. We aim to go after 'em and beat 'em." The Trokmê sentries cheered again. So did his own men.

On into Adiatunnus' holding rode the Elabonian army. The Elabonian serfs in the fields, seeing soldiers, mostly fled into the woods regardless of whether they spoke the same language. Soldiers were soldiers, and all too liable to be dangerous. "We might as well be Gradi or Trokmoi ourselves, as far as they're concerned," Duren said, watching them run.

"Remember that," Gerin told him. "My serfs don't think of my warriors that way, and yours shouldn't, either, once you've taken over at the holding your grandfather ruled."

Mischief in his voice, Van said, "But these are your serfs, too, Fox, for isn't Adiatunnus your vassal?"

"When he feels like it," Gerin answered dryly, which made his son and his friend laugh. Gerin drummed his fingers on the chariot rail. "If we win against the Gradi, he may have to decide whether he's my vassal or my foe—I may make him decide that, I should say. Till then, I'm just glad he hasn't sided with them instead of with me."

They passed that night camped by a keep that had held an Elabonian petty baron in the days before the Trokmoi swarmed south over the Niffet and was now home to woodsrunners who lorded it over the serfs at a nearby village. A lot of the men were gone from the keep, summoned by Adiatunnus to protect his western border. The Trokmê women, bolder in their habits than Elabonians would have been, wasted little time in getting friendly—or more than friendly—with the newcomers.

The night was made for such games, being unusually dark in its early states: all four moons were past full, the first of them, Nothos, not rising till almost halfway between sunset and midnight. Gerin was anything but surprised to see Van heading upstairs with a brash Trokmê woman who put him in mind of Fand. He had no doubt Fand would guess, one of these days before too long, what the outlander was up to. His ears rang in anticipation.

He sighed. He couldn't do anything about that. He wasn't Van's nursemaid. If the outlander didn't get so drunk as to make himself too hung over to stay in the chariot come tomorrow, the Fox had no call to upbraid him.

"But it's—untidy, that's what it is," he said to no one in particular. Finding exactly the right phrase satisfied him in a way even shouting at Van couldn't have done. He wrapped himself in a blanket and went to sleep.

Outriding the news of its coming, the Elabonian army descended on Adiatunnus' keep and the village—almost the town—close by it. "If I'd done as well as this when I was the Trokmê's enemy, he'd have feared me more," Gerin said.

As he'd been doing all along, he looked up into the sky. The weather remained hot and dry. He and his men were close to the Venien now. If Stribog interfered with the normal run of things, they would know it sooner and more surely than back at Fox Keep. He saw no sign of any such thing, and was relieved.

Adiatunnus rode out from his castle to greet Gerin and the men with him. "The fellow you sent ahead, he said you're after thinking of fighting the Gradi on their own ground again," he said, sounding anything but delighted at the prospect.

"It's not their ground," the Fox answered. "Some of it, in point of fact, is mine. I intend to take it back, and to drive them off it."

"You intended the same earlier in the year, and had nobbut bad cess," Adiatunnus said. "Why d'you think your luck'll be better on a second go?"

"I'll tell you why," Gerin said, and did. He finished, "I don't know whether Baivers and the monsters' gods have beaten Voldar and the Gradi crew, but I'd say they haven't lost. If they had, the weather would be worse."

Adiatunnus tugged at one side of his drooping mustaches. "It could be so," he said at last, after some thought. "Not long ago, the cold storms came rolling over the Venien one after t'other, you might say, and the Gradi looked to be gathering for a push right at us." He scowled. "Shamed as I am to own it, we'd have broken and run without your Widin. On our own, we canna stand against the Gradi. But he said he'd fight 'em with us or without us, and so I called up all the men, to give him what help we could."

Making himself stand against a foe who had trounced his folk time after time had taken courage, and courage of an unusual sort. "Widin's not the only man here with spirit," the Fox said, acknowledging that. "What happened then? I haven't heard of the Gradi crossing the Venien."

"They didna," Adiatunnus said. "Not so many days

ago, the storms stopped and it was summer again, as fine a summer as any I've seen. And the Gradi drew back a ways from the Venien. We slipped a few o' Widin's men and mine over the river to see if they could find out what was toward, and they tell me the reivers seem all in an uproar, like as if summat they'd expected hadna happened after all."

"Maybe, just maybe, I kept it from happening," Gerin replied. "And if I did, the best thing we can do now is hit them as hard a blow as we can, give them something else they aren't expecting."

"Can we do it?" Adiatunnus asked.

"Of course we can," Gerin said heartily, though he did not think the Trokmê chieftain had in fact aimed the question at him. Adiatunnus sounded more as if he were putting it to his own gods, the gods whom Voldar and the Gradi had beaten and terrified. What sort of answer would he find, whether from them or in his own heart?

After a long pause, Adiatunnus said, "Well, we'd best have a go. If we dinna go to them, they'll come to us, sure as sure, and no good will spring from that."

The endorsement, while anything but ringing, was an endorsement. "We'll move against them tomorrow, your men and mine together," Gerin said. Adiatunnus stared at him. Now the Fox glared, playing to the hilt the role of outraged feudal overlord. "Tomorrow I said and tomorrow I meant. And I mean in the morning, too, even if I have to boot every one of you lazy, sleepy woodsrunners in the arse to make it happen."

"Lazy!" Adiatunnus clapped a hand to his forehead. "Sleepy? We'll show you, you black-hearted spalpeen!"

"I hope you do," Gerin said. "But if you don't" —he waved back at his army— "I've brought enough Elabonians along to get you moving."

"Elabonians? Foosh!" Adiatunnus said. "We make no

special shivers for Elabonians. It's not as if you were so many Gradi, now."

"To the crows with you," Gerin exclaimed. Both men laughed. They'd tried to kill each other before; they might well try to kill each other again one day. Meanwhile, though, they saw they had more urgent things to worry about than their old animosity. That in itself eased Gerin's mind. He had been far from sure Adiatunnus would be able to look to what might lie ahead rather than remembering the past. For that matter, he'd been far from sure he'd be able to do that himself.

"If you're right, Fox, and we beat the Gradi . . ." The Trokmê chieftain's voice trailed away, as if he had trouble believing such a thing possible. After a moment, he started up again: "If we do that, 'twill be a braw thing you've managed: aye, a braw thing indeed."

"We'll see what happens, that's all," the Fox said. "I've always tried to take the fight to the other fellow when I stood any chance of doing it."

"That I ken," Adiatunnus said, "for you've done it to me more times nor I care to recall. May we have the same luck against the Gradi."

"Sounds like a toast to me," Van said, "and only a fool would make a toast without washing it down." It was not a subtle hint, but Van was not a subtle man: in that he matched the Trokmoi more closely than the Elabonians among whom he lived. As Adiatunnus had taken on more Elabonian ways than most of the woodsrunners south of the Niffet, he might have found Van's approach imperfectly polished. If he did, he was too polished himself to show it. Smiling, he waved Gerin, Van, and the rest of the Elabonian warriors toward his keep.

Gerin looked back at the Venien River. It wasn't a great stream like the Niffet into which it flowed; it seemed hardly enough to serve as the boundary between not just two peoples but almost between two worlds. But back there on the eastern side, Gerin had been prince of the north, overlord of all he surveyed. If he claimed to rule here, he would have to make that claim good against the Gradi.

As he had even in his own holding, he kept a weather eye on the sky. Storm clouds building in the west might give warning the Gradi gods had won their war. He saw none; the day remained fine. What he did see was Adiatunnus, also nervously eyeing the western horizon.

Catching his glance, the Trokmê looked briefly shamefaced. "It's only that I'm after remembering the last time we tried coming this way," he said. "Another summer blizzard like that—" He broke off, plainly not wanting to think of it. Gerin didn't want to, either, but couldn't help himself.

A car holding Widin Simrin's son rolled up alongside Gerin's. Widin pointed ahead. "Gradi up that way, lord prince, based at what was a peasant village." He spoke with authority; the scouts, Elabonian and Trokmê both, who had been slipping off over the Venien to spy out the raiders' doings reported to him when they returned—if they returned.

The Fox waved half the chariots off to the left and the other half to the right, wanting to hit the Gradi from two directions at once. He led the left-hand column himself. At his father's order, Duren urged the horses up into a gallop. "Speed and surprise will get us more here than stealth," Gerin judged.

Surprised the Gradi certainly were. When they spied the chariots rushing toward them they let out loud bellows of alarm. Some of them dashed back into the peasant huts they'd appropriated and then came back out with axes and a few bows. And a handful did something Gerin had never before seen Gradi do: they turned tail and ran for their lives.

Even as he nocked his first arrow, the Fox pointed to them and called, "I want some of those men taken alive. We may be able to learn a lot from them." A handful of chariots peeled off after the fleeing Gradi.

The fight with the ones who hadn't fled was as fierce as usual, but did not last long: between them, the Elabonians and Trokmoi had their foes badly outnumbered, and the arrival of the second column moments after the first threw the Gradi into confusion, for a good many of them could not decide which group of opponents to resist.

When they saw they had no hope of winning the fight, the Gradi began slaying one another to keep from being taken prisoner. Rather more of them than usual, though, did let themselves be captured. That piqued Gerin's curiosity in the same way as the earlier spectacle of running Gradi had done.

After helping see to his own men, he went to question the warriors who'd fled or been captured. They sat glumly on the ground, hands bound behind them with leather thongs. "Who speaks Elabonian?" Gerin demanded.

Several Gradi stirred. "I speak it, somely," one of them said, proving his own point.

Gerin wasted no time with ancillary questions. "Why did some of you run? Why did some of you give up?"

The Gradi looked at one another, then down at the ground. The Fox knew shame when he saw it. The prisoner who had spoken before answered, "It is not what the chiefs tell us. It is not what the gods tell us." A couple of others who understood Elabonian exclaimed, trying to silence him, but he went on, "It is so. We were to strike, not to be striked. The gods do not do what they say they do. They trickfool us. Why we do for them?"

"How did your gods fool you?" Gerin did his best to

make the question sound casual. He had to work not to lean forward and throw it out like a man casting a baited line into a pond.

And that Gradi seized the bait. "They say they help us," he answered. "They say you not can backfight. They say they chase your pisspot gods, eat them, throw dead of them on dunghill. They trickfool us."

His gray eyes were full of angry indignation. For a little while, Gerin had trouble understanding that. Then he realized he was used to living in a part of the world where the gods seldom played an active role. That was not true of Voldar and the rest of the Gradi pantheon. Now the raiders were having to do things for themselves, without their gods to help them. If this first taste of how they performed under such circumstances meant anything, they were going to have some trouble adjusting.

Gerin hoped they had a lot of trouble adjusting. Turning to Adiatunnus, he said, "You see? We're fighting just them now, not their goddess." Here across the Venien, he didn't feel like naming her, even if she was otherwise occupied.

Adiatunnus noticed that. He said, "You started well before, Fox, and then it all went sour. Finish well, now, and you'll show yourself right."

"Fair enough." The Fox spoke to the warriors guarding the Gradi prisoners: "Send them back over the Venien. The work we get out of them as slaves will pay back a little of what they've done to us."

He watched the prisoners closely as he spoke. Some of them admitted to understanding Elabonian. He saw no tries for escape, no tries for suicide, among those men or any others. The likeliest explanation was that they were cast into confusion because their gods were less with them than those gods usually were.

He very much wanted the likeliest explanation to be

true. Because he so much wanted it to be true, he distrusted it all the more.

"Only one way to find out," he said. Adiatunnus gave him a curious look. He pretended not to see it.

Whether or not the Gradi had been readying themselves to cross the Venien a few days before, they were not ready to defend against a strike from the eastern side of the river. Each group of them, gathered in villages or encamped in the woods, fought Gerin's army with an effort individually often heroic but invariably futile: those groups were crushed, one after another.

"Why don't they come together, Father?" Duren asked as the army made camp after one such little battle. "They'd be tougher meat if they did."

"I'm still not sure," Gerin answered, wiping sweat from his forehead with his sleeve. He'd earned that sweat fighting the Gradi, but it had come easy: the day was a muggy scorcher. "But I'm beginning to think they're so used to talking with their gods, and to listening to them, that they have trouble figuring out what to do when they're on their own."

"Enjoy it while it lasts," Van said. "My guess is, that won't be long. Sooner or later, they'll come out of their fog and remember they're men, not gods' toys. Life gets harder after that."

"I'm the one who's supposed to come up with cheery thoughts like that," Gerin said. "Your job is to say, 'No, no, Fox, everything will be fine. We'll whip these Gradi right out of their furs.'" He deepened his voice and gave it a slight guttural rasp, doing his best to imitate the outlander.

His friend grunted laughter. "Nobody can always see what he's going to do himself, let alone what the fool standing next to him is liable to come up with. When you threw Baivers and the underground powers at the Gradi gods, you surprised even them, I think."

"As long as they keep on being surprised." Gerin looked at the sky so often these days, he hardly noticed himself doing it. So long as the clouds stayed away, so long as the hot weather held, he would assume the monsters' gods and Baivers still kept Voldar and the other Gradi gods too busy to make trouble down on the merely mortal plane of being.

He knew how rough a gauge that was. Voldar and her crew might overcome the invaders before Stribog recovered from the supernatural wounds he'd received in his fight. If that happened, the first the Fox would know of it was running headlong into the angry Gradi gods. He did not look forward to that sort of confrontation.

Best way to keep it from happening, he told himself, *is to beat the Gradi so badly, their gods won't have much of a place to roost in the northlands.* He'd known all along what needed doing. Knowing how to do it was another matter, worse luck.

An Elabonian spy brought him news the next day that the Gradi had regarrisoned the tumbledown keep in which he'd defeated them in his earlier foray into the country they held. "They don't have much in the way of imagination, do they?" the Fox said.

When he sent scouts out to approach the place, he discovered how little imagination the Gradi were showing: their sentries seemed no more alert to attack than on his previous incursion. It was as if the idea that their enemies could bring the war to them rather than the other way round had never occurred to them. Gerin aimed both to exploit their naïveté and, having exploited it, to fill the gap in their education.

"Shall we dismount again and trick them?" Duren asked.

"They'd never fall for the same trick twice," Van
protested. Gerin got the feeling the protest sprang more
from his inability to look like a Gradi than from any
consideration of grand strategy: the outlander felt
cheated out of a good fight. No wonder he'd been able
to fathom the minds of the monsters' gods—his own
worked the same way. Could he have been projected
up into the plane of the gods, he would have had a
splendid time battling Voldar and her companions.

In the end, the Fox decided to try the same plan
again, taking advantage of the confusion the Gradi
seemed to feel without their gods leading them by the
noses. These were, after all, not the same men in the
keep as the ones his force had overwhelmed before.
He led the band of foot soldiers who approached the
keep. Many of them were wearing captured Gradi
helmets and carrying captured Gradi axes in place of
their own weapons, doing their best to make the ruse
convincing.

When the band of men on foot approached, the
drawbridge to the keep was up. He cursed on seeing
that. A Gradi up on the wall shouted something at him
and his men. A couple of the Trokmoi spoke a little of
the Gradi tongue. One of them shouted back, presumably
saying something like, *It's all right—let us in*.

And the drawbridge came down. "We *are* lucky,"
Duren breathed.

"We certainly are," Gerin said. "We're lucky enough
to run in there and see how many of us are going to
get killed. Aren't you glad to have luck like that?" Duren
nodded eagerly. Gerin cursed—that wasn't the answer
his son would give when he had a little more sense.

But then, if he'd been sensible himself, he wouldn't
have attacked this keep in the first place. He yanked
his sword out of the scabbard and ran for the drawbridge.
His men followed, their shouts making the morning

hideous. The drawbridge started to rise, but it could come down faster than it went up.

Gerin got over the bridge and into the courtyard. He ran into the gatehouse with half a dozen men at his heels. They quickly slew the pair of Gradi who had been working the big capstan around which the drawbridge chain was wound. With another shout, the Fox let the capstan spin in the opposite direction. The drawbridge thumped all the way down again, and this time stayed down.

In swarmed the warriors who had approached on foot. Gerin knew the rest of his army would soon join them: a runner would report initial success to the chariotry hanging back just out of sight. Meanwhile, how many Gradi were in the keep and how ferociously would they fight?

A good many of them fought as ferociously as they ever had. One snarling knot of men near the entrance to the great hall of the castle did not come undone till the last Gradi fighting there had fallen. But fewer Gradi manned the keep than had been here before, and not all of them chose to fight to the death. When Elabonians and Trokmoi began leaping out of chariots and running to join the fight, a startling number of the raiders still on their feet threw down their axes and gave up.

"Where is great Voldar? Where is Lavtrig? Where is Smerts?" one of the prisoners said in fair Elabonian. "How can we beat you thralls without our gods? It is not fair."

Gerin found the Gradi's notion of fairness curious, but did not try to persuade him it needed changing. Instead, he allowed himself the luxury of a sigh of relief that the Gradi gods were still preoccupied, and the even greater luxury of hope that they would keep on being preoccupied.

After he'd pressed west from the keep on his earlier

incursion into territory the Gradi held, the weather had gone bad on him. When he woke now to find the sun rising in a cloudless sky, he smiled and murmured, "Thank you, lord Baivers." Every day the god of barley and the underground powers bought for him was another day in which to strike the Gradi.

The wind did blow out of the west, but it was a natural wind, a warm wind. And, toward the end of the day, it brought a fresh scent with it, a tang he had known before but couldn't name at once. Duren noticed it, too, and asked, "What's that smell?" —for him, it was unfamiliar.

Van identified it before the Fox could. "That's the smell of the ocean, lad. We're closer to it now than back at Fox Keep, and no rain washing it out of the air before your nose can find it."

"You're right!" Gerin snapped his fingers in annoyance at himself. "When the wind swung round and blew out of the east, off the Greater Inner Sea, the air in the City of Elabon would smell like this."

"And when the wind didn't swing round, the air in the City of Elabon would smell like all the privies and stables in the world, same as it does in every other city," Van said.

"That's so," Gerin said. "When I lived there—back before you were born, Duren—I didn't notice the city stink, but by the gods I did when I first came into it. After a while, you get used to things."

Later that day, the army he led came upon a group of Gradi in a peasant village who behaved more in the manner the raiders had done before their gods made the acquaintance of Baivers and the subterranean powers. They went down to defeat, but the large majority of them fought until killed, and several of those who didn't also did not surrender, but broke away into the woods to the west.

Gerin sent men into those woods after them, but they

got away. "I don't care for that," he said when his warriors brought back the news of their failure. "They didn't look like men running for their lives. They looked more like men who wanted to take warning to their friends."

"Why do you say that, Father?" Duren asked.

"Because they all went off in the same direction," Gerin replied. "If they'd been panicked, they'd have run every which way—woods just as near these huts to the north and south as to the west. But that's the direction they went."

Adiatunnus walked up in time to hear that last. "You're after thinking it'll be harder now, Fox?"

"I wish I could say no, but I have to say yes," Gerin told him. He tried to keep the Trokmê's spirits up, adding, "Have you noticed how well your warriors have fought against the Gradi this time out? I certainly have."

"That I have, and I thank you for seeing it, too," Adiatunnus said. "It's as if a great burthen o' fear's fallen off our backs, for the which I suppose you're the man I should be thanking."

"I've taken the Gradi gods out of play," Gerin said. "Now it's you Trokmoi against them, not you against them and their gods, who had already put your gods in fear."

As soon as the words were out of his mouth, he wished he had them back. He did not want to insult Adiatunnus by calling Esus, Teutates, Taranis, and the rest of the Trokmê gods cowards. But the woodsrunners' chieftain only nodded. "Truth that—I've owned it myself. We do the best we can, is all—who can do more?" He stopped and thought about what he'd just said, then clapped a hand to his forehead. "The gods forfend, Fox, I'm after starting to sound like you."

"We've lived next to each other too long," Gerin answered. "This wouldn't be happening if one of us had managed to kill the other somewhere back down the line."

"And that's truth, too," Adiatunnus said. "We're both after having worse neighbors the now, though, the which makes me think I may be glad after all I didna overfall you. You never know till the end how these things turn out sometimes, do you?"

"No, you don't," Gerin said shortly. "If you like, Adiatunnus, and if we come out the other side of these hard times, I'll teach you your letters. They'll make your world seem wider, and you'll profit for that."

"I'll think on it, indeed and I will," Adiatunnus said. Gerin scratched his head. For years, he'd tried to preserve civilization in the northlands not least by driving the Trokmoi over the Niffet. For the first time, he wondered if, having failed to do that, he might civilize them instead. The idea made him laugh. *If they invade my country, that's what they get*, he thought.

Before he thought about civilizing the Trokmoi (and before he had time to do more than briefly wonder whether a literate Adiatunnus might prove a more dangerous Adiatunnus), he had to worry about the Gradi. The farther west he got, the bigger a worry they became. They fought harder and more cleverly than they had. He was no longer taking them by surprise, either: they knew he and his men were coming after them.

The weather worried him, too. The breeze that smelled of the Orynian Ocean was cool and moist, which made him wonder whether Stribog was no longer busy battling the underground power who had taken him on. Only when local peasants assured him summers close by the sea were generally of that sort did the worry recede—a little.

He kept scouting parties close by the Niffet, to make sure the Gradi could not use their war galleys to land a large band of soldiers behind him by surprise. That precaution paid for itself a couple of days later, when his men spotted two galleys full of Gradi going up the river. When some of the scouts brought that news back, he reversed the course of his army: two galleys' worth of warriors was not a force large enough to do much in the way of raiding upriver, and seemed likelier to be aimed at him.

Had he guessed wrong there, he might have lost the momentum that had kept his troopers surging forward. But he guessed right: his men swept down on the Gradi close by the riverside, and apparently not long after they had left their ships. The fight that followed, on flat, open ground with the Niffet against which to pin the raiders, was more nearly slaughter than anything deserving the name of battle.

Foot soldiers armed mostly with axes, the Gradi here found themselves at the mercy of Gerin's chariot-riding archers. The Gradi could neither close with them nor escape, and had no weapons able to strike their foes from a distance. One by one, they fell, until, seeing the end rapidly approaching, they began killing one another to keep from being captured.

After the fight was over, the Fox sent a party east along the Niffet to find the galleys from which the Gradi had come. Two pillars of smoke rising into the sky said they'd not only found but fired them.

"I wish they hadn't done that," Gerin said, pointing back toward the smoke.

"And why ever not?" Adiatunnus demanded. "With the boats found and all, they should be getting rid of them, eh?"

"Most times, I'd say yes," Gerin answered. "But people will see that smoke a long way. I'm afraid the Gradi army in the west just beyond our farthest advance yet will spot it and know we've smashed their friends."

"What army are you talking about?" Adiatunnus said, and then, "It's daft y'are, I'm thinking, when all we've

seen is dribs and drabs of Gradi, no proper armies to
'em at all. Not that I'm sorry for it, mind you now."

"Think it through," the Fox told him. "Why would
the Gradi have landed a force of that size behind us?
Those men couldn't have caught us, not on foot, and
they couldn't fight all of us by themselves if they did
catch us. Am I right so far?"

"Aye, belike," the Trokmê chieftain said. "What of
it, and what has it got to do with a whole great whacking
Gradi army up ahead?"

Gerin too seldom got the chance to play games with
logic. When he did, he used it to the hilt. "Think it
through," he repeated. "These Gradi couldn't have
caught us or fought us, not alone. What does that leave
for them to do? The only thing I can think of is that
they were meant to be a blocking force, to slow us down
while we're retreating and let whoever we're retreating
from catch up with us. We wouldn't be retreating from
dribs and drabs of Gradi. The only thing that could
make us retreat is an army. And so . . . does that make
sense to you?"

Adiatunnus' long, bony face was intent as he followed
the Fox's reasoning. At last, he said, "You may be after
having the right of it. What a tricksy wight y'are, to
see that army or ever you set eyes on it. Have you been
watching me the same way, all these years?"

"As best I could," Gerin told him.

"I hold myself lucky, then, for still being here for
you to keep an eye on," Adiatunnus said, "though you'll
likely tell me you'd be as pleased if I weren't."

"More pleased," the Fox said, deadpan. Adiatunnus
gave him a glare as heartfelt as he could have desired.
Then both men started to laugh. Gerin went on, "Now
let's go see what we can do to flush that army my mind's
eye sees—or find out that I'm full of eyewash."

"Indeed and I'll be surprised if it turns out y'are,"

Adiatunnus told him. "The way you laid out your thoughts, so neat and all, there I was, following along behind like you were lighting up a dark path with a torch."

"You do need to learn to read," Gerin told him. "I'll make a philosopher out of you yet, see if I don't."

"Och," Adiatunnus exclaimed, "maybe I should let the Gradi kill me instead." The Fox glared at him, only to realize the Trokmê had just taken his revenge.

Every so often, Gerin's instinct and his logic let him down with a splat. As he led his army westward, he began to wonder if this was going to be one of those times. He had scouts out well ahead of the main body of his force. They and then he passed a couple of spots where he would have judged the Gradi likely to stand and fight.

Then a scout came back from the southwest with a frightened-looking peasant clinging to the rail of his chariot. "This fellow says he knows where the Gradi are," he called.

"Good." Gerin waved, bringing his army to a halt. The scout came on at a slightly less intrepid pace, which made the elderly peasant seem happier, or at least less unhappy. "Who are you and what do you know?" Gerin asked him.

"Lord, my name is Osar Pozel's son," he answered, though Gerin wondered if he'd heard the name aright. He might have felt happier speaking to Osar through an interpreter, for the serf had a western accent that would have made him hard to understand at best, and also spoke mushily because he was missing most of his teeth.

"Well, Osar, what do you know?" Gerin repeated.

The peasant pointed back in the direction from which the scout had brought him. "Lord, there's Gradi back there, lots of Gradi. Over by Bidgosh Pond, they are. Wish somebody could do something about 'em."

"Why do you think I'm here?" the Fox said. "For my amusement? For the scenery, maybe?"

"Who knows what lords do, or why?" Osar returned. "Anyone who's smart, he stays outen the way of lords."

That saddened Gerin, but did not surprise him. "Where is this Bidgosh Pond?" he asked.

"Where is it? What do you mean, where is it? How can you not know where Bidgosh Pond is?" Osar had, no doubt, lived in his village all his life. Everything in the neighborhood—this pond, wherever it was; a hill; a forest—would be as familiar to him as his own fingers, and would no more need locating than those fingers at the far end of his hand. He'd have trouble imagining someone who'd never seen Bidgosh Pond, as he'd also have trouble imagining the terrain more than a day's walk from his village, terrain he'd probably never seen.

"Never mind," Gerin said, sighing. "Here, come up into my chariot. You tell me which way I have to go to get to the pond. If a fight starts, I'll let you jump out beforehand. Does that suit you?"

"What choice have I got?" Osar asked, the peasant's age-old bitter question. He got up into the Fox's chariot and said, "All right, back the way I came from, back toward the fields I know."

"Think what a hero you'll be to the other people in your village," Gerin said. "Now you've ridden in a chariot—two chariots, in fact—and you're going to help get rid of the Gradi so they don't trouble you any more."

"I'm going to have all these fancy chariot things churning up the fields so we all go hungry," Osar Pozel's son said. He shook his head. "Wouldn't've had much crops anyways, not with the weather so bad till just lately."

As soon as he found ground he recognized, he went from being nearly useless to being altogether authoritative, telling Gerin much more than he wanted to know about every crop, every herd, that had been on that ground for as far back as he remembered, which was about as long as Gerin had been alive. In his little corner of the world, he remembered *everything*: chuckling, he said, "Had my first girl back o' those trees, not that they was so tall in them days. Pretty little thing she was, too, and a pair on her that'd make you cry—"

After a while, Gerin cut off the flow of amatory reminiscences by asking, "How much farther to this pond?"

Osar gave him a dirty look. The Fox had trouble blaming him; remembered lovemaking was surely more enjoyable than thinking about battle. After a moment, though, the peasant pointed. "Just past that stand o' trees there."

Sure enough, through the trees came the glint of sun off water. Also through the trees came shadowy glimpses of moving figures. "Rein in," Gerin told Duren. When his son obeyed, the Fox told Osar, "You'd better get out here. Those aren't the people from your village, are they?"

"Not likely," the peasant answered, and jumped down. He scurried away from the chariots behind the Fox's, surprisingly spry. Given the fight that loomed ahead, Gerin would have been spry in his shoes, too (not that Osar was wearing shoes).

Pointing ahead, Van said, "There's a whole great whacking lot of Gradi in amongst those trees."

"There certainly are," Gerin said. "The next interesting question is, how in the names of all the Elabonian gods are we going to get them to come out into the fields and fight us on our own ground?"

Van grunted thoughtfully in response to that, but made no more definite answer. Gerin pondered the problem. Out on open land, his men in their chariots could ride rings around the Gradi and fill them full of arrows without exposing themselves to much danger. Under the trees, everything changed. The horses would have to pick their way, and the men in the cars would be hideously vulnerable to enemies leaping out of the bushes or from behind tree trunks and not seen till too late.

Gerin touched his son on the shoulder. "Ride up close to the woods," he said. "There's something I want to try." Duren did as he asked. Raising his voice to a great shout, the Fox called, "If the lot of you aren't sniveling cowards, come out and fight us!"

Against Trokmoi, the ploy probably would have worked: the woodsrunners made a point of proving how brave they were. It might have worked against Elabonians; his own people, Gerin thought, were by no means free of brave blockheads. But from out of the forest came an answering shout in pretty good Elabonian: "If you are such a great fighter, you come make us!"

It was exactly the reply Gerin would have given. Getting it thrown in his face didn't make him any happier. Neither did the cheers that rose from the throats of the Gradi who had understood their leader's answer. Only a man with a strong hold over the warriors he led could have so forcefully rejected the most openly courageous course of action. The Fox turned to Van. "You were right, worse luck. I think they've found a captain."

"And what do we do about that?" the outlander asked.

"What I'd like to do is set the forest afire and flush them out that way." Gerin bit his lip. "The only trouble being, I don't think it would work, not with no wind and not with the trees all wet and full of sap from the rains that have poured down on this place."

Van nodded. "Aye, a fire'd be slow going. They might

head out away from us, toward the pond, instead of at us, too. But what does that leave?"

Gerin looked back at the chariots full of Trokmoi and Elabonians. He looked ahead to the woods full of Gradi. The Gradi captain had rejected the obvious choice Gerin offered him. He, in turn, had offered Gerin a choice just as obvious—and just as fraught with peril.

Sighing, the Fox said, "If they don't come to us, we could go in after them."

He had hoped Van would try to talk him out of it. Instead, the outlander whooped and grinned and slapped him on the back, almost hard enough to pitch him out of the chariot. "Every now and then, Fox, I like the way you think," he said.

"I don't," Gerin said.

When the Fox shouted orders for his men to dismount from their cars and fight the Gradi on foot, Adiatunnus had his driver bring his chariot alongside and said, "Are you daft, to go fighting them under the trees? 'Tis the very thing they want you to do!"

"We'll see how much they want it once they have it," the Fox replied. "I am not wild to do this: I plainly own as much. But this is our land by rights. If we can't beat the Gradi with their gods out of the picture, we might as well leave and hand them the whole countryside."

"But they're Gradi!" Adiatunnus exclaimed—a fear-filled sentence freighted with the memories of long years of losses. "Fighting 'em in chariots, aye, or in the keep, but here—"

"If you won't, then go back across the Venien," Gerin said harshly. If Adiatunnus and the Trokmoi did go back across the Venien, the fight was doomed. His heart felt packed with jagged ice. Doomed or not, he would go after the Gradi: a sentiment the raiders might well have understood. To Adiatunnus, he added, "If I win this battle with you, well and good. If I win it after you turn oathbreaker, your turn comes next."

He meant it. Adiatunnus could see he meant it. The Trokmê chieftain bit his lip. Gerin coldly stared his way, trying to make Adiatunnus more afraid of him than of the Gradi. After a long moment, Adiatunnus said, "I am no oathbreaker. We fight beside you."

"Prove it," Gerin said, and jumped down out of his chariot. Van thudded to the ground beside him. A moment later, so did Duren, who tethered the horses to a bush that wouldn't hold them more than a moment if they seriously decided to try breaking free.

"To the crows with you, lord prince!" Adiatunnus said, and jumped down, too.

Seeing their foes descend to the ground, the Gradi began shouting, "Voldar! Voldar!" The goddess' name rang in Gerin's ears. But however loud the Gradi yelled, the Fox felt no hum of power in the air, no sign that Voldar was near. He would not have to fight against an angry goddess, merely against her angry followers, who were apt to be quite bad enough.

He turned to his own men. "Our cry is 'Baivers!' " He didn't think the Elabonian god any more likely to take part in the fighting than Voldar, but, for one thing, he might have been wrong, and, for another, maybe those cries would reach and aid Baivers up in the divine Gradihome. After a moment, he went on, "If we win this fight, I think we win the war. We've pushed them a long way back. Now we can make sure what we've done doesn't slip out of our hands. What do you say, lads?"

"Baivers!" The war cry drowned out the shouts of the Gradi and also seemed to startle the raiders, who might still have been unused to the idea that anyone or any god could presume to stand against them or their pantheon. *Too bad for them*, Gerin though. *Life is full of surprises*. He waved his arm. Elabonians and Trokmoi trotted toward the trees.

When the Gradi saw their foes on foot, some of them came out into the field to fight there. Several Elabonians and Trokmoi snatched bows from their chariots and started shooting at their enemies. After two or three Gradi went down, the rest retreated back into the woods.

Two or three we won't have to fight in there, Gerin thought. He tried to stay in front of Duren. This, whatever else it turned out to be, was going to be an ugly fight. His son had a man's courage without a man's full strength or a man's full caution. If the Fox could shield him from danger in the forest, he would. Rationally, he knew worrying about two persons' safety at the same time made it less likely either one of them would stay safe. *To the crows with being rational*, he thought.

A Gradi sprang out from behind the trunk of an oak. Shouting Voldar's name, he swung his axe in a deadly arc. Gerin batted it aside with his shield. He had to be careful not to let the axehead hit the shield square, lest it bite through thin bronze facing, through leather, through wood, and perhaps into his arm.

He cut at the Gradi. The fellow parried with his axe, beating Gerin's blade to one side. He backed up a pace, his eyes intent, wary: he wasn't used to facing a left-handed swordsman, while Gerin had had a lifetime of struggle against right-handed foes.

The Gradi chopped again. This time, Gerin used his sword to turn the axe. He rushed in close, pushing at the Gradi with his shield till the big man from the north tripped over a root and went down. Gerin used his sword as if it were a dagger, stabbing the Gradi in the throat. The man let out a bubbling scream that quickly cut off as he choked on his own blood.

Gerin scrambled to his feet. He looked around. He

couldn't see Duren, and cursed foully. The one plan he'd had in this fight was to watch over the youth, and it hadn't lasted past his own first encounter with the Gradi. The only thing left to do, then, was sweep through the woods till there were no more Gradi left to encounter.

He'd never been in a battle like this. He had scant control over it. He couldn't see more than a few feet in any direction, nor could any of the other warriors, on his side or among the Gradi. He ran from one nasty little fight to the next, helping Elabonians and Trokmoi and doing his best to stretch Gradi dead on the ground.

He was used to maneuvering scores, even hundreds of chariots as if they were war galleys out on the sea, all of them moving in accordance with his will. Not now. This was two Gradi leaping out from behind trees set close together and hacking down an Elabonian, or three Elabonians and a Trokmê slashing and stabbing at two Gradi fighting back to back till one of them fell and then swarming over the other. The woods were full of shouts and screams, full of the outhouse stink of pierced guts and the metallic odor of fresh-spilled blood.

Whenever he saw his men, he sent them toward the last band of Gradi he had spotted. Whenever he saw Gradi, he shouted for his men to come and fight them. He soon noted that he saw very few wounded men down on the ground. He didn't need long to realize each side was finishing off the other's injured men it found. He bit his lips. Fights among Elabonians, even fights between Elabonians and Trokmoi, weren't commonly so savage.

His heart jumped. There up ahead strode Duren, sword in one hand, shield on the other arm, prowling forward, his head going back and forth as he picked his way west through the woods. When the youth heard

Gerin coming up behind him, he whirled around, ready to fight.

"I'm not the enemy," Gerin said, although, to a boy first sprouting his beard, any older relative, and especially his father, was liable to look like a foe a lot of the time.

Here, though, Duren understood him as he'd intended. He asked the same question as had been in Gerin's mind: "Are we winning?"

"Drop me into the hottest of the five hells if I know," the Fox answered: quietly, so as not to draw the attention of the Gradi. That might have been excess caution, for the woods rang with cries of every description. Still, caution did no harm if exercised when not needed, while needing it and not exercising it often led straight to disaster. "I don't know," he repeated. "But we're well into the woods, and they haven't thrown us back, so I'd say we're not losing."

When the words were spoken, he remembered Baivers' telling him much the same thing in the middle of the fight against Voldar and the Gradi gods. No, he though, it probably wasn't the middle of the fight, but only the beginning—by all the signs, that fight was still going on. It might go on for days more, or, for all Gerin knew, for years more. Gods didn't need to eat or sleep in any ordinary senses of the words, and they were a lot harder to kill than mere men.

He reached out and tapped Duren's shield with his sword. "Come on," he said. "Let's see what sort of lovely company we have waiting for us."

They hadn't gone far before they came to a screen of bushes around the edge of a small clearing. Again, the scene eerily reminded Gerin of the clearings in the divine Gradihome. The battle going on in the clearing was hardly less confused and no less savage than the one from which Voldar had expelled him.

"Baivers!" Duren shouted, and ran for the fighting.

Gerin, had he had his way, would have gone into the fight without shouting first, and might have cut down a Gradi or two before the enemy knew he was there.

Well, no help for it now. "Baivers!" he cried, and sprinted after his son.

One Gradi who turned to meet Duren's onslaught died a moment later, the victim of the Trokmê from whom he'd been distracted. Maybe outrageous openness was as good at inducing surprise as stealth. Gerin reminded himself to think that one over if he ever found a moment when no one was trying to slaughter him.

If he did find such a moment, it wouldn't be any time soon. Here in the clearing, his men and the Gradi could find and fight one another. That was just what they were doing, with sword and spear and knife and axe, with stones grubbed from the ground with their hands, and with those broken-nailed hands themselves.

"Voldar!" the Gradi cried, over and over again. Gerin had heard that shout more often than he'd ever wanted, and had gauged the different ways the Gradi used it. What he heard now gave him hope: the Gradi sounded imploring, as if they hadn't heard from their goddess for a long time and desperately wished they would.

"Voldar is dead!" he yelled at the raiders. Some of them understood enough Elabonian to recoil in horror from that claim. The Fox knew perfectly well it was a lie. He didn't care. If the Gradi couldn't prove him wrong—and their reaction suggested they couldn't—he might as well have been right. Voldar too preoccupied with her battle on the gods' plane to come to the aid of the men she had intended to rule the northlands might as well have been Voldar dead.

But the Gradi remained fierce opponents even without Voldar tilting the natural order of things in their favor. One of them, shouting incomprehensible things that Gerin did not think were compliments, swung his axe at the Fox. His shield turned the stroke so that the flat of the axehead rather than the edge slammed against his helmet, but that was plenty to send him staggering. The Gradi rushed after him. He raised his sword to block the next vicious stroke, but it sent the blade flying from his hand.

Bellowing in triumph, the raider brought back the axe to finish him off. Gerin seized the fellow's wrist and twisted. The Gradi bellowed again, this time in pain and alarm. Gerin gave him another twist, spinning his foe over his hip and slamming him down to the ground. The Fox was still one of the best wrestlers in the northlands, and the Gradi, as far as he could tell, knew nothing whatever of the art.

The fall knocked the axe loose. The Gradi scrambled after it. Gerin kicked him in the ribs, then in the face. He grabbed the axe himself—it was closer than his sword. He swung it up, then down. Blood sprayed out from the wound it made. The Gradi's limbs convulsed. Gerin hit him again. He let out a snoring cough and died.

"Baivers!" shouted someone from behind the Fox. The shout was so fierce, he glanced back over his shoulder—and leaped aside just in time as Drungo Drago's son swung a sword at him.

"Drungo, you idiot, I'm your overlord!" Gerin screamed.

Drungo stared. "Oh, it is you, lord prince," he said in what sounded like sincere apology. "I saw the axe and I figured you were a Gradi. I didn't think one of us might have taken it off one of them."

Gerin sighed. Drungo wasn't much good at thinking. Drago the Bear, his father, hadn't been, either. Both of them, though, were handy men to have in a brawl.

More Elabonians and Trokmoi stormed into the clearing. More Gradi came in, too, but not so many more. After a while, no more Gradi were left on their feet in the open space. The ground was strewn with Gradi down and moaning, and with Gradi down and forever silent. A good many of their enemies lay there with them. Gerin's followers who were still upright stalked across the red-splashed grass, finishing off the wounded Gradi who still lived.

"Come on," Gerin said when that grim task was done. He pointed into the woods. "We've still got plenty of the whoresons to deal with in there."

Some of his men, even those who had fought bravely in the clearing, hesitated before leaving it for the forest. He couldn't blame them. Fighting in the open was what they knew. Sneaking among the trees was more like hunting, except that here the quarry was also hunting them.

Somewhere west in the woods, a Gradi was shouting to his comrades. Gerin couldn't understand a word he was saying, but he recognized the voice: that was the captain who'd spoken Elabonian, marshaling his troops. The Fox stopped and cocked his head and listened to the fighting. It got fiercer off to his left. He sent men of his own in that direction. Unlike the Gradi, he didn't roar and bellow while he was doing it.

Then he started moving toward that great voice. "Van was right all along," he remarked to Duren. "They've found themselves a leader who's trying to whip them into shape, Voldar or no Voldar. If we kill him, my bet is they start falling to pieces."

With their chieftain alive, the Gradi showed no signs of falling to pieces. Gerin had to fight several times as he approached the roaring Gradi leader. He was getting close when a big man emerged from behind a tree that didn't look to have been wide enough to conceal his bulk. As Drungo had, he started to attack the Fox; unlike Drungo, he checked himself without Gerin's having to scream at him.

Gerin halted what would have been his own attack. He nodded to Van, hardly more surprised than if he'd met him walking out of the great hall back at Fox Keep. "Good to see they haven't let the air out of you."

"And you," the outlander answered. "You heading over to put paid to that fellow giving orders at the top of his lungs?"

"Just what I'm doing," Gerin agreed. "Killing one man and breaking their backbone is a cheaper way of beating them than having to make the fight on his terms."

"I thought the same," Van said. "That's why I was going for him, too."

"We'll all go for him," Duren said. "Who does it doesn't matter, as long as someone does."

Van slapped Gerin on the back. "Well, Fox, you've trained up the sapling to grow the same way as the tree. And since the tree grows straight, that's a good way for the sapling to follow. Which is a fancy way of saying that the lad is right. Come on." He glided forward, amazingly light and quiet on his feet for so large a man.

Gerin and Duren followed. The Gradi chieftain kept on bawling orders to his men. He wasn't hard to find, any more than a roaring longtooth would have been. The Fox suspected he would have been about as glad to stumble over a longtooth as over the chief.

Van stretched out his arm, palm facing the Fox. Gerin obediently halted. Van didn't even point. That he'd stopped was enough. Gerin peered through the screen of bushes. A Gradi came running up to one of his fellows who stood there. He gasped out something. The other man listened, then turned to one side and shouted. This was the enemy's leader, sure enough.

"We'll all dash out together," Gerin whispered, wishing he had his bow—killing the big, fierce raider from a distance would have been safe and convenient. "One, two—"

As he said "three," another Gradi runner burst into the clearing. The Fox grabbed at his friend and son, trying to hold them back, but too late—they'd already launched themselves at the Gradi chieftain. He burst out of the woods, too, half a step behind them.

Half a dozen strides and they were on the three Gradi. That was, unfortunately, just enough time to let the raiders break free from their momentary shock, raise their axes, and fight back. The two lesser Gradi sprang in front of their chief. One of them engaged Van, the other Duren: the first two foes they found. That left the leader for Gerin.

He would willingly have forgone the honor. The Gradi was bigger than he was, and younger than he was, too. The Gradi also knew more about using an axe than did Gerin, who still held the weapon he'd snatched from his fallen foe. The only advantage Gerin had . . . Try as he would, he couldn't think of any.

"Voldar!" the Gradi shouted, and cut at his head. He ducked—and almost fell victim to a backhand cut: the Gradi was as strong as he looked, and as quick, too. Gerin made a cut of his own, a tentative one, which the enemy leader easily evaded. The Gradi chopped at him again. He took this blow on the shield, and felt it all the way up his arm to his shoulder. His best hope, he thought, was for Van and Duren to beat their men and help him. He didn't see any way he was likely to beat the Gradi chief on his own.

By the fierce sneer the Gradi wore, he didn't see any way Gerin was likely to beat him, either. He feinted once, feinted twice, then chopped again. Gerin once more managed to get his shield in front of the blow— but it hit square and true, the axehead smashing through his protection.

The very corner of the sharp edge of the axe kissed his arm with fire. He held on to his grip on the shield, though—the wound was not severe. And, when the Gradi captain tried to pull the axe free so he could strike again, he found he could not. It had twisted, and would not go back through the narrow hole it had made. He shouted in fury and alarm.

Gerin did not give him the chance to clear the axe from the shield. Instead of backing away, he moved close to the Gradi, so the fellow had no room in which to draw back his arm. The Gradi didn't like that. His lips skinned back from his teeth in a horrible grin.

He should have let go of the axe and run. Instead, he kept trying to jerk it loose, and to fend off Gerin's own left-handed blows. Since his left arm and the Fox's were on opposite sides, and since his right hand clutched the useless axe handle, he could not do it. After Gerin's second stroke got home, the Gradi groaned and his grip faltered.

The Fox hit him again, this time in the side of the neck. The Gradi let out a startled grunt. His eyes went very wide. He let go of the axe. His mouth shaped a word. Gerin thought it was "Voldar," but it had no breath behind it. The Gradi swayed, toppled, fell.

Gerin whirled to help Van and Duren. Van had his own man down, and was yanking his spear out of the Gradi's belly. A loop of gray-pink gut came with it. Duren was fighting a defensive battle against his foe. When Van and Gerin both rushed to his aid, the Gradi who opposed him turned to flee. He did not get far.

Another Gradi burst into the clearing, staring in shocked dismay at what he found there. He did escape before Gerin and his comrades could pursue.

"Come on," the Fox said. "This isn't the whole job. We can't just beat them here—we have to break them."

If he lived, he knew he'd want to sleep three days, and would wake up stiff and sore in every joint even if he did. He plunged into the woods nonetheless.

There was more hard fighting as the day wore along, but something seemed to have gone out of the Gradi when their chieftain fell. The sun was only a little more than halfway down toward the west when Gerin emerged from the woods and saw a few, a very few, Gradi running off toward the west past Bidgosh Pond. Behind him, the sounds of battle were ebbing. Such shouts and cries as he could hear were almost all in either Elabonian or the Trokmê tongue.

Half a bowshot north of him, someone else came out from among the trees: a Trokmê. He looked toward the Fox and waved. Gerin waved back. "Adiatunnus!" he called.

Slowly, Adiatunnus came toward him. The woods-runner looked as tired as Gerin felt. "Diviciacus went down, puir wight," he said. "My own right hand he was, all these years. A rare sad thing. But—" He straightened. "Lord prince, we've beaten the buggers, and in a way I don't think they'll be over soon. From here, we can clear the northlands of 'em, right out to the edge o' the sea."

"I think that may be so," Gerin answered. More men, Elabonians and Trokmoi both, came out of the woods and gathered around their two leaders. Hardly daring to believe what he'd just said, Gerin repeated it: "I think that may be so."

"It is that, lord prince," Adiatunnus said positively. Then he paused, perhaps to weigh his own words. "Aye, it is so, lord prince, and 'twas you who made it real. I couldna ha' done it: I own as much. No man but your own self could ha' done it, lord prince." He shook his head. "Nay. That isna right."

"Who says it's not?" Van boomed angrily.

"I do," Adiatunnus answered. He sighed, then went, not to one knee, but to both. "No man but your own self could ha' done it . . . lord king."

XII

From a hillock not far away, Gerin stared at the Orynian Ocean. It was not like the Greater Inner Sea, save in being a large body of water. The blue Inner Sea was calm, peaceful. The gray ocean rolled and pulsed and smashed against rocks, sending spray high into the air. It was, in its way, as barbarous and as vigorous as the Gradi who rode it.

A strong stone keep sat by the ocean, not far south of the Niffet. The Fox had driven the Gradi from most of the northlands. Their remnant lingered here. He did not think he could storm this keep. He could not properly besiege it, either, not with its back to the Orynian Ocean: the Gradi from the north could keep it supplied by a road he did not control.

Duren climbed to the top of the hillock. He looked out at the ocean for a while; he found it endlessly fascinating. Then he pointed toward the keep the Gradi still held. "What will you do about them, Father?" he asked, confident the Fox would come up with something even if he couldn't see for himself what it was.

Gerin gave him the only answer he could: "This year, nothing. We've done all we could. We've done more than I ever expected. As long as the Gradi gods are at war on their own plane, the Gradi themselves we can beat, or at least meet on even terms, which is good enough."

"What if they sally after we go away, though?" Duren said.

"I'll leave men behind—my vassals, Elabonians and Trokmoi both. The Gradi killed most of the local lords; their claims have lapsed. We'll restore some keeps, maybe build some new ones, and make this a harder land for them to overrun than it used to be. Before, all the lords were rivals to all the others. Now, they'll be able to call on one another against the Gradi—and on me, too."

"Aye," Duren said. "They can call on their king."

On his own, Gerin would not have claimed the title. Aragis the Archer, who styled himself grand duke, had stayed quiet this summer, probably hoping Gerin and the Gradi would wreck each other, leaving him to pick up the pieces—and the rank that went with picking up the pieces. What he would do when he found out Gerin was wearing the rank . . . remained to be seen.

But Adiatunnus had been a rival almost as dangerous as Aragis, and Adiatunnus had been the one to call him king. "Almost makes me think there is such a thing as gratitude," Gerin murmured.

"Father?" Duren asked.

"Never mind," the Fox answered. The Trokmoi had been as willing as his own men to acknowledge his kingship. How long that willingness would last also remained to be seen.

While it did, he would make the most of it. You could push people further if you moved them in the direction they were already going. And fear of a Gradi revival would make them want to pay attention to the man who had stopped the raiders the first time.

"We have to have ships of our own," he said. He knew he'd said that before. Without ships of his own, the Gradi would be able to rebuild their strength and assail the northlands again at a time of their choosing.

Duren had another thought: "What do we do if the

Gradi gods end up overcoming Baivers and the underground powers?"

Gerin set a hand on his son's shoulder. "I'm less worried about that now than I was before I saw how potent Baivers could be when he chose. Even if Voldar beats him, she won't rout him. If she could do that, she would have done it already. And if she does beat him, well, we may be able to stir up other sleepy Elabonian gods against her and her friends. Baivers will let them know the fight is one they need to make."

"That will put the gods more in the world, if you know what I mean, than they have been since time out of mind," Duren said.

"I've thought the same thing," the Fox agreed. "I don't like the notion—in the face of the gods' powers, the ones we have look pretty small. But if that's what happens, then it is, that's all. We'll have to make the best of it we can. One way or another, I expect we'll manage."

"You will," Duren said. Remembering himself at the age when his beard had begun to sprout, Gerin knew how rare and precious his son's unalloyed approval was. Duren went on, "You always find a way."

Is that how I want to be remembered? Gerin wondered. He tasted the words in his mind. *He always found a way.* It wasn't the sort of memorial a hero in a minstrel's song would have chosen for himself. Or was it? Gerin was himself the hero of more than one song cycle, though the Fox of whom the minstrels sang bore scant resemblance to the one who dwelt inside Gerin's body. *He always found a way.* Aye, you could do worse than that.

"When we get back to Fox Keep, my mother will be so proud," Duren said.

He was, without a doubt, right. He meant Selatre, of course. He knew she hadn't given him birth, but he hardly ever seemed to think about that; as best Gerin could tell, he didn't remember Elise any more. The Fox did. He wondered if she was still alive. If she was, he wondered what she would think, to hear him called king of the north. His mouth twisted. No point to thinking about it. He'd never know.

Knowing he'd never know, he forced his thoughts toward more immediate concerns, saying, "I'm not much worried about what Selatre will think of me. She's fond of me whether people call me king or not. When we get back to Adiatunnus' holding, though, I do want to see how the rest of the Trokmoi take to the title."

"What will you do if they reject it?" Duren asked.

"I don't know." Gerin looked sidelong at his son. "Maybe we'll have a war."

"I've seen enough of war for a while," Duren burst out.

"You're learning, lad," Gerin told him. "You're learning."

"You leave everything to me, now," Adiatunnus said as they were about to go back east over the Venien River.

Gerin laughed out loud. "I didn't get this old by leaving everything to anybody—except me."

"I named you king once now," the Trokmê chief said in some exasperation. "Am I likely to go back on that naming with your own southron warriors all around me, the ugly kerns?"

"Truth to tell, I don't know what you're likely to do," Gerin answered. As he'd hoped, Adiatunnus took that for a compliment, a tribute to his deviousness. The woodsrunner slapped his driver on the back. The driver urged the team ahead. They splashed through the Venien's ford at a gallop, their hooves and the chariot's wheels kicking up spray that sparkled in the sun.

"You don't want to let him get too far ahead, or who knows which way his mouth is liable to start running?" Van said. Even before he'd spoken, though, Duren had sped up, crossing the Venien right behind Adiatunnus and in the same style. Van rumbled approval, down deep in his chest. "That's a fine lad you have there."

"I'd noticed," Gerin remarked, which made the outlander laugh and Duren, standing there in front of both of them, fidget noticeably.

Trokmoi working in the fields called questions to the returning warriors. The shouts of victory they got back started them whooping in turn. Adiatunnus added, whenever he got the chance, "Come back to the keep, now, and I'll give you summat even more worth the hearing of it."

He didn't actually go into the keep, but gathered with his own people and the returned Elabonian warriors in the square of the large village in front of the castle. With the sense of drama any good chief had, he waited for the crowd to build—and to buzz. Serving women brought ale out of the keep and poured out dippersful to whoever looked thirsty.

When the Trokmê judged the moment right, he clambered up onto a big stump and shouted, "The Gradi are ruined for fair, sure and they are, their nasty gods still locked in a shindy and themselves pushed all the way back to the ocean." That unleashed an ocean in the village, an ocean of cheers. Adiatunnus reached down and hauled Gerin up onto the stump with him. He went on, "The southron here, he had summat to do with it—a wee bit, you might say."

Gerin was used to both the excesses and understatements of Trokmê oratory. So were Adiatunnus' listeners, who cheered the Fox. Adiatunnus warmed to his theme: "And I'll have you know I'm vassal no more to the prince of the north." That brought cheers,

too, but cheers of a different sort—the cheers of Trokmoi
bayingly eager to break free of any feudal obligations.
The Fox wondered if Adiatunnus was about to betray
him after all. Then the Trokmê shouted, "Nay, for now
I'm vassal to Gerin the Fox, king o' the north, and so
named out of my very own mouth."

Silence slammed down for a moment as the Trokmoi
took that in and worked out what it meant. Then they
and Gerin's Elabonian retainers all cheered louder than
ever. Adiatunnus gave the Fox an elbow in the ribs.
Taking half a step forward—any more and he would
have fallen off the stump—Gerin said, "I'll try to be a
good king, a fair king, for everyone, Elabonian or
Trokmê. And if anyone, Elabonian or Trokmê, tries to
take advantage of me, he'll think a tree trunk fell on
him. Is it a bargain?"

"Aye!" they roared. He suspected they were cheering
deliverance from the Gradi more than they were
cheering him, but he didn't mind that. Without him,
they wouldn't have had the deliverance. He was glad
they had sense enough to realize that—for a little while.

He hopped down off the stump. A very pretty Trokmê
girl with red-gold hair handed him a dipper of ale. He
poured it down. When he gave the dipper back, he
noticed how bright a blue her eyes were, what moist,
inviting lips she had, just how snugly her linen tunic
fit over firm young breasts. He was meant to notice;
in what seemed more a purr than a voice, she said, "A
king, is it? What might it be like, to sleep with a king?"

"If you ever come to Fox Keep, you can ask my wife,"
he told her. She stared at him. Those blue, blue eyes
went hard as stone, cold as ice. She flounced off. He
counted himself lucky she hadn't crowned him with
the dipper.

"You're a wasteful man, Fox," Van said. "The gods
don't make 'em that good-looking every day."

"I'll survive," Gerin said, "and I won't have any crockery thrown at me when I get home, which is more than I can say for you."

"You mean Fand?" Van said. Gerin nodded. The outlander rolled his eyes. "She'd throw things at me whether I futtered other women on the road or not, so the way I see it is, I might as well."

That sort of reasoning would have sent a Sithonian sophist running for cover. It sent Gerin looking for another dipper of ale, with luck one from a serving girl not quite so anxious to try him on for size just because he was wearing a fancy new title. He sighed, a little. Van was right: she had been very pretty.

A sentry up on the palisade peered out at the approaching force of chariotry. "Who comes to Fox Keep?" he called.

He knew the answer to that question. Gerin had sent messengers ahead with news of what he'd done. Nevertheless, he answered, loudly and proudly: "Gerin the Fox, king of the north."

"Enter your keep, lord king!" the sentry shouted. The rest of the men on the palisade erupted in cheers, cheers that soon echoed from within the keep as well. The drawbridge thudded down. Gerin tapped Duren on the shoulder. His son drove him over the drawbridge and into the courtyard.

He hopped out of the chariot then, and embraced Selatre. She said, "I hoped this would happen one day. I'm so glad it has, and so proud of you."

"I thought it might happen one day," Gerin answered, "though I never expected Adiatunnus to be the one to proclaim my rank. Up until the Gradi grew to be serious trouble, I thought killing him would likely be what made folk style me king."

Rihwin the Fox came over and set his hands on his

hips. "For your information," he said loftily, "I find this ever-swelling titulature of yours in questionable taste." Then, grinning, he clasped Gerin's hand.

"You're impossible," Gerin told his fellow Fox. Rihwin's mouth opened. Gerin beat him to the punch line: "Bloody implausible, anyhow."

"The king!" Geroge shouted. The monster, still short a fang, held up a jack of ale in salute. "The king!"

One more feast, Gerin thought. *One more big feast and I can send my vassals back to their own keeps and let them eat their own food.* The fields past which he'd ridden on the way back to Fox Keep looked to have good crops coming in. He hoped they would; that would let him begin to rebuild his stores, which were painfully low. If his vassals had good harvests, too, they might even be able to send grain west to the lands across the Venien, which had had such a dose of Gradi-style weather that their fields were unlikely to yield much this year.

Then the Fox stopped worrying so much about the fields and the harvest. Dagref, Clotild, and Blestar came rushing out of the great hall and swarmed over him and Duren. "I want to hear everything that happened after you left," Dagref said. "I want you to tell it to me now, in order, so I don't get anything mixed up."

"I'm sure you want that," Gerin said, hugging his eldest by Selatre. He was also sure that, having heard everything once, Dagref would be able to correct him on details for years afterwards. And the boy would be right, too, almost every time: Dagref could be quite alarming. Gerin went on, "I'll tell you everything soon, maybe even tomorrow. Right now I want to—I need to—spend time with my vassals."

"It's not fair," Dagref protested. "You'll start to forget things."

"It'll be all right," Clotild told him. "Papa has a pretty

good memory—most of the time," she added with a small sniff.

"Papa!" Blestar said happily. "Papa!" Gerin hugged him, too. He wasn't finding fault with his father: probably, though, for no better reason than that he was too young.

Selatre gave Gerin a jack of ale. He poured a small libation down onto the ground and said, "Thank you, lord Baivers." As with the battle cries there in the woods not far from the ocean, he had no idea whether the god of barley and brewing heard or was still too busy fighting the Gradi gods to pay any attention to mere mortals. He didn't care. He was grateful, and willing— no, eager—to show it.

He went through the keep—into the great hall, back out to the courtyard—several times, drinking, eating, clapping his vassals and their vassals on the back and telling them how splendidly they had fought, something which, in most cases, had the virtue of being true. They were doing much the same thing themselves, though less systematic in their mingling. He got called "lord king" often enough to begin to get used to the new title, even if he still wondered what Aragis the Archer would do in response to his wearing it.

Night fell. So many torches burned, people hardly seemed to notice. And then, here and there—on benches in the great hall, in quiet corners of the courtyard— the warriors who had returned to Fox Keep with him began falling asleep. Gerin remembered wishing he could sleep for three days after that fight in the woods. He was still far, far behind, and likely would be for . . . oh, the next twenty years, if he lived so long.

Not far away from him, Fand demanded of Van, "And how many wenches were you after sleeping with this time?" She sounded half-drunk and more than half-dangerous.

To Gerin's horror, Van, who had drunk a good deal

himself, began counting on his fingers to make sure
he got things right. "Seven, it was," he announced at
last, as proud of his precision as Dagref might have
been.

"It's an old man you're turning into," Fand told him.
"You said a dozen the last time." Her voice rose to a
screech: "Keep your breeches on, curse you!" She dashed
her jack of ale into his face. Dripping and sputtering,
he roared at her. She roared back, even louder.

Gerin's head started to ache. He looked around for
his children. The younger ones, along with Van's son
and daughter, were curled up on the rushes not far
from the doorway to the great hall, but well away from
the path people used to go in and out. Someone had
spread a couple of wool blankets over them. They were
fine where they were; he saw no point to waking them
up and taking them to their bed. They might not fall
asleep again for half the night.

He didn't see Duren at all. That probably meant his
eldest was finding a way to celebrate his return that
would have made his wife shout as Fand was shouting
at Van. Since he didn't have a wife, though . . .

The Fox did see Selatre. With Dagref, Clotild, and
Blestar conveniently asleep, he also saw an opportunity.
He caught her eye, then glanced toward the stairway
that led up to their bedchamber. She smiled and nodded.

With only the two of them in it, the bed seemed
uncommonly large, uncommonly luxurious. Making love
without having to hurry or to worry about the children
waking up at an inconvenient moment seemed
uncommonly luxurious, too.

Afterwards, Gerin thought of the pretty Trokmê girl
who hadn't managed to tempt him into imitating Van.
Chuckling, he told Selatre the story, then asked her,
"What might it be like, to sleep with a king?"

"I," she said, "like it."

✦   ✦   ✦

Geroge looked dubious as Gerin walked up to him carrying a small bowl filled with fine, moist clay. The monster's thin lips skinned back from his teeth. Those teeth looked so extremely formidable, Gerin wondered whether he wanted to go through with what he had planned.

He decided he did. "Open your mouth," he told the monster.

"You're going to have me eat clay?" Geroge protested. "You didn't tell me I'd have to eat clay."

"You don't have to eat it," Gerin told him. "You just have to let me press it up against your teeth so I can get the shape of the fang you have left. I'll use the mold you're giving me to make a gold tooth like it to put on the other side, to take the place of the one the gods under Ikos took."

"It'll taste horrible," Geroge said. "I don't think I want to do it."

"It's only dirt," Gerin said. "It's not even very dirty dirt, if you know what I mean: it's the fine clay they use for baking pots." When Geroge still shook his massive head, the Fox sighed and said, "When we're done, I'll give you a jack of ale to wash away whatever taste there is."

"Oh, all right." Geroge still sounded reluctant even after Gerin's promise, which showed how unwilling he had been before.

"Open your mouth," Gerin said again.

Eyes rolling, Gerin did. The Fox brought the lump of clay up to it with more than a little trepidation: if Geroge chose to bite down now, he'd spend the rest of his days one-handed. Geroge grunted as Gerin made the impression of his fang and the teeth near it. He went from grunt to growl, but held still.

"Splendid," Gerin said, gently freeing the clay. "If

you'd wiggled there, I would have had to do this all over again." *Oh, what a liar I'm getting to be*, he thought. Doing it once had been hard. Doing it twice . . . He didn't care to contemplate doing it twice.

Geroge peered down with interest at the marks his teeth had made in the clay. "They're big, aren't they?" he remarked. "I didn't know they were that big. I thought they were more like yours."

"Did you?" Gerin said. *That's what comes of living among humans all your life—we're your touchstone, your standard of comparison.* That probably made Geroge and Tharma a lot safer to be near than they might have been otherwise.

He took the bowl with the impression to the oven the potter used in his trade and fired it, as the potter would have fired a platter or a storage jar. When it came out and had cooled, he took it to the shack where he worked his magic. He had no intention of doing anything magical to it, but had a small furnace of his own there. In it in another small bowl he put some armlets and rings from his treasury: loot taken from the Trokmoi. He stoked the little furnace and used goatskin bellows to make the fire burn hotter yet.

He'd carved his tongs himself, of wood, and faced them with bronze so they wouldn't char so fast or even catch fire at an inopportune moment. With them, he lifted the bowl and poured molten gold into the mold he prepared for it. The mold took almost all the metal he had melted; Geroge did indeed have big teeth.

When the metal had cooled, he broke the mold. He used a bronze chisel to cut away the gold that filled the impressions of other teeth near the fang, then polished the fang by shaking it in a hide bag full of fine sand. After he'd attached a couple of thin wires to the base, he took the gold tooth to Geroge.

This time, the monster opened his mouth willingly

enough. Gerin put the gold tooth in the gap the monsters' gods had left when they ripped the real fang from Geroge's mouth. He used the wires to anchor the artificial fang to the genuine teeth on either side of it. "What do you think?" he asked Geroge.

The monster explored with his tongue the change in his mouth. "It feels all right," he said. Then he opened his mouth in an enormous smile. "What does it look like?"

"Your other fang, except it's gold," Gerin answered.

That was literal truth, but it wasn't what Geroge wanted to hear. He waved to Tharma, who was walking across the courtyard, and pointed to Gerin's dentistry. "How do I look?"

Like a monster with a gold tooth, Gerin thought, but held his tongue, waiting to see what Tharma would say. "I think you look very handsome," she replied after grave contemplation. Geroge preened and swaggered. Gerin didn't know whether the answer, and Geroge's response to it, pleased or worried him more.

Chariot wheels rumbled on the paving blocks of the Elabon Way. Along with the chariots, Gerin led a good-sized force of men riding horses. The army he headed was smaller than the one he had taken west over the Venien against the Gradi, but more than large enough to be formidable. Like the force that had traveled west, it included both Elabonians and Trokmoi, Adiatunnus having sent a contingent of woodsrunners at Gerin's request.

Van looked back and chuckled. "If this doesn't have 'em ready to piss their breeches, nothing ever will."

"That's the idea," Gerin answered. "Anything worth doing is worth doing properly—or worth overdoing, if you'd rather think of it like that."

"Aye, that suits me pretty well," the outlander said.

Considering his excesses whenever he got out of Fand's sight, Gerin had to agree with him.

Duren pointed ahead. "There's the border post between Bevander's holding and Ricolf's."

"No, that's not right," his father told him. "There's the border post between Bevander's holding and yours. And if anyone has any doubts about that, well, I expect we can convince him to change his mind." He waved back over his shoulder to show what he meant.

The guards on Ricolf's side of the border stared in popeyed wonder at the army bearing down on them. Gerin started to tell Duren to stop and parley with them, then decided to hold his tongue: Duren was going to be the baron here, not himself. Duren did stop. In a shaken voice, one of the border guards asked, "Who, ah, who comes to the holding formerly of Ricolf the Red?" He sounded as if he couldn't decide whether to sell his life dear or flee for the nearest woods.

His companion at the border crossing added, "Not just who—why?" He was gawping at the Trokmoi, as if wondering if they'd decided to settle down in the neighborhood.

"I am Duren Gerin's son, grandson to Ricolf the Red and heir to this holding through my mother, Ricolf's daughter Elise," Duren answered. "Having completed the service I owed my father, I have come to take my rightful place as baron here. From this day forth, I stay in this holding."

"Brought a few, ah, friends along, have you, lord?" the first guard asked. He was looking at the Trokmoi, too.

"He has my support, as you might have guessed he would," Gerin put in.

Both border guards nodded. "Oh, yes, lord prince," they chorused.

Gerin, Van, and Duren grinned at one another. Being

at the forefront of news was always enjoyable. To the guards, Duren said, "Allow me to present you to my father, Gerin the Fox, king of the north, so proclaimed first by Adiatunnus the Trokmê after we all vanquished the Gradi together."

In a way, Gerin thought, it was too bad the two guards had already been staring. Their eyes couldn't get much wider; they jaws couldn't drop much farther. The first one, the one with the slight hitch to his speech, said, "I would, uh, be glad to have more of that, uh, tale, lord."

"And I would be glad to give it—another time," Duren answered. "Now I want to settle myself in the keep that is mine." He flicked the reins. The horses began to trot. Because he was driving the lead chariot in the army, that was the best signal he could give for the rest of the cars to enter the holding that was now becoming his.

On the way down to the keep that had been Ricolf's, peasants who saw Duren's army fled for their lives. "I don't like that any better than you do, Father," Duren said, pointing to serfs running for the shelter of the woods.

"I worry about it less here than I would otherwise," Gerin answered. "For one thing, this is a good-sized force, and all the more frightening on account of that. And for another, remember, we've got Trokmoi with us. The woodsrunners haven't been seen in these parts since just a little while after they flooded over the Niffet."

"Aye, that's so," Van agreed. "And the reason they haven't been seen in these parts for so long is that you've held them away from these parts—not that anybody around here will want to give you credit for it."

"I didn't do it to get the credit for it," the Fox said. "I did it because it needed doing." He chuckled. "Besides, the only thing a baron in one holding is liable to give his neighbor credit for is catching unpleasant diseases from his sheep." Van snorted. So did Duren, although he, unlike the outlander, tried to pretend he hadn't.

Lying by the Elabon Way, the keep that had been Ricolf's was well positioned for its holder to keep an eye on north- and southbound travelers. The frantic stir and bustle on the walls said nobody there had seen anything like the approaching army for a long time. The cry of "Who comes to this castle?" betokened not just curiosity but genuine alarm.

Duren needed no prompting from Gerin to answer as he had at the border: "Duren Gerin's son, come to claim the lordship here, which passes to me from Ricolf the Red through his daughter Elise, my mother." Then he added, "Let down the drawbridge this instant, Ricrod." He did not say *or suffer the consequences afterwards*, but his meaning was plain to Gerin.

It was evidently plain to Ricrod, too, for the drawbridge came down in short order. Duren drove over it into the courtyard of the keep, followed by so many other cars that resistance from the men already inside quickly became hopeless. As he snapped orders, some of Gerin's men took charge of the doors into the great hall of the castle, to make sure they could not be slammed shut against the newcomers. Gerin approved: he would have taken charge of the keep the same way.

But instead of a host of armed men, only Ricrod the steward came out of the great hall. He looked round in amazement at the force that had come to install Duren as baron. The size of that force drove from his head whatever objection he might have had. "Welcome, lord," he said to Duren, and then, to Gerin, "And welcome to you as well, lord prince."

"My father's style these days, with the Gradi beaten, is 'lord king,' " Duren said.

That made Ricrod stare and several soldiers exclaim. In the holding that had been Ricolf's the Gradi had never been more than a name; as he had with the Trokmoi, Gerin had shielded the lands belonging to his former father-in-law from the onslaughts of the invaders. But if only a name, the Gradi were a potent name to the men here, and the importance of the name only grew if beating them had been enough to let Gerin assume a royal title.

After the tale had been briefly told, Duren said, "Ricrod, send messengers at once to Authari and Hilmic, Wacho and Ratkis. Order them to report here to my keep at once, that they may give me homage and fealty." The look he gave the steward was less than warm. "I know you can get messages to them quickly."

"Er—yes," Ricrod said. To Gerin, he sounded nervous. In Ricrod's boots, the Fox would have been nervous, too. The messages he'd sent the last time Duren had been through this holding had almost ended up getting its rightful overlord killed. Ricrod coughed a couple of times, then bowed low. "It shall be as you say, lord, in all things. With dawn tomorrow, the messengers go forth."

"That will do," Duren said grudgingly. He still stared through the steward. "Did you wait till the next morning to send them out when I left this keep on the way to Ikos?"

"Lord, I did," Ricrod said. He nodded toward the altar that smoked close by the hearth. "In Dyaus All-father's name I swear it."

"Very well," Duren said, mollified by the answer. Gerin thought his acceptance wise unless he planned to remove Ricrod, in which case it didn't matter. But if he was going to keep the steward and work with him, he needed to show he trusted him. Otherwise, even if Ricrod hadn't been inclined toward plots, he was liable to acquire that inclination in a hurry.

The Fox's eyes went to the altar dedicated to Dyaus. He wondered if the head of the Elabonian pantheon noticed when someone swore an oath in his name. From what Baivers had said, Dyaus was even further removed from the material plane than the rest of the Elabonian gods. Voldar, now— Gerin didn't want to think what the Gradi goddess might have done to one of her people who falsely swore by her (except, perhaps, one who swore falsely to gain advantage over her foes). But Dyaus seemed to ignore such transgressions. Would Ricrod know that, or feel it somehow? Gerin studied the steward. He had trouble deciding.

He shook his head. It wasn't properly his concern, or wouldn't be for long. This was Duren's holding. Duren would choose whom to believe here, whom to doubt. If he chose wrong, he'd pay for it.

To Duren, Ricrod said, "Er, lord, with the lord prince your father now become the lord king your father, do you hold this keep as a free and independent baron, or as his vassal?"

Gerin's respect for Ricrod's wit, till then low, rose sharply. That was a good question, and one whose answer every petty baron in the holding would want.

"I am my own man here," Duren answered. "I have sworn vassalage to no one for this keep, nor has anyone asked me to swear it. If you think I will deny I am my father's son, though, you are making a mistake."

He'd said much the same thing here shortly after his grandfather's death. It had seemed theoretical then. Now it mattered, and mattered a great deal. Ricrod smacked his lips, tasting the reply. "I could not ask you to speak fairer, lord," he said at last, and sounded as if he meant it.

Several of the soldiers at the keep also nodded. "Well said," came from one of them. Gerin grinned to himself. Duren was starting off here as well as anyone could hope. What would happen after Authari and the other leading vassals arrived was liable to be a different story, though.

Up on the wall of Duren's keep, Ricrod looked away toward the southwest. "Why don't they come?" he muttered fretfully, glancing over to Gerin, who stood beside him. "They should have begun appearing a couple of days ago."

"If they don't come soon—Authari Broken-Tooth especially—I'll go pay them a visit, and we'll see how they like that," Gerin said.

"It would keep your men from eating this keep out of food," Ricrod muttered. Gerin didn't think he was supposed to hear that, so he politely pretended he hadn't.

The first of Ricolf's leading vassals came in that afternoon. Gerin would have bet on Ratkis Bronzecaster's arriving before any of the others, and would have won that bet had he made it with anyone. Ratkis wasted no time in going to one knee before Duren and saying, "Good to have a lord again in this holding."

"Good to be here," Duren said. "I'm sure I still have a lot to learn. Some of that, I expect, I'll learn from you."

Ratkis got to his feet and turned to Gerin. "He's already learned a good deal from you, sounds like." He raised an eyebrow. "And did the messenger have it right that you're calling yourself king these days?"

"He had it right," Gerin answered, and waited to see how Ricolf's vassal—now Duren's vassal—would respond to that.

"I hope you get away with it, lord king," was all Ratkis said. Considering that Gerin hoped he would get away with it, too, he didn't see how he could complain about Ratkis' answer.

Authari Broken-Tooth, Wacho Fidus' son, and Hilmic

Barrelstaves all arrived within a couple of hours of one another on the following day. Each of them came with a large force of chariotry, no doubt as large as he could muster; in his mind's eye, Gerin saw messengers hurrying from one keep to another. The sum of their three little armies, though, was about half the size of his, as they were crestfallen to discover.

"Got their line nibbled by a bigger fish than they expected," Van said gleefully. "Instead of pulling him up onto the bank, they find that they're going out into the creek."

"So they do," Gerin said. "And do you know what? I'm not the least bit sorry for them. Maybe now, seeing what I can do if I like, they'll realize they aren't big enough to quarrel with me, and they'll settle down and be good—or at least not impossible—vassals for my son."

If that was what the three vassal barons had in mind, they didn't show it right away. Authari stomped up to Ricrod and, all politesse forgotten, demanded, "Has your messenger gone daft? What's this nonsense about kings he was babbling?"

Glancing nervously toward Gerin, the steward cleared his throat and answered, "Ah, lord Authari, no nonsense to it. There stands the king of the north."

Authari clapped a hand to his forehead. "You haven't had enough of lording it over men who are by rights your peers?" he snapped at Gerin. "Who named you king, anyhow? Did you do it yourself?"

As the Fox had more than once already, he took considerable pleasure in answering, "No, the first man to use the title was my vassal, Adiatunnus the Trokmê."

Authari's jaw dropped. Hilmic and Wacho both gaped at Gerin. All three of them must have known how much trouble Adiatunnus had given him over the years, and had probably hoped to match his thorny independence.

Authari found his voice first: "What did he go and do that for?" He sounded not just disbelieving but outraged.

"For driving the Gradi back to the edge of the ocean and for embroiling their gods with others so we could pin 'em back there," Gerin answered calmly.

"If you'll think back," Van added, "you'll recall the Fox here was the one who put paid to the monsters a few years back, and to the wizard Balamung a few years before that. So he's done a thing or three to deserve being called a king. What in the five hells have *you* done to deserve to say he doesn't?"

Several of Authari's men nodded when they heard that, which made Gerin work hard to keep a stiff face. He said, "What I've done doesn't matter, not here, not now. This trip isn't about me. It's about my son here, and about the oaths you swore after you heard what the Sibyl had to say about him."

"I said I had to serve my father before I came and ruled this barony on my own," Duren put in. "Now I've done that, and now I'm ready to take up my rule here. Does any man in this keep say I have not the right?"

There it was, a challenge set out with more blunt force, perhaps, than Gerin would have used, but with undeniable power. The crowded great hall in the castle that had been Ricolf's and was now passing to his grandson grew very still. Men leaned forward to hear if any of Ricolf's vassals would challenge that succession.

Always a temporizer, Authari asked, as Ricrod had before him, whether Duren intended to hold the barony as his father's vassal. As Duren had before, he denied it. "It doesn't matter," Authari said then, gloomily. "We're still going to be in the middle of this kingdom, whether we're a part of it in name or not. Bah!"

Gerin thought he was right about that. Everyone outside Duren's barony with whom he would deal would be one of the Fox's vassals . . . unless he tried dealing with Aragis the Archer, in which case Gerin would make him regret it faster than he'd ever imagined.

Authari, still looking for a way to play ends against middle, hadn't noticed all the implications of what he'd said. Wacho, for a wonder, did. "Give it up," he said. "We're fighting somebody too big for us now."

"You say that?" Authari demanded angrily, his suave manner eroding with his hopes.

But Wacho nodded, and so did Hilmic, who said, "Look around you. He's got too many men for us to fight, he's got Adiatunnus' Trokmoi backing him instead of making his life a misery—"

"And how did you manage that?" Authari snapped at Gerin. "Aren't you the one who was always prating about what a pack of savages the Trokmoi were and how we Elabonians shouldn't do anything with 'em except drive 'em back over the Niffet?"

Since Gerin had done a good deal of prating on exactly that theme, he answered carefully: "When you've seen the Gradi, it's amazing what a bunch of good fellows the Trokmoi seem alongside 'em." He looked down his nose at Authari. "Not that you've ever seen a Gradi, of course."

Authari's scowl was a joy to behold till the Fox remembered he was trying to get the petty baron to accept his son's overlordship, not to make an enemy for life of him. Scowling still, Authari said, "Had they come here, we'd have beaten them back."

"Maybe we would, Authari," Wacho said, "but the point is that they didn't come here, and the reason they didn't come here is that the lord prince—uh, the lord king—beat 'em back before they could."

Gerin studied Wacho in some bemusement; he was showing more in the way of common sense than he'd given any hint of having till now. Hit a man over the head with an idea often enough and he sometimes got it.

Authari Broken-Tooth was getting it, too, but not caring for it once he had it. He set a hand on the hilt of his sword as he glared at Ratkis Bronzecaster. "If you hadn't shown up at the wrong time, we'd all still be free," he snarled.

"What, there on the Elabon Way when the Fox here was coming back from Ikos the second time?" Ratkis asked. Authari nodded. Ratkis, by contrast, shook his head. "I heard about what happened there. You could have squashed him, but you funked the job. And you've got no one to blame for that but yourself." Under his breath, he added, "Not that you will."

And, sure enough, Authari snapped, "That's a lie." But it wasn't a lie. Gerin knew it, and Authari probably knew it, too, down in his heart of hearts: he lacked the gambler's nerve that would have spelled the difference between a petty baron and something more prominent. He looked around the great hall, out toward the courtyard, and out toward the encampment some of Gerin's men had made beyond it. The Fox could gauge the moment when he accepted that he could not change what he saw. "Bah!" Authari said. "We might as well get this over with." He looked around again, this time for Duren.

Ratkis Bronzecaster did more than look. He waved, and got Duren's attention. Gerin waved, too: if Authari was going to give homage and fealty, the opportunity had to be seized, not wasted.

Duren hurried over. Gerin used elbows to help clear a space in the crowd where Authari and his fellows could kneel. Ratkis Bronzecaster had already sworn loyalty to Duren, but had no objection to doing it again. On the contrary: when he gave his new overlord homage and fealty, he obviously meant what he said, which exerted extra pressure on the other three men who had formerly been Ricolf's vassals to mean what they said, too.

After they had given Duren homage and fealty, he said in a loud voice, "Now we see how the prophecy Biton delivered through his Sibyl at Ikos is fulfilled. May the omen prove good!"

Gerin's men cheered raucously. So did a good many of the ordinary troopers Hilmic, Wacho, and Authari had brought with them. That in turn cheered the Fox. If ordinary soldiers favored his son, their leaders would have a harder time making trouble for Duren. And reminding the folk here of the oracular response also struck Gerin as clever. Duren could claim—and claim truthfully—he took the barony with the support of the gods.

The Fox made his way over to his son. "It's yours now. Use it the best way you know how. If you have trouble, you know you can call on me."

"Yes, I know that." Duren nodded. "I shouldn't do it save in direst need, though, or people will think I can't handle my own troubles."

"That's the answer a man gives." Gerin thumped his son on the shoulder.

Duren might have sounded like a man, but he didn't look like one, not in that moment. He looked about the way Gerin would have expected a youth leaving the only home he'd ever known to look: worried and a little afraid. "I'll have to make my place here," he said. "I won't have it on account of who you are."

"That's so," Gerin said, choosing to misunderstand him a little: "Your place here comes from your grandfather . . . and your mother." He wondered again what Elise would think if she learned her son had taken over her father's barony. He wondered again if she was still alive. Then he wondered what he'd think, what he'd feel, if he found out she was alive. All things considered, he hoped he'd end his days content just to wonder.

"My place here will spring from *me*, from what I do and what I don't do," Duren persisted. "If I'm right, if I'm clever, I'll do well. And if I'm not, I'll have no one to blame but myself."

"You're my son, all right," Gerin said. Duren looked puzzled. Gerin explained: "Most men—aye, and most women, too—will blame anything and anybody but themselves for everything that goes wrong in their lives. If you know better, that puts you ahead of the game from the start."

"I know better." Duren dropped his voice. "I'm not Authari, to try to blame Ratkis because he didn't strike hard when he had the chance."

"If Authari were as bold in truth as he dreams of being, you'd have more trouble with him, sure enough. With him as he is, though" —Gerin also spoke quietly— "the most you'll have to fret about is poison in your soup. Unless I miss my guess, he'll never try to fight you straight up."

"If you do miss your guess, I expect you'll avenge me," Duren said.

"Bite your tongue—hard." Gerin gestured to turn aside the evil omen. "I've tasted revenge too many times already, and it's a dish I'd sooner not eat of again."

"As you say, Father." Duren matched the Fox's gesture.

Gerin set a hand on his shoulder. "You'll do fine, lad," he said. "The men jump when you talk to them, and that's a gift straight from the gods: if it isn't there, you can't bring it out. And you have a head on your shoulders, even if it's a head without much beard on it right now. Don't take too much for granted, don't fall head over heels in love with the first pretty girl you find down here—or even the third pretty girl—and try to learn from your mistakes. Do that and you'll make a fine baron."

"Good advice," Duren said. Maybe he would turn out to be the one young man in a hundred who actually took good advice. More likely, he'd have to do a lot of learning from his mistakes. *So long as he doesn't make one that kills him*, Gerin thought. *Hardly anybody learns much after that*.

A servant came by carrying a pitcher of ale. Gerin held out his drinking jack. The servant filled it. He drank. As far as he could tell, he badly needed more ale in him if his mind filled with such gloomy thoughts in the aftermath of a good-sized triumph.

The ale didn't make him stop worrying. Maybe he would do that when they flipped earth onto his shrouded body. On the other hand, he was liable to be thinking they weren't doing a proper job of burying him. That was a morbid thought, too. It made him laugh anyhow.

Authari, Wacho, and Hilmic took their men back to their castles the day after they acknowledged Duren as their overlord. Ratkis Bronzecaster, who was on better terms with his new suzerain, stayed a day longer. Then he too departed, leading his retainers off to the southwest. Ricrod looked visibly distressed when Gerin didn't leave the next morning.

"You think they're liable to come charging back as soon as they decide we've upped and gone?" Van asked.

"I don't know," Gerin answered. "I'm not what you call dead keen about finding out the hard way, either. And if the steward here wants to grumble about us eating the storerooms empty, let him." He lowered his voice so only Van could hear: "If I'm not crazy, I'd say Duren picks himself a new steward as soon as he has his feet on the ground."

"You are crazy, Fox, but nobody ever said you were

stupid," Van answered. "Nobody ever said that about Duren, either, which means you're almost sure to be right."

None of the reluctant vassals tried anything untoward, so Gerin and his army rode north three days later. Duren stood on the wall of the keep now his, waving till a bend in the road took his father out of sight. The Fox was waving, too. When high ground hid Duren, he felt it had robbed him of a piece of himself, too. He wondered how long he would take to get over the feeling. He wondered if he ever would.

Up in the watchtower of Fox Keep, the sentry winded his trumpet. "A chariot approaches from the south, lord prince!" A moment later, sounding embarrassed, he corrected himself: "Lord king, I should say."

Still not being altogether used to his own royal title, Gerin did not take offense when those around him had trouble remembering it. He hurried up onto the palisade to see who had traveled almost to the Niffet to pay him a visit. A couple of the men up there shouted out a challenge to the newcomer.

From his chariot, he shouted back, at formidable volume: "I am Marlanz Raw-Meat, sent to treat with Gerin the Fox by my overlord, the grand duke Aragis the Archer."

That got complete and attentive silence from the men up on the wall, Gerin included. He'd been sure he would hear from Aragis about his assumption of the kingship. He hadn't expected to hear so soon. He called, "Marlanz, you're my guest-friend from ten years ago. Use my keep as your own for as long as you choose to stay here." Hearing that, the men at the gatehouse lowered the drawbridge so Marlanz could ride over the ditch and into the keep.

Aragis' envoy was much as the Fox remembered him:

a big, strong, muscular fellow, smarter than he looked and now a bit thicker through the middle than he had been ten years earlier. Gerin also remembered he had a streak of wereblood in him, but the moons had not come full together in clumps of late, and so Marlanz remained wholly human in form.

He clasped Gerin's hand in a grip few warriors could have matched. "Good to see you again, Fox," he said. "It's been a long time. You look well."

"I was thinking the same of you," Gerin answered.

"That was your son heading up what was old Ricolf's holding?" Marlanz asked. "Word came down Ricolf had passed on."

"It's true, I'm sorry to say." Gerin looked sharply at Marlanz. Maybe he hadn't come about the title after all. "Has the Archer a quarrel with that? Unless I were going to claim Ricolf's barony for my own, which I've never wanted to do, it has no other heir but Duren. If you doubt me, go speak to the Sibyl at Ikos."

Aragis' envoy spread his hands and shook his head. "You haven't meddled in the grand duke's part of the northlands, so he has no business meddling up here. And, so far as he knows, what you say about your son's claim is true. But—"

Gerin realized his first guess had been right after all. "Go on," he said.

Marlanz Raw-Meat coughed, as if to advertise he spoke hesitantly. He'd gained in subtlety since his previous trip north. But the point of the visit could not be delayed: "Is it true, Fox, what the grand duke has heard, that you've taken the title of king for yourself?"

"Actually, I had it given to me," Gerin answered. "By Adiatunnus the Trokmê, of all people."

"We heard that, too, but had trouble crediting it," Marlanz said. "If you say it's so, though, I'll believe you.

The question grand duke Aragis would have me put is this: what do you mean by it?"

"When Adiatunnus offered it to me, I kept it, because I think I've earned it," Gerin answered. "If Aragis disapproves—"

Marlanz broke in to repeat, "What do you mean by it? When you style yourself king of the north, do you lay claim to the whole of the northlands? Do you claim to be overlord to the grand duke? If you do, I am to tell you he rejects out of hand any such claim."

"Oh," Gerin said, and then, "Oh," again, because that let him make noise without obliging him to make sense. It also gave him a chance to think, and think he did. He felt as he had when light returned under the shrine of Ikos after he and the monsters' gods finished their strange parley: no longer altogether in the dark. "I see what troubles Aragis. Tell him no, Marlanz. In my own lands, my style is now king, not prince. But I do not claim any lands I did not claim before simply because of my new style. As far as I'm concerned, the grand duke Aragis is lord of his own lands, and is not obliged to me in any way for them."

"That is the question I was asking, yes," Marlanz said gratefully. "The grand duke will be pleased at the news I bring him. You and he have lived side by side with each other for a long time now. He may not be your closest friend, but he respects you."

"And I him," Gerin said truthfully. He was glad he had earned Aragis' respect. Aragis, from all he had seen, either respected you or fell on you like a landslide and crushed you. He was a man with no middle ground in him.

"He has always thought so, Fox," Marlanz replied. He did not call Gerin *lord king*, possibly because Aragis had told him not to. Gerin gave a mental shrug. He was not about to fret over trifles. Marlanz looked thoughtful, then went on, "You said you claimed no new lands because of your new style. Do you claim new lands for some other reason?"

Gerin eyed him with considerable respect. A decade earlier, he wouldn't have noticed such a subtle point. The Fox would have been just as well pleased if he hadn't noticed it now. But, since he had noticed it, he had to be answered: "Aye, I do. Most of the land between my former western border and the Orynian Ocean has passed into my hands by right of conquest over the Gradi."

"We've heard somewhat of this down in the south, but the tales are new and sound confused," Marlanz said. "What really happened?"

That was a dangerous question to ask a man who'd studied historical philosophy down in the City of Elabon. It was a particularly dangerous question to ask in this case, where the quarrels of the gods, which mortals could at best only partly understand, clouded (or, with Stribog's discomfiture, unclouded) the picture. But Gerin knew Marlanz didn't want the truth, or not all of it. What he wanted was a story: the truth set into an interesting framework. That the Fox could give him.

"Come into the great hall and drink a jack or two of ale with me," he said easily. "I'll tell you what happened."

In the hall sat Geroge and Tharma. Marlanz reached for his sword, then checked himself. "These are the two of whom I've heard, not so?"

"Yes," Gerin said. Marlanz Raw-Meat, when his were streak came out, hadn't looked much different from Geroge. The Fox decided mentioning that would be imperfectly tactful, and so kept quiet. He introduced the monsters and Marlanz to one another.

"Pleased to make your acquaintance," Geroge said politely, speaking as he usually did for the two of them.

"Uh, pleased to make your acquaintance as well,"

Marlanz answered, perhaps taken aback by the spectacle of a well-mannered monster but doing his best not to show it. His best was good enough to satisfy Geroge and Tharma, who were less than exacting critics. They both smiled at him, which left him taken aback again. Warily, he said, "I hope you don't mind my asking, but is that tooth made of gold?"

"Real gold," Geroge agreed. "Lord Gerin made it for me, to make up for the one the gods under Ikos tore out of my head. It's not as good as a real tooth, but it's better than a hole in my head."

"Yes, I can see how it would be," Marlanz said. Turning to Gerin, he asked in a low voice, "This is what you spoke of earlier? By the gods under Ikos, he means the gods of his own kind?"

"This is what I spoke of earlier, aye," the Fox said. "As for the other, he does mean the monsters' gods, but he never calls them the gods of his kind or anything like that. He may well be right not to call them that, too, for he and Tharma are of the monsters' blood, but they don't act like them."

"I would not presume to quarrel with my host," Marlanz replied, by which he meant he thought Gerin was spouting nonsense. Then Gerin remembered the hunt on which he'd joined the monsters earlier in the year, and Geroge's excitement—in every sense of the word—after he'd killed. *Maybe I am spouting nonsense*, the Fox thought. *I expect I'll find out.*

Instead of pursuing that, he changed the subject: "I brought you in here for ale, but we've been standing around talking instead."

"Don't let it worry you," Marlanz told him. "Ale I can get anywhere, even the meanest peasant village. Here at Fox Keep, I have many things to see and to talk about that I think I would find nowhere else in all the northlands."

Despite that, Gerin did get him a jack of ale. Only after he'd handed it to Marlanz did he pause to wonder about the propriety of pouring ale for someone else now that he was a king. Since Marlanz accepted it without comment, he decided not to make an issue of it himself. "Is it all that different at Aragis' keep?" he asked, half slyly, half from genuine curiosity.

"It is," Marlanz answered. "The grand duke is, you will forgive me, of steadier and more orderly temper than yourself." Yes, he had learned the arts of diplomacy in the years since Gerin had last seen him. The Fox, who knew Aragis, had no trouble extracting the reality from the bland phrasing: anyone who made Aragis unhappy once was quickly disposed of so he never got the chance to do it twice.

Gerin knew that could happen to him. The best way to keep it from happening was to be—or at least to seem—too strong for the grand duke to attack with any hope of success, but not so strong as to put Aragis in fear of him. The balance between those two was delicate. Picking his words with care, the Fox asked, "How will Aragis respond to my taking the kingship once you've made it plain I intend him no harm?"

"That depends," Marlanz said. "If he believes me when I tell him—if he believes you for what you've told me—all should be well. If he decides not to believe me, or rather, you . . ." He let Gerin draw his own pictures.

None of the pictures his fertile imagination conjured up filled him with delight. Aragis the Archer was a long way from the best of rulers. Obedience through fear worked, but not well. But as a soldier, Aragis was not only as direct and aggressive as a Trokmê, but also more cunning than any woodsrunner, even Adiatunnus. Going to war against him, even with superior force, carried distinct risks.

The Fox said, "I hope you'll be convincing, Marlanz,

for your sake and the grand duke's." *And mine*. But that was one more thing he would not say to Aragis' envoy.

He wondered if Marlanz would cast about for some incentive to be convincing. The bluff young warrior he'd known a decade before would never have thought of such a thing. But this Marlanz was subtler, smoother; Aragis had felt no need to send an older, more polished man with him, as he'd done the last time he'd used him as ambassador.

Marlanz took a long pull at his ale. Gerin eyed him narrowly. That sort of thoughtful pause was exactly what a man looking for a bribe would give in an effort to demonstrate that the notion had only just now occurred to him. The Fox wondered how much in the way of gold and silver he had left after a summer spent campaigning with his warriors and feeding them when they weren't in the field. Carlun Vepin's son would know—or, if he didn't, Gerin would either have to train up a new steward or go back to doing the job himself.

But all Marlanz said was, "I think I will be, Fox. Will you give me your oath by Father Dyaus that what you've told me is true?" He held up a hasty hand. "Not that I doubt you, mind: I mean no offense. But if I can tell the grand duke you've sworn it—"

"I understand," Gerin replied, and gave him the oath. Even as he said the words, his eyes traveled to the altar to Dyaus that stood close by the hearth. He wondered once more if the All-father paid any attention to oaths offered in his name. From what Baivers had said, he had his doubts. But you didn't want to be wrong about something like that. Best to go on as if Dyaus were as immanent in the material world as Voldar had been before Baivers and the monsters' gods distracted her.

He wondered what would happen if one day Voldar won her fight up in the divine Gradihome. He'd told

Duren he could deal with her, and still thought he was right, but, again, he didn't want to have to find out.

"Do you know," he said to Marlanz, "sometimes the most you can hope for is to stay ignorant."

"I'm ignorant of what you mean," Marlanz answered, smiling.

"Good," Gerin said, and slapped him on the back.

The Fox began reckoning achievements in negatives: Voldar did *not* come down to the material world against him, and Aragis the Archer did *not* go to war. The monsters did *not* burst out of the caves under Biton's temple at Ikos, one more worry he'd had, and Authari, Hilmic, and Wacho did *not* join together to overthrow or slay his son.

As the days flowed past, one after another, he began to believe those negatives might hold together for a time. That let him savor the positives: a good harvest and peace among his vassals, even including Adiatunnus. The best surprise of all came from Carlun. Once the harvest had been gathered and payments in kind brought into Fox Keep, the steward came up to Gerin with parchments in his hand and a surprised look on his face.

He thrust the parchments at the Fox, saying, "Lord king, if I've reckoned rightly, we have enough here to get through the winter. I never would have believed it, not with all those gobbling warriors trying to eat the keep empty."

He still thought like a serf. "If it weren't for those gobbling warriors," Gerin reminded him, "you'd be explaining how this keep is set for supplies to some Gradi chieftain—if you were lucky. More likely, you'd be dead."

"I suppose so," Carlun admitted, "but it seems—wasteful." He made the ordinary word into a curse.

"Why fix a roof in summer, when the weather's fine

and looks like staying fine for a long time?" Gerin asked. "The same reason you have men trained in war: sooner or later, you know trouble's going to come. Being ready ahead of time is a better idea than trying to fix things at the same time as they're falling apart."

Carlun chewed on that for a while, then reluctantly nodded. Gerin, meanwhile, checked the steward's figures with meticulous care. As far as he could tell, everything gibed. That meant Carlun was either a very clever cheater or too afraid of him to take any chances. He suspected the latter. That suited him fine.

Winter was the quiet time of the year, serfs and lords alike living on what they'd stored up in summer and fall. When they hadn't stored enough, what they got was famine, which, all too often, brought peasant uprisings in its wake. To try to head them off, Gerin did send what grain he could west of the Venien, to the lands where unnatural summer weather, courtesy of the Gradi gods, had ruined the crops. He scored another negative success: the serfs there did *not* revolt.

"In a horrid sort of way, I understand why things are quiet there," he said to Selatre one day. "They don't have much food, but there aren't many of them left, either, not after living under the Gradi for a while and then after the war. What little they've got, along with what little we could give them, is somewhere close enough to get them by."

His wife nodded. "Life for farmers is never easy." Having grown up a peasant's daughter, she knew whereof she spoke. After a moment, she added, "You've done everything you could, and more than most lords would have dreamt of trying."

"It sounds like an epitaph," Gerin said, laughing. A moment later, as with Duren, his hand and Selatre's twisted in a sign to avert the evil omen. That done, he let out a long sigh. "We got through it."

Selatre nodded again. "So we did. And after what we got through, it has to get better, because how could it get worse?"

"That's why we go on living," he answered: "to find out how it could get worse." Selatre poked him in the ribs, and he had to admit (though he didn't have to admit out loud) he deserved it.

As winters went, this one was mild, again to Gerin's relief: he'd feared the Gradi gods, if they got free at that season of the year, would do their best to freeze the northlands solid. Nothing of the sort happened, though, and in due course winter gave way to spring. Leaves came out on the formerly bare branches of oaks and maples, apples and plums; fresh grass sprouted on the meadows, pushing up through the yellow-brown dead growth of the year before. The peasants yoked their oxen to the plow and planted wheat and rye, oats and barley. Gerin blessed Baivers, and hoped the god heard him.

He had one more worry in the middle of spring: Elleb, Math, and Tiwaz came to fullness on successive nights. No reports of werebeasts ravaging flocks or peasants reached him, though. He hoped Marlanz Raw-Meat hadn't given way to his lycanthropic tendencies during the run of full moons.

And then, when for once he saw no trouble on the horizon at all, the midwife came rushing up from the peasant village near Fox Keep to let him know Fulda had been delivered of a baby boy. He thumped his forehead with the heel of his hand, angry at himself for letting the imminence of the event slip his mind. "What's Mavrix's bastard like?" he asked.

"Lord king, you'd better come see for yourself," said the midwife, a sturdy, middle-aged woman named Radwalda.

And so the Fox followed her down to the village. She

pointed the way to Fulda's hut, but showed no eagerness to go into it herself. Shrugging, Gerin stepped through the low entrance, ducking his head as he went.

His eyes needed a moment to adjust to the gloom. When they did, he saw Fulda sitting up on the bed. She didn't look nearly so worn as other women he'd seen just after childbirth: one more advantage of divine parentage, he supposed.

Smiling, she held up the newborn baby. "Isn't he beautiful, lord king? I'm going to call him Ferdulf."

"Hello, Ferdulf," Gerin said.

Ferdulf's eyes, which had been closed, came open. "Hello yourself," the infant demigod said in a distinctly unbabylike baritone.

Gerin looked at Fulda. She nodded. "Oh, dear," the Fox said.